FAMILY BUSINESS

MIXING BUSINESS WITH PLEASURE SERIES
BOOK THREE

Ace Gray

Editing by:
Kathleen Payne

Book formatting by:
Perfectly Publishable

Cover compilation completed by:
Rebecca & Harper Graham

To Bex, Emma, Mel and Mix
You guys are the bright white in my darkest moments

ACKNOWLEDGMENTS

Each time I start these, I stare blankly for a while at the screen. I mean how do I ever properly articulate a thank you to the people who have been instrumental in making my dreams come true? Because that's what my acknowledgements are, a very deep, very real thank you for letting me indulge my every fantasy, including being an author.

Thanks and massive sabering-the-champagne toast to . . .

Pat, my hubs, my light. Thank you for always being proud of me. Thank you for encouraging me to keep going. I'd fight for you just like Kate would Nick. You are the real fairy tale deal baby.

Mom and Dad you guys taught me everything I know. The older I get, the more I realize that you taught me everything that matters—kindness, generosity, love, perseverance, tenacity, and hard work among many other things—I've applied each and every lesson to my life, and of course, this book.

Bex, Emma, Mel and Mix, aka my Ladyfaces and Ladyloves. Thank you for always answering my heinous messages. Thank you for often agreeing to marry me, accepting my flaming poop, being my movie premiere date and being my constant dick pic supply. You guys keep me going when the author business gets hard. I can always count on you four. There are no words for that kind of friendship. There are, however, lots of emoijs . . .

Karrie for tolerating my terrible snapchat singing.

Kathleen for accepting *You can take that feedback and sit on it* as a legit response to editing my books. (P.S. check the italics. Sorry, there aren't more commas).

BB for letting me get the tattoo. And being worth every single drop of ink.

AM Johnson, A Wilding Wells, M Andrews, Martha Sweeney, RK Ryde, and TR Cupak for simultaneously being my heroes, my friends, my idols, my inspiration and some of the best friends a girl could ask for. I can only hope to be like you guys when I grow up.

Selin for being my Care Bear.

Amanda for letting me keep her AND Devon Sawa.

Simmy for everything, particularly being you.

Sahara and Morgan for making me feel like a celebrity.

Kellogg for reading my books despite anal.

Stephanie for giving it to me straight even when I want it curvy, but always over cocktails.

Stella and Jill for being badasses and angels and saints. And saintly, badass angels!

Be (again) and Harper for being what I needed, when I needed, without question. I'm still crying . . .

And the rest of my squad, like @authordeeellis, @authordeegarcia, @taylors_pages, @smutty_men, @marthadita, @cozy_dita, @gizzygrl11, @little_monkey12, @wondertre, @abdulia_ortiz, @ash.loveofbooks, @booksandlooks30, @bookmarkbelles, @karen_sedg68, @winlocklane, @book_bf_lover, @book_lovin_misfit, @librenjady, @bookminx25, @j.valentine702, @authorameliaoliver, @kinky_n_smutty_book_addict, @ms_kyle29, @bl_harvey_, @innergoddess_booklover, @ratherbereading143, @danireneauthor, koko_moe_, @cassie_mags, @lizziminto, @love2read_, @lakerl24vr, @73jem, @cindymrls, @authorscole, @bellelovebooks, @kinkygirlsbookobsessions, and I'm sure a million others, you guys are my universe. (Ask my hubs, he thinks I'm on Instagram way too much). Like Tinker Bell get strength from clapping, I get strength from you guys, from your likes and love. My heart has grown a million sizes since finding you guys!

"This is a business of love and labor."
~ Chester Bennington

PROLOGUE

Flesh. Supple, pale, taut, perfect flesh.

That's what my step-brother was enjoying as his whore performed for him just beyond the windowed wall of his office. Kate Elliott's delicate skin and dangerous curves were on full display, well, where they poked out of that tight leather jacket and tiny lace panties anyhow. Her dark wavy hair framed sparkling hazel eyes and luscious pouty lips that cried out repeatedly.

Nicholas Bryant was a bastard. His self-righteousness and refinement had made my skin crawl since before I could pinpoint or define the terms. Now, the way he handled his woman, the way he pawed at her, spanked her, shoved his dick into her with zero sentiment, made me jealous. And for the first time, not in a way that had me wanting to choke him.

I wanted to choke *her*. I wanted to see her body writhe beneath mine. I wanted to watch the fight and fire leave her eyes for just a moment before *my* thrusts brought her back to life. The way she responded to each and every one of his touches, hard or soft, was perfect. *She* was perfect. She was the kind of loose woman, with loose morals and a tight pussy that would let me beat her to orgasm.

Nicholas won after all . . .

The thought made me snarl. He always got everything. The good grades, to be team captain, the love of a mother, the success, and now this. This . . . creature was his. This creature that let him take her ass, sans lube, only to crumble beneath him rather than turn to slap him.

I'd planned to end it once and for all tonight. He deserved a bullet in the head for what he'd suffered me. And when they hadn't been in the master suite of Kate's Hampton estate, I'd shot her fucking pillow in pure, unadulterated frustration. When I saw my brother screaming at security along Highway 27, hope filtered back in. Hope that I could still make him pay for everything. And soon.

But watching them now . . .

There was a decidedly different way to make Nicholas pay for the offenses he'd laid against me. It was her. Kate Elliott was my ticket to destroying my dear, dear *brother*. I could take a woman that had spunk, and would likely swallow mine, from him. I could do it in front of him—do *her* in front of him—and he'd crumble in a far deeper sense than simple death.

He'd made it obvious just by looking at her. There was love and adoration—maybe even worship—and I could smother it. I could wreck *everything*. And the beauty was that the game was entirely in my hands. Did I want to shoot her? Now? In front of him? It would be particularly tragic. He would cradle a blood-addled body to his chest and cry gut wrenching tears.

Well to me, they'd be wholly satisfying tears but . . .

If I waited, I could toy with them.

I pocketed both the silencer and the gun I'd been contemplating using in favor of watching. I was treated to her agonized cries and became even more sure of my choice. She wasn't with me, but I could feel her coming in my bones. In my cock. I'd gotten hard when I watched Kate barrel into the office, shouting, but now . . . now I hurt. She was fiery, furious, and did things a back alley hooker charged far too much for.

I patted my gun as I switched the ankle crossed over my knee. There was no sense in using it now. It was far more gratifying this way. They were fucking against the windows, draped across the leather, then back again. Kate was going limp when I started to stroke myself. They were just too good together not to.

Porn had nothing on my brother and his scene. I hadn't wanted to tie a woman down, hear her shriek, and shove my dick in her mouth to cut her off this badly since my little sister-in-law. But what was even more tantalizing than Aribella was Kate. She made me thirsty. The kind of thirst that not even a wet pussy would quench. Only days and days of abuse and penetration would soften the likes of my desperation. And, once she was broken, I'd win. Because broken Kate equaled decimated Nicholas.

Yes, death would be far too simple a solution for my dear, *dear*, brother. He had to feel loss and desolation as deeply as I did. Kate was the key.

They fucked. Everywhere. And God damned if it wasn't so good I jerked myself off. Hot cum still speckled my sleeve as he scooped her up from the couch. A moment later the lights flickered off one by one in their apartment, leaving me to bask in the hazy, faded dark of a New York night.

I sat there for what felt like hours, both making sure the lights were out and remembering the details of the fucking my step-brother had just handed down. My dick twitched again when I recalled his hand around her throat.

When I was sure they weren't going to come back to the main floor, or call security up for that matter, I deftly unlatched the office door and stepped into the chic surroundings of Nicholas' One Madison office. I ran my fingers over the couch they'd fucked on.

I even bent to smell it, catching the hint of her womanly, musky, but sweet scent. Filling my lungs with the smell of her made me twitch again. The fact that she was mixed with a flavor I still remembered was Nicholas, made me harder still.

Revenge was a heady drug.

I casually walked through the massive apartment, taking in all of what could have been mine. Had he not stolen attention, had he not stolen Aribella away, had he not been him . . . The name, the reputation, the businesses, they would have been mine for the taking.

I made sure my fingers touched everything to etch the memory into my flesh for days to come. The bar. A discarded scotch glass. His priceless artwork and ornate furnishings. Her high heels . . .

Slow, silent footstep, by slow, silent footstep, I made my way to their bedroom on the third floor, relishing pieces of their life as I went. Luckily, they hadn't shut the door and I could creep in to watch them as easily in the master bedroom as I had from the veranda.

A stark naked Kate had fallen asleep, nuzzled into the chest of a bastard-ass Nicholas. Soft white sheets waved and rippled around them giving this marshmallowy dream-like quality to their intimate pose.

Kate clung to my step-brother so tightly; her hand curled into his chest, begging to claw at flesh. My little angry kitten wanted to claw his heart out too, even if she wasn't ready to admit it.

My hands were moving toward her before I even thought about it. Every fiber of my being was desperate to touch her, to have a response from her. I tucked her hair behind her ear then I let my fingertips follow down her neck, her shoulder, and then toward her breast. I couldn't help myself when I reached down and grabbed her pert nipple and twisted it between my fingers. It hardened at the same time she moaned and her body bowed toward my step-brother.

I wanted to jerk off all over again. I wanted to see my hot cum covering her, not my God damned sleeve. The thought of my jizz polka-doting Nicholas was an equally gratifying turn on. He would know immediately what I'd done. What I intended on taking from him.

But for all his faults, and all the ways I wanted him to suffer, I couldn't show my hand just yet. He'd gotten smarter. She'd made him stronger. And giving away hints would put my newly formulated plan in jeopardy. I'd likely pay before I had the chance to bury my cock in the sweet folds Nicholas called his. Before I could take the thing he held most dear.

Her.

So I twisted her nipple once more, gently this time, and watched as both her and my brother's bodies rolled against each other. Her pale flesh goose bumped as I traced back down her forearm and let my hand fall away.

Oh God, how I wanted to see those goose bumps rise in fury and panic as I took her by force . . .

So slowly, silently, I turned around and walked as light footed as I could back downstairs. Back to the office, back to the veranda. And with all the skill I'd developed in the hopes of destroying all things Bryant, I slithered down the air ducts with a new, and decidedly more appealing mission:

Obliterate everything that was Kate Elliott.

1.

Ugh. I'm going to murder someone.

Dawn shown a blush pink on the tips of the skyscrapers of New York—a site that always made me nauseous and more than a little irritable. Anything before 8 a.m. did. I rubbed my eyes, and groaned. It didn't help that there was a layer of ick coating my skin again. For the past week, I'd felt dirty when I woke. I shook the feeling and tried not to stumble on the stairs as I walked down to the kitchen.

Why am I doing this again?

I sighed. *Of course* the answer was Nicholas Bryant.

Nicholas Bryant, the man I'd left sprawled in bed, was swiftly becoming my universe. Part of me hated being dependent—being *that* girl—but I'd learned the hard way I couldn't live without him. We'd been up, down, together, and apart over the past few months. I fully expected we'd turn left or right at some point, but I wasn't going anywhere. My heartbeat had tuned to his, my breathing too. We made each other stronger, but we also made each other crazy. Bat shit crazy. And lately, with increasing frequency.

I took a deep breath and pulled the turkey from the fridge so it could continue thawing. I turned back to the stairs, still having a hard time coaxing my eyelids open. All I wanted was to slip back into bed, and with any measure of grace, I'd do it without waking Nick. He rarely slept a full night, and lately it had gotten worse.

I froze when I found him not only awake, but sitting up, his perfectly chiseled and tanned torso bent over his Blackberry. His brow furrowed deeply where it peaked out of the longer waves of his dark chocolate hair as he stayed focused on the screen. His beautiful blue eyes had undoubtedly shifted to dark and stormy. For the first time, that look didn't trigger my urge to console, it flared my temper.

Neither of us took time off from running our respective empires, but we'd promised to leave it be today. Actually, *he'd* made *me* promise. The more I recalled of the conversation—okay, *fight*—the more worked up I got. I scoffed and he didn't flinch. The clock hadn't even hit seven and he'd smashed his own demand all to hell. I turned away from him and shoved my hands through my hair.

"What's wrong now?" he asked, exasperated.

I rolled my eyes at my reflection in the bedroom windows; he hadn't even looked up. Heat rose in my cheeks and a few choice swear words hitched in my throat. Rather than engage, I stomped over to my side of the bed far louder than was absolutely necessary.

"Nothing." I whipped back the comforter then plopped into bed and yanked the covers back up. I made sure to *humph* as I spun away from Nick.

"Kate, I asked you why you're throwing a temper tantrum."

"Fuck you. I'm not throwing a tantrum."

"Kate," he warned as his eyes studied the exposed nape of my neck. My skin always reacted when he stared intently, this time blanching. "Answer me." His gritty voice betrayed his temper, fraying just like mine.

"It's not even seven and you're on your God damned phone, Nick," I shot back as I burrowed further into bed.

"It can't be helped." He turned icy.

"It was your idea to disconnect, not mine."

"Kate." If my name before hadn't been a warning, this time it certainly was.

"What's so important? Tell me, perhaps I'll understand," I said, attempting to dial back the edge in my voice.

I was challenging him and he knew it. Sharing wasn't Nicholas

Bryant's strong suit and we'd fought repeatedly on the subject. Every moment silence filled the room rather than an answer my irritation ratcheted up.

Until I broke.

"Right," I quipped. "I forgot. We don't *do* that. You don't include me, I get upset, someone gets hurt. It's kind of our thing." I shoved the covers again, this time to dart back out of the room.

Keep your temper, keep your temper, keep your Goddamnedfuckingshitty temper.

My fingers balled into fists, nails digging into my palms, and my shoulders tensed further as I muttered multiple profanities under my breath as I stomped back down to the kitchen.

I kept up the banging, reveling in the ruckus of pots and pans. The noises that echoed through the glass box that was our apartment were guaranteed to reach Nick's ears. Not once did I consider whether Jaime, Colton, Terrence, or the three new security detail members were being subjected to my mood.

Who the fuck cares anyway?

When I was rational, I blamed the recent friction between Nick and I on lack of sleep and the gunshots that'd been fired in my Hamptons house. Right now, I blamed it on Bryant's bastard-ass BlackBerry, his distance, and 6:48 a.m. I growled and slammed the bowl in my hands down a few times on the cutting board, letting my frustration out.

"This is the definition of a temper tantrum. And FYI, it doesn't suit you."

Nick had appeared and was leaning against the breakfast bar, watching me with arms crossed. There was a spark of humor in his eyes that made anger swell further.

"Funny, being an ass seems to suit you quite well."

I propped one hand on my hip, the other still holding the bowl, and glowered. He dropped his arms and righted himself. The humor evaporated from his beautiful face.

"I don't appreciate being called an ass."

His voice was frigid and I should have reined in my snarky mouth.

Instead, I barreled on. "Then I would suggest you stop being one." I matched his tone perfectly as I held his gaze across the breakfast bar.

"What do you want me to say, Kate?" My name was sharp and pointed when it left his lips. "Do you want me to tell you that my foreign properties are still being dicked with? Or perhaps that I received my own cryptic message from Victor Alexander? Seems he's switched his attention from destroying your business to destroying me. Perhaps you need to know my personal favorite. Christopher, my delightfully fucked up brother-in-law, has liquidated his assets and is operating on a cash-only basis. Which is something I can't track. He could be fucking *anywhere*."

His hands fisted and his muscles flexed just before he cocked back to punch the stool closest to him. When it clattered and clashed to the floor, I jumped but otherwise stayed silent.

"Is that what you wanted to hear, Kate? Am I allowed to be on my fucking phone now?"

All the tension left my body. My anger too. I circled the bar, trying to hold his intimidatingly gray gaze.

"I'm sorry. I didn't . . ."

"You weren't supposed to know. This isn't how our first Thanksgiving is supposed to go." He spoke harshly, even as I wove my hands around his waist.

"It doesn't have to go a particular way, baby." I stayed soft and consoling but it wasn't easy. "Tell me more. Talking about it might make you feel better."

"That's fucking ludicrous."

The jagged, rugged notes of his voice echoed off the kitchen glass, and his hands didn't move to hold me back. I circled my fingers to soothe him but he shrugged me off. I exhaled loudly, frustration back in full force, and dropped my hands from his body. I circled the bar and returned to prep work.

"Do you get tired Nick?" I cocked my head and dramatically timed a *thwack* of my chef knife through a potato on the cutting board. "I mean, constantly pushing me away has to get exhausting."

"Excuse me?" Nick asked as his eyes turned darker.

"You heard me." I halved another potato and arched my eyebrows.

Nick took two giant steps and positioned himself directly behind me. It made me nervous that I couldn't see his eyes. I whacked the next potato anyway, doing my best to ignore him and the way he made my skin vibrate.

His hands came to the countertop on either side of me, and I watched his forearms flex as he gripped the marble.

Shit.

Despite our *disagreement,* my wayward mind imagined those hands flexing into my hips. I flushed automatically, even across the back of my neck, and Nick hummed with approval when he saw. The temperature in the room skyrocketed and the knife clattered out of my hand as my fingers scrambled to pull at the neckline of my shirt, desperate for extra breathing room. Try as I might, I couldn't clear my throat.

"I won't be chastised like that, Kate." He pressed his body against mine.

"Then don't give me a reason to do so." My voice was almost a whisper as I crumbled beneath him.

"Perhaps I should teach you to stop questioning my motives."

I stared, steady and unblinking, down at the potatoes catching his meaning immediately. I had a decision to make. Get an answer or get some. I straightened my spine deciding on the former and to stand my ground. But then my ass rubbed against his solid erection and my body trembled in response. The heat was so undeniable between us I couldn't help that my breathing hitched. I held out as long as possible but caved, slouching against the counter. He read me like a book.

"Good girl." Nick's voice was positively wicked.

I gulped as his hands came to my hips, and everything except pure, unadulterated lust flew right out the window. He pulled me along the countertop to a clear space and used his body to press my hip bones into the edge. His hands skated up and down my arms before he unceremoniously pressed my chest down to the marble.

Mercifully, the stone was cool beneath my cheek, the perfect contrast to my skin, which caught fire as he rolled up the soft fabric of my oversized t-shirt. My heart thudded when I was fully exposed to him. I knew better than to shift but when his finger swept from my clit to ass, I couldn't stay still.

I breathed deeply despite the sizzle of my skin and tried to still myself; he would only start playing once I was composed. But the longer he kept me waiting, the greater my desire became. My wiggling started without any conscious thought.

Knowing it would still me, but not even remotely satisfy me, Nick started tracing a circle on the small of my back with a single finger. His touch worked me up into a tingly frenzy even though he was barely throwing me a bone. My body melted and I exhaled, my breath fogged against the stone. I was focused on the circle evaporating when a loud swat landed across my backside. I gasped at the delicious sting that moved through me then pooled in the shape of an exceptionally skilled and incredibly manly hand on my ass.

"If you hadn't left my bed, I wouldn't have woken." Nick's voice was even and businesslike. Another smack landed firmly across my ass, just to the side of the first. "If I hadn't woken, I wouldn't have checked my phone."

Everything in my body clenched in anticipation, but before he spanked me again he shoved me further up on the counter so my toes couldn't touch the floor any longer. They swung the slightest bit when a third swat landed far harder and closer to the mark left by the first. I cried out and my hands scrambled to defend my bare ass.

"You didn't even give me a chance to explain."

His voice betrayed that his irritation was quickly being replaced by lust. A fourth smack landed harder and lower than the others. I couldn't help but moan his name, even as my hands moved to shield my raw skin.

"And I was going to," he breathed.

Nick shifted behind me and before I could even think, his hard cock shoved into me. He began thrusting deep and urgent making me cry out beneath him. His hand gripped at my t-shirt, fisting between my shoulder blades. He kept me pinned down while rolling his hips against mine, zinging the fresh welts from his smacks each and every time. My hands scrambled to grasp at anything and, depending on the intensity of his thrust, sometimes still my ass.

Nick bent over to reach for my wrists. As he did, he moved deeper inside of me, and I shrieked. He yanked my arms back and used his vise grip to pull my body back onto his erection. Repeatedly. My forehead rolled on the marble as I lost control of every fiber in my body, simply at the mercy of his rhythm. The countertop remained fogged beneath my whimpering lips, and after a few fierce rolls of his hips, I couldn't feel my toes. I honestly wasn't sure if it was from the stone digging in or pure ecstasy.

When I'd become completely nonsensical, he lifted me to yank my shirt up and over my head. My toes returned to the floor, tingling, and couldn't gain traction. When my balance faltered, Nick cupped my breasts and used them to pin my back to his chest. He hadn't moved from inside me, just shifted, and he started thrusting again, using my nipples to pull me down to meet his motion.

My ankles rolled repeatedly forcing Nick to pull out and turn me so our chests could press together. He violently kissed me, his teeth digging into my lip. He still had my wrists trapped in his or I would have pulled his face roughly to mine. He picked me up and pushed me onto the counter. The second my backside hit the stone, I winced. Nick didn't falter as he yanked my hips to the edge so my legs were wide open and I was completely accessible to him. He pushed back in making me scream, then returned to a punishing pace.

Everything in my world was consumed by his touch, his taste, his feel. I loved this man, and I loved the things he did to me. Even the edgy things.

Particularly the edgy things.

The wave of desperation to hold his skin against mine hit me hard and fast. I tried to sit up and press my body to his. He stopped me part way with his hand against my throat. He gently pressed to keep my body angled, hovering above the marble. My hand splayed back across the countertop to help support my weight while the other reached out for him. I pulled again, this time harder. I only meant to get his bare skin against mine, but he slipped out of me and climbed onto the counter top instead.

He hovered over top of me, studying my trembling chest, and gasping lips. His long lean muscles rippled, and his blue eyes churned with lust. That look was enough to make me come but I bit my lip and made myself wait for him to get back inside.

Nick prolonged the torture, resting his cock on my stomach as his breathing slowed infinitesimally. He could always read my body, and how close I was, then choose whether to keep going or let me explode. Today he wasn't being kind. When I whined, he smirked then sunk back in. Slowly.

He began to thrust purposefully, prolonging each movement, each moment. He was just *so* good at this.

Passionate kisses trailed across my lips, then my chest, both in time with his expert thrusts. Each kiss pressed hard then lingered on my skin. Thank God my hands were free to roam up and down his body. My nails drug down his back, eliciting a primal moan from him just before his lips locked back on mine.

One of his hands slid to my hip and dug in. I arched my back off the counter in response. The slight shift of my pelvis allowed him to slide slightly deeper, and I couldn't stave off my orgasm any longer. I cried out desperately, unable to stay focused on anything but the waves shaking my body. My hands fell from his body, and my head rolled to the side, gasping.

Nick kept thrusting, using my body to reach his own climax. He groaned through gritted teeth when he shot into me, then again when he collapsed on top of me. We stayed a pile of flesh on the countertop for a few moments, both of us trying to breathe again.

"Better?" He moved his forehead to rest against mine.

"Yes." I sucked in a giant breath. "I'm sorry I got so worked up."

"I know you're exhausted but cut me some slack. I'm more than happy to fuck the attitude out of you on the kitchen counter but it's not always an option." A brilliant smile spread across his face and it paired perfectly with breathtaking eyes.

"It has nothing to do with being exhausted." I rolled my eyes. "It's about you keeping things . . ."

"I'm . . ." he interrupted me but I stopped him in his tracks. He'd been saying one particular phrase on a loop since we met.

"If you say *I'm trying,* I will murder you. It won't matter that you're still inside me."

"Sweets, I was going to say I'm sorry." He glared playfully and nudged his semi-hard cock inside me. I rolled my eyes then swatted him. "I really was. This all just happened. I'm not trying anymore, I simply *will* be better."

His head fell against my chest and his lips pressed to the skin above my heart. I took a deep breath and let any irritation go, determining to enjoy the smell of sweat, sex, and Nick.

"Kate, I'm thankful you're mine. That you somehow manage to deal with me." He kept his lips against my skin and I liked the way he growled *mine* at me.

MMMmmm.

Only one phrase made my heart thump more furiously than that.

"I love you."

That was the one.

My heart jackknifed in my chest and I trembled against his cheek. He murmured my name and arched up to take my lips roughly with his.

"I love you too, Nick."

I gasped in between fevered kisses. He twitched inside of me and my fingers slowly returned to his skin, my nails raked across his broad shoulders again on their own accord.

MMMmmm.

A BlackBerry buzzing from the floor interrupted my pleasured purr. Nick hesitated against my lips. A small part of me wanted to spank him the way he would have me—No, *had* spanked me—but the other part of me understood.

"Go ahead. Grab it."

He slid out of me and I whimpered. It never ceased to amaze me how much I missed him the moment he was gone. My pained sound brought out his beautiful crooked smile, and he flicked my clit just before bending to snatch the buzzing phone from his discarded pants pocket. The second he had it, his hand moved back toward my still trembling sex.

I swatted his hand away and jumped off the stone as quickly as my Jell-O legs would allow.

Nick's hand pushed back between my thighs and danced across my slick slit while he barked into the phone. We'd played this game before but I shoved on his arm, having zero desire to stay silent while being fondled today. His brow knit together, and he pinched on the sensitive nub between my thighs hard enough to make me cry out. His eyes swirled at the sound.

"Don't," I hissed.

He tried to push his fingers inside me, insistent. My temper swelled. Every ounce of me wanted to shout *fuck off!* but I knew we'd brawl if I provoked him. Instead, I waited for the moment he relaxed to shove him again. I used both my bodyweight and momentum, which caused him to stumble.

I managed to scamper just out of reach while he recovered. He let me walk away but the tone of his conversation betrayed his aggravation.

He couldn't see me roll my eyes or that my previous pique returned despite the sexing. He probably figured it out when I bent and snatched up my shirt with far more force than was necessary. If not then, perhaps when I stomped up both flights of stairs, knowing full well he could hear every sound as I went.

2

"I'm done fighting with you today." Nick's quiet decree came while I was yanking on skinny jeans despite my smarting ass.

A heartbeat later, he wrapped his arms around my still naked chest; I struggled against him.

"Kate," he warned as his grip got tighter. "I mean it."

I sighed and sagged into his grip.

"Yes, sir." I rolled my eyes.

"I like that."

Nick nuzzled into my hair as he started circling on my skin with his fingertips, but his grip didn't lessen. Matter of fact, his hold got tighter the longer we sat there. When he started fidgeting behind me the all too familiar boulder of anxiety dropped into my stomach. All the telltale signs were present, Bryant bad news was coming my way.

"Spit it out." I made a point to stay relaxed in his arms, his fingers clenched anyway.

"I have to go to Hong Kong in two weeks."

"For fuck's sake Nick!" I pushed against him, wanting to throw my arms up. He managed to keep me pinned.

"Knock this shit off right now," he commanded roughly against my ear.

"Don't tell me what to do." I still wrestled with his grip.

"Kate," he warned.

"Let go of me Nick." His name was equally pointed on my lips.

"Not until you calm down." He squeezed. "Why are you losing your shit over this?"

"I don't want you to go, okay?" The admission just vomited out. "It scares me. And for a whole myriad of reasons, not the least of which is the shit you told me this morning."

Every muscle in his body tensed when I brought up the list he'd snarled not long ago.

"You're coming with me."

"Like hell I am."

He let me go and I swiveled to look him in the eyes. I caught him staring directly at my swaying breasts rather than up at my face. I couldn't help but burst out laughing.

"You're a dirty bastard." I shook my head and went back to picking a shirt.

"A dirty bastard who's taking you to China December 14th."

"Not possible. I'm too busy with Vesper. You know that."

"I'd never jeopardize Vesper, *you* know that. Look, Kate." He sighed and circled away to sit on the ottoman. The tufted leather creaked underneath him as he slumped to rest his head in his hands. His posture and tone changed so dramatically that he had my attention. "I'm asking, not telling, okay? I need someone smart who I can trust to help me figure out what the hell is going on over there. You're the most intelligent person I know, and you're the *only* one I trust. Please." He spoke with starling sincerity.

Please?

He never said please. *That* word on *those* lips made my stomach flip. I knelt down and gently pushed his hands aside so mine could cradle his face instead.

"What's going on, Nick? And don't placate me."

He leaned into me but kept his gaze on the plush carpet.

"In the last week, I had the tires of an entire armored car fleet slashed, an assembly line fall apart, and a security checkpoint leveled. Then there's this facility that keeps toying with me. I was trying to buy the plant but they're fucking with me and don't think I can tell. I need to figure out why."

Nick went quiet and his face morphed into the one I hated. The one I was always compelled to fix, no matter the personal cost.

"Why not send Jaime? And fuck the plant." I climbed up onto his lap, straddling him, and making the leather furniture protest against my shuffling. My arms wrapped around his neck and I pulled him to my chest.

"I can't. *I* have to figure out what's coming. *I* have to stop it."

I half expected him to tell me he had to protect me. But he buried himself in my breasts instead.

"Nick." I laughed lightly and playfully smacked him. "Stop." He paid no attention, nuzzling all the further.

"I like Thanksgiving. I'm quite thankful for your perfect breasts."

"Oh my God." I pulled away. "I don't think that's quite the spirit of the holiday."

I took a breath and studied him. As much as I wanted to question him on the whys of Hong Kong, or insist he didn't have to personally go, I caught the turmoil in his eyes and folded.

"I'll go. Of course, I'll go. I'll just need to arrange it with Gemma." I stood and yanked on the nearest shirt.

"It's already done. I took care of it."

"God damn it Bryant!" I banged my fist on the doorframe as I walked out of the closet.

Nick caught up to me, grabbed my wrists, and, with a twirl, pressed me up against the nearest wall. My body hit with a thud. I was about to snap at him when his lips snatched mine. He kissed me desperately then pressed my ass firmly up against the wall. I yelped into his open mouth.

"People will be here soon . . ." His breath was warm against my lips. " . . . but if I have to remind you to check your temper with another spanking, I will." He took my lips again and used his knee to spread my legs apart.

"People, including your mother." My words were jagged, a little pained, and a lot breathless as I tried to shove on him in between kisses.

"I'll make sure to be extra quiet." He dropped my wrist and slid his hand between denim and my naked skin, angling to slip between my thighs.

"Nick, I have to cook." It was a pitiful plea.

"Fine," he said nonchalantly as he yanked his hand out of my pants, dropped the other one, and seamlessly turned me toward the door.

He chuckled and my knees wobbled as I shuffled toward the stairs. When I was almost out of reach, he smacked my ass all the same. I yelped and jumped as my hands naturally covered my backside before skittering down the stairs.

"Not sleeping well are you?" My best friend Laura, complete with frosty martini in hand, slunk up as I put the finishing touches on squash.

"Why do you ask?" I tucked my chin, knowing full well I'd spent far too long trying to cover up the dark circles under my eyes.

"I've known you for a *very* long time. You cook when you need to unwind. And you get wound pretty tight when you don't sleep." She looked at me sideways over the rim of her glass.

"I'm cooking because it's Thanksgiving. Call me sentimental." I arched an eyebrow at her.

"You get emotional when you're tired, too."

"Fuck off."

"Language." She took another sip. "It's a holiday after all."

"So I should get a free pass," I said then changed subjects. "Who's the guy?"

Laura had shown up with a cute guy who was nowhere near her usual fare. I hadn't even paid attention when she introduced him, knowing full well he wasn't Mr. Right, he was just Mr. Right Now. Generic guys were becoming more and more commonplace of late.

"I told you, he's Gabriel. He's an investment banker. We've gone on a few dates." She pinched her eyebrows.

"A few dates and you bring him here?"

"He's from Vancouver. He doesn't have any family here and he's kind to me."

"Kind, huh?" I rolled my eyes, sure kind had nothing to do with it.

"You're a jerk."

"Funny, last Thanksgiving you were in a serious relationship, and I was the slutty one with the bad attitude."

She turned and walked away without a response. I looked up, watching her return to our family. Right before her hand slid around Mr. Right Now, she flipped a very pointed bird in my direction.

My eyes wandered across the faces filling my home, searching for one person. Deep down, my body knew Nick wasn't in the room simply because the ever present tingle that accompanied him wasn't humming across my skin. When I noticed Jaime was gone too, I bit my lip.

Shit.

As if on cue, Nick's stormy eyes, and Jaime's furrowed brow ducked out of the office, neither of which reassured me. My eyes met Nick's for the briefest moment. He had to see my unasked question but simply turned away. For the first time I got the feeling it actually meant not now rather than don't ask. I appreciated that development but it didn't stop my mind from spiraling.

I dropped my gaze to the food at my fingertips as my mind tripped over the list of things he'd mentioned this morning. My shoulders tensed with each item, threatening to swallow the hoops I was wearing, until strong hands slipped around me, and Nick nuzzled into my hair.

"What's up baby?" I exhaled deeply as I twisted to kiss his jaw.

He didn't answer, instead he purred quietly so only I could hear. My body reacted, my nipples pressing against the leather of my shirt. I was trying to contain the natural rock of my hips when one of Nick's hands slipped below the waist of my pants. I gasped. Our family was just feet from us and his roving hands, their conversations still going strong. Scarlet spread like wildfire across my skin and forced my eyes to fall to the countertop. Anyone would see sex written plain on my face if they caught my gaze. The change of view was zero help; potatoes two ways was sitting where my bare ass had been just a few hours ago.

My temperature skyrocketed as his hand leisurely skated from hip bone to hip bone. I did my best to answer a question Ari yelled. I barely managed words before giving up completely and collapsing back into Nick's chest. Mercifully, everyone was absorbed, paying me absolutely no mind.

I wiggled against him and he laughed lightly. I was both embarrassed and turned on. His hand slid lower, shielded from view by the breakfast bar as I whisked gravy. My whisk chattered against the metal when he hit his mark. No one flinched as I tried to pick it back up. My butterfingers dropped it all over again; I was barely able to breathe as he gently stroked me.

Nick was killing me, and his bastard-ass chuckle said he knew it too. He went so far as to start up minor conversations with the others; his posture seemed natural and his voice completely even. I nodded along hoping no one would ask me a question, sure my voice would betray me if they did. I didn't know how I would keep the inevitable orgasm quiet if he kept up.

The elevator dinged mid-stroke and Nick's mother stepped off. His hand froze. I didn't know if I wanted him to finish or get his hands the fuck out of my pants so I could attempt respectable. He made the decision for both of us and pulled out. I couldn't help the heavy sigh that left my lips as he untangled himself and circled toward the elevator.

But just beyond the breakfast bar he stopped and turned back toward me. Nick waited the slightest moment to catch my eye. He pressed the fingers that had been inside me past his lips and into his mouth. He purposely hummed then added a sultry, "Delicious" as he arched an eyebrow.

It wasn't possible for me to turn a darker shade of red.

"Are you stealing bites?"

Neither of us had noticed Ari rising to greet her mother. She was close enough to overhear Nick's comment and elbow him in the ribs. I coughed loudly, choking on a knot of embarrassment and lust. Nick didn't miss a beat though. "Yes I am. The gravy is wonderful." He winked over at me and my whole body blanched.

I'll kill him.

He seamlessly turned to his mother and hugged her. When she pulled back, she looked him up and down.

"Nicholas. Is what Frank said true?" Julia's eyes were cloudy; so similar to Nick's when he was agitated, but a flat and far more sad color.

"I have no idea what you're talking about, Mom." His perfectly crafted mask fell into place, saying he knew exactly what she was asking.

Julia greeted Ari with a big hug around the shoulders but her gaze stayed fixed on Nick.

"Nicholas Bryant," Julia snapped and Nick's hand rose to his temple and rubbed.

"Mother," he mimicked her tone perfectly.

"What's going on?" Ari chimed in and the two of them were exact mirrors as they narrowed their gazes in his direction.

"Not now," he growled.

That tone gave away everything, and made my stomach churn. *Christopher.*

As they continued to pepper him with questions, their faces pinched, and Nick deflated. My heart tore a little for all the burdens he carried. His shoulders slumped and his eyes were flat. A few weeks ago, I would have badgered him to tell his mother and sister the truth, now that I knew more, I just wanted to defend him.

"Julia." I forced a smile as I set down my whisk and rounded the breakfast bar. "So glad you could join us."

Her perfectly polished smile pulled into place and she reached to gather me in a hug. I managed to keep a perfectly passable look on my face even though our hug felt wrong. Forced. Her snipping at Nick bubbled up a bitter taste in my mouth.

I thought I'd let any pique with her go, but there it was, snarling in my chest. Apparently, I was still conflicted over her roll in Nick's past and our current problems. I creased my brow as I rubbed her back gently and focused on Nick over her shoulder to avoid more awkwardness.

He mouthed *I love you* when our eyes met and my whole body relaxed.

When I pulled away, Nick took Julia's elbow and introduced her to everyone. Julia was undeniably sweet and perfectly at ease despite what had transpired moment's ago. Her socialite mask was so perfectly polished she beamed. Because Christopher was back in the mix, the mask bothered me more than usual today.

Luckily, dinner kept me occupied. If my fingers were busy, it wasn't so hard to focus my mind. I was finishing plating when Julia wandered back into the kitchen.

"I'm very thankful for you young lady. For the life you've given my son."

She carried a flute of fizzing pink bubbles as she patted my shoulder. I shied away from her touch the slightest bit then forced myself to stand still.

"I can't imagine my life without him." I didn't have to force the response or smile as my eyes shifted to where Nick was laughing by the bar.

"Darling, I know you're upset with me."

"I . . . That's not . . . No . . ." My eyes dropped back to my fingers while they worked.

"It's okay, Kate." She watched me intently. "I get angry with myself sometimes too."

My head snapped up to find her eyes. They gave things away just like Nick's, and I hoped they'd give me clarity now. Something about her serene but sad look reminded me of Nick's when he needed consolation. My wall melted. The words were out of my mouth before I gave them much thought.

"Why you don't you just leave Francis?"

"Ari said Nicholas told you everything. That's what this is about?" She sighed a sad sigh as I nodded. "Because I'd do anything for my children. Then, and now." She shrugged as if it was a simple, obvious answer. "It wasn't until you that I trusted Nicholas was taken care of. But it worries me there's still so much trouble. And I lose sleep over Ari every day."

"We can take care of Ari." My voice was quiet but urgent, hoping I could finally be the one to help her see.

"Someday when you're a mother, you'll understand. Anyone and everyone can tell you they'll take care of your children, but until you feel it in your bones . . ." She shook her head and a smile danced on her lips again.

"I'll have to take your word for it." I couldn't help but scoff.

"You and Nicholas will be lovely parents. You'll have breathtaking children." Her voice lightened completely and her excitement mirrored Ari's uncontrollable jitters.

I finally found a full-blown smile for her. It was accompanied by an incredulous laugh and severely crinkled eyebrows. Julia laughed along and I breathed a sigh of relief that we'd landed somewhere far less heavy.

But when I really thought about parenting, I couldn't stop laughing. Julia looked quizzically at me and, when I shook quite thoroughly, she took the plates out of my hands and over to the table. My palm pressed into my chest as I bent over and slapped my knee with the other.

"What are you cackling about?" Apparently, Laura had forgiven me even though her voice had gotten snarkier since switching to tequila.

"Julia thinks we'd be good parents." I still couldn't right myself.

"That *is* hilarious." She started laughing with me, throwing an arm around my shoulders and pulling me into the dining room to feast.

3.

I was near comatose in the theater room after dinner when Julia bent over the chair Nick and I were cuddled in. As soon as she said she was leaving, Nick's eyes went lifeless and he slipped out from behind me. They wordlessly walked out with Ari close on their heels. Everything in their posture read defeated.

My insides churned. Did I follow Nick? Or did I give him space since he hadn't pulled me downstairs with him? When shouting drifted up from the living room, I was up and out of my chair before I made a conscious decision, bolting down the stairs.

"Hey," I hissed as I skidded down the last few, "everyone can hear you."

"I'm not overly concerned with what they can and can't hear," Julia snapped and I arched back like I'd been slapped.

What the hell?

"Don't yell at her. She's right. This is family business." Nick came to my side as he came to my defense.

"So you admit that it is, in fact, my business?" Julia arched an eyebrow in Nick's direction before adding a small, "Sorry sweetheart" in mine.

"We need to know, Nicholas," Ari piped up.

"Neither of you need to know. It should suffice when I say I'm taking care of it," Nick growled beside me.

Of course I knew how infuriating that answer was but I had no desire to fight with Nick. And honestly, at the end of the day, I had every faith that he would, in fact, take care of things. I stayed silent.

"I don't need to be pandered to," Julia said harshly.

"Me neither Nicholas." Ari's tone dropped.

"Can't we just let him handle this?" I hadn't meant to sound so flippant, or roll my eyes.

"That's easy for you to say, Kate," Julia sneered. "You know what *this* actually is."

"Yeah, he tells you everything." Ari crossed her arms on her chest.

"Yes, I do," Nick growled, "and I will continue to do so."

"Nicholas, Kate hasn't seen it first hand. She hasn't felt it all bear down on her." Julia was growing louder again. "And you're going to tell *her* and not me? You're going to let me walk into trouble unseen?"

Julia didn't follow up with a small apology this time and defensiveness flared in my chest.

"That's not even remotely funny, Mother. You know I wouldn't let that happen. And Kate knows a rough outline. She's had her fair share of trouble because of the Bryant name. I had to tell her something."

He let out a deep sigh and stepped away, pulling both his mother and sister into a giant hug.

"Mom, I had to placate Kate."

My mouth dropped.

"It was the only way to get her back."

I vividly pictured slapping him.

"It's the only way to appease her temper. If she really understood, like you do, she'd let me handle things. She can be nothing if not dramatic."

Hurt replaced my trademark temper and threatened to consume me. For a moment, I was drowning in it. Tears pooled in the corners of my eyes, and I had to bite my lip to keep it from trembling.

"Nicholas!" Julia shouted at the same time Ari mumbled, "Dumbass."

"Nicholas Bryant, I taught you better than that. Don't ever belittle a woman," Julia shrieked. I couldn't find my voice.

"I wonder if Kate even has a temper when she's not dealing with you, fuckface," Ari added.

The ball of emotion in my throat was slowly choking me.

"You two stop. Now," Nick growled. "Mother, I will take care of whatever Frank mentioned. Ari, I will take care of you."

Ari's face pinched and Julia shot Nick a withering look, holding his gaze even as she started speaking to me.

"Kate, I'm sorry about snapping. I'm sorry about everything today." Julia frowned and let her hand rub down my arm reassuringly before turning to sweep into the elevator. Ari was still mumbling under her breath as she turned toward the stairwell. I watched both of them go, wondering who I should stomp after. Anguish and fury each screamed different directions.

"Kate?" Nick's tentative tone told me he could see the tension rolling off me in waves. Something about that tone made me break.

"You've been *appeasing* me?" I didn't even recognize my voice. "You don't really give a shit about being equals?" My words were short and choppy.

"Kate."

"Don't *Kate* me!" My vision was tunneling. All I could see, all I could feel, was a black inky ball of heartache that enveloped me. "After everything? After *FUCKING* everything, I'm still just a possession to you?" I hadn't made the conscious decision to scream at him, but there I was, screaming.

"That's not what I . . ." Nick stuttered before I interrupted.

"What is it going to take?" I shoved against him. Ari had circled back and Laura was jogging down the stairs, both piping up trying to diffuse the situation. When I went to shove Nick again and he swiftly captured my wrists, they started shouting and grabbing at him. Neither stopped him from using his grasp to shove me up against the wall.

"I've told you everything willingly. I just wanted my mother to leave it be. Believe it or not, I still don't like sharing this shit with everyone. She'll let me take care of it if I say the right thing."

"Well why the fuck say *that*?" My voice broke.

"Because I thought you would know the truth. We've talked about trust a million times and you always read me so well." The blue in his eyes and the loosening of his grip told me it was true. He really had thought I'd understand.

"You thought I knew better than to believe you when you say our reconciliation was built on lies?"

"Yes. You know me better than myself." Nick let go of my wrists and I rubbed each one tenderly.

"According to you, actually, I don't understand. I *can't.*" I sneered on the word.

"It's my mother that can't understand. I swear," he pleaded with me.

"So make her understand. Make her leave that house."

"She's my mother. I can suggest and beg and plead but I can't force her. I've been trying for fucking years, Kate."

"Sure you can, Nick. It'd be one of the best ways to wield your high handedness."

"Is that what you think of me?" he snarled. "You think I'm arrogant and temperamental? Why the fuck are you with me, Kate?"

"You know that's not what I meant." I stepped toward him and Ari and Laura reappeared at our sides.

"I told you earlier to stop questioning my motives. Why the fuck can't you do *one* thing I ask?" Nick asked, exasperated.

My mouth fell open. I couldn't believe he'd just said that to me.

"What the hell is your problem Bryant? I'm not asking for the world, I'm suggesting you stop playing games with me and take care of your mother." I threw up my hands.

"You've forgotten what it's like to respect your mother and her choices. It's been so long since you had one. Since you had to give a damn about a family at all . . ."

He stopped short when my face contorted. My body staggered back and slumped against the wall like Nick had punched me with a very real, leaden blow. My breathing became forced, my shoulders slumped, and my knees quaked. The small part of my brain that was still functioning noticed his whole posture had changed, and his hand reach out for me. I would have batted it away if Laura didn't beat me to it.

"You're a bastard!" she bellowed as she stepped in between us and reached to steady me.

"You really are a fuckface. That was uncalled for," Ari scolded.

"Kate, I didn't . . ." Nick was trying to find a way around Laura.

"Don't touch her!" Laura shouted again.

The racket was creating a low level ringing in my ears and contributing to a severe headache.

"What's going on down here?" The cacophony had finally attracted Jaime, Gemma, Gabriel, and Ari's friends from upstairs.

"You should hear what this asshole . . ." Laura started in and her voice seemed amplified in the glass box that was our apartment.

"Shut up!" I shouted. "Everyone shut the hell up!"

The room went silent except for the thundering of my heart. Every pair of eyes stayed fixed on me but I couldn't bring myself to meet any of them. Not even the disasters that had to be Nick's.

"Kate, come on. We're going home," Laura said as I wordlessly pushed away from the wall.

My body was numb, dead even, as tears pooled in my eyes. But even here, even now, I wouldn't cry in front of everyone. I shuffled toward the stairs.

Laura's "Kate," Ari's "Jesus," and Jaime's "What the hell is going on?" all piled on top of each other. I didn't know what to say or who to say it to, I just slowly waded through the people toward the stairs.

"Sweets?"

I was half way up the stairs when Nick's pained question rang through the apartment; his voice made my insides twist. I froze but couldn't bring myself to turn.

"Sweets, are you leaving?"

"Of course she's leaving. You just called her an orphan, you diminished her pain, her loss!" Laura's succinct summary was sucker punch number two. Orphan sat pretty damn poorly on my shoulders.

"Kate, I didn't mean . . . I didn't think." Honesty and terror were thick in Nick's voice.

The very fact that he was scrambling publicly spoke volumes, but

I couldn't bring myself to reassure him. Or any of them for that matter. I started back up the stairs.

"Kate. Sweets, please." Nick's heavy footfalls pounded up the stairs after me.

"Stop." At my command, he froze.

"Kate, get your things, we're going," Laura said shrilly from below us.

"We'll have pizza or tequila or something," Ari agreed.

"Please . . ." Nick's voice was only a whisper, barely audible above the rest.

I took the biggest breath I could manage but my shoulders wouldn't relax.

"You." I turned and leveled my finger at Laura. "Cannot continually assume the worst of Nicholas." She sputtered but the look I gave her clammed her up quickly.

Nick's hopeful, " Sweets?" followed a moment later.

"And you," I shifted my gaze and my pointed finger to him. When I noticed it was shaking I shoved it in my pocket instead. "Don't you dare follow me."

"*I'll* escort you if you're leaving the building, Kate." Jaime fell into duty without anyone having asked.

"I'm just going to bed." I narrowed my eyes in Nick's direction. "Alone."

Sound erupted behind me but I started moving, completely unconcerned. I barely made it to a second floor guest bedroom before tears streamed down. I tucked in and slammed the door behind me so they could fall unashamed. I'd been battling the memories and emotion all day, Nick's shitty comment and Laura's orphan jab had cut extra deep.

I slumped down against the door and let my head fall into my hands. My tears rolled across my palms and down my wrists. Maybe five minutes passed before Laura came and hammered on the door. I didn't even flinch. When Ari followed her, I stood and walked away from the wood all together to collapse onto the freshly made bed.

Piece by piece, I shrugged out of my clothing then slid under the sheets. I wasn't even remotely comfortable, the mattress was foreign, lumpy even. I started counting panels on the ceiling to relax and dozed off around 82, a pool of dampness beneath my cheek.

4.

The faintest moonlight shimmered in through the windows when my eyes fluttered open. The floor to ceiling glass was familiar but the view was off, the bedding too. I turned and stretched, feeling achy in the way only whirlwind emotions could leave me. With an exaggerated groan into the dark, I rolled over.

Dark eyes caught my attention and my breath. Nick was awake and watching me intently from a bedside chair. For a moment neither of us spoke. Or even moved. I didn't know what to say, and I guessed he didn't know where to start.

Nick finally let out a deep sigh. "It's not even remotely sufficient, but I'm sorry. So sorry. I was such an unbelievable bastard." He lowered his head into his hands for just a second. When I stayed silent his hurt, swirling eyes shifted back to meet mine. "I can't believe you stayed. I thought I'd finally blown it and you'd be leaving for good. I would've deserved it."

His tone was so broken, cracked even, that I couldn't help myself when I reached out for him. His eyes went wide when my finger crooked as a signal to come to bed with me. He crawled in quietly, watching me as he did. I still didn't know what to say, but I hated watching his heartbreak in the sliver of shimmering moonlight.

"I'm so sorry," he murmured into the sheets as he snuggled into bed. "Please tell me you forgive me. Please, please, please."

It was harder to see his eyes now, my shadow obscured his face, but I was certain they were inconsolable. Before I gave it much thought I reached for him. My fingers itched to touch his skin; knowing it would ease the emotion bubbling in my stomach. No matter how angry I was, Nicholas Bryant was my talisman. I yanked at the hem of his shirt and used it to pull his muscular frame toward me.

"Kate," Nick whispered as he slid across the sheets. "Do you forgive me?"

I didn't have an answer. I didn't really forgive him, but I didn't want to fight either. Or talk at all for that matter. I wanted his lips on mine, and to forget about the crappy day, the family stress, Christopher, Victor . . .

God damn that list.

Nick was speaking again—probably begging forgiveness—but I didn't even bother listening. I just cut him off mid-sentence by swiftly straddling him and locking my lips on his. His hands flew to my naked hips and squeezed as he tried to keep talking. My tongue threaded between his lips and tangled with his, effectively ending any apology.

My hips started to roll against the soft fabric of his sweats, coaxing his erection to grow in the notch between my thighs. My hands slid to his and I laced my fingers in to pull them up beside his head. The cotton encasing his cock was slowly growing damp with the arousal spreading between my thighs. I hadn't let his lips leave mine, and I dug my nails into his hands where I held them. He growled at me. I snarled right back but let go of his hands and sat up swiftly.

"Kate?" Nick questioned as his hands found my hips again.

I shushed him, making my first sound since waking up. My hips kept their rhythm, I was fully focused on gentle gyrations.

"Talk to me. Tell me you forgive me." His breathy plea was a wholly tortured sound, and my compulsion to comfort him almost took over.

Almost.

I shoved his tone to the back of my mind and made the conscious choice to surrender to the ball of lust now thoroughly churning inside me. I reached under his waistband to explore the familiar contour of his sculpted hips that led to his perfect rock hard cock. In a swift move, I shoved the fabric aside and positioned him beneath my slick slit.

"Kate, please," he groaned and this time I didn't know if he was asking for forgiveness or to take him. I barely hesitated to figure it out.

I had to bite my lip as I guided his shaft into me. I wanted to cry out, something loud and mangled, but I didn't want to give Nick the satisfaction. My breathing hitched anyway as I sat still, him buried deeply inside, while I tried to calm my body. I shifted slightly and he slipped in deeper; I had to choke back another delighted gasp. My hands moved to his chest and flexed as I started rolling my hips against his.

I purposely moved along the length of his shaft, testing his resolve by almost letting him slip out then slowly gliding back down. His hands gripped at my hips in a way that would bruise, and his pleasured cries rang out into the night, but he didn't take control.

The longer I kept up the painfully slow rhythm, the more Nick trembled beneath me. My legs ached and my fingers were uncomfortable where they dug into his chest. The feeling had begun as exquisite but now . . .

I wasn't anywhere close to coming.

"Sweets," he gasped beneath me. "Please let me apologize." He moaned at the end of his sentence. "Forgive me and let me apologize." His words were truly agonized and I honestly didn't think it was from pleasure.

He was biting his lip and trying desperately not to squinch his eyes shut. Every single muscle in his forearm was rigid from how he held onto my body. Even his chest was fully flexed, rock hard beneath the bright red angry marks my nails had made on his flesh. His misery was a fully formed, living, breathing being in bed with us. He needed my forgiveness, and control, probably even my moans of pleasure and hammering heartbeat against his.

It *was* how we communicated best.

When he let his lip fall from between his teeth and I saw he'd broken skin, I caved. My sharp intake of breath sounded different than just a moment ago; softer, more sensual.

"Please," he whispered, sensing the shift.

"Nick, I . . ." My voice trailed off then stilled but he waited for me to speak. His hands changed from vices on my hips to tracing small, familiar circles. "You hurt me," I managed, "in a way only you can."

"I was the worst kind of bastard. I'll do anything to make it up to you." He nudged his hips against mine. "Anything." Bright blue—my bright blue—was slowly overtaking the sad color his eyes had been since I woke.

My body trembled as I sat above him. It had already forgiven him. My heart thudded once when he murmured, "Please" again but this time in a husky, deeply sexual tone.

Before I thought much more about it, I eased down along his chest and gently took his lips. I sucked ever so slightly and tasted the saltiness of his broken skin where there were welts from his teeth.

"I forgive you," I murmured, brushing his lips with mine as I spoke.

He didn't say anything in response but his demeanor shifted instantly. His intense grip on my hips returned and he used it to flip me. I winced when he slipped out of me. His fingers quickly took his cock's place. I couldn't help but roll my hips up to meet his hand where it teased my slit.

Nick's other hand slowly wrapped up and around my leg. His fingertips dug into my inner thigh as he pulled my leg up and over his shoulder. He slunk down my body, kissing every inch of skin before his face disappeared.

His nose brushed against my clit just before his tongue started to explore my quivering sex. My whole body shuddered when his tongue pressed inside and lingered, slowly exploring every inch he could reach. Nick's breath was warm against me, and I used my grip on his shoulder to buck against his face. His grip grew tighter on my thigh, and I knew it would wear bruises that matched my hips. The image made me groan desperately into the quiet night.

His nose, lips, and tongue were working overtime to touch and tease everything between my thighs.

"Nick," I gasped after a particularly naughty nip.

I felt his answering smirk as he lapped against my arousal like it was some kind of life blood. I was pretty far gone but I noticed when one of his fingers brushed along my thigh. Desire coursed through my veins and only ratcheted up at the idea of him swiping across my G-spot.

I jumped when he traced his finger lower and pressed it against the pucker of my backside.

"Fuck," I whispered the expletive when his tongue assaulted me at the same time his finger pushed inside.

Nick knew how to massage me gently, hitting spots that made me twitch and jerk. The hand that wasn't inside me slid up to pin my hip bones. His nose and teeth still alternated at the apex of my thighs, nudges and nips driving me crazy. I cried out and my heel dug into the flexing muscles of his back. My hands scrambled against the sheets below me. The finger in my ass was slowing making me crazy.

I was about to burst. My whole body tensed, every muscle bunched, and Nick noticed, pulling back slightly to watch. My hands flew to his gorgeous hair and I brought him back against me. His finger kept thrusting, his tongue lapped leisurely and I swore he smiled against my skin when I yanked a little too hard.

There was an extra burst of wetness between my thighs when the waves of an orgasm finally took my body. I jerked on Nick as I shrieked and ground my hips against his face. That feeling of satisfaction slowly spread from my stomach and filled my limbs like thick, warm honey. Then everything in me, every piece of me, melted to the sheets below.

Nick sat back when I lost control of my fingertips, just enough to watch me fall apart completely. The second I stopped violently shaking, he leaned in and kissed my clit. My body trembled as his lips travelled up my body, my arousal glistened on his chin and cheeks. He tenderly took each of my nipples and sucked before gently flicking with his tongue. My back arched off the bed in response. I was still breathing hard when his lips locked on mine. I could only gasp for air in between his passionate kisses.

"Why didn't you leave?" he murmured between lip locks.

"Ahhhh." I wasn't ready to make sentences.

"I need you." He sighed. "And I want you." He nudged his still rigid cock against me. "But I don't know why you stayed. Why you forgave me."

He kissed my chin and cheeks and eyelids before pulling back to look me full in the face. He sat there, waiting for me to catch my breath and answer. Part of me didn't want to break my silence, reveling in the sex, and the sensation was enough for me. But I couldn't override the desire to comfort him any longer.

"I said I'm not going anywhere and I meant it, Nick. I love you."

He folded down beside me, nuzzled into my neck, humming a pleased sound.

"And you're not angry with me despite the fact that I'm a fucking asshole?" He sounded completely unsure. And, honestly, it was totally appropriate.

"I never said I wasn't mad at you." I was still trying to catch my breath as I shoved my hands through my tangled hair. "I said I forgave you, that I love you, but I never said I wasn't pissed."

"Sweets?" His tone and the way he almost swallowed his voice said he hadn't expected that answer.

"Nick, I love you but a good orgasm isn't always going to fix our problems." I sighed and turned over in bed. I was staring out the windows when I continued. "I mean, thank you. I do, in fact, feel better, you're fucking phenomenal in bed, but it doesn't erase what you said."

There was a heavy silence in the room when I stopped speaking. It was almost stifling when Nick broke it.

"I don't know how to do this part, Kate."

I didn't respond and after a while Nick fidgeted behind me.

"Kate?" he murmured, "can I hold you? I need to hold you right now."

"I guess." The words were barely out before he pulled my back to his front and cocooned me. His fingers started to circle on my skin but they had an unsteadiness to them. I sighed a loud exasperated sigh, and his hand froze and dug in instead.

"Please don't hate me," Nick breathed, rustling my hair.

"Oh for fuck's sake, Nick, I don't hate you. I'm just not very good at this part, either."

"I wasn't thinking when I said it. I'm trying to get everyone to understand without laying *everything* out there. I'm trying to protect all of you at the same time, and it feels like so many balls are up in the air that I'm bound to drop one. At least one." He sighed and kissed the back of my head. "I dropped a ball tonight, and it's not an excuse, I just want you to understand. I hate myself for what I said."

My body was moving before I even thought about it, turning in his arms. My lips brushed his chest and I stopped to kiss above his heart.

"It'll be okay, Nick, but tonight, just stop talking." I sighed again and tangled my legs up in his so I could burrow deep into his chest. "You wanted to hold me, so do that. Hold me."

He didn't utter a word but let out a deep breath just before he adjusted his grip on my body, squeezing a little too tightly.

5.

The light shone in from the wrong angle in the spare room. Everything was off just enough to remind me of Nick's stupid, shitty words, and our stupid, shitty fight. He was still asleep, wrapped tightly around me, but his brow was creased and appeared to deepen as I watched him.

That crinkled face bothered me. Not only because he looked troubled, anxious even, but because the urge to make it go away was so strong that a very large part of me was willing to forget about last night completely. And I didn't want to sweep it all under the rug. At some point, we'd have to face our sharp, stinging issues head on.

I need a fucking run.

I started to weasel out of Nick's grip hoping not to wake him. I wanted out of the house without additional discussion on the matter. I managed to tip-toe upstairs, change, and brush my teeth without the slightest sound echoing through the apartment.

For a moment, I thought I'd get to sneak away but Nick's groggy voice greeted me when I bent over to throw my hair up in a ponytail.

"Did you change your mind?"

"Huh?" I snapped up, pulling my hair tight in the tie.

"Are you running from me after all?"

"I'm going for a run." I managed to keep any snap out of my voice. "Big difference."

"Why?" he asked mid-yawn as he rubbed sleep out of his eyes.

"You know why, Nick." I arched an eyebrow.

His whole face sobered. "You aren't going to run through the park are you?" The fear in his eyes melted me.

"No, baby, I'm not." I managed a small smile for him. "I think I'm gonna go into the office."

"We agreed to work from home. To actually take a four day weekend," he said softly.

"We agreed to a lot of things that got shot to hell yesterday." I couldn't swallow my exasperated sigh in time.

"Kate . . ." His voice trailed off and his eyes shifted to that sad silt color.

"It's also because of Hong Kong. That trip, along with Christmas, will effectively end my operating year two weeks early. I have to shift my priorities." I crossed my arms and leaned against the counter.

"You're still coming to China with me?" The tiniest twinkle crept into his eyes.

"Of course." I rolled mine.

Nick reached for me as I passed by and I let him pull my body to his. He kissed my forehead and breathed in my scent deeply.

"I'm running with you."

He turned toward the closet without further conversation. I raised my eyebrows even though he couldn't see. I wasn't particularly thrilled with the idea but I didn't want to fight anymore either.

Nick was moving slowly, and I ended up making coffee and waiting for him at the breakfast bar. Without thinking, I jumped up and sat on the stone. I was the tiniest bit sore when I landed but shook it off, purposely pushing the memories of yesterday morning from my mind. I was sipping coffee and answering emails when Nick finally plodded down the stairs.

He was wearing black sweats that hung sinfully well from him hips and a matching hooded sweatshirt that managed to hint at the muscles underneath. He was gorgeous. I still couldn't decide if he was more attractive in workout wear, casual clothes or one of his perfectly tailored suits. Lately I'd been leaning toward whatever he happened to be wearing at that particular moment. Or naked. He was perfect naked. My thoughts betrayed me when my chest and cheeks flushed. He ran his fingers through his hair, and he pulled out a small, crooked smile for me.

"I love you on the breakfast bar."

"Not this morning, Nick." I shot him a look even though it was my wayward thoughts that'd started it.

"I can't help myself when your skin turns that particular shade of pink." He was trying to stifle a wider smile, one that wanted to split his face.

"You're a dirty bastard."

"With you, yes, undoubtedly."

Nick moved between my legs and grabbed my hips. He pulled me roughly toward his body and rested his chin on my chest. He looked up at me, and the textbook definition of adoration batted up at me from under long lashes.

"Are we ok?" He wrapped his arms around my hips and lifted.

Sometimes I forgot how strong he was, how completely he could dominate me. Here, with my legs wrapped high around his chest and nothing but his arms supporting my weight, I remembered and flushed again. My body had obviously made up its mind as I unwound from his and slid slowly down his chest.

"We're ok." My mind was getting there too.

I leaned in and gently curved my lips up to his. I'd only meant to coax a gentle, chaste kiss from him, but he took full advantage. His hand came to my chin and held me still. The other moved swiftly back to weave into my ponytail and pulled. Hard. I gasped toward the ceiling when he opened my neck to his lips and proceeded to kiss a tender trail slowly down to my collarbone.

He pulled away a moment after but still had my ponytail wrapped around his wrist and my head tilted back. My breathing was a little more ragged than I cared to admit.

"We don't have to go. There are other forms of exercise you know." He chuckled.

My lips parted to scold but he leaned over me and winked as he let go then called the elevator. As soon as I stepped toward him, he grabbed my hand and gripped it tightly.

Jaime was in the lobby waiting for us, and his concerned eyes flashed first to mine, then Nicks and settled on our hands clasped together. He had to be expecting fall out. Nick purposely brought my hand to his lips and kissed the back of my palm. I rolled my eyes and Jaime nodded knowingly.

Nick must have caught a glimpse of my face because he stopped short. His fingers unlaced from mine and took my hand with both of his. He brought my palm to his lips and kissed the center ardently. It was the first tender gesture we had ever shared and he used it as his secret weapon now, knowing full well it made my heart flutter.

"I love you, Kate Elliott."

Jesus those words make me weak in the knees.

My favorite bright eyes peered over my fingertips. When he knew I was watching, he ducked down again and kissed my palm every bit as lovingly as before. He closed his eyes and held his lips to my skin for a few moments then wordlessly wrapped his hand back around mine and pulled me toward the front door. I couldn't help the genuine smile that broke across my face; Nick squeezed my hand all the harder.

A handful of photographers waited for us, and Nick kept his vice grip on me as we followed Jaime; he wove through both them and the pedestrian crowd. Nick's grip was uncertain, fidgety almost, until a small crack opened in the sea of people. Without warning, he yanked me free from the clog so we could really run.

When we hit our stride, he let go and gestured for me to move ahead of him; I hesitated for a second. He scowled playfully and I easily jetted in front. My breath puffed rhythmically in the cold air surrounding us. I tried to focus on the swirls but Nick occupied my thoughts.

He was staying close—*too* close—even getting his feet tangled with mine. I swore loudly but reined in my temper, keeping our tentative truce. The second we had to stop for traffic, he was there, his hand reached out for me a few times, but I didn't look around to see why. When we reached Vesper, he let out a massive sigh as I pushed open the large glass door. I caught a glimpse of troubled eyes before he could look away.

"Is this about the fight?" I shot him a look as I asked.

"No," he answered succinctly.

"Then what's wrong?"

"Nothing."

"Bryant." I clenched my fists and stomped my foot.

There'd been too much shit in the past 24 hours for me to tolerate his overused and evasive responses. I glared at him as he grumbled rough monosyllables at the elevator door where we waited. The moment the doors slid open he pushed me into an empty car, continuing his silence. I shook my head in the elevator, trying desperately not to break skin where I dug my nails into my palms, furious we were back at square one.

"I'm scared, Kate. I was scared yesterday and I'm fucking terrified today."

Whoa.

Nicholas Bryant didn't do emotions regularly. Or ever, really.

"Everything is off. Fighting with you makes it that much worse. And that run was awful. All I can think about is how I might lose you. How I have lost you . . ." His words trailed off.

I slumped against the elevator wall and looked him over before I responded.

"I get scared too, Nick. I lost you too. And I'm just as terrified I'll have to go on without you at some point. That something will happen beyond our control. When you don't tell me things, I immediately assume it will be sooner rather than later."

His steely gaze slowly swept over me when I laid bare my deepest fear. I hadn't fully voiced it to anyone, maybe not even myself, but as soon as I gave it life, I felt the honesty deep in my bones. I did worry about losing him, worry it was too good to be true. Every. Damn. Day.

I swallowed hard as Nick pushed off the wall and crossed the small space between us to grab me. As soon as the doors opened, he pulled me out of the elevator, stopping just outside to kiss me deeply. His hands moved up to weave into my hair and pull me onto his lips.

When he came up for air, he leaned his forehead to mine.

"I'm not going anywhere." His whisper was warm against my skin.

"You don't always have a choice in the matter. I mean, my parents . . ." I couldn't finish that sentence. "And with Christopher . . ." Emotion balled in my throat making that one even harder.

"Kate, I was never *that guy*." He chuckled at himself. "And it's corny as hell, but now I know not even fate would keep me from you. It wouldn't fucking dare."

He wove his hand around mine and pulled it up so he could kiss each of my knuckles. For the first time, since he'd told me about Victor and Christopher, I relaxed. I couldn't even replay yesterday's *orphan* debacle anymore. My entire world revolved around the way our skin molded perfectly together where it entwined.

"Oh my God, that's it!" Nick interrupted our moment as he spun from me, stroking his chin, and staring at the lobby floor. "Why didn't I see it earlier."

"Nick?" I arched an eyebrow.

"Jaime take care of Kate, I'll be back." Jaime had arrived in a separate elevator just in time for Nick's outburst. My eyes darted between the two of them. Jaime was just as confused as me.

"Nick. What the hell is going on?"

I reached for him but he shoved at the emergency door and rounded the corner into the stairwell without even hesitating. For a moment, I debated going after him. His reaction worried me until I remembered his eyes had been crystal clear. I didn't know what was going on but that alone told me I could let it play out. I shook my head with a small, baffled laugh as I headed into my office and settled in to answer the mountain of emails that had piled up in a little over 24 hours.

A production delay quickly captured my attention, and by the time I looked up, I'd been working for two hours without hearing from Nick. The all too familiar dread clenched in the pit of my stomach. I was about to call Jaime when there was a knock at my door. Those knuckles wrapped a familiar, homey sound and I exhaled loudly.

"Come in."

Brennan, the head of my Tech Department, followed Nick into my office, carrying a stack of papers and a small box. The hair on the back of my neck stood up at the sight of that godforsaken box. It was the bane of my corporate existence, housing every failed prototype of the fitness device I'd been developing.

Or rather, trying to develop.

My eyes narrowed, glaring at the innocuous black box, and the familiar signs of my temper welling almost replaced my words with a haggard roar.

"Why did you bring that damned thing in here?"

I sat back in my chair as I waited for them to begin. Nick chuckled while Brennan took the lead.

"We've solved everything, we'd like your approval."

What the . . . ?!

My mouth dropped open, and I gracelessly launched forward as my fingers scrambled for the papers Brennan was handing me. I glanced at the documents, grabbing my glasses and shoving them on before refocusing. I didn't know if I needed them because of disbelief or to actually read the text. Nick's heated gaze and arched eyebrow didn't escape my notice. I purposely lifted the paperwork to block my view.

Before me was a simplified algorithm that took into account every different piece of a song; bass lines, vocal lines, downbeats, *everything,* so we could accommodate a variety of paces with one track. Users could select a genre then a program we'd carefully curated played over six hours of music based on their cadence.

"You're sure this will work?"

"Yes." Brennan's eyes lit up.

"We tested it downstairs," Bryant added.

I folded the corner of the paper and looked over my glasses at him. "Why wasn't I included?"

"Oh, um, Mr. Bryant . . ." Brennan stammered.

"You were busy. My understanding is that you have two weeks versus the usual four before year end." Bryant's words were thoughtful, his smirk, on the other hand, was beyond smug.

"We tested the reprogrammed chip in the old prototype. Works pretty great. You're welcome to try it out." Brennan pulled the old and suddenly-not-so-upsetting device from his box and set it on my desk.

"And the clip?"

I couldn't help but raise an eyebrow. It was the other massive hurdle I'd run into. And bashed my head against. Multiple times.

"Well that was all Mr. Bryant."

"Bryant?" I cocked my head as I questioned him.

"I started to think about skin curving against skin."

My eyes narrowed as I calculated whether I could reach his face to slap from where I was sitting. He was undoubtedly referencing personal things. Whether the contours of my skin in Patrić's photos, us tangled in bed together or . . . Then the glimpse I'd caught of our intertwined arms mere hours ago came to mind, and the sentiment suddenly seemed undeniably sweet.

Nick pulled the smallest shell from the box and it'd been transformed. My eyes lit up. Neoprene contoured out from the plastic casing, sort of like a wave or a sideways, thick, barely bending letter S. It wasn't even as long as the finger he placed it on for me to inspect. And inspect it I did before my face fell.

"It's nice, beautiful even, but how's it going to stay on. I specifically wanted something low cost to manufacture that would make the device accessible to anyone, wearing any type of workout gear without having to purchase separate cases, adapters, Vesper clothing, etcetera."

Heat rose into my chest and up into the tips of my ears.

We've been over this.

"Magnets." He shrugged with his nonchalant reply.

"Magnets?" I peered over my glasses at him again. He shifted ever so slightly and a smug smile threatened to pull at his lips. "Care to elaborate?" My jaw clenched at his reaction.

His eyes lit up just before he leaned across the desk and wrapped the fabric around my finger. There were magnets hidden in the fabric that easily clasped around my finger. The aesthetic was a surprisingly stylish, almost brash cocktail ring. I tried to stifle a gasp, sure I needed to play the cynic.

"I don't know how practical a ring is unless the consumer is willing to purchase the wireless headphones."

Bryant had to know he was winning me over when I stayed focused on the pretty little device despite my protest. Without a word, he pulled my arm back across the desk. He took the ring from my finger and moved to my sleeve. He laid it out, almost like a watch but on top of the fabric. With nimble fingers he slid two small, opposing disks in place on the underside. There, without a clip, without a bulky armband, and on normal clothing, it sat firmly in place. I shook my sleeve gently then crescendoed to a wild flap; the device stayed perfectly set on my sleeve.

It can go anywhere!

"Magnets," Nick repeated.

"I love it." My voice was a mix of awe and adoration. I didn't even try to stifle it. They really had fixed everything and fixed it beautifully.

Nick smiled. "Cost of production will make you love it even more."

"Thank you both so much. Brennan, thank you for working on this, today, of all days. Bryant . . ." I let my voice trail off.

Would it be completely inappropriate to lunge across the table and kiss him?

A long-oppressive weight fell from my shoulders, and a deep exhale left my lips. My gaze shifted from one man to the other and back. I couldn't help the massive smile that spread across my face. When I let loose a loud hearty laugh, both men joined in, the room itself feeling infinitely lighter.

Brennan was collecting his things when Nick's eyes latched on mine. The pure blue was hungry. He wanted to devour me—all of me—and not just my flesh. My heart swelled and everything below my belly button clenched, goose bumps travelled up my skin. Nick noticed and, with a positively beaming grin, he ushered Brennan to the door.

As soon as the door shut behind him, before he was even able to turn around, I murmured, "I love you, Nick."

He turned and looked directly into my eyes. "I love you too. More than words can say."

"How did you . . . ?"

"I'd do anything for you." He strode purposefully to my side. "And I'm particularly interested in making amends at present."

Nick lifted my hand, device still attached, and kissed the inside of my palm.

MMMmmm.

Carefully, he pulled the magnets free and tucked the design back into his pocket.

"I'm glad you like it. I'll get the specs to production right away." He turned to go.

"Wait!" I almost dove after him. "How did you magically fix this in one morning?"

Had he been holding out on me?

My temper flared a little at the thought.

"I had the right kind of motivation." He smiled warily and took a deep breath. "Your skin has always been an inspiration to me." He winked and I swallowed any irritation. "Holding your hand today got me thinking about the shapes possible. About how something could mold to the contours of a body."

"It really is beautiful, babe. I never imagined anything better." I smiled widely and he stepped back to reach for my cheek. "That doesn't explain the cadence issues?" I turned my voice up at the end so he'd know what I was asking.

"When we were running I was so nervous I started humming. People walking would match other beats or rhythms in the same song. It was so obvious. I should've realized a long time ago that one song could work for a ton of paces if I factored in something besides down-beat. We just had to rewrite the algorithm to accommodate."

"Why didn't you tell me?"

"I wanted to surprise you." He bent and kissed my forehead.

"You are truly brilliant, Nick. People see the savvy but they don't see the utter genius behind it."

He tried to hide an embarrassed smile. "Kate, I don't . . . That's not . . . You're the brilliant one."

I rolled my eyes just before launching my arms around his neck and yanking him down into a smoldering kiss. He bumped up against the desk but caught me firmly. His smile was broad and full against my lips. He pulled back just far enough to speak.

"I thought you had to get all sorts of work done." Every time he let his lips graze mine as he spoke, my skin caught fire. My insides liquefied when he nudged his erection against me. "Not happy about leaving the bed now are you?"

He laughed as I slumped against him and shook my head against his shoulder. Emotion pooled inside me and sentiment bubbled up in full force.

"Nick, I want to say something before you leave, okay?"

He pulled back and the corners of his eyes crinkled. I could tell by the set of his shoulders that he was holding his breath. I tried to smile but tears threatened to choke me instead, making for a confusing and contorted face.

"You are my other half." I cleared my throat. "You are the only person I trust with my business, and more importantly, my heart. I know last night was not great but I swear to God or on the moon or on this business, whatever you want, I'm in this."

I didn't even really get the last bit out before he mashed his lips to mine. They were confused, trying to consume mine, and press gently all at the same time. His hands worked against me, trying to pull me closer but cradle me too. There was some sort of rolling wave of tingles resonating through me when he let his tongue wander into my mouth. My hands moved into his hair then traced down along his shoulders in the same sweetly frantic motions.

My breath caught when he scooped me up and carried me to the couch. Nick kept an arm around me while he shoved cushions to the floor then laid me on the soft gray fabric.

Nick slid ever so gently over top of me. His hand caressed my thigh and notched behind my knee, barely squeezing as he hitched me up and started a slow roll between my thighs. So many times sex was urgent and rough between us. This had none of that frenzy.

He slowly kissed down my body, lifting my shirt to expose my belly button, then continued down my stomach. When he finally pulled my top off, goose bumps spread across every exposed inch of me. He moved in closer, finding a way to cover me completely while his lips wandered around, tracing passionate trails.

Not a single thought crossed my mind except Nicholas Bryant. His taste, his smell, his skin, and his unique brand of adoration filled my senses. My mind was foggy, and all I remember was sensation; skin on skin rather than him actually stripping me naked. There were kisses and hands and stroking as he pressed his perfect naked body up to mine. His arms wrapped around me, cocooning my head as he bit down on my bottom lip and pushed slowly into me.

6.

I looked up at the couch for the 800th time and blushed.

Damned couch.

That damned couch where my damned sexy boyfriend had his damned way with me.

And God damn was it good.

So good in fact, I'd had a hard time refocusing and was still working at 11 p.m.

Jaime had settled into a seat long ago and had almost finished reading an Ian Flemming novel. In all that time his phone only buzzed twice. The relative peace was almost as distracting as the memories flitting through my mind. I'd started absentmindedly chewing on my cheek in an effort to concentrate, but I had a better chance of actually breaking skin then I did of focusing.

Jaime's phone buzzed a third time, and I let out a deep breath I hadn't realized I was holding. He barely had time to check the screen before I spoke up.

"Is everything ok? Is Nick ok?"

"Give me a minute." His brow furrowed as he read his screen. Almost as quickly as he looked down, Jaime looked up with a warm smile on his face. "Everything is perfectly fine." "That was just Colton checking in. If you'd like to stay much longer he'll relieve me."

"Oh," I said and arched back, making a face.

I was sure Nick would have been harassing one or both of us to get home by now. Apparently, the confusion read loud and clear in the way my face contorted.

"Mr. Bryant asked once how long we were going to be. When I told him I didn't know but could ask, he simply told me not to bother you."

I started chewing on the inside of my cheek again.

"Is he mad at me?" He'd gone silent on more than one occasion for that exact reason.

"Kate?" Jaime looked up from his book, his warm smile had shifted to quizzical, complete with arched eyebrow. "Why on earth would he be upset with you? In my opinion, you let him off a little too easy this time." He chuckled softly.

"He usually hounds one or both of us at this hour."

Jaime understood that it just didn't feel right. "I believe he's trying out this novel thing called patience." His shoulders shook from his husky laugh.

"Huh." Patience was so unexpected, I honestly couldn't think of anything to say.

"When you came back, Kate, something shifted. I have every faith that he'll do whatever he can keep you. Including show some restraint."

I nodded again, still at a complete loss for words.

"If it makes you feel better, there's probably a punching bag or Hong Kong executive that's taking the brunt of it." Jaime capped off his statement with a roll of his eyes and even though it wasn't funny, a loud "Ha!" escaped my lips.

The truth behind Jaime's words was what finally made me give up. I wasn't here to punish Nick or anyone else for that matter. Jaime smiled even wider when I asked him to call the car service then packed my things.

As predicted, Nick was shouting into the phone at some poor soul when I walked into the apartment. In Cantonese, no less. I leaned against the office doorframe for a few minutes, watching him pace around the room like a baited animal, muscles flexing and coiling under the fine fabric of his clothes. When he started gesturing wildly with his free hand, I pushed away from the dark paneling and walked toward him.

He sensed me and lifted his arm so I could slink in underneath when I got close enough. All his rigid tension melted as I wove my hands around his waist. Even the tone of his voice changed; I shook my head at the response. The moment his tirade stopped, he leaned down to kiss my forehead where it was tucked beneath his chin. His fingers started circling along my ribs, and a shiver ran up my spine at his touch.

"I'm glad you're home," he said against my skin. I wasn't sure when he'd hung up the phone.

"Me too." I nestled in under the crook of his jaw.

He held me like that until his phone started buzzing again. He simply reached into his pocket to silence the BlackBerry.

"Baby, is everything okay?" I pulled back so I could see his eyes when he answered.

"Same shit." They were mostly gray but a little bit of blue danced around his irises.

"We never got a chance to discuss the list of issues you rattled off at me. What did Victor's note say?" I tensed in anticipation of an answering onslaught.

"To watch out. That I'd pay for what I did but he swore to God, it wasn't his doing," he answered without hesitation.

I choked back the bile that bubbled up to my throat. "What's he getting at?"

"I wish I knew. He's making it sound like he's a player in someone else's game."

"Could it be . . ." I let my voice trail off, not even wanting to say Christopher's name. The way Nick's eyes went flat, I was glad I hadn't.

"I hope . . . God . . . I don't know." His voice choked off. "I mean . . ."

"What?" I barely breathed.

"It would be weird. They don't know each other. They have no reason to, but . . ."

"But?" I murmured.

"I can't find *him*." I couldn't tell if it was fear or anger that tinged Nick's growl when he referred to Christopher. "Anyway you'll let him go for the moment?" he asked, softly.

"Sure." Nick had shared openly at my request; I'd stop at his. I looked for a change of subject, catching Christmas lights hanging on a distant window. "Hey, do we have any plans for Christmas? Laura will be in Portland."

"I hadn't really thought about it." He sighed. "I doubt you'll be surprised but I don't really do Christmas."

"Oh, Nick, I . . ."

"It's okay, Sweets." Nick's finger came to my chin and pulled my eyes up to his. "It was partially because of my step father, but also because I don't usually have time."

"You don't have time for Christmas?"

"Julien buys my gifts and has them delivered. I take the day off and buy a particularly rare, exceptionally delicious scotch and try to relax. I don't often succeed."

"No decorations, no movies or carols or cookies?"

"No." He smiled. "You make time for all that?"

"Well, I try but I guess Laura always did most of the work. Or towed me home to Oregon with her." I shrugged remembering how she'd recruited her ex-boyfriend to get a twelve-foot live tree into their seventh floor apartment last year—he'd had to hire four movers—but we caroled drunk beneath it while I burned cookies.

"I'll see if I can arrange for something." He was businesslike but his face had lightened. I pulled his body back flush with mine and let my lips graze along his neck and jaw where I could reach.

That was the last moment I stood still with Nick for almost two weeks. Surprisingly, it wasn't the only time he'd been overly sweet though. We fell into a new pattern that made our relationship seem completely normal.

I hated it.

Nick was usually gone or already shouting Cantonese on a conference call by the time I woke. I was at the office late enough for

Colton to relieve Jaime most nights. When I dragged my weary ass home, there was only a fifty-fifty chance Nick was there to meet me. When he was, he wordlessly took me to bed and lavished attention on my clit until I pierced the quiet of our apartment with the shrieks of a joint rattling orgasm.

At Nick's command, Jaime provided me daily updates on the problematic men in our lives. He also accommodated my every request to run, albeit usually with beefed up security.

I'd been gifted with Nick's take on Christmas decorations—chic and simple modern decorations to compliment the architecture and interior design of our immaculate penthouse. Normally chic sleek silver and simple shimmering white were the epitome of my aesthetic but there was no red or green, nothing homey or comforting. All my childhood decorations were still tucked in boxes at Laura's.

It felt wrong.

Matter of fact, it *all* felt wrong. There was zero conflict between Nick and I. He was exercising patience and understanding in *everything*, and it didn't sit well. It was obvious he was trying—hell, it was obvious he was succeeding at being a better boyfriend. But in the end, I questioned whether that made things any better between us.

Even the sex was focused fully on me. I couldn't recall whether he'd come since Thanksgiving. He'd pulled out all the tricks my body responded to and had me coming hard and fast daily. But all without his cock inside me. We certainly hadn't done anything kinky. I couldn't recall if we'd lasted more than 30 minutes . . .

Is he masturbating in the shower?

I would have been. The thought was downright depressing.

The more I dwelled on the dynamic, the further I spiraled. Was this what a life together would be like? Once our major conflicts were resolved, were we this boring? Could I be satisfied with that sort of relationship? Could he? Neither of us signed up for white picket fences.

I got myself so worked up that I convinced myself I couldn't feel the electricity between us anymore. And, of all the ways I thought I might lose Nicholas Bryant, morphing into beige and growing tired of *us* hadn't one of them.

I was panicking—regularly—and rather than hyperventilate like a normal person, my temper flared. Spectacularly. Every employee at Vesper had cowered on the other side of my desk at one point or another. Nick and Jaime had both gotten their fair share of pinched looks and icy growls as well.

I shot Jaime one such look when he cleared his throat around 4:30 p.m. the day of our Hong Kong flight. His subtle hint was the first thing that pulled me from the contact sheets marketing had sent over two hours ago.

"One minute, Jaime. I have to get Callista on board with the campaign and her PR firm behind Vesper before I leave."

He made an excessively sour grimace at my request, but let me yank out my BlackBerry nonetheless. As always, Callista tried to steamroll me for Bryant related-details the second she answered. When we started bickering, Jaime wordlessly began gathering the items I normally did, effectively packing my bag.

Out of the corner of my eye, I saw him hand my belongings off to Gemma, then circle back to collect me. When I held up my pointer finger asking for another minute he simply used my outstretch wrist to pull me up out of my chair and toward the elevator.

4:47 p.m. Motherfucker.

I was running over fifteen minutes late. The old Bryant would have flipped, this new, patient Bryant would probably apologize to me for some imagined slight. Nauseated at the idea of a simpering conversation, I let Jaime corral me. I even walked quickly to the waiting Bentley.

When Callista tried to circle back to personal PR issues, horns started blaring in painfully slow traffic. My shoulders inched up to my ears, and my free hand balled against the leather beneath me. My temper was moments away from erupting in a way that threatened to shatter me.

But then my phone vibrated and buzzed beneath my ear. Then again. And again. Soon they rolled in almost on top of one another, each text message resonating like a tiny expletive. When Jaime started receiving a similar flurry of buzzes and his face contorted, I guessed exactly who they were from. And what they were saying. A little over two weeks ago, they'd been commonplace. My blood boiled and, as sick and twisted as it may have been, it surged excitement rather than fury through my veins.

Perhaps he still has a backbone.

The more buzzes that resonated beneath my ear, the more I wanted to hang up on Callista, call Nick and yell, "We're on our fucking way!" then hang up just to fan the flames. It was masochistic but something about bickering felt *right*.

I resisted the urge and was still mid-conversation when we pulled up to the heliport. Nick paced in front of the helicopter with Colton. The storm in his eyes told me far more than any of the texts would have. I was in even more trouble than I'd guessed. Not a single hint of the cool, calm, collected Nick from the last two weeks was on the tarmac.

As soon as I walked up, Nick lunged for my phone. Mercifully his fingers missed tangling into my hair as he snatched my cell from my ear and barked, "Ms. Elliott is running late. She'll contact you later." He hung up as forcefully as possible then pocketed my phone just in time for me to screech and shove him. He stutter-stepped and my back bristled when he steadied himself and glared at me.

"That was important!"

"Being on time is important," he shot back.

My heart thudded as he took one powerful stride toward me, curled his fingertips around my arm, and pulled me toward the helicopter. My phone ring was barely audible from his pocket over the whir of the blades. I scrambled to reach for it.

"You should be glad I decided to come in the first place." I was shouting but it had nothing to do with the cacophony of mechanical noise.

"If you were going to make me late and embarrass me in front of potential associates, perhaps you shouldn't have!" He managed to keep me away from my cell and get me up into the helicopter.

The door shut behind us but it did little to dampen the noise. I put extra volume into my voice to shout, "Screw you" as I crossed my arms and turned away from him, refusing to take the headphones he held out for me.

"Kate, put these on," he snarled, "before you make things worse." I kept my arms crossed and my eyes fixed out on the water surrounding the pier. Without warning, the giant headphones scraped down my ears, stinging and shoving my sunglasses into my lap.

Without thinking, I turned and slapped him hard and fast across the face. He looked so stunned I almost backpedaled to apologize. But then his whole face pinched. He took my phone out, fiddled momentarily at the side then snatched the sim card and handed me the empty, dead case of a phone. I contemplated chucking it out of the rising helicopter or smacking him again. Or throwing the phone *then* slapping him.

True to form, Jaime's eyebrows almost climbed off his forehead before he picked somewhere else to look.

After a few strained minutes we touched down at Teeterboro, and the helicopter blades came to a stop in front of a hanger. Even though we were fighting, Bryant reached his hand back to help me down. I pursed my lips then purposely ignored it, reaching for Jaime's unsuspecting shoulder instead. When my hand clutched his suit, Jaime turned to help me down. Nick eyed us both then stormed off, his blazer whipping behind him in the wind. I kept a hold of Jaime's arm as I click-clacked across the tarmac after Nick.

"We *were* late." Jaime leaned in, murmuring, trying to ease the tension before a 24-hour flight.

"He's being a dick."

Jaime tried to stifle a laugh at my retort. He almost succeeded but I still caught a small scoff.

The plane was decorated in the same beautiful pale fabrics and dark woods that were a trademark of Bryant spaces. Warm, recessed lighting filled the seating area making the plush couch and recliner-style seats infinitely more inviting. A few pillows and soft furry blankets accented the various seating options. Nick had chosen an individual seat with a narrow tabletop in front of it. There was a single seat next to it that had newspaper scattered over its cushions. When I walked up, he shuffled to collect the papers.

I eyed the seat, then him, trying to decide where on the temper tantrum scale I actually was. He refused to meet my eyes, instead making an overly dramatic gesture telling me to sit.

Go fuck yourself, Bryant.

Deciding I was somewhere between nine and nine a half, I pursed my lips and walked straight to the flight attendant making drinks in the back. She'd just finished pouring a scotch and looked up, beaming, only for her face to fall when she realized Nick wasn't the one hovering behind her. I snatch the scotch from her hands all the same.

"Thank you."

I smiled so wide it had to come off phony. Jaime cleared his throat behind me, and I whirled around, throwing a scowl in his direction. He waved his hands in surrender.

"Is there a phone that I can use during take-off?" I asked sharply, and Jaime pointed to a closed door. I shoved past both him and the flight attendant into the small room.

The office was obviously Bryant's. It was a small replica of his office at The Venture Group, dark leathers, light whites, and a chic cigar club feel. I sunk into the chair and picked up the phone. I punched in Callista's number and propped my feet against the edge of the desk. Bryant's frigid barks rang through the cabin in between dial tones, but when Callista answered I started right back in where we left off, paying him absolutely no mind.

I stayed on the phone for at least 45 minutes. When I hung up I didn't mean to slam the phone down, but my temper was barely contained. Neither scotch nor Callista had done anything to improve my mood.

For a second I thought about going out to find Nick, his skin would soothe me, but then I pushed my hair behind my ear and brushed the scrapes from where he'd shoved my headphones.

"Ahhhh!" I snarled, and it resonated in my chest.

I fired up my laptop and aimlessly reviewed everything for the spring line. It didn't really need doing but I'd be damned if I was going anywhere near Nicholas Bryant.

7

The soft hum and chatter of the plane was the only thing interrupting what should have been soothing silence; it had me gritting my teeth. Vesper business was making my temples throb. I plugged in my headphones, hoping a mellow playlist would do what ambient noise couldn't. Instead, fury flared every time Alt-J, Glass Animals, or even Chet Faker came on because I could vividly imagine sex with *him* to those songs.

When the next one played, I mashed the skip button on my laptop hard enough that it crunched beneath my finger.

"Do tell, did the laptop do something completely reasonable, like ask you to be on time?"

I jumped in my seat, the chair clattering against the wall behind me when he spoke. Being caught off guard was the only reason I looked up into the swirling pools he called eyes. For a moment I got lost, barely able to swallow from their intensity fixed on me.

"Well?"

He questioned with the most patronizing voice I could imagine. To prove a point, I pinched my face and assaulted another button on the keyboard.

Bryant's eyes narrowed as he stalked over and grabbed my fingers with one hand. He held them just above my keyboard, and I tried to yank them free. I was still pulling when one long finger from his other hand came up and hooked into my earbuds to jerk them from my ears. They clattered against the computer.

He adjusted his hold to my wrists and pulled me; I landed less than an inch from his face. Tumultuous eyes met mine as his fingers tightened around my bones. The more fierce his grip the more brilliant his eyes became.

I wrestled with him and, when I couldn't budge, I swore his eyes sparked. He used his hold to angle me against the bookcase then used his whole body to pin me down. He held me for just a moment, studying me. His breathing went ragged, and his heartbeat pounded against mine, but then he dropped his hands.

Instinctively I rubbed my wrists, noticing the slight redness. Those marks made my knees knock together.

God damn I miss the marks.

I bit my lip as he slid his arm around the small of my back to escort me out of the office and rather than plant myself, I reluctantly obeyed. As soon as we stepped out of the office, the flight attendant was on him; she reached to smooth his t-shirt. Heat raced through my veins all over again.

"We will be in the back and are not to be disturbed." Nick barely glanced at her as he pointed toward another door. She *humpfed* and I wheeled on her, feeling the clench of my jaw every bit as tightly as the squeeze of my fists where they'd balled. Her eyes went wide as I took a step. Nick's hands wrapped around my shoulders and he wordlessly turned me back toward the room. When I fought him, he actually growled at me.

"Now," he said sharply, and I finally obeyed, my temper still seething at the surface.

The back room Nick had referenced was a barely lit bedroom. I wasn't sure whether the venue was good or bad considering our moods. I plopped on the bed, crossed my arms and legs, and waited for him to follow me in. When he finally did, he had a bottle of Glenfiddich and all but slammed the door before locking it behind him.

"I don't like it when you pick fights with me." He set the bottle down on the bedside table.

"I don't like it when you treat me like a child," I retorted.

"I didn't treat you like a child, but you certainly insisted on acting like one." He loomed over me, his arms crossed like mine.

"What was I supposed to do? Take your rudeness in stride and simply apologize?"

"An apology would've been very nice."

"Okay, I'm sorry." My tone was anything but remorseful.

"I don't believe you." He stepped toward me and lifted my chin, staring deep into my eyes.

I jerked my chin away, still being petulant. Nick's low rumble filled the room as he bent down to lift my shirt anyway. I swatted at his hand. Sex was an easy out. And if it was just him eating me out, I had no desire anyway.

Nick reached again and I swatted again.

But this time he anticipated it and captured my wrist. His grip stung a little on the raw skin he'd left moments ago. I yanked and his grip got tighter. I balled my fist and reached with the other hand fully intending on ripping it out of his grasp, but he captured that one too. Bryant shifted his weight and pushed me back along the bed, forcing my arms to stretch out overhead. I bucked and struggled underneath him as an undeniably gritty, sexy rumble resonated in his chest.

Nick straddled me, pinning me firmly to the bed. He shifted toward the pillows and reached under one of them. When he pulled out handcuffs and deftly pushed them onto my wrists, I shrieked in protest.

"Why the fuck do you have these on the plane? Do you make it a habit of . . ." My outburst was quickly interrupted.

"You will stop yelling right now, Kate."

He moved off me and, in one swift motion, pulled me partially off the bed and twisted me so my chest was flat on the mattress. My cuffed hands had landed balled under my chest, and my knees sank to rest on the carpet. This position served my ass up on a platter for him.

Like hell he's going to spank me!

I tried to stand up but as soon as I got one foot under me he pushed me back to the bed. He shoved his forearm against my back while his other hand tugged at my high heels.

"Bryant!" I screamed at the top of my lungs while he held me down. It was more in frustration than anything else.

"They will all hear you if you keep this shit up," he hissed inches from my ear.

"I don't care." I was seething.

"You don't care that you're subjecting Jaime to this? I know you're spiteful enough today to enjoy the thought of our flirtatious flight attendant hearing, but him?"

He'd said it to shut me up, knowing full well how terrible I felt that Jaime always caught us in compromising positions.

"Answer me." Smugness was thick in his voice as he shifted his knee to press against my calves while his arm kept me firmly in place. He started to work my leggings down, leaving my naked skin exposed.

"This is embarrassing," I mumbled, still struggling beneath him.

"I was rather embarrassed this afternoon."

At that, I lost it. I shot up forcefully enough to surprise him. For just a second he was off me. But then he lunged to hug me, grasping again for my wrists. He unclasped one cuff and pulled me toward the bedpost hoping to restrain me but my free hand flew to his hair and wrenched his head backwards. His answering groan was more pleasure-laden than anything else.

My heart hammered, my chest vibrated—I was alive, and the singe of our electricity crossed my skin. Judging by the sound that Nick had let out, he felt the same way.

He pushed his body harder against mine as he tried to capture my free arm. The plane hit slight turbulence and it was enough to knock me off balance. I fell backward against the bed and shot my hand back to brace myself. He took the opportunity to gain control again.

This time he twisted me away from the bed and pushed my face down to the carpeting. He shoved my knees forward and used the cuffs to pull my wrists together behind me and into the crease of my knees. I was left with the option of either putting weight onto my forehead against the plush carpet or sitting back onto my heels and pressing the biting metal of the cuffs into my thighs and wrists.

Since I couldn't do much more than shuffle, Nick picked up the little ball that was my body and set it on the bed. When he pulled off his shirt and climbed up behind me, I yanked up my shoulders and endured the sting of the metal against my thighs. I writhed, hoping I could somehow maneuver to knee him. One hand came to my hip and held me in place. I screeched.

"Your temper has been exceedingly short of late. Particularly when it comes to me. And all I've tried to do is apologize."

Nick's full, open hand came to my ass and my breath caught. I twitched and contorted; I did *not* want to be spanked. Not like this. Electricity or no, feeling alive or no, that seemed demeaning after this particular tussle. His hand fell away, and I almost yelled *no!* but he redirected and simply found new skin to skate across.

"Kate, I'm trying."

"I know." I was quieter, most of the acid leaving my voice as he touched me.

Nick's voice was unreadable when he spoke again. "What did I do? What did I fuck up now?"

His hand unexpectedly slipped between my legs only to skate through dripping arousal. Our wrestling had been the epitome of us, downright fiery and laced with lust. Of course I was turned on.

"Na, nah, no . . ." I stammered as he pushed his finger inside me.

"Are you sure?" He purred as he added in a second finger.

"I just don't feel like myself," I managed.

"I can help you find yourself."

His fingers stroked leisurely in and out. He bent and kissed the small of my back. I'd expected a spanking, and I wasn't sure if this gentle teasing was a good or bad surprise. He kissed me again, pressing his lips to my skin reverentially.

"Oh, Nick."

Anger melted from my body when he lingered on my skin like that. He bent down so his tongue could replace his fingers inside of me. His hands were at my hips, pulling apart my cheeks and digging deeper into my skin. Like always, he dug in hard when he was enjoying himself.

His tongue flicked and twisted at the sensitive spots between my thighs. When the plane shook with his tongue inside me, I couldn't help but moan. Loudly. He darted in and out while I trembled.

Based on the last few weeks, I thought I could predict what was coming next. He'd twirl around the tiny hub of nerves in my clitoris whether with fingers or mouth. I would have pushed him away if I had control. I was so tired of this. He flicked my clit with his finger at the same time I begged, "Baby don't . . ."

But then Nick didn't sneak his lips lower, he drug his tongue higher.

He's not going to . . .

But he did. Nick's tongue rimmed around my *other* opening and I jerked. Well, as much as I could anyway. His hands flexed harder into my hips and he pulled me back onto his tongue. I couldn't stifle my cry. Jaime and whoever the hell else be damned.

His slow, steady tongue thrusts into my ass had me clenching, jerking, and moaning into the comforter beneath my forehead. When he pushed two fingers roughly into my sex and danced up against his tongue, the all too familiar feel of pre-orgasmic tension wracked my body. I was about to come spectacularly.

Nick read my mind, or body, or whatever he did, and swiftly moved to undo the cuffs. I wanted to slowly stretch my limbs but, before I could move my aching shoulders, he twisted me to face him and yanked my shirt up over my head. He had my bra off only seconds after. I noticed his pants were already gone when he cuffed my hands in front of me. Nick's head shoved between my elbows, bringing my wrists to rest flat against his neck as he pinned me beneath his heavy body. Before I had time to react he was pushing up into me.

I would have cried out if he hadn't locked his lips on mine. He kept them sealed as he hammered into me, over and over, right up until he turned us. I stayed flat to him as he started guiding my pace.

Nick put a hand on my chest and pushed my body up as far as the cuffs would allow. The way he arched my back was intense, and I couldn't help but whimper. When I quaked above him, he sat up, taking me along for the ride. He was still thrusting into me as we wound closer together. Sitting like that, entangled like that, with his hips moving like *that*, was building a deliciously sexy sheen between us.

The friction was borderline unbearable. Every single inch of me tingled, trembled, or both. I bit my lip, desperate to prolong this feeling. When Nick pushed my hips high enough to slip out of me, I cried out.

"I just want to turn you around, Sweets." His lips grazed my skin as he spoke.

Hearing he wasn't done with me was enough. I did as I was told, pulled my arms free, and shuffled to put my back to his front. He wrapped his arm around me and slipped his hand between my legs, lifting my hips. His cock rested perfectly in the crease of my ass.

Nick kept his fingers playing with my clit as he inched into the space his tongue had scandalized minutes before. He was gentle, and I relaxed allowing him to push in.

"Oh God, your ass is always so tight. So perfect and so tight. I was going to spank you but I wanted this so much more. I wanted you to give me this."

He sucked in deeply as he pushed me the rest of the way down onto his shaft. My head rolled back onto his shoulder and I twisted back into his neck, biting down in lieu of screaming when I took him all.

His fingers slipped inside my slit and stroked against his shaft through my thin skin in between. He started alternating the thrusts of his fingers with those of his cock, the rhythm almost hypnotic. I thought I'd lose it completely when his free hand flew to my nipple and pulled. Hard. But it was enough of a change to stave off the building explosion. And thank God, because each time the plane shook he settled deeper into me and my blood boiled a bit more.

In one blissfully perfect moment, it all came together; thrust, yank, turbulence, and tremors. I shattered. And when the ripples of my orgasm rolled through my body, Nick wrapped his hand softly around my throat. His fingers curled up over my chin and crossed my lips before flexing into my mouth. I bit down to keep from screaming out and was rewarded with a strangled grunt of his own.

His muscles bunched, and his telltale quiver timed with the clenching I couldn't control. He came while I trembled against his perfect chest. My gasps were stifled by his fingers. He bit into my shoulder and grunted, quiet and pained, against my skin while he emptied into me.

Nick was still firmly notched inside me when we collapsed together onto the sheets. He nuzzled into my hair as his heart raced against my back. We panted as the plane chattered again.

"Oh God Kate, I love you. So much." He tangled his legs with mine and breathed warm against my neck. "I don't want to fight with you anymore. Just tell me what I have to do."

I was breathing hard, clutching the sheets under me even though my hands were still bound. "Well, you could un-cuff me."

He shifted for just a moment, then returned and cocooned me even tighter as he unlocked the cuffs.

"Now, without the smartass remarks. Tell me what I have to do."

I thought over the doubt that had been weaving through my mind these past two weeks. Giving voice to them was a wholly terrifying thing. But staying stagnant with Nick, not being able to read our future, was the only thing worse.

"Where do we go from here?" I breathed the words, barely shaping them. "The past two weeks have been so straightforward. No games, no bullshit, no fights, and they felt utterly wrong." I bit my lip, not sure how he'd take it.

Absolutely terrified, actually.

"Me being patient and understanding felt wrong to you?" His voice was even, contemplative maybe.

"Not wrong so much as normal. A normal man coming home to a normal women, having fine sex, and I know that's not going to fly long term. Normal feels like a cage. A cage we'll both tire of. You'll get tired of me." My pulse rose just like my voice.

"Tired of *you*?"

He pulled out and I gasped at the shock to my system. He grasped my shoulder and pulled me, flattening me so we could be nose to nose.

"Never," he breathed. "I was just trying to make amends for being such a prick. Repeatedly. Believe me, it wasn't easy. You've been hell on wheels. But I had to do *something*. Every day I want you more. I need you more." His hands wandered over my body. "I never thought I'd get married, but now I know, I *will* marry you."

"What?" I exclaimed.

Fuck! What did he just say? Married? Goddamnedshitpissfuck!!

I couldn't rein in the sheer terror crossing my face.

"You heard me." He smiled my favorite crooked smile. "You said you won't run but I'm going to make sure you can't."

This was the moment to bring up my commitment issues I could elaborate on why I thought fate would take it all away, regardless of what we wanted. That fairy tales weren't real. That regardless of what we wanted or deserved, life made other plans. I could remind him both Christopher and his stepfather were proof of that. That my family had all but evaporated into thin air. I would force myself to keep my cool while I explained.

Or you could shut your mouth and snuggle into him and his painfully sweet notion.

With that thought, something unfamiliar thumped through my veins. It was an undeniable yearning, a need much the same as air or water, but this time for a forever. Picturing a future with Nick, simple, complex, or otherwise, was kind of amazing.

"It's not funny to joke about a wedding." I meant to be snarky. If I had managed, maybe all those fears would have come to light, but it came out small and breathy.

"I didn't think so either." He kissed my forehead.

8.

The moment we deplaned and greeted our hosts in Hong Kong, the all too familiar and irksome boulder of dread settled in my gut, and settled down deep. I got nauseous as I shook hands and bowed to our would-be associates. Everything was wrong, but almost imperceptibly so. I couldn't put my finger on the real issue any better than Nick.

The moment there was a lull in the conversation as one of the businessmen left the dinner table I caught Nick's attention.

"I see what you mean," I said plainly over my martini glass as if we were seamlessly continuing the conversation from Thanksgiving morning when Nick had asked me to come in the first place.

He nodded and it was the only interaction we had until we returned to our suite.

"It doesn't seem right to you, either?" Nick asked, his voice businesslike as he loosened his tie.

"No. I don't trust them at all."

"Me neither," he grumbled as he slammed his jacket on the coffee table in dramatic fashion.

I wanted to take in our view of the night lights but Nick's eyes were the shade that pulled at my heartstrings. I followed him to the bedroom, slowly peeling off jewelry as I went. When I walked in on a ball of rage, blindly bumbling at his cufflinks, I was glad I'd trailed behind.

"Any idea what it might be?" Nick asked through gritted teeth.

"No baby, sorry. Not yet anyhow."

I slipped off my shoes and stepped toward him, deftly pushing his hand away, undoing the cufflink for him. He took a deep breath and a little light filtered into his features. I think he even managed a small smirk as he turned and walked away, continuing to shed his accessories and shoes.

Now that he'd relaxed fractionally I allowed myself to walk over to the windows and look out on the harbor. The floor to ceiling glass reminded me of home, but the electricity that bubbled up to the 118th floor was uniquely Hong Kong. The life of the city danced against the glass the way electricity hummed between us. A two-finger scotch came over my shoulder as Nick pressed up against me.

"It's amazing up here." I sipped slowly. "Makes Times Square look understated."

He chuckled softly. "I suppose. You should see it from where I'm standing." I smiled to myself, loving the line he'd used the very first night we'd spent together. "Beautiful," he added. I smiled my biggest smile and sipped my scotch before gripping the rim and letting it rest by my thigh.

Nick pressed his erection against me; it twitched just before he took the glass. I was wearing a fairly conservative outfit compared to our first night. This time Nick had to work to pull the gray knit blouse out of my high waisted white pants. His eyes locked on mine in our reflection.

"A little more work than the last time you had me up against the windows." I laughed a small, husky laugh.

"More sexy now than you were then."

His hands wandered up underneath my shirt and pushed the cups of my bra down, freeing my breasts. His fingers stayed hidden as they gently flicked and tugged on me, making my nipples taut and slickness spread between my thighs.

MMMmmm.

My purr had his hands at the hem of my shirt and pulling. Once my chest was exposed, it didn't take long for him to undo my zipper and let my pants billow to the floor. As soon as I was naked, he pressed my body against the windows; the cold glass made me jump and my breath fogged the window beneath my lips.

Nick kissed each of my shoulders then backed away to pull off his shirt. I ached for his skin to press up against mine. Instead, he turned me and pushed me down to my knees. I folded beneath him and let him run his hand through my hair. He leaned in and braced himself against the window.

When he gently caressed my cheek, I knew what he was asking and undid his fly, freeing his cock. I moved to catch him in my waiting mouth. As soon as he felt my wet lips around him, he slammed in. It was unexpected, but oh-so delicious. I hummed, holding him tight, as I rocked back and hit the glass with my shoulders.

My throat burned as he picked up pace, thrusting repeatedly between my lips. He leaned heavily on the glass, and his free hand laced into my hair as he held me. I let him move deeper than I would have pulled him in on my own. I focused on the twists of my tongue rather than the growing strain on my jaw. My hands wrapped around his thighs, and I wished they grasped at skin rather than his lightweight wool trousers. At least I had the presence of mind to change that.

As he controlled my mouth, I scrambled to work the waistband down his legs. He paused to let me, then pushed the fabric to the side with his toes. When his focus returned to me, he used his hand, still tangled in my hair, to hold me perfectly still. I was trapped. His hips pistons against me as he took the liberty of fucking my face.

He loved this, control like this. I loved his expressions and moans as he fell apart above me. Even the lightness he would radiate afterward. This was the natural rhythm of our relationship and that was what made everything inside me clench. Nick banged his fist against the window and I simply hollowed out my cheeks and sucked as hard as I could.

Little waves wracked his body the way they usually did mine. He went rigid a single heartbeat before he shot, hot and salty, into my mouth. His fingers pulled on my hair hard enough to bring slight tears to the corner of my eyes. He moaned as my throat rippled along his still-hard shaft. I swallowed as best I could but some of his cum spilled out of the corner of my mouth.

When he finished, Nick stumbled backward slightly. He dropped to his knees in front of me while I stayed resting against the window, trying to catch my breath. His eyes caught fire when my tongue lapped at the cum drizzling from the corner of my mouth. Nick's thumb reached for my chin and wiped off the last little bit. When I gasped it made it all the easier for him to press his salty coated finger between my lips and against my tongue. I arched my eyebrow as I closed my lips around him and sucked. Hard.

He moaned again before lunging and pinning me by the lips to the window behind me.

"God damn." He pushed his tongue into my mouth. "Sweets." His tongue tangled with mine. "You are . . ." He nibbled on my lip. " . . . sexy." Nick devoured my lips in a kiss again.

His strong hands reached for my hips, and he lifted, rearranging me so I could slip under him on the soft carpet. His phone rang but he didn't pause. He kept up kissing and nipping, this time at my inner thigh as he slowly pulled my thong down along my legs.

Nick's phone rang again. Part of me wanted to urge him to answer. The other part of me didn't give a damn. I fully focused on his lips as they brushed my ankle. Then my phone rang.

"Should we get that?" I gasped.

"No." His answer was short and sweet.

Good enough for me.

My attention snapped back to him, the sensation of my skin against his, and the way his tongue lazily explored my inner thigh. The intense drumming of my heart filled my ears and the way I tingled where his hand held my legs open made every inch of me flex.

A knock at our suite door settled my bowing back to the carpet. Nick grunted but didn't waiver. Jaime's voice accompanied a second knock, asking to speak with him immediately.

"I'll kill him." Nick grimaced as he sat back on his heels.

I was breathless on the carpet. "*You'll* kill him?" I was more than ready to strangle Jaime myself. My fists balled and I banged them back against the floor.

"Sorry." He helped me off the floor and kissed my forehead before turning away. There was another knock. "Coming!" he roared at the door. I grabbed a robe while he pulled back on his suit pants.

Nick whipped open the door and growled at Jaime. God love Jaime for only looking mildly taken aback. "Sir, I apologize for interrupting but it's important."

"What could possibly be *that* important?" I was relieved not to be on the receiving end of that tone.

"Should we discuss this in private?"

"No," Nick answered sharply and I let out a deep breath I hadn't known I was holding as I settled into a plush chair.

"Sir, it's Christopher."

My eyes went wide.

"What?" Nick bellowed. His tone was dangerous enough that I got up and went to him. I put my hand on the small of his back hoping my touch would calm him the way his did me.

"He was found today." Jamie's shoulders were braced against the coming onslaught.

"Where?"

"Ari's apartment. Neither she nor Laura was home but every indication was that he intended on waiting for them."

"Are you serious?" Nick's voice became a wholly unearthly sound.

"Nick." I tried to calm him even if it was slight. "Jaime wasn't there, you can't yell at him."

"Of course I can!" Nick swiveled and roared in my direction. "Can you imagine if they *had* been home?"

I cringed away from him and he swallowed when he saw his harshness reflected back. His demeanor softened. "I would be twice as angry if we were talking about you." He kissed the inside of my palm and then walked away.

Nick poured another round of scotch and sank onto the couch. He held out my glass and signaled for me to come next to him. As soon as I did, he pulled me tightly to his side. His hand wrapped around me and he started to make circles on my skin through the robe, pushing harder than normal.

"Sit, Jaime. Explain," he commanded.

"The new security system went off, unbeknownst to Christopher, just as planned. Upon arrival Colton found the deadbolt dismantled."

Nick's hand stopped circling and started gripping, slowly getting tighter and tighter. He was downing scotch faster than normal too.

"He swept the apartment and found Christopher in Ari's room, digging in her, um . . ." Jaime turned green. " . . . unmentionable drawer."

My stomach lurched and Nick went stone faced, his eyes a matching slate. His hand clamped harder on my hip.

"Ouch, Nick." I didn't swat him away, but pain was pain, particularly when it lacked pleasure. Wordlessly he switched back to circling.

"And . . . ?" Nick questioned.

"They fought. Christopher fled the scene. Colton is dealing with the police now."

"Where did he go?" Nick's voice dropped to low and lethal.

"Colton pursued but due to injuries sustained he couldn't keep up. By the time backup arrived Christopher had disappeared."

"What injuries?" I piped up, my worry for Colton overtaking any sense to keep quiet.

Nick's eyes swept up my body then fixed on Jaime, waiting patiently.

"A black eye and a broken nose, Kate." The corner of Jaime's mouth turned down the smallest bit but fell right back into place.

My body went rigid, my shoulders shooting to my ears, waiting for the tempest next to me to break.

"Thank God Ari's in France. Where is Laura now?" Nick's voice was choked rather than angry.

"Work, but we've reserved a suite at the Waldorf. We plan to tell her rats were found in the kitchen and that we're bringing in an exterminator."

"You shouldn't lie to her," I said without pausing to soften my tone.

Silence greeted me as I looked from one man to another.

"I'm trying to protect her." Edge was back in Nick's voice. "For you."

"And thank you. But she's a smart, intelligent, *sane* woman. If you tell her what's going on, she'll play by the rules. After what happened in the park . . ." I swallowed on the words, and Nick went whiter if possible. " . . . she knows when you say there's an issue, there actually is an issue."

I turned and stared at Nick's profile. His jaw clenched and flexed, a muscle on his neck seemed particularly interested in staying defined. Steely eyes flitted toward mine a few times but he wouldn't meet my gaze full on.

"Fine." He shattered the silence.

Nick's eyes locked on mine and I shrugged. We stayed frozen for a moment then his hand started moving again but it had a hard time making even circles.

"Should you be dealing with this?" Nick grumbled at Jaime; his fingers paused and flexed against my skin again.

"I trust Colton." Jaime was adamant. "I wish I was there. I wish we all were, but it's only because I feel a little powerless from here."

"The feeling's mutual," Nick mumbled his agreement.

"I could stay here with Jaime, take the meetings for you," I offered.

"No." Nick's tone switched back to harsh.

"It was only an offer. With you in mind, Nick." I was comfortable getting sharp right back.

"I'd never leave you." He clenched too hard on my skin again.

"I'm sorry I suggested it." I let sincerity color my words.

"Keep tabs on it, Jaime, and let me know what's going on. If you need to go, I'll manage here." Jaime stood to leave before Nick added, "Make sure they keep police involvement minimal. You know how I feel about that."

Jaime nodded briskly then headed for the front door. The familiar feeling of fear churned wildly in my stomach. I'd never been able to shake the feeling that last time, had there been a police report, a restraining order, *something,* Ally may have kept her distance. Every bit of me screamed that we should be following the proper steps this time around. I bit my lip though, recalling the scars law enforcement had left on Nick's childhood.

The moment the door closed behind Jaime, Nick stood and silently walked away. He filled another glass of scotch and pulled out his computer. He slunk to the desk space in our bedroom, and I let him go.

I wanted to go to him, to hold him, to discuss this whole madness, but he hasn't asked me to join him. He needed space and a brawl would do nothing to chase away what was brewing in his eyes, so I made myself bite my lip, curl onto the couch, and answer emails. Swallowing my words tasted a bit like chewing on wood.

"Did you want to talk about what's going on at home?" Nick reappeared in the doorway and stood watching me with an arched an eyebrow. I squinched my nose and shifted to chew on my lip instead of answer. "Kate, I know you have opinions on the matter."

"I do. Have an opinion that is. But we've had a discussion once or twice about trust." I made sure to roll my eyes as wildly as I could. "Nick, you made a good decision to tell her. I'm grateful for that. I'm not completely unreasonable." His mouth dropped. "I want you to protect my family to the best of your abilities."

"Who the hell are you, and what have you done with Kate?" He wasn't quite playful but relief colored his features.

Any remaining tension melted when he walked over, pushed my hair behind my ear, and kissed the sensitive skin just beneath, paying extra attention to the spots he'd scraped with headphones just yesterday.

When I got around to calling Laura, we went ten rounds about Nick, his family, and all the shit that followed in his wake. Our conversation ended with her shouting, "You're a masochist, you know that right?" I'd mumbled something at her, completely defenseless, before she added, "And thank you for looking out for me."

Someone forgot to tell my stomach that Laura was safe, and I'd been forgiven; it churned all night. I woke feeling off but since I wasn't shooting up, gasping for air, I took it. Nick was already awake, hunched over a screen, and didn't budge when I stretched beneath the comforter. He even waved me off when I told him I was sneaking to the gym, letting Jaime take me without comment.

My stomach summersaulted.

Nick's mood did not improve over breakfast, or in the car, or even once we arrived at the massive building that housed his associate's corporate offices. As our day rolled on, I found myself glowering and my jaw clenching too.

We should write this facility off. Ulterior motives be damned.

I would have told Nick as much except he'd made it clear with monosyllabic grunts he wasn't really in the mood to chat. I distracted myself with coffee and lots of it. After what had to be a whole pot, I had to use the restroom. I only half listened to directions, desperate to break free of the stagnant thickness filling the conference room. My lack of attention landed me significantly deeper in the offices than anyone intended.

When I rounded a corner, trying to find my way back, a man caught my eye. My feet followed him before I gave it a conscious thought. There was something hauntingly familiar drawing me toward him. And when he stopped to chat with someone in a side office, I caught his profile and my back bristled. Victor Alexander was slithering down the hallway in front of me.

Oh you fucking bastard!

Instinctively I flattened into a recess as Victor spoke animatedly and in casual, friendly Cantonese with some nameless executive. I watched as he bowed, and when he rose, he twisted the slightest bit and his beady little eyes raked over me and my chest seized.

Victor pulled his shoulders back and furrowed his brow. He'd been caught red-handed but rather than look contentious, remorse colored his face. He turned toward me slowly, making every inch of my skin crawl.

We stared at each other for what felt like an eternity. Victor's mouth flopped open and closed like a fish. My heart pounded so hard I couldn't tell if he made a sound. In the end, he moved first, starting toward me but then reconsidering.

"It's Christopher, Kate." He almost choked on the words. I almost choked on the shock. "I'm sorry, I didn't understand . . . I just wanted revenge. And now I'm in too deep . . ." His voice trailed off. "Tell Bryant to be careful."

Victor turned without another word. My mind had stalled out completely. *That* name on *those* limps made my heart hurt. I was torn between running after him for an interrogation and rushing back to Nick. Victor Alexander's hatred of us ran too deeply for me to believe he would legitimately warn us of anything.

Right?

The mere mention of Christopher had me doubting that. After all, how else could he even know?

My knees wobbled damn near violently, but I pushed out from my hiding place and did what I could to sprint back the way I'd come. Or the way I thought I'd come. Slowing down, breathing, and looking normal was difficult with the tempest whipping up inside me. Finding the right door was too.

Nick's eyes narrowed infinitesimally when I finally pushed back into the conference room.

"I was beginning to worry," he hissed as I plopped back into a swivel chair. "I need you to listen to this. It's why I brought you." I was about to snap back when he silenced me with a pointed look.

I whipped out my phone.

Victor Alexander is here. Christopher is involved.

My fingers mashed on my BlackBerry buttons. Nick had to hear the furious plinking of my keys but he took no notice; not even of the buzzing in his breast pocket. When he didn't flinch, I shifted in my seat and picked up my leather portfolio. With it close to my chest, I leaned back hoping he'd have full view of the paper. I did my best to discreetly scribble the same note.

I felt it every bit as much as heard it when he saw the scribbles on the paper. The sharp intake of breath was only slightly more noticeable than the dramatic temperature drop and teeth-chattering waves of anger that began rolling through the room. I folded the folio and pushed it back onto the table so I could sneak a peek at his face. His jaw had clenched and every muscle in his neck stood at attention. The unnervingly flat and lifeless eyes he wore made my heart stutter, even without the deep ridges of his furiously furrowed brow.

He held my gaze for one agonizing second then stood without saying a word. To anyone. The executive that had been speaking trailed off mid-sentence, as tension became a living, breathing being sharing the room with us. Every pair of eyes fixed on Nick, except mine. I swallowed the ball of emotion in my throat and scanned for Jaime, wordlessly pleading with him to understand.

Something about how the wide-eyed look he wore said he already did.

My fingers itched to reach out for Nick, to soothe him, or at the very least, to get him to unfreeze, but I stopped myself. At this point, being unprofessional was just going to be icing on the soon-to-explode cake. My breath cut off when Nick's shoulders really started to heave.

"It seems this office hasn't been completely truthful with Bryant Venture Group." Icy tendrils of Bryant's most bone-chilling voice wormed their way through the room. "I knew you were fucking with me but Victor Alexander?"

It wasn't lost on me that he refused to say Christopher's name.

"Jaime," Nick snarled, "call the car."

All I got was the jerk of his chin in my direction. I shot him a look, tempted to tell him how well that bullshit sat with me, but again swallowed my snippy words. I'd be adding fuel to a raging inferno and if I was being honest, I had zero desire to get burned. I collected my things and wordlessly followed Nick from the room.

Both stilted English and furious Cantonese chased after us until the moment Nick shot the businessmen and women a withering glower as the elevator doors sealed shut.

The second we were alone in our car, Nick started shouting. I listened to the stream of consciousness for a while, but when Jaime started shouting back I gave up, doing my best to block them out by leaning back to study the small paths in the suede on the roof. They looked like some small child had been tracing figures on the ceiling and I found myself imagining giraffes and elephants to help filter out the ruckus.

They carried on that way, through Hong Kong, through the lobby, up the elevator, and into our hotel suite. I didn't mean to slam the door when I barricaded myself in the bedroom, but my temples thudded in time with the bass notes of their voices.

For a second, the room on the other side of the door went silent, and I smiled hoping I'd snapped them out of it. Turns out, they'd just been catching their breath. I shoved my headphones in when the barrage of voices started back up.

I was answering emails in bed when Nick came charging into the room.

"Get dressed and get packed, we're leaving," he bellowed and my earbuds did nothing to muffle him.

"Leaving to go where?"

"Home," he snapped, like I should have guessed then turned on his heel to stride back out.

For a moment, I pictured my hands around his throat but let the image go with an exhale that came all the way up from my toes.

The calm was momentary, tension gripped my shoulders as soon as the boom picked back up in the suite. When I appeared, suitcase in hand, Jaime deftly took it from me, shouted at Nick and ushered us both toward the elevator.

The volley continued. Back down the elevator, across the lobby, in the car, and even in the airplane hanger.

Just as with our inbound flight, I couldn't bring myself to sit next to Nick in the main cabin. Assuming he chose to sit at all rather than pace like a feral animal. Instead, I opted for the small bedroom, slipping into bed still clothed, and yanking the comforter over my head as I went. The down did little to dampen the fury ricocheting off the cabin walls, so I wrapped the nearest pillow around my head and settled into the relative silence.

The soft hum of the jet in flight qualified as utter silence when my eyes fluttered open. I reached for Nick, assuming the calm meant he'd run out of steam at some point and had come to join me. I launched up and my head whipped around when my hand only found cool cotton. A low chuckle gave him away. He was folded in the plush chair to the side of the bed, his ankle crossed on his knee, his arm bent so a glass of scotch could rest against his temple.

"Hi." I rubbed my eyes as I climbed out of the bed and slunk over to him.

He set his drink down and opened his arms to me. I yawned as I curled into his lap. My head nuzzled into his shoulder, and I sagged into this sweet, non-shouting version of Nicholas Bryant. His hands automatically started circling on my thighs. When he let out a heavy sigh, he rested his forehead against mine but still said nothing.

I let him stay quiet, listening to the soothing beat of his heart. It was about to lull me to sleep when he whispered against my skin, "Will you ever forgive me for putting you in Christopher's path?"

"What?" I sat up, groggy and slightly confused.

"I brought you into a problem with Christopher." His voice trembled in a way it never had. "Mother fucking Christopher," he added under his breath.

"No, Nick, I can't." His fingers clenched into my skin. "Because there's nothing to forgive. You had no way of knowing and I'm sure if you did, I wouldn't have been allowed to leave the apartment, let alone the country."

I was trying to lighten the mood. He didn't bite.

"Nick, I mean it. I love you and I would've come regardless."

"Don't *ever* knowingly put yourself in danger. Especially not this kind." His voice was fierce even though he stayed quiet and close to my ear.

"I wouldn't. I won't," I scrambled then added, "Unless it'll protect you."

"No, never." He almost growled at me. "Promise me never."

Despite his forcefulness, his breath was steamy against my neck, and his nose traced my earlobe. His hands had returned to circling against my skin. His heartbeat and breathing were the only things that rose above the subtle hum of the jet.

"I promise."

I couldn't begin to explain what had possessed me to speak. Particularly because I knew deep down it was a promise I would break. Without hesitating. Something somersaulted inside me as I realized there was a very real possibility I'd have to prove it.

But Nick sighed heavily and melted into the chair. His heartbeats slowed, and his gentle touch continued in the silence of the cabin. Nestled right against his neck, I lost my battle with sleep, once again trying to ignore that dread had come in and nestled in the pit of my stomach.

9.

New York had landed in the middle of a holiday themed snow globe while we'd been in Hong Kong. The next few days were as blurry as the flurries outside. Despite being my favorite time of year, I really only saw Christmas lights from where they twinkled beneath Vesper's office windows. I really only saw Nick in that building too. Or when one of us slunk to bed at some godforsaken hour. But we were good in business and in bed; we were *us*.

Christmas Eve was particularly hectic. I had something in the ballpark of 200 emails to answer and three projects to finalize. I barely took the time to breathe. Every deadline bore down on me, snarling in time with my ticking clock, reminding me that I was actually taking a vacation. I'd promised Nick to disconnect, despite how poorly those promises had gone on Thanksgiving.

He'd just made this time seem so damned important.

And his eyes had been a really weird color . . .

Night had blanketed New York as thickly as snow when the familiar rasp of Nick's knuckles landed on the mahogany of my office door. He walked in without introduction, and I kept my head down, talking to the footfalls in the room.

"I know I'm running late. I'm sorry. I can't help it. Jaime was supposed to tell you I'm trying."

"He did and it's fine." Nick didn't even hesitate.

"Ten minutes." I was still speaking to my desk instead of him.

"Is that a real ten minutes or something closer to a half an hour?" Amusement colored his voice and that finally stole my attention from the papers in front of me.

He was a breath of fresh air as he casually leaned against my office wall. He'd shoved his hands in his pockets, barely rumpling his skillfully tailored three piece black suit. He was almost too formal, too scrumptious for a workday.

"Ten minutes, I promise." I smiled broadly, ten minutes was all I had before getting entirely distracted anyway.

Nick answered my smile and finally strolled fully into the room to fold into a seat across from me. The moment I returned to the paperwork in front of me, his eyes roved over my body making my skin react. I shook my head a few times and shuffled my papers hoping to shake the diversion. I snuck a look up at him just to catch piercing eyes staring back at me. He wore a lopsided grin as he rested his head on his hand, his long finger pressed into his temple.

Good fucking Christ.

I shook my head desperate to shake increasingly filthy thoughts from my mind.

He rose and I tried to keep my head down even though my heart hammered. The version of Nick across from me was a force of nature, a damned Adonis with a devious smile and a bespoke suit. I tried not to let a smile creep across my face. I was sure that if I looked up, I'd get completely off track without hope of ever getting back.

Out of the corner of my eye, he materialized a small black velvet ring box. My breath caught. He swiftly used it to pin the papers in my hands to my desktop, gaining my full attention. My heart stopped cold. Only one thing came in little black boxes like that.

Oh God. Oh my God. Oh my holy fucking God.

Nick stayed silent as he scrutinized me. My chest rose and fell far too fast and my cheeks flushed. Everything in my body went haywire. Nick had to hear my heart the way it thundered in my chest.

Can I say yes?

I didn't know. Marriage was always an abstract thought for me.

Acceptable for others, but not in my cards. Fate was too cruel for happy endings. I'd hardened my heart against that ages ago . . .

But can I say no?

That question made things a little easier. I wouldn't lose him. I just couldn't unfreeze to say as much.

"Just open it." Nick's voice was a mix of humor and something I couldn't quite place.

Nothing inside me reacted normally. My stomach seemed to vibrate, backflip, and melt into a puddle all at once. I watched, oddly detached, as my hand trembled across the desk. I had to ball it into a fist before I could steady myself enough to wrap my fingers around the velvet.

The box was heavy which made me swallow. Hard. I had to muster strength to pop the slight top. As soon as the soft snap of the case broke the silence, my jaw fell open and my eyes shot to his. A twinkle of laughter met me, and I debated reaching across the desk to smack him.

The finished device, Vesper's FiTech, sat on a pillow inside the small box. I picked it up and the product came alive in my hand. The soft blue screen emitted a soft glow, and the magnets Nick had devised held fast in a ring shape. He took it and slipped the FiTech on my pointer finger then pulled the matching bluetooth headphones out of his pocket. The buds slipped into my ears and music started to play, crystal clear, through them. The song was slow because I was sitting, but Nick's smile made my heartbeat quicken then the music pick up pace.

"I'm quite happy with it as well." His voice was a little smug but that emotion I couldn't place was still edging in.

"Nick, I can't believe it. It's everything I ever imagined." I looked up and it was the man in front of me, not the device that choked me up. "I couldn't have done this without you." I ditched the headphones as I circled the desk to hug him tightly. "Baby, thank you. For everything." I took a deep breath, relishing how his strong, manly scent reminded me of home. "Every bit of my life is better because of you." I kissed the corner of his jaw.

"No, Kate, I've caused so many problems. This is the least I could do." His face fell as he reached for my hand and kissed my knuckles just below the FiTech.

"You're wrong, but I refuse to fight with you today. It's Christmas Eve and I want to go home to be with you."

His smile returned as he wrapped his arms around my hips and lifted. I seamlessly wrapped my legs around him, and he carried me out of the office. Jaime collected my things while we waited for the elevator. Nick let me slide down his chest only for his churning eyes to meet mine before he turned away.

"Did you think I was purposing to you?" He wouldn't meet my gaze but I could tell the unnamed emotion was back. And thick.

"Yes," I admitted, he'd sensed as much already.

"It looked like you were trying to figure out how to say no."

My heart sank as low as his voice.

"Nick, that's not it . . ." My hands scrambled to reassure him.

"What is it then?"

"It scares me how much I love you, how much I need you. Marriage really hasn't crossed my mind. Ever. I didn't know what I'd say if you ever asked me until that exact moment."

"And?" I could tell he was holding his breath.

Something about admitting I wanted to marry him, admitting my answer was yes, unhinged my joints and liquefied my insides. My throat felt the tight squeeze of tension. Giving shape to the words made it all far too real. As much as it would soothe him, I had to dodge.

"Someday you'll have to ask and find out."

Outside, small flakes drifted in swirls and zigzags down to my eyelashes. I was bundled in my favorite trench but burrowed deep into Nick's side anyway. He gladly pulled me in and directed me to the car. Christmas carols floated like the snowflakes on the wind. We were about to slide into the backseat behind Jaime when I stopped.

"Nick." My face lit up. "Let's go see the tree at Rockefeller Center."

"Kate." His eyes clouded. "That's rather cliché."

"Nick, come on. You're allowed to be cliché at Christmas. We didn't do anything. Nothing traditional anyway." I yanked playfully on his arm.

"Kate, it's too crowded." His voice sharpened and I caught the implied meaning.

Right. Shit.

Christopher hadn't come up frequently since Hong Kong, just a whisper of trouble here or worry there. I'd been too busy to press him.

I forced a smile. "I got carried away."

"Sweets, I am sorry and I will make it up to you." He kissed my temple, brushing his lips across my skin as he apologized.

"I know." I shrugged as I slipped into the waiting car.

"Not quite sure I'll ever get used to the level-headed version of you." Nick watched me intently with a smile that packed so much emotion, so much awe, that I shifted under the weight of it.

"Don't. Get used to it, I mean. There's not a chance in hell I'll ever be a Stepford *Wife*." I spat the word out, meaning to be snarky but coming off sharp instead.

Something sat on the tip of his tongue in response. I watched as he formulated and reformulated whatever it was. The way his face twisted and contorted was so uncharacteristic I shot him an arched eyebrow.

Nick rolled his eyes as he turned away from me but his reflection betrayed how his face had gone steely. "You'd never be a Stepford Wife. Of that much I'm sure." There was only the slightest hint of humor in his voice.

I cocked my head as I evaluated the man reduced to a ball of weird emotions sitting next to me. It was so faint I could have been mistaken but I thought I heard him whisper, "Let's just hope I'm sure about the other part, too."

What? What other part?

Before I could ask, his eyes cleared and he snatched my hand. He shot me an absolutely mouthwatering look before he bent to kiss my palm. My skin still blushed a furious scarlet when he was so tender, and the color had transformed his smirk into a shy, disarming smile. Whatever emotion he was bottling up was downright bewitching.

When he pulled me into the elevator of One Madison, I shuffled against him and pinned his body into the corner. He looked devilishly handsome in his perfect suit, pressed leisurely against the wall. His new, dangerously delicious but somehow timid and naive smile grew as he melted and pushed his hands into the long wavy strands of my hair.

I happily lay my body against his and snaked my hands into his back pockets. I arched up and planted a soft kiss on his jaw. When he purred, I replaced my lips with my teeth, dragging them up to nip at his earlobe. He swore when the elevator dinged softly behind us. Nick shook his head, and his smirk returned as he arched off the wall. We were slow enough that he had to shoot his arm out to stop the elevator door before closing.

I stayed woven against him, unconcerned with our legs tangling and my stilettos teetering, until he nodded his chin toward the open living room. As soon as I turned, my face was bathed in soft, warm white light. My hands flew to my mouth to stifle a squeak then I couldn't pry them loose. My body had gone rigid, too locked up to even breathe.

There in my living room, the one that had been treeless and sported simple silver tinsel this morning, was a gigantic Christmas tree enveloped in soft white Christmas lights. All the ornaments I'd inherited and collected over the years hung alongside cranberry and popcorn garland. The way it draped in perfect swoops mirrored the pine that crept up the stairway banister. Nick had somehow managed to outline our massive window panels in beautiful lights too. It was the homespun Christmas I'd been dreaming of.

A gigantic lump welled in my throat that I couldn't swallow around.

"Sweets." Nick's hands came to my rigid shoulders. "Do you like it?"

"It's beautiful." I couldn't help that my voice came out as a small, choked whisper. "How did you . . . ?"

"Laura helped me. Well, Romana more but . . ." His tone wavered as he slipped his arms around me. "You really like it?" he asked again, so unsure.

"I'm honestly fucking speechless."

At that, he turned me and gently pressed his lips to mine.

"Language," Nick playfully scolded.

He chuckled as his long fingers set upon my buttons, undoing my coat and pushing it off my shoulders. I returned the favor with his jacket and started for his vest. He laughed and gently clasped my hands.

"There's more."

He smiled and punched a few buttons on a large remote before Bing Crosby echoed through the room. My broadest smile broke free as I slipped out of my heels. I left them in a pile as I gravitated toward the tree. My ornaments—my beautiful, bittersweet memories—dripped from the branches. Everything from baby's first Christmas to our last family vacation was reflected back at me in the form of brass or hand-blown glass shapes.

As my fingers grazed over each glittering orb, warm tracks trickled unbidden down my cheeks. My hand delicately traced those too.

"I hate that I make you cry." Nick's voice was low and raspy as a mug appeared over top of my shoulder.

"I miss my family most on days like these." I sucked in a few unladylike sobs.

"Hey." He kissed the back of my head and pressed his perfect body up against mine. "I'm yours." He slid around me and extended the mug again. "I know it's not the same but . . . any way that could be enough?" he breathed.

Nick's timid little smile and downcast eyes almost shattered what was left of my heart. In the best way possible. Who was this man? Could he possibly be a version of my domineering, severe lover? If so, how did I keep him forever?

"You're more than I ever thought to ask for, baby. I love . . ." A sob choked off my words.

"Not as much as I do, Sweets," he barely breathed. "Swear."

I bit my lip as weird-yet-wonderful bashful Nick pulled me and my cup of Christmas toward the private elevator then our bedroom.

"This is for you." He gestured toward a snuggly robe and silky romper laid out on the bed, both crisscrossed with candy cane stripes. "Get comfortable." He pulled me a little more urgently to his lips than last time and his tongue reached deep into my mouth. His hands squeezed on my hips in that almost violent way he had but then his hold dropped without warning and stepped away still gasping.

He held my gaze for a moment, putting all his vulnerability on full display. My breath caught and, for a moment, I was going to tumble into his deep blue pools and get lost. But then he turned, and disappeared into the closet. When I unfroze, I undressed and slid into his gift.

When Nick reappeared, he was in one of my favorite fitted V-neck tees and matching candy cane pajama pants. I couldn't help but burst out laughing.

"Who are you, and what have you done with Nicholas Bryant?"

"I'd do anything to make you smile." He looked me over in the short silky shorts and his hands reached for me but he stopped himself. "Give me five minutes downstairs, okay?"

I nodded and the moment he turned to clip down the stairs, my brow crinkled. I plopped down onto the edge of our bed and aimlessly kicked my feet as I thought over the Christmas gifts I'd purchased for Nick. They paled in comparison to this new side he was showing of himself.

Even now, Nicholas Bryant could surprise me.

When I slipped down the stairs, Nick had pulled something close a hundred pillows and a fluffy comforter underneath the tree. A small flat screen sat on the coffee table nearby. Takeout containers peppered the table and more cocoa steamed where it basked in the glow of the tree.

"Nick, what's going on?"

He smiled and patted the comforter next to him; the down puffed into an oh-so-inviting pillow. "Garlic Chicken?" he offered without a solid answer.

I plopped down and studied him carefully while my hand blindly reached for Chinese. His eyes were churning, but with different shades of blue, and he alternated between staring too intently and finding anywhere to look but my face. I arched an eyebrow over a piece of broccoli but he didn't seem to notice.

What in the ever-living fuck?

At least I was asking without fearing the answer. Nick was happy—no, beaming—so I didn't speak up.

I grabbed a piece of shu mai, my takeout container, and leaned into Nick. He wrapped his arms around me then picked over my shoulder to eat out of my box. The ever present tingle that crawled across my skin in response to him was amplified tonight. It even shot straight to my heart, making it go a little haywire.

What the hell is up?

Nick slid out to reach for the remote that controlled everything, easily turning off the stereo and flipping on the TV. I couldn't help but lick my lips as I watched his muscles bunch and flex when he moved. And if that wasn't enticing enough, the emotion I'd been struggling to place all evening was back on his face and making lightness reform his usually sharp features. I started to wonder if Nick had finally cracked.

"I have it on good authority this is your favorite."

The opening scenes of *White Christmas* distracted me. Nick came back to the comforter and stretched out, then patted his chest so I'd snuggle into it. I gave him a look then settled in all the same. The heady smell of Nick and pine tree filled my senses, and my eyes fluttered shut as an *MMMmmm* escaped my lips.

"Sweets," he warned, "watch the movie."

"That's exactly what I'm doing." I let my hand skate down toward his waistband.

"No." His hand wrapped around mine. "You're being naughty when I've gone to great lengths to be nice."

I was about to quip about being punished when I shifted and caught his face. My brow crumpled as I studied the anxiety etched firmly around the corners of his wonderful-but-weird eyes.

"Nick, what the hell is going on?" I sat up and cocked my head.

"You really do have the mouth of a sailor," he joked as he wrangled a smile that threatened to split his face in two.

"Answer me! Something's off. Something's weird." My skin

vibrated and my bones hummed in response to everything he'd said, everything he'd done. It wasn't the same boulder of panic I'd been crushed with over and over but something *was* coming. Of that much I was sure.

"Nothing's wrong, Sweets. I swear." He held his hands up in surrender.

"I didn't say wrong, I said weird. Something is up. And if I have to, I'll happily spank and or fuck it out of you." I bent to snatch his pointed nipple between my teeth. My tongue flicked gently on him and even with a t-shirt in the way, he shuddered at the sensation.

"Stop . . ." Nick gasped. " . . . please." He laughed breathily at me.

I didn't even hesitate as I let my hand wander down his body. Lower and lower.

"Kate, I have something else for you tonight." I barely paused my risqué trail at his waistband. He pushed on my shoulders forcing me to sit up as he all but shouted an urgent, "Stop. I'm begging you!"

10.

The desperation in his voice made my heart swell and my hands fall away as I sat up.

"Nick, you don't have to do anything else." I tried to soothe him with my softest, warmest voice. When he didn't relax, I bent down to nibble on his lip. "Well, I can think of one other thing you should do, but in my personal opinion, it's really more of a two person job." I let my words puff across his skin then tried to slip my tongue between his barely parted lips. His big hands wrapped back around my shoulders and pushed me away. Again.

My brow furrowed as I recalled memories of us together, only once had he stopped something physical between us. He was taking steadying breaths as he ran his hands through his hair beneath me. His eyes were those insane, unearthly blue pools again.

"What's wrong? And you better answer me this time." I couldn't quite keep the bite out of my voice.

His mouth started once or twice, searching for words but he couldn't find them. Instead, his crazy eyes traced my face a few times, as he took in a deep breath and held it. He it blew out when his eyes fell away then roved over the tree the way they'd done me.

"Kate, there's a special ornament on this tree."

What the fuck?

My whole face pinched like I'd sucked on a lemon and he smiled at my perplexed face.

"It's a small porcelain snowball that your father put your first diamonds in. Studs, if I'm not mistaken."

"How did you know that?" I gasped; something sentimental was the last thing I expected.

"Laura." He sat up and nuzzled gently against my jaw with his nose.

"How did Laura even remember?"

"Find your last present tonight, Sweets."

"Nick, baby, I don't need anything." I kissed his nose as my insides back flipped.

"I know but *please* . . ." he trailed off.

I sat back, studying him once more. His eyes had settled on a deeper, darker, but electric blue. One I'd *never* seen before. The color may have been completely new, and utterly foreign, but it made my breath hitch and my heart jackknife all the same.

"Okay . . ." I drug out the word with uncertainty as I unfolded toward the tree. My eyes started searching for the familiar golden-rimmed, circular jewelry box ornament, then paused to look back at him. "You know the evening is already perfect." I smiled warily over my shoulder.

"I do, and that's why I need to give you this now." His eyes danced as I returned to my search, wondering what on earth was wrong with him.

Normally we'd be naked by now. I could conjure up a game to play under the Christmas tree, involving a big sparkly ribbon and his candy cane. Hadn't he called me naughty earlier?

That's when I saw it. The shiny, stippled porcelain snowball hung daintily from the branch on a thin gold string that wove through its small green holly leaf and matching red berries. The way my father's diamond studs looked pillowed on the velvet inside was etched into my mind, and my fingers fluttered against the clasp, hesitant to change that memory. Could whatever was inside even live up to that special Christmas morning?

I carefully pulled it off the branch then stalled, staying frozen except for cocking my head to the side. "Nick, you should open one of your presents."

He waved me off.

The white lights danced on the porcelain in my hands. Whatever was inside was heavier than the studs had been. My fingers ran across the gold rim, my mind lost to a different time.

"Kate, open it," Nick whispered from the floor.

When I still didn't budge, he stood and reached for my forearms. He pulled me ever so gently toward his body and kissed my forehead. I let his lips linger there. My fingers itched to chuck the snowball and cradle his face.

"Please."

He has never said please this many times . . .

I honestly didn't know why I was hesitating. Yes, my stomach was trying to tell me something. Yes, his eyes were speaking volumes. I just didn't know what either was saying. Or why they would make me waiver.

The sigh that escaped my lips was heavy, wary, and Nick's hands jittered on my skin in response. I stepped back slightly, just so there was enough room to hold the ornament between us. His fingers curled into my skin. Without further hesitation, I popped it open.

I felt like I'd been punched hard and fast in the stomach. I couldn't breathe. It took every ounce of my concentration not to drop the ornament. Nick's grip tightened when I started to tremble.

There, in place of diamond studs, cushioned on velvet was the most beautiful ring I'd ever seen. The center diamond was about the size of a dime, and it had pinhead-sized diamonds circling it. In between the round stones were tiny square-shaped emeralds. The setting was art deco, and the ring was definitely antique.

Was my body humming or shaking? Could my lungs expand or was my breath simply caught in my throat? Would my heart shoot straight out of my chest?

"Kate Elliott, I love you so much." Nick's voice broke and he cleared his throat. "I wish I had something eloquent planned out but . . . I . . . All I can do is tell you that you mean more to me than anything ever has or ever will. You make me feel alive and complete and I wouldn't know how to live without you anymore if I tried. I love fighting with you. I love making up with you. I just love *you*. Every day, all I think about is you. Every day, everything I do is for you. I need you Kate, I need to know you're mine and that I have you forever. Marry me?"

His hand still rested at the crook of my elbow, and he had to feel my racing pulse; the jackhammer radiated throughout every inch of my body. His thumb kept circling on my sensitive skin. Those constant circles were trying to calm me, even coax me to speak, but words just wouldn't come to my short-circuited brain.

"I'll beg. And plead. Please, please, please marry me." Nick shifted so he could hold my other arm too. I rested the ornament on his chest still too stunned to react. His voice got quieter, desperate. "I'll get down on one knee if I need to."

That snapped me out of it.

"No, please don't," I whispered and Nick swallowed as his face fell. His fingers curled into me the way they always did when he got scared. I wasn't sure when tears pooled in the corners of my eyes, but that's when the sob broke free of my throat. "Kneeling is so cheesy. I wouldn't want you to spoil the best moment of my life by being cheesy."

Tears started down my cheeks and quivered on my lips. My voice was a sultry rasp, ragged from my body's overwhelming reaction.

"Yes, I can't live without you either."

He let out a huge sigh and cracked a breathtaking smile. In that moment that unnamed emotion and the deep, crisper blue I'd seen made sense. This was love. The real kind that had a hand in everything from fairy tales to Shakespeare tragedies. The kind that laid a soul bare, gutted, and bare.

Nick gently took the ornament from me and pulled the ring out. Those deft fingers—*my* deft fingers—slowly slipped the silver down my finger. The ring, despite its size, was delicate, as was Nick's touch where he lingered on my skin.

"Do you like it Mrs. Bryant?"

Mrs. Bryant? Huh?

Well I sure as fuck had never thought about being a wife, let alone changing my name, but I liked it.

"It's perfect." My head snapped up and I gazed into those new deep pools.

He set the ornament down on the coffee table, and his electric touch came back to me as his fingers slid under my robe, gently pushing it off. It fluttered to the floor behind me, and I blushed for no other reason than his touch still lit my skin on fire. Maybe even more so now.

His crystalline eyes locked on mine and without breaking my gaze his fingers traced along my collarbone. Nick noticed my skin reacting more than normal and he kissed the bright red tracks. Much like the first night I'd been with him, he kissed first one shoulder and slipped off one spaghetti strap, then repeated the same tender gesture on the other side. My romper followed my robe to the floor.

"You, my fiancée, are the most beautiful I've ever seen tonight."

I smiled shyly then realized I agreed. The fact that he was mine made everything infinitely more delicious. I slipped off his t-shirt and laid my hands on his chest. I kissed the precious skin underneath my fingertips. His body shuddered, and he groaned before picking me up. I gladly wrapped my legs around his waist.

My thighs squeezed hard on his hips and my arms wove tight around his neck, then he dramatically tumbled to the down nest beneath us. His fingers dug into my ass and he squeezed. Hard. Something was different, possessive, almost domineering, about his grip. I thought he'd held on tightly before but this was pure unadulterated ownership of my flesh.

He kissed and nipped down my breastbone, swirling his tongue on my flesh then biting hard enough to make me yelp. When my fingers started to lose feeling and fell away, he took advantage and flipped me onto my front. He pinned me facedown beneath his strong body and stayed heavy against me as he scraped his teeth in delicious tracks down my neck and shoulders then soothing the skin with supple kisses. Nick nipped lower and lower. I gasped loudly when he moved low enough to bite my ass. Hard. He kissed the exact spot and then sat up and pulled back. I whimpered when he stopped touching my skin.

His hand plunged roughly between my thighs and pushed my legs apart. His other hand laced into my hair and pulled. My head arched up from the comforter. He leaned in, draping himself across my body and kissed the corner of my mouth just before he shoved deep inside of me. I groaned loudly when his thumb pushed just as harshly into my backside.

"Will you give yourself to me, body, and soul?" Nick snarled in my ear before nipping mischievously at it. I couldn't focus well enough to answer so he pulled my hair like a savage and arched my neck further. I moaned out in pleasure.

"Body and soul?" he breathed.

"Ye . . . yeah . . . yes," I gasped.

My reward was a swipe with the perfect amount of pressure across my G spot. I went limp and, as honey sped through my veins, his hand slowed and massaged in hypnotic circles. Arousal spread across my thighs and Nick's hand, making his skin extra wet. He hummed in pleasure and shifted his weight off me, likely so he could watch his fingers glide in the slickness. He kept hold of my hair but relaxed the arc of my neck a little.

His greedy hand cupped my sex, grasping at the wetness while his thumb still thrust gently inside me. His knees shuffled up and pushed against mine, encouraging me to spread my legs wider. They automatically inched across the soft fabric. I pulled my arms up, curled them under my chest and my forehead slumped to the comforter beneath me as his hand collected the arousal between my thighs.

Nick sighed loudly and let his hand fall away. My breath was jagged, raspy even, and it was the only sound in the apartment until I shrieked as he plunged two lubricated fingers into my ass. My body jerked and my sound twisted, contorted into something so primal it couldn't be muffled by the linens. I went back and forth between delight and agony as he thrust and stretched. I barely registered that his fingers were back lacing tighter into my hair.

His other hand twisted so his thumb could roll around my clitoris then start plunging into the slick of my sex. These were shallow, teasing motions, and more torturous than the stretching of my ass or the yank on my hair.

I was trembling when he stopped. He untangled his fingers and let my head return to the blanket. I couldn't breathe, or feel my toes for that matter, but I certainly didn't want to be left hanging.

"Nick." The agonized word was all it took to bring his hand back to my body. He pushed me hard against the floor and his cock notched between my cheeks just before he draped his body along mine.

His other hand reached down and clutched into my ass, pulling me open and letting his dick settle in closer. He rested his hard tip against me, and I couldn't help but writhe when he pressed in. I wasn't lubed enough as he shoved and I scrambled and bucked beneath him. His hand moved to my hip and pushed it back down forcefully to the floor. I groaned into the blanket and balled my fists where they were trapped beneath my body.

Nick kept pushing his cock further into me. His pelvis weighed heavy on me, and I couldn't quite writhe anymore. I settled on biting the shit out of my lip until I needed to suck in a deep breath. He gave one more forceful nudge. I clawed the floor as his pleasured moan rang out in time with him sinking all the way into me. I started to wiggle again—I couldn't help myself—I bucked up into his body. He moved his legs to the outside of mine and squeezed, once again forcing my body to still.

He sat there for a moment, nestled deep inside of me. "You're marrying me. You're finally mine. Completely mine."

"I always have been." I was able to say softly in return.

He started moving in and out, his breath warm on my shoulder.

"Mine. Fucking all mine."

I moaned when he pushed back in.

"For-God damn-ever." Nick picked up speed, and I lost my breath completely. My skin caught fire where it was smothered by him. Nick was grunting through gritted teeth behind me, and I didn't remember making a single sound but my *Yeses* and cries were echoing through the living room.

His thrusts picked up to such a fevered pace they were brutish. He was going to decimate me with his strokes. His grip would leave his usual bruises on my hips where he held me, and I was pretty sure his knees might do the same on the outside of my thighs. The way Nick was taking me was past edgy. He was claiming me, and as his most cherished possession, marking me as such too. I loved every minute of it.

He leaned back, changing the angle of his shaft and I yelped. The sound had barely left my lips when he spanked me twice, incredibly hard, on the side of my hip.

Fuck!

An orgasm shot through my body without any warning and my muscles clenched down hard on Nick as I cried out. I was unhinged, numb, and unable to collect myself. He'd scattered the pieces of my soul into the wind with the way he'd just owned me. The only way I would become whole again was if Nick pieced me together. I knew it, even here, even now, gasping, almost choking on the feather down beneath my lips—I *was* his.

I vaguely noticed him coming right afterward, but I couldn't really focus. My lungs wouldn't fully expand under the weight of Nick's body; I wasn't really interested in making them. Satisfaction oozed from my every pore. He shifted on top of me and the sting of his spank resonated but it couldn't lessen my delight.

When my ragged gasps rattled against Nick, he gracelessly rolled off me. I yelped as he slid out of me and clattered against the low hanging ornaments on the tree. Heavy panting echoing off the glass was the only sound in the room beside the soft clink.

"Oh Mrs. Bryant you amaze me." He smacked my ass again when his breathing slowed.

"God damnit Nick!" I cringed and my neck tensed.

"Calling you Mrs. Bryant or the smack?"

"The smack. That stung like a sonofabitch." I melted into the comforter again. "Surprisingly, I like Mrs. Bryant."

I still hadn't moved the rest of my body; I couldn't bring my limbs to do *anything*. He, however, propped himself up on an elbow so he could study me, jostling the ornaments again.

"Careful," I playfully warned.

He smiled and started tracing circles on my back in his familiar gesture.

"I wasn't sure you'd change your name. No one, including me, would've blamed you for staying Elliott."

"I'm doing a whole lot of shit I didn't think I would lately. Selling the business, getting paddled, getting married . . ." I smiled. "But it has a nice ring to it."

He let one long finger trace the handprints on my backside.

"Mrs. Bryant," he repeated softly, disbelieving. "Mrs. Nicholas Fucking Bryant," he added as with a low, smug rumble.

"Language," I hummed and turned toward him. He wrapped his arms around me and pulled me flush to him. I snuggled into him and he tangled his legs around mine. I stayed wrapped up in my fiancé—*fuck! fiancé!*—under still twinkling Christmas lights.

11

Soft daylight reflected off the giant ring now resting on my finger. I sighed as I picked my hand up from where I'd been drumming on the dresser.

Mrs. Bryant. Mrs. Fucking Bryant.

Five blissful days where Nick had paddled me, drank scotch out of my belly button, fucked me until I couldn't walk or swallow, and photographed me with bows covering both my tits and clit were a bubble I would have lived in for eternity if it were possible. We'd pushed both Christopher and work aside and reveled in the pleasures of each other.

I'd been claimed.

My only wish was that I had a tangible way to mark my territory in return. Or, at least show *him* that he was mine. I wracked my brain for a token that would say I'd chosen him, a daily reminder he could look at and know I'd pledged myself to him and this marriage too. Something that complimented the extravagant but perfect ring he'd given me.

The perfect gift hit me like a ton of bricks.

I turned and scrambled across our sprawling bed to where my phone rested on the nightstand. It only took a moment to dial and even less time for the familiar voice to answer.

"Hey kiddo, Merry Christmas." Jenkins, the caretaker of my Hamptons house, was bright on the line.

"Hi Jenks. Did you have a good holiday?"

"It was nice and quiet, just the way I like it. You? Were you with that guy?"

I sucked in a deep breath. Here it was. The first time I had to tell someone who wasn't Laura, Ari, or Julia I was engaged. The words were sticky, slimy almost, in my throat.

"Well, about the guy . . ." My voice trailed off.

"He was a good one," Jenkins interrupted.

"How do you know? You didn't meet him, you barely saw him when we were there." I laughed lightly.

"I saw the way he looked at you. That was enough for me."

The sappy sucker smile I'd been wearing for five days pulled back into place.

"Well, that was enough for me too. I'm marrying him." I blew out a deep breath.

"Oh Kiddo, that's awesome. Congratulations."

"Thanks, Jenks."

"You doing okay?" There was a faint chuckle in his voice now.

"Oh you know me . . . I'm terrified." He laughed flat out at that and I joined him. "But I love him, and I can't live without him, so . . ."

"So." He picked up for me. "What can I do for the happy couple?"

"Ms. Elliott." The concierge's voice crackled across the line mere hours later. "There is a package here for you."

I practically jumped as I hung up the landline and bolted toward the stairs. I was barreling down only to stop short on the second floor landing. Nick was below practicing his speech for the annual New Year's Eve Gala benefitting the Carter Foundation but tension radiated off his shoulders.

He paced the length of the windowed wall, half reading, half mumbling words that were on the notecards in front of him. I stayed frozen, watching him prowl. When he snarled, swore, and ripped his notecards in half, my feet started down the stairs all on their own.

"Baby?" I was headed toward him but he waved me off.

"There's coffee on the counter."

"That's nice, but I don't give a damn." I shrugged my shoulders as

I crossed the softly sunlit living room. "What's wrong?"

"This speech . . ."

"Try again," I interrupted. "You're a brilliant speaker. If you're having trouble it's something else."

He looked me over—twice—before he sighed. "Grab your coffee, I'll explain."

Nick slumped into the wingback chair in the living room. Rather than take a seat on the couch, I knelt on the floor in front of him and let my fingers dance on his kneecaps.

"Christopher disappeared again."

My hands automatically clawed in. "What?" My voice was sharp and my eyes were wide as saucers.

"That reaction doesn't help, Kate."

"I'm sorry. It won't happen again." I squared my shoulders and closed my eyes to take a deep, cleansing breath.

"It will." Nick smiled when I opened my eyes but it was a pained, rueful thing. "And with Christopher, I suppose in some sick and twisted way, I'm glad you understand he's such a problem. You know I'm handling it, right?"

"You know I'm your ally, right?

His smirk shifted, now more genuine. I found my lips moving toward his. He easily laced his fingers into my hair and pulled me firmly against his lips. Nick kissed me once gently, then pulled back to speak, his lips brushing against mine.

"I'm scared, Sweets. Scared he could take this away from me. From us," Nick's whispered confession pulled on my heartstrings.

"Stop," I begged.

"I'm just being honest." His hands wove all the more thickly into my hair, his fingers clutching at me.

"I know. And I'm grateful." I curled my fingers into his shirt, grasping the cotton the way he gripped at me. "But stop with the doubting, stop with the questioning. I worry too. Every day. But . . ."

"But what if I bring something down on you? What if I bring *Christopher* down on you?" His lips still leisurely brushed across my skin, his fingers almost trembled.

I didn't know the details of Christopher's wrath, only that it made Nick's blood run cold. He'd done unspeakable things to Ari and blamed Nick's good fortune and naturally kind heart for both raping her and attacking us. Honestly, none of it mattered.

"Nick, I said yes knowing damn well there's a good and a bad side to loving you. Knowing there is a way I end up complete and a way I end up completely destroyed. But I think you'll find being all-in, fear of decimation be damned, is the only option we've got."

"This is why I need you. Why I'm terrified, but why I need you." He finally pulled me up into his lap and let his lips trace up and down my jaw.

"That reminds me . . ." I trailed off and pushed away from him. Grabby fingers followed me but he let me go. "I'll be right back." I practically skipped to the elevator and I pressed the call button multiple times even though I knew it wouldn't speed things up.

Nick had risen to follow me and just before the elevator closed, he shoved his hands on his hips and furrowed his brow. The moment the elevator arrived in the lobby I bolted barefoot to the concierge stand then hefted the large package into my arms. As soon as I set it down in the elevator, I swallowed. Hard.

The sentiment behind the gift was what put a strangle hold on my throat. Nick had said such sweet things when he proposed. He needed at least that much from me. He would recognize the size and shape of the package immediately. I'd have to be short, sweet and vulnerable.

Fuck.

The elevator doors opened to a still frozen Nick. When his stormy eyes fell from mine and took in what I was holding, he cocked his head and blue filtered in.

"Is that really for me?" His eyes came back to mine.

"Of course. Who else would it be for?"

"If it's what I think it is, I don't know why you'd give it to me." His voice was low and thick with emotion.

"You deserve something special, something that tells you I chose you every bit as much as you chose me. That I ask you to pledge yourself to me the way I did to you. Something that shows I'm all in, and I want you to be all-in too. Forever." I bit my lip as I handed the butcher paper clad rectangle over. "I doubt you'd like a diamond ring."

I held my breath but he wasn't paying attention to me. He was staring at the soft brown paper where his fingers skated along the edge.

"I've wanted to see it since the day you told me it existed, but always thought better of asking." He picked at the twine tied around and into a bow. "Just knowing it existed inspired me to start photographing you."

"You dirty, dirty bastard." I shook my head.

"I'm not the one posing naked for photographs." He winked at me then ripped into the paper. His face lit up when it fell away. "Kate," he breathed.

I could picture what he was seeing. Patrić, the photographer responsible for the sensual photos of me in our theater room, had only taken one long shot of my body. Only one that showed anything private. He'd stood on a ladder over top of me, and shot in the same dim light and shadowy setting as the ones already hanging in our penthouse.

This one captured me from lips to mid-thigh. I had on dark red lipstick and matching crimson fingernails skated across my torso. Besides the pops of red, the photo was black and white highlighting shadow and sensuality. Beneath me was a soft white satin sheet that appeared to ripple against my skin. The contours of my body were on display just like the ones Nick had purchased. Only this time he got *every* curve and contour.

"This is the most beautiful gift." He swallowed hard. "It's you." He sounded shocked.

"You have lots of naked photos of me Nick." I smiled shyly and my eyes dropped to study the back of my engagement ring. "Many far more scandalous than this."

"But none you gave to me. And Patrić's photos are what got us here in the first place. I held onto hope because of the woman in those photos. I held onto you even when I was drowning."

He was still staring in disbelief when I grabbed the frame and slid it to the side. I wove my hands around him and whispered, "You're mine, fucking mine" into his ear.

We kissed tenderly as his hands explored the contours from the photograph in person. My hands returned the favor over his sculpted hips then up along his broad back. I scraped my nails down making him groan into my open mouth as I went. I smirked and unceremoniously shoved my hands down his pants.

He arched away from my hands. "Hey, stop. We've got things to do today."

I didn't even falter, I just grabbed his dick and started stroking.

"Kate," he warned as he grabbed my wrist and squeezed.

My knees knocked together. Just his grip, firm and possessive as it was, made me wet. I pushed my breasts up against him. He snarled.

"They say the second you get married the sex dies." I added an exaggerated sigh as my hand fell away.

"Ah, the vow I forgot. I promise, my fiancée, to fuck you into oblivion from now until forever." His hand found his way back into my hair and he yanked, craning my head up toward the ceiling, opening my throat to him. He kissed my neck, sucked hard, then bit just as roughly. It would leave a mark and I groaned. "But I need to take you dress shopping first."

I rolled my eyes and relented. Nick pulled my hand from his pants and lifted it to kiss the center of my palm.

"Fuck, I love it when you smell like me."

With that, he pulled me into the elevator. When we met Jaime in the lobby, Nick's eyes clouded again. I followed Nick's line of sight only to find the photographers that always greeted us. If my eyes changed color, they would've turned a dejected shade too. Our reality was overwhelming sometimes.

At least it's ours together.

I turned to face my fiancé and my hand automatically moved to cradle his face. I played with the edge of his hairline then let my hand roll down along his neck. He still had a hard time looking directly in my eye.

"Kate, I have the worst request." Nick's voice was a wholly tortured thing.

"Anything," I replied unequivocally.

"You haven't heard it yet."

"The fact that you're making a request is enough for me." I smiled as I ducked into his line of sight.

"They can't know yet. About the engagement. Not with *Christopher* . . ."

I cut him off, "Nicholas Bryant."

"Sweets," he scrambled, "please let me explain."

"No. *You* let *me* explain. I couldn't care less if the press knows. Ever. I told you a long time ago, I don't need you to shout about this from the rooftops. Just between us is all I ever need."

His shoulders sagged and relief seeped into his eyes. Without warning Nick's arms flung around me. He gathered me into his chest, his arms around my neck, and my face gracelessly mashed into the crook of his shoulder. All I could do was wind my arms around him and run my hands up and down his back. When he pulled back, he smiled down on me.

"If you wait right here I'll run up and take my ring off." I patted his back and tried to turn for the elevator.

"No." His arms got tight again around me. "Don't ever take that off. It's a symbol. It's a promise."

I wanted to quip something snarky about taking it off to shower or swim—or give him a hand job—but he was just so earnest. I swallowed the words, and when he laughed, loud and bright, I was sure he noticed.

12.

When we crossed the wide curb toward Bergdorf's entrance, my shoulders crept up toward my ears. Depending on the day, society women could be worse than shutterbugs when it came to privacy invasion. But Nick pressed his palm to the small of my back and I melted.

The doors opened in front of us and we were greeted by my personal shopper, Beatrice. I introduced Nick as nonchalantly as possible—as if he wasn't Nicholas Fucking Bryant—then snaked my left arm around his torso. The moment I snuggled into Nick, Beatrice squealed a holy unearthly sound, bringing the sales floor, customers and associates alike, to a screeching halt.

My heart seized in my chest and worry filtered into my insides. Nick tensed beneath my fingers. Something blood curdling like that could only mean trouble. Both of our gazes started sweeping the floor, but when nothing seemed out of place I turned to sweep up my fiancé's face. A giant sparkly diamond caught my attention. *My* giant sparkly diamond. The one Beatrice was laser beam locked on.

Murmurs broke out as an unfortunately timed ray of sunlight made my engagement ring appear even more ostentatious.

So much for secrets.

I turned toward Nick and a truly scared rather than horrifically angry man greeted me. I thanked my lucky stars that only I'd be able to tell the difference in his pinched face.

"I think that's quite enough." Thankfully Nick's voice boomed through the marble corridor then silence once again blanketed the room.

Beatrice's eyes widened and when her brain lurched into gear, she stammered an apology and ushered us up to the fourth floor salon.

Nick sat diligently as I tried on gowns. Beatrice worked extra hard, extra quietly, bringing me dresses she deemed appropriate for our New Year's Eve gala. I showed the first six to Nick, each one receiving a mild-manner nod. The spark he got in his eye when he liked me in something, or even better, the hungry look he got when he wanted to peel me out of it, was decidedly missing. The seventh started a downhill slide.

I stepped out and Nick pursed his lips and scrunched his brow, searching for a words.

"It's okay to say it Nick. I know it's the dress." I arched an eyebrow and flicked the hot pink train behind me on the pedestal.

Is she delusional?

"It's not that it's bad." He rubbed his chin still looking perplexed. "But it's pink."

Jaime tried to stifle a laugh behind us.

"And you don't really *do* pink. Ever." Nick crinkled his nose and Jaime let out a genuine laugh behind me.

Beatrice was losing all three of us quickly. *Very* quickly. I sighed as I wondered if I could call in a favor with Zac Posen and chalk the whole afternoon up to a massive loss. Nick noticed my restlessness shifting to temper and stood.

"I'll take a look."

Without waiting for an answer, he walked out of the fitting room. I turned to watch him go and caught Jaime's eyes instead. His look made me break into giggles. I was so obviously not a hot pink girl even he knew it. I went back into the fitting room, still laughing to myself as I shimmied out of the dress. Beatrice hung it for me and started removing the rejects.

"Try this."

Nick was back and there was the soft whisper of fabric rustling on the other side of the curtain. Moments later Beatrice stepped in with a dress that looked like liquid shimmering champagne. It was made to hug curves and had a small pooling train. The top was a sculpted bodice with a deep cut down the front, making an incredibly risqué sweetheart neckline. Even on the hanger, it was gorgeous.

Better yet, it was soft on the inside and easy to climb into, I could even zip myself with the hidden side closure. The J Mendel gown was beautiful. And it made me feel incredibly sexy.

"Well?" Nick was waiting on the other side of the curtain.

"It's beautiful. It's the one."

"Are you coming out?"

"Nope." I unzipped it and handed it back to Beatrice. As soon as she walked away, he whipped behind the curtain.

"Are you purposely being naughty?" He pressed me up against the wall in my lingerie and I chuckled as I curled my hands into his shirt.

"I just thought about the look in your eyes the first time you see me in it." I pulled myself closer and whispered in his ear. "I want you to be desperate for me the way I'll be desperate for you in your tux."

"Oh Mrs. Bryant, you are a cruel, cruel woman," he whispered in my ear and dug his fingers into my hips.

Jaime cleared his throat as a signal; we were about to have company. Nick didn't seem to mind, he pressed me flush against the wall and kissed me. He bit and nipped at my lips, and I could only sigh into his open mouth. His hand snaked between my thighs finding nothing but slickness consuming the thin strip of lace of my thong.

"I think we're done here. Get dressed now."

I nipped his earlobe then let him pull away. He slipped out of the room only to swear under his breath.

"Piper." Nick's growl sent shivers up my spine and the name made my fists ball. "What are you doing here?"

"Nicholas, we need to talk." Her purr made my jaw clench. Fire flushed across my chest too.

Before I realized what I was doing, I shoved the brocade curtain aside and lunged at her. I'd be damned if she talked to my *fiancé* in that bedroom voice. Neither Nick nor Jaime expected my lingerie-clad ass to spring out at her, hands headed for her throat.

She yelped like a wounded animal as soon as I got my hands on her. I had her neck and I started squeezing just before she wildly clawed at me. Her talons dragged down my right arm hard enough for me to drop my hold like I'd grabbed something flaming hot.

"You bitch," I screeched.

The anger I'd harbored against her bubbled up in spectacular and volcanic fashion. I wasn't remotely satisfied with one tiny assault and scrambled to find something else to pummel. I got to her ponytail first with one hand and her throat again with a second. I yanked and dug as hard as I could.

She screamed again, louder and more anguished than before. The sound gave me the slightest bit of satisfaction.

Nick's arms squeezed around me. They were strong and sturdy without being aggressive, but they pulled my arms away from Piper's body without even trying. He gathered me into his chest even as I fought to dive at Piper again. She was out of reach with Jaime similarly restraining her. I breathed heavily and my heart hammered against Nick's forearm, shaking my body even more than vengeance itself.

"Sweets, I get it. Swear I do. But do you really have to do this here?" Nick whispered in my ear with the hint of a smile. I still squirmed in his arms. The desire to throttle her had me seeing red and little else.

"Kate. Leave it." Nick squeezed me a little as a warning then kissed the back of my neck. "For me?"

I melted a little into him and finally his grip lessened the smallest bit. He didn't let go.

"Why are you here Piper? What the fuck do you want?" Nick snarled a little too loudly in my ear and I automatically elbowed him.

He grunted then let me go. Well, mostly anyhow. His hand found its normal place on my hip and his fingers curled in exactly the amount I expected under the circumstances. I would bruise but because of *Piper*, I didn't care.

"Yes, do tell, Piper? You haven't ruined everything completely so you thought you'd come back to try and finish the job?"

"Ruin? You think your life is ruined? From where I'm standing . . ." I didn't let her finish.

I broke out of Nick's hold and bolted toward her. "No thanks to you!" I screamed and once again went to choke her.

"Stop. Please stop!" She managed in the most broken tone possible.

My hands fell away. Not because she'd asked but because she was so close to tears, it surprised me.

Nick had his hands around me a moment later but his grip lacked authority. He'd heard her break to.

"Did she hurt you?" Nick asked, still cold.

"No, it's not that." She yanked down the collar of her turtleneck, revealing deep purple bruises. "It's these." My mouth fell open and the longer I stared the more I recognized their familiar shape.

Handprints.

But they weren't mine. My hands were smaller and I doubted I could squeeze that hard, even to save my life.

"Did he do this to you?" Nick asked like it was a continuation of a conversation from earlier. His snarl rumbled in his chest, vibrating against my back. I was the one who wanted to growl. How could he read her so easily? My temper was back and threatened to be even more volatile than before.

"Who is *he*?" My voice was raw but as soon as I spoke, I knew.

"Christopher," they said it in unison, in matching dejected and pained voices no less.

I sucked in deeply. Sure, I imagined how my hands would fit in the edges of those bruises but my heart also twinged a little. If she was still involved with Christopher, there was something brewing that a cat fight couldn't resolve. No matter how good it would feel.

"Why are you still involved with him? After everything that happened, I thought you'd have enough sense to get out, Piper. I told you to get out." Nick had shifted to his cooly detached and all together scary voice. I shivered in spite of myself.

"I'm not. I mean I did." She cowered under the weight of that voice. "Get out, I mean. But that doesn't mean he was done with me."

She gulped. "He's been watching . . ." her voice trailed off in one of those gut wrenching ominous tones.

"Watching what?" I snapped.

"Everything. Everyone. Me." Her eyes lifted then narrowed. "You."

"He's watching Kate?" Nick lunged out from behind me only to roar in Piper's face.

Her eyes dropped and her shoulders rounded beneath Nick's withering gaze.

"Piper, I asked you a question."

Jaime and I both stepped toward Nick when his hands balled at his sides, fury rolling off him in visible waves.

As if on autopilot, she fell to her knees and placed her palms flat on the floor, keeping her eyes on Nick's shoes as she went. It was so automatic and so naturally submissive, I felt like I was glimpsing an intimate moment between them. My stomach heaved.

"Get up Piper." Nick was softer now and it made the feeling in my stomach all the more violent. When she didn't move, he added, "Get up and speak to me like an adult. That's all you are to me now."

She sat back and looked up at Nick with giant puppy dog eyes. The urge to pummel her all over again swept through my veins. Nick must have read me perfectly because his hand returned to my hip and pulled me to his side.

"Tell me what you know, Piper. Now."

"He has enough blackmail on me to ruin my life. My master's too. No matter how high ranking he is, we can't bury this kind of stuff." She gulped and her hand went to flit around her throat.

"And what exactly is he blackmailing you to do, Piper?" Jaime's deep baritone voice took over asking the questions.

When I looked from him to Nick and back again, I got the feeling Nick already knew. Piper must have gotten the same sense because she reached for a bag that laid by Jaime's feet. She shuffled around in it, searching for something, until she pulled out a small manilla envelope and held it up to Nick.

"Just take this. Please," she whined a little.

"I'm not taking that from you, Piper." Nick's bone chilling voice was fading, his grip on my hip was not.

"Yes, you will. You need to know what's coming, Nicholas." Piper found a little bit of confidence in her voice and stretched her arm out even further.

"I'll figure it out some other way." Nick looked away, off into the distance, and then over at me. His gaze swept all the way from my eyes down to my toes and back again. The deep coal his had turned wasn't lost on me.

Piper stood and stepped closer to the two of us.

"Take the envelop Nicholas. He's blackmailing me to help with your destruction. And I'm not the only one."

Nick's body went rigid. I swore his heart stopped beating. Piper tried to manage a small, apologetic smile as she attempted to tuck the envelope into the crook of his elbow. When he squeezed so hard, she couldn't, Piper turned and handed it to Jaime.

"A storms coming, Jaime. Don't let it destroy him."

Jaime took the envelope and all three of us wordlessly watched her walk out.

"Baby, what was in the envelope?"

Nick didn't say anything, he didn't even acknowledge that I'd spoke. He was facing away from me, drinking scotch, watching the city go dark. He hadn't said anything in the six hours since he'd all but dragged me out of Bergdorf's. I hadn't pressed him either. Instead, I studied the tuxedo that molded to his perfect frame.

"Kate." He sighed and sipped again. "Is there any way you'd leave it? Just this once? I'll beg."

He sipped again, watching my reflection in the massive wall of windows that was our living room. Judging by the bottle next to his shiny Prada shoe, this wasn't his first or even second glass. And if his rigid shoulders were any indication, they weren't helping. My heart broke at the obvious anxiety that riddled his body. My mind, however, was at war. I was just as desperate for answers as I was to console him.

"Is that a let it go permanently or just for now?" I asked quietly.

He turned to face me and studied me. His face fell as he did. "I'd beg for permanently but I don't think you'll let me." His voice was even quieter than mine.

If the whole world hinged on Nicholas Bryant, that look said he was going to let it fall. He was going to let it fall to the ground and smash into a million pieces. Based on whatever had been in that envelope, he just couldn't hold it up any more.

I scrambled to catch it, determined to hold it up for the both of us.

"Permanent is good." I shrugged and bit my lip.

His brow furrowed as he cocked his head to the side.

"Come on Nick, I'm not completely unreasonable."

That made his scowl break, replaced by a wistful smile.

"Just this side of it I think." He set the scotch down and walked toward me. "Unreasonable or not, you're gorgeous." When he leaned in toward my lips I ducked away.

"Don't. You'll ruin my makeup."

"Who said I was going to kiss you?" His lips brushed against my skin and his fingertips curled into the romantic wisps of hair I'd left free. "If I kiss you now I'll have even less desire to leave."

His eyes fell from my face but I caught fear filter in anyway. My hands went to his chest on their own accord. I definitely did not mean to flex them into his pecks.

"Are you trying to kill me?" It was our long standing joke but there was absolutely no humor in his voice tonight.

"I didn't even realize . . ." I let my voice trail off as I renewed my assault under his jacket and up against his low back.

"Well you do now." Amusement colored his voice as he went back to playing with tendrils of my hair. His other arm wove around me and his fingertips started playing at the hidden zipper. "Tell me we don't have to go. Tell me we can stay here tonight." Nick's tone, breathy and desperate up against my ear, pulled on my heartstrings.

"They're honoring you and your contributions, Nick . . ." My fingers disagreed as they clenched into him.

"I shouldn't have to do anything but peel this gorgeous dress off my beautiful fiancée."

Oh God, yes please.

I wanted him. Desperately. Just as I'd foretold. And not only because the all too familiar wetness was spreading between my thighs, but because it was the first time his eyes had lightened, albeit infinitesimally, since Bergdorfs. I wanted nothing more than to keep them that way.

My body caved before my mind, sagging into him and angling so he had even better access to my zipper. "Screw it," was on the tip of my tongue when the elevator dinged behind us and Jaime, Colton, and Terrence all stepped off in classic tuxedos.

"Sir, everything has been prepared as requested, even at the venue. Are you two ready?"

Nick looked longingly down at me, and something about his face was so distraught that all my breath left me. It was like a massive kick to the stomach, and that nauseating feeling of dread landed at my core with a thunk. Before I could even think, I spoke.

"Nick I don't . . ."

His, "We're all set" rang out over top of my words, and his hand seamlessly slid to the small of my back as he pulled my now-leaden feet toward the elevator.

13.

The ballroom where I'd first laid eyes on Nicholas Bryant had been transformed. The room was covered in black, silver, and green gossamers, all shimmering with an iridescence that reminded me of the way my insides felt when Nick was near. Touches of holiday still lingered in the centerpieces, holly mingled with silver dusted globes and snowflakes. If that damned feeling hadn't been gnawing at me I would have relished the splendor.

"Sweets?"

Nick noticed me studying the carpet rather than the ethereal ceiling. I met his eyes and everything in me lurched.

"Something's wrong." I didn't think before I said it.

"What? What's wrong?" His eyes went flat and his frown marred his gorgeous face. All I could do was shake my head.

He gave me a severe look, and would've questioned me if family hadn't found us, Ari cutting off our words with a giant hug around Nick's neck and a giddy shriek in his ear. Julia grabbed me before I could pull my hand from Nick's, making for the awkward lump of people standing by our table. I was able to manage a small smile and wave at Laura as she worked her way over behind them.

Whether we liked it or not, whether something was afoot or not, we were thrust into the very public role of gala honoree and new fiancée. The whole thing was disconcerting and knocked me off my game.

I couldn't give Laura shit for another new man, or be grateful there was no awkwardness with Julia. I couldn't be myself or clear my thoughts. Dread had started snarling in my stomach like a caged and baited animal. The whirl of faces, fabric, and chatter around me was quickly drowning me. Only one voice could help me surface, and even then, I barely reacted when Nick whispered in my ear.

"I have to make my speech," he said and my insides clenched. "Please stay right here, where I can see you." I had to dig my fingernails into my palms to keep from reaching out and stopping him.

Laura took Nick's place when he strode toward the stage. I jumped when she laid her hand on my shoulder.

"Whoa, what's wrong?"

"Nothing," I snapped and slammed my champagne.

"Don't lie to me." She was speaking aside to me while we clapped for Nick's introduction. In the twenty seconds since Nick had left my side, his eyes had gone colder. Shit had seemingly gone very wrong, very sideways, and I almost couldn't breathe.

"Is *I don't know* sufficient?" I asked quietly and narrowed my gaze, still unwavering from Nick.

From the corner of my eye I saw Laura furrow her brow, and I was in no mood to reassure her. Honestly, I couldn't.

"Champagne miss? For the toast?" I turned on autopilot to grab a flute from the tray.

The man carrying it was just a shock of blonde hair and blur of a silver vest. I noticed he hadn't made eye contact but almost nothing else registered. Something thudded inside of me and my head snapped back to the stage.

Nick was right where my eyes had left him, still perfectly attired, breathing calmly, eyes flipping between note cards and me. But then he looked past me; his face fell and his eyes turned black. My heart jackhammered as I looked around. Nothing seemed out of place but Nick was morphing up on his pedestal. His fury was becoming less and less contained. I slammed my second glass of champagne, immediately making a face.

"That's what you get for chugging champagne," Laura quipped

beside me.

"It tasted funny," I said as I refocused on the end of Nick's speech.

"Kate, what's going on?" Laura, was shifting between my face and Nick's.

He'd finally cracked enough that others could tell. He was beet red and a vein popped out of his neck. His teeth gritted together so tightly that his razor sharp jaw was somehow more defined, and a dimple hollowed near his ear. Nick was even inadvertently balling note cards in his hand; I couldn't look away.

"This is way more than funny tasting champagne."

Laura's eyes bored into me; studying, evaluating. And she wasn't the only one. The weight of the room fell to my shoulders.

"I need a scotch."

Before I start shaking.

"Did someone say scotch?" The voice interrupting was vaguely familiar and I turned to take the amber glass from the same blonde server that'd circled not two minutes ago.

"What the fuck are you doing?"

Nick's voice roared inches from my face only a heartbeat after he finished his last word on stage. The whole room froze when he bellowed and my body reacted immediately, goose bumps covering my skin and hair standing up on the back of my neck.

"It's just scotch, Nick," I spoke softly hoping to soothe him.

"I wasn't talking to you."

I looked up and saw the glower he'd fixed behind me. Everyone nearby was fixated on us, on the pure hostility radiating off my fiancé. Movement toward us pulled my attention from Nick. Jaime, Colton, and Terrence were all jostling people and shoving furniture to reach us.

What the fuck?

Nick answered my unspoken question and finished his thought with one dreadful sentence.

"I was talking to Christopher."

The shock took my breath away. Even more so than the painful grip Nick used to pull me back or the wildly terrified look on Jaime's face.

Christopher Winthrop was shockingly blonde and dressed to disappear into the ballroom, but once I really looked at him, his sick, sadistic smile made him stand out. It hung naturally on his face—like he didn't have to work to keep it there—and his eyes lit up with an eerie, smoky light that made his skin all the more waxy in appearance. Had I never heard a word uttered about him, that face would have made my skin crawl. Something in that gaze shifted to hungry when his eyes locked on mine. My stomach bottomed out and I tried to keep my face from betraying me.

"She's even better in up close Nicholas." Christopher's laugh cut straight through me, down to my very bones. I didn't even notice Nick's hands had left me until they were clawing at Christopher's vest.

"Not here, not now." Julia's voice came from somewhere behind the wall of men, every bit as assertive and icy as Nick's could be. "You will not make a scene in public."

"Keeping up appearances Julia? Wouldn't want anyone to know that Nicholas isn't perfect, or that he's marrying a delicious whore."

I balled my fists, Nick growled again, and this time even Jaime joined in.

"Upstairs, now." Julia narrowed her eyes at Nick and Christopher. Nick's fingers were turning white on the satin of Christopher's vest. "Now," she commanded, marginally louder.

Nick was completely unconcerned with a scene as he yanked Christopher toward the staircase. Christopher couldn't keep up and his feet wheeled and scrambled beneath him. Jaime lunged to Nick's side and the two of them manhandled Christopher up the sweeping stairs.

"Take her home now," Nick shouted over his shoulder to Colton.

"Wouldn't want her to know the truth?" Christopher laughed.

The comment should have pissed me off, but this time around, it simply freaked me out.

"Christopher," Nick warned, his temper fraying.

An odd ringing started in my ears. The further they moved away from me, the harsher the sound became.

"I'm not going anywhere. Not without Nicholas." I pushed past Colton's outstretched arm, following everyone else up the stairs.

"What's going on?" Laura was beside me the moment we made it to the second floor. "More of that *you don't know* stuff?"

"I knew you wouldn't tell her." Christopher was watching Laura and I intently behind Nick, that smile still hanging on his lips. The ringing in my ears got louder.

It's okay Nick didn't share. It's okay Nick didn't share. It's okay Nick didn't share.

My pulse raced.

"Your damn right I didn't tell her. Why would I subject her to that?" Nick shoved Christopher down an empty hallway, toward the balcony from our first evening.

"Whores don't have feelings. Tell her whatever you want." Christopher snickered.

Excuse me?

My whole face contorted and that familiar ball of acid welled in my throat but I didn't dare speak. Christopher stumbled a little in Nick's grasp but he recovered quickly, those evil eyes laughing at me all the while. One of Nick's hands cocked back and his whole body coiled before crushing his fist into Christopher's jaw and sending him crumpling to his knees.

"You will not call her a whore!" All of us cringed when Nick bellowed.

"But she is one." Christopher shrugged as he regained his footing. He acted as if he hadn't been punched, as if there was no crunch reverberating through his bones. He didn't even check the blood coming from his lip.

"Christopher, stop this," Julia scolded.

"I've seen the things she lets you do to her." Christopher kept speaking as if nothing was happening to him.

What?

Jaime and Colton both muscled over to him and pinned him

against the wall. With him restrained Nick paced closer, more livid than I'd ever seen. Every inch of him quivered.

"I will kill you." Nick's voice was low and menacing in a way that made my blood run cold.

Laura gasped beside me but I kept my eyes on Nick. Nothing else mattered in that moment but him. I wanted to go to him. I wanted to put myself squarely in between the brothers and beg Nick to come home. Even apologize for letting us leave the house in the first place.

"I know you like whores. Whores that do dirty things. Whores like Piper. And now Kate. Just another set of holes that likes filthy, dirty things."

Even from behind, I could tell the effect those words had on Nick.

"Shut the fuck up!" I shouted without thinking. Everyone turned except Nick when my voice rang out. "You're the disgusting one. And you will not speak to Nicholas like that. Not about me, nor about our relationship. Not about anything." I'd managed to speak with a snarl that should have made Nick proud.

Instead, I saw his shoulders slump and his being deflate at the same time Christopher's eyes flashed with a truly unholy glint.

"She's feisty, too. Even better." A laugh rang from Christopher's lips that made my skin crawl and my insides twist.

Before anyone else reacted, a few things happened all at once. Jaime stepped back to pull his weapon as Christopher lowered his shoulder to crash into Colton. Colton went flying backward into a potted plant and Terrence tried to shove between Julia, Laura, and myself to get to the wide open hallway Christopher bolted for. Laura grabbed a frozen Julia and hauled her out of the men's way. I barely noticed any of it as I watched my fiancé fracture rather than sprint after, or even seethe at, what had just happened.

Colton scrambled, sending soil flying across the perfect white carpet, then tore off after Christopher. Jaime ran past me just a breath later, making the material of my dress rustle. Nick still hadn't flinched.

"Laura, take Julia and find your date. If one of the new guys is downstairs send him home with her. I'm assuming Frank got Ari out of here the second they realized Christopher was here."

"They did." Julia was thawing but there was something in her eyes when she met mine that unnerved me.

"What about you?" Laura asked while Julia's bleak gaze shifted to her son.

"I'll be fine." I don't think anyone believed me.

I waited for them to turn down the stairs before I crept toward the statue of a man in front of me.

"Nick," I whispered as my hand rose to his shoulder. He flinched when I set my hand lightly on the soft fabric of his suit. "Baby?" He shifted again, this time I followed to wrap my arms tightly across his chest.

He sagged into me.

"What have you done?" he asked, no louder than a whisper.

"What do you mean?"

Nick turned in my arms, I still held him as tightly as possible. I was prepared for him to push away, to scream and shout, maybe even foam at the mouth, but he simply wormed his arms out of my grasp and wrapped them tightly around my neck.

Huh?

He didn't pay attention to my hair as he pulled me tighter to his chest. Or to my makeup as he kissed one eyelid, then the other, before landing with his lips pressed against my forehead.

"Oh Sweets, what have you done?" He lips brushed against my skin as he whispered.

The particularly uncharacteristic softness flat out frightened me.

"I don't know, Nick." My voice shook all on its own. "Tell me and I'll fix it."

He didn't say anything. The silence was more unnerving than any fight we'd ever had. He was looking down the hallway in the direction the men had sprinted, but I couldn't tell what he was seeing. I didn't know why he wasn't the one leading the pursuit.

"Come home with me?" His lips were still against my skin.

As soon as I nodded, Nick pulled me toward the ballroom, his hand faithfully stuck to mine. He didn't breathe a word, his eyes didn't shift from their awful new shade. He didn't even try to keep up appearances as we tore through the party and out the front door.

In the backseat of the car, I tried to listen for his heartbeat or his usual, deep, even breathing. For the first time, neither registered. He traced his familiar circles on my thigh but they weren't angry, grippy things, they were tentative and shaky. Each gesture, each moment that ticked by, showed me this completely unfamiliar man and that man had panic gripping my chest.

As soon as we were home, Nick went straight to the office. I let him; sipping scotch in the living room suited me just fine. Jaime, Colton, and Terrence weren't too far behind, and I simply pointed to the office door when they arrived. The door opened and closed unceremoniously when Jaime announced himself. There was no shouting, no slamming of things, none of the angry Nick trademarks. Nor did I have any desire to burst into the room and demand to be included. Matter of fact, I wanted to be as far away as possible.

When exhaustion hung heavy on my eyelids, I went up to bed. I couldn't help but tiptoe the whole way. Even in my own closet, I was tense and my heart beat far too fast. My eyes fluttered shut and I took a deep breath as I slowly pulled pins from my hair and let it fall. I unzipped my gown and let it pile on the floor around me. A loud exhale echoed behind me.

"Nicholas." I turned toward the door to see fixated, stormy eyes. I reached out for him and, to my surprise, he crumbled to his knees in front of me. "Nick." I cried out as shallow breaths wracked his shoulders.

I went to kneel down but he stopped me by wrapping his arms around my legs then holding tight like a stone statue.

A horrified, broken, petrified statue.

14.

"Love, talk to me," I begged.

He didn't answer.

My hands wandered through his hair as we sat like that for what felt like eternity—me hesitating, him statuesque. I was getting cold and trying to think of something to say when he nuzzled into my bare skin. The proof of life urged me to try again.

"Nick?" His hands dropped from my body and he looked up. I melted down to the floor. "Baby, are you ok?"

"You have to be freezing." His words weren't what I expected but I was glad he was speaking.

"Yeah, but that's ok." I smiled tentatively, now nose to nose with him.

He grabbed my shoulders and crushed me to his chest. When his grip loosened the smallest bit, I twisted to sit in his lap and he adjusted his arms around me. As always, his touch warmed me, even tingled slightly. I leaned my head back on his shoulder and breathed in his purely Nicholas scent.

His hands automatically went to my chest. For a moment, he simply traced the swell of my breasts, and I purred into the cool air. Then his hand slid down to my nipples and yanked roughly. I arched against him as my purr shifted to a loud groan. The sound egged him on, and he pulled even harder. I started gasping and panting just before he dropped my breast and both his hands plunged between my thighs.

My shocked cry echoed off the glass and Nick growled in response. One finger slid into me and the other immediately dug in to my thigh. I couldn't help but arch away from his chest, even as I pushed myself further onto his hand. He massaged my G-spot over and over, and I couldn't help but grind my hips in time. Arousal dripped down my leg and dampened his sleeve where it rubbed against me.

When my limbs went limp, he used his grip to push me up to standing. My vision tunneled, my thighs tried to press together—my knees wanted to buckle—but he kept his hand inside me to prevent me from crumbling. Nick gracefully unfolded from the floor and used his fingers, still dancing on my G-spot to lead me to the bedroom.

His hand fell away when I stood next to the bed, and he jerked his chin toward the mattress. I climbed on, and had to consciously keep from flopping gracelessly to center.

"Play with your nipples," Nick purred his command when I laid back and my hands moved without hesitation.

I tugged and twisted and pulled the way he would. I arched up off the bed into my own hands. He groaned as his tuxedo pieces started to hit the floor. When he was naked, he bent over *the* drawer before climbing back onto bed and bending over me.

"I need some control back tonight, Sweets. Will you give it to me?"

I nodded, never ceasing the tugs on my chest.

"Tell me you want me to feel in control again."

"Yes," I gasped.

"Yes, what?"

"I want you to be in control Nick, feel in control, whatever you need." The words were a plea to take me. However he damn well wanted.

"Good girl." His voice broke.

They were the right words but not the right tone. He was sorrowful like the day he'd told me about Christopher in the first place. Something was still very wrong, and I tried to focus long enough to see his eyes.

He leaned down to fasten my hands to the headboard and tucked his chin, bending to hide his eyes and take my nipple in his mouth as he clamped the cool metal of handcuffs to my wrists. As soon as I was secured, he yanked me down, forcing my arms to stretch straight overhead. His eyes fluttered shut as he continued to roll my breast between his teeth.

Now I was too preoccupied to care what color they'd been.

Nick pushed my legs up, each heel as close to my backside as possible, then he started kissing on my inner thighs. When he got to my clit, he kissed lightly then started sucking. Slowly the light touches of his tongue turned into assertive thrusts. I twitched with each and every one.

I was so focused on his mouth I didn't pay attention to his hands. They'd left my hips and were now playing with black satin ribbon. The fabric danced against my skin as he looped circles around my bent legs, intersecting each loop with one soft, barely there knot up against my calf. He bound each leg tightly on itself keeping my knees bent and me open to him.

That was when the real torment began. Nick's lips slowly moved across every inch of skin. Not just my aching sex or beaded nipples, but every single inch. And I couldn't move in any way; I had to take it, feel it, relish it, and only wish to God I could give it back somehow. His hands followed his lips, tracing my every contour, memorizing every line.

MMMmmm.

"Sweets," he murmured and the sound was still broken.

His cock twitched against me, his fingers dug into me but he wasn't enjoying himself. Despite all my pleasure, that voice made my heart hurt.

"Baby." My hands yanked against the cuffs, reacting only to my urge to console. "It's okay, baby." My last word turned into a groan because his tongue waved and rolled inside me while his fingers traced the edges of the ribbon.

His touch was reverential but distant, covering every inch firmly, but not rough. It seemed like he was prolonging the experience and trying to get it over with all at the same time. Nick's tongue inside me just felt *different* than usual. But at the end of the day, my G-spot was still a trigger, and when he stroked it all I could do was shake my head side-to-side and moan.

Just before I came, he pulled away. I was left gasping, hands balled where they were cuffed, hips writhing as much as they could with the way I was tied, praying he'd come back to my body. Instead, I saw him shuffle to the side of bed and reach back into the bedside drawer. A matching satin blindfold tickled over my skin as Nick leaned in to tie it. I caught the unearthly slate of his eyes just before my world went dark.

I would have asked him about it, even here, even now, if he hadn't roughly taken my lips. This kiss was harsh and tender all at once, just like his touch had been. He bit down hard on my lower lip and when he broke skin, he whimpered. I gasped, feeling both my heart jump and my stomach clench.

His tongue took advantage and slipped into my mouth. He explored and tangled, desperate to taste and leisurely enjoy my mouth the same way he had the rest of my body. Every once in a while he came back across his bite mark on my bottom lip and lapped at it.

MMMmmm.

Without warning, he scrambled and his cock replaced his tongue. His signature salty, sweet softness pierced my lips and pressed in, all but choking me. I simply hollowed out my cheeks and sucked. His hips quivered over top of me. The warmth of his flesh radiated across mine and his constant groans of pleasure filled my ears. I let him piston against my lips. I even twirled my tongue and let him lace his hand into my hair to pull me up to meet him. When his fingers went rigid, I figured he was going to come.

But he pulled away leaving me panting. My heart was thundering—freakishly so—and sweat coated my body, staying clammy on my skin and making the ribbon stick where it wrapped my skin. I was pinned and I couldn't feel my fingertips or toes.

All the shit was long gone. The gala, Christopher, Nick's eyes; my brain had officially blanked, consumed by only the picture of Nick's body lowering to mine.

When he finally settled between my thighs, I gripped him with my knees as best I could and shoved my hips up to meet his.

"I love you," I stuttered between erratic heartbeats.

"Not as much as I love you."

His words were still fragmented, anguished even. The feeling that always balled up in the pit of my stomach was trying to cut through the sexual fog. But Nick's thrusts were so perfect, his rolling so expert, I got lost in the movements. In the taste of him. And the feel of our skin against each other.

Nick's lips moved between my lips and breasts, his fingers between my clit and ass, and because of both soft satin ribbon and steely cuffs, I was powerless to stop him. I wouldn't have even if I were free. I was building toward some sort of spectacular orgasm as both of our bodies bunched and coiled up against each other.

"You're the love of my life," he whispered, never breaking pace.

"Nick . . ."

"Remember that always." For the first time today he was sharp with me; his voice was low, sexy, domineering, but again, *different*. I got the impression that he needed me to understand deep in my core, down in my bones, like he wouldn't be there to remind me. My heart popped against my rib cage.

"Always." I gasped. "Forever."

His lips pressed above my left breast, over top of my jagged heartbeat while his hips kept moving perfectly against mine. Nick lowered himself flat, pressing his full weight to me. One hand gripped my ass, his other arm wove further around my neck, and those fingers snaked down to flick my nipple. I don't know if it was the actual moves or the sheer closeness of our bodies that shoved me over the orgasmic edge.

My restraints protested as my arms and legs and hips tried to move. It was excruciating to be pinned and absorb the waves that wracked my body. My cries got more intense and the chattering of the metal handcuffs echoed in the room. My body was desperate to hold him and prepared to break steel to do it.

"You were mine," Nick growled as he came brutally inside of me, even slipping out part way and shooting hot cum onto my skin. My body tingled everywhere. Everywhere that I hadn't gone numb anyway.

I didn't even notice the past tense.

Nick collapsed on me and I wasn't sure how long we stayed there. Every so often he'd nuzzle against my skin or kiss my jaw where he could reach. I would have let my fingers comb through his hair or trace circles on his back but he hadn't unlocked the cuffs. Or untied either ribbon.

"Just this once can I keep you chained to the bed like I've always wanted?"

His breath was warm against my skin. I could tell this was a plea more than anything. Even post climax, Nick was distraught. My compulsion to soothe took over.

"Yes," I breathed. "Anything for you."

"I'd do anything for you, too. You know that right?"

I nodded as Nick found new spots to kiss me, wandering leisurely across my skin. I sighed repeatedly, pulling every once in a while on the cuffs, knowing full well there would be bruises tomorrow. If I were being honest with myself, I would have wondered if the emotional ones were going to match.

I had to be dreaming.

I was completely unbound from both steel and silk, and my engagement ring was gone, though the sting of bruises was noticeable on my wrists as I reached out for Nick. Every bone in my body ached as I patted across the soft fabric.

A hand caught mine and I let out a deep breath, my eyes closing tightly. Nick gently twisted my arm and kissed the inside of my palm. He followed it up with a kiss where my ring had been. My body instinctively moved closer to the hand but there was still no matching hard body there to curl into.

"Nick," I moaned into the night air.

Something in my stomach flipped when he didn't answer. Suddenly it seemed critical to open my eyes, but I couldn't; sleep still weighed heavily on them. I tried to pull on his outstretched arm too, but my body was too weak to move him. The softest, saddest sound left his lips in response.

"I knew you were too good to be true," he murmured and I gathered he was sitting in that same side chair he'd slept in so many times while watching me.

Things were far worse than I suspected.

Open your eyes Kate, look at him.

"I never deserved you," Nick continued.

Oh shit, open your eyes!

"And my selfishness almost cost you everything." His voice broke.

Kate! For the love of God! Wake the fuck up!

"For the briefest moment I had you and I was happy. But I'm not meant to be happy." I'd only heard it twice before but that tone was etched into my being; it accompanied Nicholas Bryant's tears.

This wasn't a dream, this was a nightmare. My worst nightmare. My body wouldn't move again. My eyes wouldn't open. Nick's voice was so real, the sheets beneath me so soft. Even the dread churning inside me was normal—awful, but normal.

"I'll always be yours, even if you can't be mine," he whispered oh-so quietly.

Please, please, please wake up, Kate. Pry your mother fucking eyes open!

A new agony appeared alongside the dread in my stomach. This pain was lodged squarely in my chest.

He pushed his hand through my hair. His fingers wove into my long, tangled strands. When he cradled the back of my head my body nuzzled into his touch.

"I love you, Kate Elliott."

My body thrummed like it always did when Nick was close. The sounds of him moving only preceded his lips brushing against my forehead, down beside my eye and across my jawbone by a heartbeat. Then his lips pressed against mine. I willed mine to respond. Just like my arms and eyelids, they wouldn't, instead staying limp while he chastely planted a trembling kiss to my lips.

I love you Nicholas Bryant.

My body finally allowed me to react. I was allowed to cry. The tear tracks started wet and warm down my cheeks. Then, with just one deep breath, it was all gone. Nick, the tears, everything faded into the dark.

15.

Oh holy mother of God it hurts.

I shot up in bed, clutching my heart. There was a very real, very sharp pain shooting through my chest. I was gasping for breath as first light showered the apartment in rosy hues.

"Nick!" I could barely yell, pain firmly lodged in my throat. Nothing stirred in response. "Nick!" This time I put everything I had into shouting.

My call just seemed to echo even deeper into the cavernous apartment. A pain closer to lightning than anything else shot through my heart.

I need to go to the hospital.

I shoved out of bed when the realization came crashing down on me. I wasn't handcuffed to the bed anymore. I wasn't bound by ribbon either. The chair was exactly where it should be if my dream had been real. A snifter sat on the floor.

No!

My mind wouldn't—no, *couldn't*—process that the nightmare had been real. *Those* words couldn't have been uttered. The goodbye couldn't be real.

The lightning in my chest rolled again and my hand clawed at my skin. That's when I realized my engagement ring was back on my hand, diamonds and emeralds exactly where they should be.

What the fuck is going on?

"Nick!" I screamed this time, letting all the terror welling in my chest screech out.

Now I was scrambling from the sheets, desperate to figure the mystery out. I snatched a robe and started wheeling about the house in between horrific heartbeats. I was about to call out in the living room when I saw it, or rather didn't see it. The photo, *my* photo, the one I'd given him as a symbol was gone. I knew damn well that meant Nick was missing.

My knees gave way and I crumbled gracelessly to the floor. Why had he left? What had happened? What had he said last night? Why the fuck hadn't I been able to open my eyes? I could have made him stay!

I squeezed tighter across my chest and held my body together until I caught my breath. Even after that I sat, staring dumbfounded at the spot where my photo had been.

I'll be damned if I'm losing him again.

Clumsily, I stumbled over to the phone. I jammed on the buttons hard enough to chip a perfectly manicured nail. It was the least of my concerns as his cell phone rang. And rang. And rang, and rang, and rang. I dialed the office next. To my surprise, and despite the early hour, there was an answer.

"Bryant Venture Group, Julien speaking." The familiar voice of Nick's assistant came across the line.

"Julien, it's Kate." I muffled a pained wail. "Is he available?" I was only asking as a formality.

"Ummmm . . ."

"Julien," I begged.

"I'll check, Ms. Elliott."

Ms. Elliott?

I waited for Nick's voice, unsure if it would be icy or abrupt, *or timid,* but wanting the reassurance that coursed through my veins when I heard him regardless.

"Ms. Elliott?" Julien was back on the line. "He's unavailable."

"What?" My mouth fell open and I stuttered, "Ahh." My heart

thudded, and I wasn't sure if Julien caught the ragged sound.

"He's unavailable," Julien repeated but his voice wavered and he added in a whisper, "I'm really sorry, Kate." He hung up before I could collect my thoughts and respond.

I sat staring at the phone as if it had betrayed me. Nick always took my calls. I called his cell phone again and even left a desperate voicemail. He didn't respond to that attempt either. It was 9 a.m. before I gave up. Nick hadn't called, Jaime hadn't come to collect me. For the first time since meeting Nicholas Bryant, I was actually alone. My heart started crashing about in my chest and my hand clutched at it.

My fingers dug into flesh or fabric above my breast as I got ready. The only time my hand left my chest was when I got woozy and needed to steady myself—something that happened far too frequently. Out of habit I called out for help when I tumbled to my knees after a particularly painful thump. The hospital still sounded smart but I was running late and Vesper responsibilities won out.

Even in the office, I couldn't shake the pain in my chest. My hand kept digging into my heart and rubbing, hoping to keep it from busting straight out of my rib cage. With each mini-heart attack, either my face scrunched or my knees went weak.

I was rolling my palm into my skin, face contorted, as I walked down to the conference room for a staff meeting.

I wonder if he'll show?

"Ahhh!" I had to steady myself against the wall at the errant thought.

"Kate! Are you alright?" Gemma rushed to my side.

"Is he here?" The words came out through clenched teeth.

"What?"

"Is *he* here?" I snarled, still massaging my aching heart.

"Not that I'm aware of." She frowned. "Jaime didn't mention anything." Gemma wasn't overly concerned with the boys, she was fully focused on my frantic movements. "Are you all right? Perhaps I should call him? Or a doctor?"

"No."

I shoved off the wall and shuffled into the conference room.

I began without pretense and had to check myself a few times from screeching in pain or adding flippant comments about Nick's absence. I had to hold back tears for the exact same reasons, too.

Nick didn't come to the staff meeting. Or Vesper. Or home. All week. My heart was horrible the entire time, reminding me every thirty seconds or so that Nick was gone. My temper and my tears warred with each other the whole time.

Each time I called Nick, my heart would start racing, my breath got short, and the pain picked up. Eventually, his voicemail would pick up and fury would override everything. When I'd gone and gotten real worked up, usually mid-tantrum, the cadence of my heart would become worrisome all over again and I'd plop into the nearest chair to practice deep breathing. I should've learned my lesson—or gone to the hospital—but instead, I stayed at One Madison and kept right on calling.

There were about eight million other *should's* throughout the week too. I should have laid off the coffee. I should have checked my temper. I shouldn't have ripped up half of the fall line sketches in front of Elena's face. I shouldn't have smashed Nick's favorite scotch glasses. I should have tried to sleep. And I definitely shouldn't have cried alone against the big glass windows of the living room every night.

The bags were worse under my eyes Thursday evening, a deeper more phenomenal purple than I'd ever seen. Even the bruises from our most dirty exploits hadn't been that dark. The thought made my heart hurt. Literally.

My fingers started dialing Nick's number before I even thought about it. His brisk "This is Bryant, leave a message" greeted me. Again.

"I don't know why you're doing this. I honestly can't fucking figure it out. I've tried." My voice broke. "I really have. I know you have a reason. I'm sure you think it's a good one. But bottom line is, it doesn't matter. Please come home." A single sob strangled my voice. "Please." I hung up, wrapping my arms around myself, wishing desperately they were his instead.

I need you Nick.

In bed, I stared at the ceiling and started counting panels. *82.* I counted the window panels in the room and then all the ones on all the buildings nearby. *147.* I even counted the stones in my engagement ring as I twirled it around my finger. *18 circles, 12 tiny emeralds, one massive stone.*

Thursday night faded to gray, and Friday morning turned to a light pink—gray hurt my heart and I never was a pink girl. I glared at the sky, wanting to rail at it too, but it set my heart thundering.

The mood I eventually left the house in most closely resembled that of a starving animal, one forced to stare at food out of reach. I actually snarled at my doorman. When Gemma's hand trembled slightly while handing me my coffee and a thick black envelope, I sagged.

"I'm trying to rein in the temper, I really am, it's just . . ."

"He's still not home?"

I shook my head and slumped onto the edge of her desk.

"I need him Gem, I really need him."

I popped open the note, knowing damn well I didn't want to read what was inside.

You think a desperate plea is going to change his mind? He's making it too easy for me to have my way with his whore.

Christopher!

The letter broke me. It was all far too much. Particularly because I didn't have Nick to turn to. A solitary tear ran down my cheek. I tried to wipe it away before Gemma saw but I wasn't quick enough. She threw her hands around me.

"I can't today Gem, I just can't."

She nodded against my shoulder and reached for the phone. One hand kept rubbing my shoulder while she busied herself punching in numbers and canceling appointments.

"Anything else, boss?" She smiled at my puffy face when she wrapped up the last call.

"I know you and Jaime speak." I cleared my throat, almost

choking on the ball of emotion there. "I need you to get this to him." I handed her the letter, unconcerned with whether she read it or not.

I picked up my coffee, my Birkin, and the sorry excuse that was myself and headed back out to the snowy street. I wandered to Prada and Chanel and even Alexander McQueen but I couldn't focus on anything. The word *Nick* was rattling in time with my jittered heartbeats. Eventually I found my way to S&C.

Laura.

For the first time in a few days, I genuinely smiled. As soon as I was upstairs, she waved me into her corner office. She was wrapping up a phone call as I plopped down and threw my feet up on her desk. She rolled her eyes at my dramatics and then pulled a smug smile into place.

"Taking the day off? That's . . ." She let out a quick short laugh. "Odd."

"Fuck you."

"Language, Kate. That was uncalled for and the curse word was just unnecessary."

"I'm having a shitty day, Laura. No, I'm having a shitty week."

"On a scale of one to ten how bad is it?"

"Shitty." I arched my eyebrows and enunciated every letter.

"Scotch or Tequilla?" She arched an eyebrow right back.

"Remember that time we were eighteen and killed a bottle of Fireball?" I asked and she let out a low whistle.

"Well, well. That night was an epic train wreck, or at least what I can remember. You still have that scar?"

I pinched my face and absentmindedly rubbed on the raised skin on my shoulder.

"Only one person can get you that worked up nowadays. Are you moving out and smashing glassware as you go?" She cocked her head. "I'll help, but I refuse to drink Fireball."

"Whiskey will do just fine," I grunted.

"You rarely make good decisions while drinking whiskey." There was amusement twinkling in her bright blue eyes.

"Thanks Mom, I hadn't realized . . ." I hadn't meant to sound as snarky as I did.

"I won't go anywhere with you if you take this out on me." She shot me a deadly look from behind her desk. I immediately slumped in resignation. "I thought so," she quipped and started shuffling her paperwork. When I let loose a world weary sigh, Laura picked up the papers and shoved them in her bag.

She grabbed my elbow and led me out of S&C and toward a bar. My heart jackknifed and made my ankle wobble as we crossed the threshold. Laura's brow crinkled in response but she let me choose a large booth away from the front windows without question.

Our drinks came quickly and my whiskey neat went down far too easily. The worry I'd been consumed with mellowed but wouldn't melt completely, not even with the too sweet amber liquor.

Ugh, this is why I drink scotch.

"Where are your shadows?" Laura asked.

"Haven't a clue. They disappeared with Nick and I couldn't even begin to guess at why." I rolled my eyes, thinking it over for the tenth time in as many minutes.

"Do you want to talk about it?"

"Not really." I shrugged my shoulders as I stole a cherry from her drink.

"Is it about the naked photos?" If I'd had a mouthful I would have spit it out at her, totally unconcerned with the mess it would have spattered everywhere. I ordered another drink with a quick, curt gesture.

"What the fuck are you talking about?"

"Kate . . ." She went to chide me but I cut her off.

"No. Nope. Don't even think of Kate-ing me. What naked pictures?"

"Well they aren't so much naked pictures as they are pictures of you and Nicholas in the middle of . . . well . . . you know."

"No, I don't know. This is all news to me. In the middle of what?"

"Don't make me say it," she whined.

I simply arched an eyebrow and pursed my lips. I pulled my fresh whiskey to my lips and let it burn across my tongue and down my throat.

"Fine." Laura glowered at me. "Fine. They're of you two having sex."

"When?"

How? Why? Was I tied up or getting paddled? Motherfuckinggoddamnshit.

"I don't know when."

"How bad are they?"

"I don't know." She sipped on her cocktail. "Ari told me about them. I don't ever need to see your naked ass all twisted up with Nicholas."

"Ari knows?" My volume was rising.

"Yeah, she called me the day after the gala."

"So everybody knows this shit except me?"

"Christopher was right, Nicholas loves to keep you in the dark."

Christopher was right?

I didn't even bother responding to her. I shoved out of the booth and stomped to the bar. Laura yelled after me but I crossed my arms and gritted my teeth as I slid onto a barstool.

How dare she agree with Christopher. On Anything. Ever. Even something fucking tiny!   Sexual photos explained a lot. Nick's adamancy that, this time, I would actually be hurt. Christopher calling me a whore. The security ramifications were even more worrisome. He would have had to be close—too close. Maybe even inside the apartment.

"Looks like you need a drink worse than I do."

A snicker interrupted my spiraling thoughts from the corner of the bar. The bearded ginger-haired man across the way was vaguely familiar but I couldn't place him.

"No, thank you, I'm engaged." I tried to soften the tone of my voice.

Sort of.

"I'm not trying to hit on you kiddo, just offering a drink to another angry soul."

"I am not an angry soul," I enunciated each word sharply. "And I don't want your fucking drink."

"Okay, okay." He was chuckling again as he raised his hands in defeat over the bar.

The laugh made him seem all the more familiar but even wracking my brain, I couldn't figure him out. The creepy feeling he gave me was easier to place.

"Glenfiddich. Neat, please." I angled myself away from the lowlife and toward the bartender.

As soon as the scotch hit my lips, it tasted wrong. There was something slimy about it and the usual notes were muddied, the aftertaste acidic as hell.

Everything is wrong today . . .

After a second sip, my head cocked back and I scrunched my face. That's when the laughing began.

No, maniacal chuckling.

I looked over and it clicked. It was the sadistic smile that hung on the ginger man's face that was familiar. Satan's grin itself made all the features I'd missed snap into place.

Christopher.

I couldn't think about him or the implications of his presence, because my head started to swim. I swayed on the stool.

"You're so predictable, Kate. Just like Nicholas."

My fingers curled into the marbled bar as I swayed again. My knuckles turned white. My heart was hammering faster than I'd ever thought was possible, it was shaking my body, shooting pain up and down my limbs. I couldn't help but reach for my chest, and when my hand left the bar, I pitched further.

Like a lopsided bag of potatoes, I started sliding from the stool then tumbled into a heap on the wooden floor. My body tingled and not in the blissful way, in the oh-God-it-fucking-hurts way. Voltage shot through my body and I was fairly sure I knew what it felt like to be electrocuted. And what was worse, I couldn't feel much else. My hand fell away from my ribs, as my body lost motor control. My vision tunneled but I could see Christopher slinking toward me.

"You keep your hands off her."

Laura.

She sounded like she was underwater.

"I'll help you get her in a cab." Christopher's voice made me want to shove or shout but I couldn't move. I could barely breathe.

"Back the fuck away!" Laura screamed just before I blacked out completely.

16.

A small, piercing beep rang repeatedly through my subconscious. I was cold, colder than I should be. The light was dim but somehow still harsh even through my closed eyelids. I could hear voices drawing me out of a deep, miserable sleep.

It's your fucking fault. The woman's voice was shrill.

I would give my life for hers. Had I known, I never would have let this happen. The male voice was pained and ferocious but still ran like warm butter across my skin.

You would have known if you'd been around. The woman's voice was getting more agitated. I finally processed that the voices were fighting.

I had to keep my distance to protect her. All I do is think about her. Every God damned moment of every single day. The man's voice sent small shockwaves down my spine.

You keep telling yourself that. The words were acidic as they dripped off the woman's tongue.

Ms. Gold, Mr. Bryant, if you would please continue this discussion outside. This was a new voice. Deeper, kinder. Somehow more forceful too—authoritative.

The clipping of heels and shuffle of shoes faded out of earshot. Only then did I let my eyelids flutter slightly. A wheeze escaped my lungs when unfamiliar cold fingers pressed to my wrist. The pressure on my wrist tightened but no one spoke.

After a few seconds he questioned, "Ms. Elliott?" There was something small and round and cold at my chest.

"Nick?" I muttered.

"No, Ms. Elliott, I'm Dr. Chambers." He scribbled on a clipboard at the foot of my bed. "Mr. Bryant is just outside. How are you feeling?"

I didn't really know yet.

"Fuzzy," I grumbled. My voice didn't sound like mine.

He chuckled softly. "That's to be expected. Anything else?"

"Cold."

"I'll make sure we get another blanket for you. Do you remember what happened?"

I tried to get my brain to kick into gear. I remembered drinking then . . .

"Not really."

"You were drugged," he spoke matter of factly. "Quite heavily actually. We had to pump your stomach to prevent you from succumbing to an overdose. You passed out and suffered a head contusion as you fell. Your CT scan came back clear. However, there are still toxins in your blood. Preliminary results show it was amphetamine based, so until it's thoroughly through your system, I expect you'll feel pretty awful."

No shit, Sherlock.

"We're going to keep you one more night for observation but if you continue to make improvements, we should be able to release you tomorrow. You're expected to make full recovery with rest and time." He smiled warmly as he tucked a tablet under his arm.

He was about to continue when all hell broke loose outside. Dr. Chambers immediately went to find the source of the uproar. I knew. I finally understood Nick and Laura were brawling. They'd been in the room bickering as I woke up. And apparently things had escalated.

Dr. Chambers added to the cacophony, his voice rising above both of them, threatening to remove them from the hospital. I rolled over, hoping to drown them out. And stop the room from spinning.

Different cords and tubes twisted and protested as I shifted. One slipped off and the machine behind me started squawking. The commotion as they all poured back in the room overshadowed the piercing sound. There were frantic movements and barked commands but I couldn't make myself turn back over to greet them.

"She's fine, machine slipped." Concern still colored Dr. Chamber's voice.

"Sorry," I croaked.

"Sweets?" Nicholas's voice was almost as bad as mine.

I closed my eyes, letting the sound wash over me anyway. Even scared and angry, it was him. And he was what helped steady the whirring room. I wasn't ready to answer though. I wished I was myself, and that spite and stubbornness had me punishing his silence, but I just honestly couldn't force my mouth to move.

"I'll get him out of here, just say the word." Laura was still back there too.

"I'll have *everyone* removed if needed, Ms. Elliott."

I seriously thought about Dr. Chambers offer. I didn't turn when the silence turned heavy behind me.

"They're fine." I pulled the blanket up to my chin, burrowing away from all of them.

An ear-splitting phone ring reverberated through first the room and then my teeth. Laura answered and her voice hesitated before she click-clacked out of the room. Dr. Chambers was quiet at my side, readjusting whatever monitor had broken free.

"If you change your mind, or need anything else for that matter, please call the nurse's station. All you have to do is press this button." The blue button was more comforting than his sweet smile. "One of us will happily come running."

I tried to muster a smile in return but couldn't quite manage. He understood and squeezed my shoulder gently before striding out of the room. Only Nick was left behind. His breathing filled the room. His body was nearby too—the telltale current between us told me so. I didn't particularly want him to go, but I wasn't ready to deal with him either.

To his credit, he let me sit in silence. Something creaked and crinkled as he took a seat on whatever was behind me. I let my eyes wander over the tiled floor and up the clinical walls. The survey was taxing and I almost nodded off before Laura click-clacked back into the room.

"Best, can I get you anything?" I imagined her glowering at Nick when she said it. I raised a hand and waved her off. She couldn't make the nausea or headache go away. "I'm here to help," she continued. "I can go anywhere, get anything. I can start moving things out for you. Whatever you want."

"Moving things out?" Nicholas's angry growl rolled from his corner of the room. "What on Earth do you mean?"

"I think she should move out, you obviously don't care about her. Look at her."

"You think I like this? I would have done anything in my power to prevent it."

"Except stick by her, be by her side." They were shouting again. I pulled the blanket up over my head, trying to hide from the noise.

"Stop it right now, Laura. You're bothering Kate."

"You're bothering Kate," she snapped back.

"Shut up," I wheezed as loud as I could.

The words hurt my throat and my head, but Nick and Laura went silent at my command. I stayed with my head tucked under the blanket.

"Kate?" Laura questioned.

"Please leave me alone," I rasped.

"I . . . I can . . . I guess I'll come back after lunch." I could tell she was hurt, but I said a silent thanks that the fighting would stop. My eyelids sagged even though I'd just woken up.

My thoughts drifted to Nick. They hovered there for quite some time. I wanted to hear his voice, feel his touch, then fall fast, fast asleep. I'd been devastated before blacking out but now I was just hopeful. Whatever had happened to me, whatever had happened in that bar, I was alive and Nick had stayed. If he was here, I would be okay.

I pulled the covers down to find him inches from the bed. He'd pulled a chair over to my bedside and was sitting with his head in his hands, his elbows on his knees, staring at the floor. I didn't speak as I studied him. I hadn't seen him in what felt like forever.

He was frazzled. No, *tormented*. His hair was disheveled, and he wore a dangerously sexy five o'clock shadow. I'd never seen him scruffy. Ever. His suit didn't look overly fresh or clean either. The upper buttons were undone and his tie hung loosely around his neck. I silently reached my hand out and let my fingers run through his hair. My touch surprised him and he jumped.

"Sweets." He sucked in a deep breath.

"I missed you." Even at a whisper, my voice sounded horrible.

"I missed you more." He looked so scared I had to reach for him.

I cupped his cheek and he nestled into my hand. His tentative fingers reached up and wrapped around mine. My skin warmed where he cradled it.

"May I?" He gestured to the bed. I wiggled to make more space for him. I couldn't help the wince that crossed my face. "Kate?" His face filled with panic.

"I'm okay."

He eyed me suspiciously before slipping out of his jacket and tie and sliding into the bed next to me. Warmth blanketed my body where we touched. I slowly moved into the crook of his shoulder and laid my cheek on his chest. I finally felt a familiar feeling course through my veins.

He'd need one hell of an explanation for almost leaving me. And for taking Jaime with him. But right here, right now, I didn't want it. The moment was actually beautifully, and wonderfully peaceful.

Another familiar voice filtered into my blurry thoughts.

"Please don't wake them, Dr. Chambers. Please. She needs her rest and he hasn't slept in over a week." By the rise and fall underneath my cheek, I gathered Nick was still beneath me, which meant he was the one who hadn't slept.

"I need to check her vitals. The drug she ingested doesn't normally affect people so severely. I'd be lying if I said I wasn't concerned. I need to make sure she made it through the night okay, and Mr. Bryant is on her monitor."

I was processing faster now. They wanted to wake Nick to make sure I was okay. I recalled how rundown he'd looked.

"Jaime," I whispered. "I'm fine. Please let him sleep."

"Ms. Elliott may I take your blood pressure?" I nodded and lifted my free arm for Dr. Chambers. The room was quiet while he pumped, only Nick's steady breathing and monitors disrupted the silence.

"May I listen to your heart and lungs?" I twisted, trying not to jostle Nick, and he slid a stethoscope under my gown. I let out a deep breath when Nick didn't flinch. Dr. Chambers stepped back and started to scribble on the tablet attached to my bed. "Rest for the next few hours. We'll make sure you can keep some food down and have you complete a simple set of daily activities, but as long as you feel alright after, we'll be able to discharge you."

"Thank you, Dr. Chambers." I smiled genuinely then melted back into Nick's body. "What time is it Jaime?" I smiled at him and his protective position in the chair I'd found Nick in not too long ago.

"Just after 5 a.m."

"What day?"

"Thursday." That was a shock. I'd passed out on a Friday. "He's been incredibly worried about you." Jaime jerked his chin toward the lump of man meat beneath me.

"If he was so worried, why haven't I seen either of you for a week?"

"I'll answer that. When you're home. In my arms, in our bed." I hadn't noticed Nick was awake until he mumbled, his words rustled my hair. I nuzzled into him and he hummed appreciatively. "What food sounds good? Jaime will get you anything." Apparently, Nick had been awake for the entire exchange with Dr. Chambers.

"I most certainly will." Jaime nodded and smiled at me.

"Chicken noodle soup sounds alright," I answered as Nick ran his fingers through my tangled hair, gently combing out knots. Jaime didn't even hesitate, he simply nodded and left.

The room was silent except for the electric hum of all the monitors when Nick whispered so light I barely caught it. "I'd never forgive myself if you weren't okay."

"Me neither," I whispered back with a smile.

He gently kissed my forehead. It sent a jolt of electricity through my body. We both chuckled when it registered on the machine to my side.

I was able to keep the soup down but my stomach had a hard time. I masked it as best I could; Dr. Chambers bought it. Bryant knew damn well how hard it was. He kept his mouth shut too. After that, different therapists popped in and out.

Nick's disapproval with each one became more blatantly obvious. His eyes churned gray then went flat. His jaw clenched so tightly I thought he might split his teeth as we walked slow, small step, by slow, small step down the hall. I wanted to tell him to relax but it was almost too charming.

The trip made me overly winded; my knees wobbled, and my heart thundered. I didn't know why, but my neck and shoulders tensed too. They were so tight I thought they might snap.

But in the end, I made it.

Dr. Chambers read my heart monitor after the lap and got worried all over again. He ran what had to be a thousand tests, taking a million more measurements and bringing in two specialists. I wanted to whine, *You said I could go home* but I kept my mouth shut and endured every little bit.

In the end, I was rewarded with a thick stack of discharge paperwork. As soon as I signed the last sheet, Nick's arm wrapped around me. He was pulling me into his arms when a wheelchair arrived. A snarl rumbled in Bryant's chest when the staff insisted I be pushed rather than carried out. He relented, plopping me down, only to snatch me back out the second we breathed fresh air.

I hadn't thought of the press or what had been reported in the days I'd been unconscious. When we walked out of a service entry, I knew something extravagant had made the papers. I couldn't bring myself to care. I couldn't find the strength. I didn't need to. Nick had enough for both of us and he put it to good use, carrying me as he barreled through the press to the front door of One Madison.

We were in the bedroom before he set me down. I chewed on my lip as he rolled down the covers. I gingerly made my way underneath as he disappeared into the closet. Part of me couldn't believe I was even remotely tired, let alone exhausted down to my very bones. Part of me didn't give a damn and stood at attention when Nick came back dressed in soft pajama pants and nothing else. I let out a deep, loud sigh.

In that moment, I decided that was the way I liked him best, forget the power suits, tailored tuxes, and perfectly fitted jeans. His golden skin rising from his low hung, soft sweats as he slunk toward me, made me smile, and my heart shudder. My wide grin wasn't lost on him, and his answering one was beautiful. It had a certain sadness that mixed perfectly with tenderness.

When he climbed in, I let him pull me to his chest and then with one finger, he lifted my chin. He kissed me firm and full on my lips. Despite my utter exhaustion, my body reacted immediately. My hammering heart was completely manageable as he rolled on top of me and kissed me over and over. It was comforting to be wrapped up with him, firmly back where I belonged.

He pushed and pulled on my lips until they throbbed. Only when he pulled away did I notice how bad my jaw and throat ached. My back and head too. I couldn't help the pitiful whimper that escaped. The sound made Nick pull back to study my face. I sagged into the bed and let my eyes close.

After just a moment, he rested his forehead to mine, and I forced my arms to tighten around him despite the throb it sent shaking through my bones. Nick slid down beside me and picked up his familiar circles on my skin. I shifted so I could rest against his taut chest. I kissed the hard muscles under my lips as I went. Nick let his hand on the small of my back wander down between my thighs. I couldn't help that my hips arched up to meet him. Nor the pathetic sound that slipped from my lips immediately after.

"Sweets?" He hesitated long enough to question me, his voice a mix of worry and frustration.

Sorrow seeped into his eyes. He didn't want to stop; he wanted to be inside me, relishing my body as our familiar rhythm reassured him that I was okay. That I was alive and unharmed. It had always been the way we communicated best. And I wanted sex for the exact same reason.

But I just couldn't. My head throbbed so thoroughly I couldn't force my body to follow through. I curled into a smallish ball against Nick in a gesture of defeat.

"Can I do anything?" His lips brushed against my forehead.

"I just need to sleep." I was already dozing off when he started to gently play with the ends of my hair.

It was then that Nick started speaking.

17.

"I don't know when Christopher decided on vengeance. I don't even know what he thinks he's getting revenge for."

I wouldn't have stopped Nick, even if I'd had the strength to do so.

"My heart stopped when I saw him standing next to you at the gala. I told you once I never believed in something bigger before you. Even after, I was unsure *what* I believed in." He let out a heavy breath then bent to kiss my shoulder. "But when he was there, smirking at you, I prayed. I prayed that I really would be able to protect you." Nick was snarling, and though my heart pumped painfully at that sound, I kind of enjoyed it.

"You've said that once or twice." I smiled and let my hands wander over his skin.

"This time I needed it to stick."

My heart beat its new erratic, startling beat.

"Kate, you don't know what he's like. You couldn't have known, and that was my fault." Nick's fingers leisurely traced along my spine. "He's been watching you for a while. And I mean watching *very* closely. Just like Piper said." Nick sighed. "And why wouldn't he watch you?"

I let his question hang in the air.

"Everything about you piques his interest. You're powerful, smart, sexy as hell, and worst of all, *mine*." Nick's voice broke. "Laura said she told you about the photos. What she didn't tell you is that there is set after set. Graphic pictures. Close up pictures. When you stood up to him I knew why he'd taken them. He knows what you can take and he likes it when women struggle. He made up his mind to have you, when you sparked in front of him at the Gala, I saw it."

Nick's fingers stopped circling, and just dug in instead. I made sure not to flinch.

"My world crashed down around me, Kate. I died a little knowing what I'd brought on you. All my selfishness went out the window and I knew what I had to do."

His voice seemed to stick in his throat.

"You had to leave me." There wasn't a question in my voice.

"Tried to." He adjusted so he could look me in the eyes.

After a moment, his lips brushed against my forehead and his fingers started back into their circles. "I was going to follow through, then, at the last moment, I saw the photo. Your body highlighted by shadow, given freely to me, completely and for forever . . . All the memories slammed into me. The good, the bad, the sexy, the sweet." His fingers came to mine and wove in.

"That's when you put my ring back on."

My words slipped out.

"What?"

"Nothing."

"Sweets . . ." Nick's grumbled warning rattled against my ear.

"I was awake when you were leaving me. Or not quite awake. I was . . . I don't know. I thought I was dreaming, I was untied, ring missing. I tried to say something but just . . . couldn't. I tried to reach out for you. It was surreal." I shook my head at the memory. "I mean why would you leave me? *How* could you leave me?"

"You were so pissed. I could tell the moment you stepped out of the building that morning, hair whipping around, dark lipstick, and *that* look." Nick chuckled. "When I couldn't follow through I kept hoping your temper would get the better of you and you'd take my ring off."

"What do you mean?" My temper threatened to get the better of me now. "You wanted me to have some sort of tantrum and break it off?" I tried to push away from him.

"Yes, I counted on it." He held me in place and let a small smirk cross his face.

Asshole!

"I opened the paper everyday hoping to see the headlines," he said honestly as I struggled harder, feeling my heartbeats soar. Hadn't he gone on about it not just being a symbol but being a promise?

"Well I'm incredibly sorry I disappointed you," I growled. "I'm sorry that I stayed faithful just as I fucking promised!"

Ouch.

Sparring literally hurt my heart; it labored both furious and wild. I clutched at my chest as it constricted then shuddered.

"Shhh, Sweets. Please."

Nick's brow crumpled when pain shot across my face but he started to rub up and down on my arm. I took a few steadying breaths and closed my eyes as my heart started to slow. His big hand left my shoulder and cocooned mine. I fought it at first but then he bent and kissed my engagement ring.

"I was worried when my plan didn't work, but I was over the moon that you didn't waiver. It meant more to me than I can possibly say. I was so scared, but I knew I had you."

"Always." I was still short of breath. "But if you're really interested in forever, this shit can't happen anymore. You have to treat me like your partner. You have to fill me in."

Nick sighed and buried his head in the pillow. "I know you hate to hear it, but I *am* trying."

"Try harder." I laughed a little bit, certain I didn't want any kind of a fight right now.

"It isn't funny, Kate. He watched us fuck. He watched you sleep. He was in here and I can't figure out how," Nick roared but this was purely a scared sound.

My hand instinctively went back to my chest and Nick swallowed hard. I made sure my free one found its way to his chest and rubbed soothingly. Nick sighed and let his hand cup mine.

"I lost all confidence in myself to protect you. I resorted to figuring out a way he might lose interest." Nick gulped; his distress pulled on my heartstrings. "I had to pull everyone to make it look real. He obviously knows our lives *intimately*."

"In that case don't try harder, be smarter," I said softly. "I would've taken it off. I would've made a scene. If you'd asked, I would've done anything."

I couldn't help but weave around him and kiss him passionately, hoping my affection would ease his pain. When he hummed into my open mouth and rolled me on top of him, I knew I'd succeeded. Eventually Nick rolled me again, this time depositing me back on the bed and innocently pulled the sheets back up.

"Hell no." Nick snarled as he walked into the closet bathed in morning sunlight. I didn't even flinch. I just opened my jewelry drawer to look for accessories. "Kate, I said no."

I turned to look at him, my hands immediately coming to my hips. "No, what?"

"I don't know why you're getting dressed. You sure as shit aren't leaving this apartment."

"Nick, I feel fine and the product launch is in a matter of days."

"You've been in the hospital, mostly unconscious for a week" His voice rattled the furniture as he balled his fists and clenched his jaw. My heart started to race but I didn't let it affect my face. "The doctor said time and rest."

"Nick," I turned and started digging in my drawer. "I'm . . ."

"No. There is nothing you can say, nothing you can do. You are resting and that is final." My heart twittered a little more but it wasn't too painful. Yet.

"Actually, I'm not." I found my giant faced gold watch and matching gold hoops. I shut the drawer and yanked my hair back to a ponytail before turning to face him. Bright, sparkling blue eyes greeted me despite his pinched face. "I know you're worried baby, but I'll be okay. Really." My heart shuddered a little but I kept talking. "Going to work isn't a health hazard. I'm going to be fine."

He stared at me hard, drinking me in from head to toe. His brow was crinkled as he evaluated every inch. An unspoken tension built between us but I stayed firm. His eyes hadn't stormed and that was my saving grace. I wouldn't break on this one unless it was going to break him.

Nick took two powerful steps toward me. I did my damnedest not to flinch but couldn't completely contain it. He noticed and smiled just before bringing his hand to my heart and letting it rest there. I flushed under his touch and my heart did pick up pace. He arched an eyebrow.

"You do that to me. You always have." I sat patiently under his hand.

When I saw his eyes swirl, I ducked out from under his hand and dove for a pair of crisp white ankle boots and scampered out of the closet before he could object.

Nick humored me, even holding the door as I click-clacked across the sidewalk to the waiting Bentley. We sat silently in the backseat, both attending to our BlackBerry's, but it was a comfortable quiet. His hand came to my thigh at some point and started circling. Slowly but surely his circles got more firm.

"Ouch, Nick," I mumbled without taking my eyes off my screen.

His hand fell away immediately and he sharply inhaled.

"If that hurts you shouldn't go to work."

"It hurts because you're digging in not because of my heart."

"I don't like this, *Kate*." His antagonistic growl filtered back into his voice.

"Noted, *Nick*." I shot him a sideways glance.

He studied me, tension obvious in his lips, his shoulders, even radiating from his frame.

"I have to go to the Venture Group first thing, but I'll be at Vesper as soon as I can. Don't get on a spin bike. Don't yell at Elena or Brennan. Behave." He started circling on my leg again. "Kate, I can handle a lot of shit, but . . ." His voice changed again; it had a lump forming in my throat.

"Nick, baby . . ."

"No, don't Nick or baby me. I'm allowing you to work, you will allow me to finish a sentence." I put my phone down, crossed my arms. and waited. "Good girl." He watched me roll my eyes. "I just wanted to say, I can handle a lot of shit, but losing you is not one of the things. I can barely deal with your heart hurting."

Sarcasm bubbled up but he was so earnest, the words stuck in my throat. He smirked when I sucked in a deep breath. He leaned in to kiss my forehead, but I straightened up and went straight for his lips. Of course, my heart reacted to the spark that was Nick.

"I said behave," he spoke against my lips.

I simply smiled, leaned my forehead against his, and took two deep breaths.

In one of his oh-so-smooth movements, Nick slid out of the car before I even knew he was gone. He reached back to pull me out. He scanned the crowd but tried to cover his motion with a smile shot back in my direction. Christopher's smile inadvertently flashed into my memory and I blanched. Nick pulled me into his chest, and I let him, unconcerned with what the paparazzi caught or printed anymore.

He kissed me at the revolving door and left me smiling as I pushed into Vesper's lobby, relishing his tenderness, and letting my heart get ever so slightly out of control. I was rubbing my chest gently when my name boomed across the lobby.

I froze.

18.

The voice was familiar but off. It made my skin crawl. The normally smooth buttery sound of Kevin's voice, usually punctuated with laughter, was now scratchy, raspy, and downright furious. When I turned, a truly haggard man stood before me.

"What are you doing?" I asked, incredulous.

He was the last person on earth I expected to see.

"What the fuck are *you* doing, Kate?"

My heart thudded but I managed to narrow my gaze all the same.

"No need to make a scene." I walked toward him but Jaime stepped between us, his hand already on his holster. "Jaime, it's okay, he's not going to hurt anyone."

"Yeah, she's the only one that goes around abusing people."

The amount of venom in Kevin's voice surprised me. It went against every memory I had of him, of his soft, gentle support when I'd seen him in Portland.

"He's not supposed to be here." Jaime cleared his throat, his gaze shifting from the entrance to the elevator and back again. I sighed.

"Noted, Jaime."

Ugh, my heart.

"But I'm overriding. I'll deal with Bryant later."

An exaggerated scowl overtook Jaime's face but he nodded.

"Kevin, let's go upstairs."

"No."

My heart thunked against my rib cage when his voice echoed off marble and stopped people passing nearby in their tracks.

"Look, Kevin, we've got fifteen, maybe twenty minutes. And that's if Nicholas made it very far."

"He's going to drop everything and run over here because of me?" he sneered. "Doesn't he have better things to do?"

"He's going to drop everything and run over here because of *me.*" I pointed at my chest. "Good to know how highly I rate with you these days though." My voice dropped to icy.

"I never took you as the type of girl who needed her boyfriend to deal with an ex. You want him to kick me out? You want him to cut me down to size? Or do you just want to hold his hand while you deliver the final blows?"

"Jesus Christ, Kevin!" I shouted, banging my fist on the lobby chair next to me and sending my heart soaring; suddenly the damn thing felt like it was going to explode. I hunched a little. "I will not be spoken to like that. I get that you're pissed, but you're delusional if you think I need a man, even Nicholas Bryant, to do my dirty work."

Kevin hadn't noticed my labored breathing, and couldn't tell that my fingertips were going numb. I certainly should have taken note, instead I railed on.

"It just so happens that my fiancé is a tad overprotective, and he'll want to make sure that you're not here being a prick. So far, I'm guessing he's going to be sorely disappointed." I let out a strangled cry as I completely doubled over still desperately trying to steady my heart and ease the shooting pain.

"Kate . . . I . . ." His anger and defensiveness deflated and he stammered, "Are you okay?"

Jaime appeared at my side and protectively threw his arm around my shoulders. He snarled a Bryant-worthy snarl at Kevin.

"Sit down." I gasped loudly for air. "And tell me what you came here to say."

He sat as directed but kept shifting toward me. Jaime's position prevented him from reaching out for me.

"He will be here shortly, Kevin."

When he finally spoke, it was a defeated pout. "You're going to marry him?"

I held up my left hand, showing off my ring.

"Really?" he groaned.

"Yes, Kevin. Why wouldn't I?" I had to look uncomfortable as I wheezed; I couldn't calm my heart. I tried to soften my tone to be sympathetic, but I couldn't catch my breath.

"Oh I don't know?" He cocked an eyebrow and pulled attitude with me. "Maybe because he's going to hurt you? Maybe because he'll walk out on you the second you need him? Maybe because you can do better?"

He's going to kill me.

He had worked his way up to shouting again.

Shitshitshitfuckshit OUCH!

My heart was thrumming and my vision tunneling. My arms wound around my body and clutched.

"All I know is that I love him, more than anything." The words were ragged and interspersed with giant gulps for air. "I need him!" I shouted before trying to take a huge breath.

"And I will never leave her or hurt her ever again." Nick's dangerous voice came from the revolving door, echoing through the stone and glass lobby. The rhythm of my heart changed a little, partially relieved, and partially on edge because of the instant fury pulsing through the room. "Why are you here Kevin?" Nick sent shivers up my spine.

Kevin stood, and rounded away from the lobby chairs to stand toe to toe with Bryant. Nick was taller and more muscular but not by much. Nick's presence was what made Kevin appear small. He looked polished in his perfect suit but downright feral because of the storm churning in his eyes.

"I'm here to offer her an alternative to the screwed up life she'll surely have with you," Kevin spat the words in Nick's face.

"Go fuck yourself!"

I noticed Terrence slip into position behind Nick. Jaime flinched, wanting to follow suit but since he was shielding me, he didn't budge.

"You don't deserve her." Kevin stepped even closer to Nick as he yelled, "She deserves someone who'll actually care for her. Be there for her!"

"You're right, I don't deserve her, but I intend on trying. Every God damned day, with everything that I have. And I *will* be there for her through anything."

My heart twittered for a very different reason.

"I've been there twice when you blew it all to hell!" Kevin bellowed, and Nick lunged for him, latching onto his shirt to haul Kevin in close.

"Stop it. Stop it right now." I stood and shouted at them, pressing hard into my rib cage again. "Please."

"You want to hear what he has to say?" Nick paused, radiating pain.

"No, Nick. I don't want you in a fight. In public no less." I arched my eyebrows. "It's not worth it."

"Did you just say I'm not worth it?" Kevin's voice cracked.

His twisted face and halting speech didn't affect me nearly the way Nick's did.

"Yes, Kevin. I did. I can't handle this, my heart can't handle this." I tried to push in between them to really end the standoff but Nick angled to keep me out.

"Sweets, is this hurting your heart?" He looked over his shoulder at me.

"Yes," I groaned.

"You hurt her heart?" Kevin went back to shouting.

To my surprise, Nick's hands left Kevin's shirt but not to let loose a punch. He simply pushed Jaime's hands aside so he could grasp my shoulders.

"I would gladly take all of her pain, *any* amount of pain, to protect..."

"Pain I can do, asshole," Kevin interrupted and cocked his hand back before Nick or I could react.

Nick's reflexes were good enough that he shoved me out of the way, but the flying fist still crunched into his cheekbone.

"Nick," I gasped as he stumbled from the force of the blow.

My heart was about ready to thud out of my chest but it didn't matter. I zigzagged after him and my hands flew out to slow his fall. I sucked in a deep breath as I caught his muscular frame.

"Fucking shit!" Nick shook his head trying to deal with the instant pain.

It only took a single heartbeat for Nick to gain his footing, push away from me, and swing at Kevin. He landed a quick right hook followed by an even faster jab to Kevin's stomach. Kevin doubled over and I thought he might puke on the marble floor.

Nick stood, seething over his heaving body. When Kevin regained his composure, he took a run at Nick. The brick wall that was my future husband stopped him short. Nick took the opportunity to bear hug Kevin and punch him hard in the kidney. Repeatedly.

It was the wrong time to realize Nick was an exceptional fighter. He was going to seriously hurt Kevin if I didn't stop him. I went to step in but my feet faltered after a painful shot from my heart. While my body hesitated, Kevin found the strength to shove on Nick again. He caught Nick off balance and they both toppled over an armchair and thudded into a potted plant.

I had to stop things before Nick got hurt.

Or I die.

Still rubbing my chest, I managed to shove my way in between them as they scrambled back to their feet.

"Stop!" My shout pulled Nick up short.

When he saw both of my hands frantically pressing and rubbing at my heart he forgot about Kevin. Ever so tenderly his hands wrapped around mine. He pulled me close to his chest, which rose and fell every bit as fast as mine.

That's when Kevin lunged at Nick and landed a hard hook to his jaw. I was so tangled up in Nick that I tumbled in a heap of limbs. Grunts and groans mingled with my pathetic whimpers as we careened to the marble floor. My body crunched even though I could tell Nick was trying to soften my fall. As soon as I could compose myself my hands flew to his face and the purple splotch blooming across his jaw.

"God damnit Kevin! What is wrong with you?" I was in searing pain as I alternated piercing words and haggard breaths.

"What the fuck is wrong with *me*? Are you really asking that?" he shouted back.

"No, on second thought, I'm not. Because I don't give a fuck anymore." I rolled off Nick and onto the floor, trying to still my heart.

I was completely unconcerned that a crowd had gathered in the lobby, I was just hoping my heart didn't shatter or give out completely. My fingers clutched at my flesh.

"Are you ok, Sweets?" Nick's voice was not what I expected it to be, he was soft, gentle.

My head rolled and I found myself nose to nose with my fiancé. Weakly, one of my hands moved to cradle his face. The tenderness that plainly greeted me soothed me and my trembling bones.

"I'll live. I think. You?"

"I'm fine but I want him gone," Nick said, more businesslike than anything. "Gone for good. Out of our lives." Those perfectly blue eyes focused in on mine.

"That's not your choice asshole!" Kevin bellowed.

"No." I stopped Kevin short with a wave of my hand, still breathing far too loudly from my puddle on the floor. "It's not his choice. It's mine. And we're done, Kevin. As friends, as anything more, as anything period." I took a deep breath—well tried to anyway. "I am marrying Bryant. Not because of any stupid reason you've conjured up in your head, but because I can't live without him. I refuse to even try. If you can't respect that, then I can't respect you." I honestly didn't know how I still managed to string words together. "You should go." I gracelessly pointed to the exit from the floor.

Nick's fingers searched for my free hand still resting on the floor. His hand crunched on mine. Past him, Kevin's face had fallen—no, worse than fallen—it was pure desolation.

"Do you mean that?"

I barely made out Kevin's whisper.

"I do." And I pictured saying those words to Nick and I gained strength.

Even here, even now, lying on the cool marble floor, I wanted to say them to him. I was excited to have the big white dress, the solemn ceremony, and to really pledge my life to him.

If I hadn't been focused on the painfully beautiful image—well, that and the jackknife pummel to my insides—I would've heard Kevin walk away; a slow, sad shuffle against the stone of the lobby. And Jaime's phone call to Dr. Chambers. Instead, the thundering inside my own chest, and Nick's ragged breathing beside me, filled my senses.

"We're going home," Nick said simply beside me.

"Nick, I need to work."

"You'll work from home, or not at all." He turned and pulled me into his chest where he laid on the lobby floor.

"Nicholas . . ."

"Fuck you, Kate," he shot gruffly. "I know damn well your heart is going crazy."

I sighed loudly. The all-consuming reality was I couldn't feel my fingertips.

"Nicholas, Kate, may I suggest we move off the lobby floor." Jaime leaned over us, a bemused smirk on his face.

For some inexplicable reason, Nick burst out laughing. His hand still held mine but otherwise his body twisted up in full body shaking giggles. It was the last emotion I expected after what had just happened. His reaction made me chuckle too.

When he caught his breath, he pushed up onto his elbow. "Is that a yes? And an, 'I'll go home without a fight?'" He was still smiling that perfect crooked smile. As much as he could with the bruising anyway.

"The doctor said to bring you in if the symptoms didn't recede with rest. *Bed* rest." Jaime emphasized even through the smirk he tried to hide.

"Fine."

He didn't even wait a breath before standing and scooping me up to carry me to the revolving door.

"You can put me down, Nick."

He didn't react to my words, and I rolled my eyes as I settled into his chest while he waded through photographers. Hearing his heartbeat eased my thundering pulse. He cradled me in the backseat of the car and, as he carried me back up to the apartment, I playfully swatted his chest when he snarled at my request to walk into the building myself.

When I slid down Nick's rigid torso, the delicious musculature underneath wasn't the only steely thing to greet me. His erection pressed into my belly. I flushed and bit my lip. Of course my declaration—probably even my obedience—had turned him on. My heart started racing, but in the normal, Nicholas Bryant way. I made a point to fidget up against him.

"Stop." Nick was stern and forceful.

I looked up to see swirling, stormy eyes.

"I know you want to." I arched an eyebrow.

"I always want to. This time I damn near need to, but I won't. Besides, I'm supposed to be at work."

"Please?" I leaned in to beg, all breathy, against his ear. Suddenly nothing in the world sounded as perfect as the fluid motion of us weaving together.

"I'd love to spank you for being so reckless with your heart."

"Why don't you?" As soon as I said it, his face dropped.

"You know damn well why I won't." I pushed out of his arms in the entryway and reached for his hand. I placed it over my heart. "Kate," he growled.

Damn it Nick, just listen.

He had to feel the difference for himself but he kept trying to pull away.

Skin against skin always spoke volumes for us. I shrugged out of my trench and let it crumple to the floor. He pulled his hand away, stepped back, and watched me curiously. I yanked my sweater off without hesitation.

The bra I was wearing pushed my breasts up, making the tremble of my heart obvious in the swell of my flesh. I held his gaze while I removed the bra, letting my breasts fall and bounce ever so slightly as I did. My nipples reacted to the cool air, and Nick's eyes reacted to the view. He didn't move toward me and, for a split second, I was glad. My heart responded to his hunger a little more forcefully than I'd anticipated. I kept this tremor in check though, my face and knees held strong.

Thank God.

I closed the tiny gap between us in one step and reached for his hand. His fingertips would understand now. I picked up his hand and for a moment, he wouldn't let me move it.

"I'll beg."

He eyed me suspiciously then let me take control. I pressed his palm back to my chest. I smiled when his fingers flexed into my skin. He stared into my eyes for a moment and then his fingers curled again. This time he sucked in a loud breath.

"Sweets."

Oh thank fuck.

I made my voice as sultry and suggestive as possible. "I'll be in the bedroom."

19.

I sprinted to the bedroom as fast as my heart would allow, yanking off my heels, and peeling out of my leggings, only to dump them unceremoniously in a pile by the side of the bed.

"Excited are we?"

Nick's smooth, velvety purr came from the doorframe and sent shivers up my spine. Without turning, I simply nodded.

"Good."

Ah, God, that voice.

"Me too." Just his tone was getting me wet. "Stay." His command was even more arousing. Desire ran rampant through my veins.

He purposely brushed against me as he walked over to the bedside table. My skin scorched where he touched me and my heartbeat skyrocketed again. I was worried he would hear it, or my knees would give out, and then the game would be over. I had to find a way to settle myself.

Nick reached into his drawer of toys and pocketed things in both of his front pockets. He slipped out of his shoes before he turned to face me. He looked me up and down, drinking in every inch, and I couldn't help but flush. My heart hammered again, but his priceless smile told me I was able to mask it.

Nick prowled around me, then stood close to my back. Wordlessly, he reached around and laid his hand over my heart. Thankfully, it was at a moment when I had the damn thing under control. It only beat for him.

His hand brushed across my body then whispered down my arm. I gasped when his touch suddenly changed and he yanked my arms, folding my forearms on each other. He held them in a box shape with his vice-like grip. I was consumed by the singe of his skin until soft silk brushed my backside. The long black ribbon danced across my skin leaving goose bumps in its wake.

"Keep your arms just like this."

I did as I was told despite having to shift because of the slickness building between my legs. Nick's soft chuckle reverberated through me when he understood why I was wiggling.

He wrapped the ribbon first around one wrist, then tightly circled it around my forearms where they laid on top of one another, until he could bind the other with a satin bow. Nick wound tightly so my chest pressed out and the nicely wrapped package of my arms swayed at the small of my back. My fingers could only drum at the crook of my elbow with anticipation.

I watched his reflection in the window turn and stride out of the bedroom. Once the soft shuffle of his feet faded the jackhammer of my heart flooded my senses. I gasped and had to work to keep my knees from crumbling. Nick was the key to keeping my reactions under control.

I closed my eyes to picture Nick, shirtless, sweats hanging low on his hips. I particularly liked it when he wasn't wearing his usual boxer briefs underneath and every contour of every bit of him was on full display. I made myself breathe deep as I pictured every inch of muscle diving under that soft waistband. I finally shut out the deafening noise of my heart by thinking of the V of muscles that highlighted his hips and how those small dimples above his ass looked peeking out over fabric. When I visualized the downright scandalous way they would hug his swoon worthy dick, my knees knocked together for a completely different reason.

MMMmmm.

My thoughts went to kissing him there—any *there*, whether above or below his waistband. Then his neck and jaw, or running my lips across his taught skin. Or devouring his perfect full lips.

Oh God.

Very real arousal was dripping down my thighs as my heart's hammering shifted back to its familiar only-for-Bryant race.

When I thought about his eyes, deep, dark crystal blue, the way they only shown for me, I faltered.

"Kate." Nick was back in the doorframe.

Shit! Of all the moments to come back.

"I won't . . ."

"It's not that. I swear. Feel. Please." My interruption was strangled.

He *had* to believe me. I would fucking explode if he didn't. Mercifully, he stepped to my back again and took a moment to wrap his hand around my body, squishing my arms between us. His hand laid over my left breast and electricity shot through my body.

"It's just you," I said, sultry.

He groaned and let his hand slide down to my hard nipple. He pulled and I arched back further into him.

MMMmmm.

He dropped his hand and walked away from me, letting his fingers trace along the footboard. On the bed was the reason he'd left the room . . . the camera. Nick motioned to the floor in front of him.

I strode over, notched myself between his knees, and waited.

"Lean over," he commanded in his bedroom voice.

My body easily dipped to where he was casually sitting on the edge of the bed. He held something besides the camera in his hand. When I pushed my chest squarely into Nick's face, his hand leisurely traced down from my collarbone to my slightly swaying breasts. When his fingers found my nipples he pulled one and then the other, rubbing and flicking until they were rigid. I whimpered when his hand left my body.

His hand unfurled to reveal the dark jewel nipple clamps we'd played with before. Nick let his fingertips circle each nipple before clipping each one onto me. They weighted my breasts to hang even heavier and I groaned. He flicked each jewel, sending shockwaves through my body, then wove his hand up into my hair. He used his grasp in my long locks to pull my lips to his.

Nick rose as he kissed me roughly. His grip flattened me, complete with jewels, to his chest.

"Don't ever be reckless with your heart again." He breathed a moment before he smacked my ass. Hard.

I shrieked. I hadn't been expecting to be spanked standing, tangled as we were. The swat jump started my heart. It thudded against his chest making him pause. He sucked in a deep breath but didn't let it go, instead he stilled his whole being to listen. He'd plastered me up along his body for this exact reason.

Calm down, calm down, calm down.

He sucked in a deep breath just before he spanked me twice more in quick succession.

"I just need you. Here. With me." His voice got rough as it cut through my wild cries.

Slap.

My heart was drumming damn near audibly now.

Crack, crack. And I was writhing against his torso.

"Forever!"

He slid a long finger in between my legs, feeling the arousal there. I moaned out oh-so-loudly, the tortured sound echoing off the glass.

"I can't live without you." He pulled his finger out and lightning fast, sank back to the bed and splayed me across his knees only to spank me three more times.

I jolted with each sting and the nipple clamps shook and swayed. I didn't know if the stones or the spanks were responsible for more of my mangled cries.

"I need this heart and I need this body for as long as we both shall live."

He rimmed his finger through the slickness between my thighs then cracked against my backside twice more. My heart was thundering but only for him. My body trembled too. Nothing existed in the whole damn world besides Nicholas Bryant.

Without warning, he shoved his fingers into my hair and arched

me back toward my bound arms. The motion sent the jewels swaying and I winced. He wasn't watching my face, just the stones as they
swayed hypnotically back and forth. I couldn't breathe and had to find
his eyes to settle my heart. Deep, pure blue colored every inch of his
irises. For a moment, my entire universe existed in the profound pools
of his eyes. I almost came right then.

As always, he sensed how close I was and let his hands dropped
from my body. I sagged, still helplessly tied, back to his thighs, gasping
for a decent sized breath. It wasn't lost on me that a sizable erection
now pressed into my arm.

Nick turned his attention to the camera and snapped a photo of
me.

"Jesus, that's perfect," Nick said as the camera went crazy.

I stayed put and turned to face him, my vision blurry. Nick
snapped furiously as I indulged him, looking up in the direction of the
shutter snaps as best I could from under long eyelashes. Lying across
his lap was doing nothing to ease my desperate want.

"Please!" I broke.

He snapped two more photos then chuckled as he set the camera
down. Gently, he lifted me from his lap only to drape me along the
bed. He quickly pitched his shirt and vest then fidgeted at his belt. His
cock pressed hard against the fabric, keeping his pants in place. My
fingers took to drumming against my forearms again, wanting nothing more than to reach out and strip him. I didn't mean to dig my
nails into my own flesh when he finally got naked, but I couldn't help
myself.

Nick crawled onto the bed and pulled me to my knees. We sat
nose to nose, with me squirming against the ribbon still wanting to
run my fingers over every inch of him. He curled his grip into my
smarting ass and lifted me again. Nick held me so I hovered just above
his erection and my greedy sex pulsed with anticipation. When I
dripped onto him, he held me just out of reach, his smug smirk firmly
in place.

I bit my lips and wiggled my hips, hoping he would falter, and
I'd fall onto his perfect, waiting penis. His hands curled into my fresh

welts and stilled me. I was rewarded with a devilish smirk, and the tip of his dick teasing at my slick slit. When I bit my lip to keep from begging again, he pulled my hips down. Hard. I cried out and couldn't help but scramble.

Nick didn't flinch. He sat buried inside of me and only when I stopped bucking did he lean forward to press his ear to my chest. I should have known there was a reason he'd chosen this position. It was a different type of toe-curling to know he cared that much.

Once he was satisfied with my heart beats, he angled me backward. His chin nodded, encouraging me to glide up his cock. At the last moment, right before he fell out of me, he used the dangling nipple jewels to pull me back down.

"Ahhh!" I screamed as all sorts of sensation shot through my body.

When I arched away from him, writhing wildly, his hands roughly shoved into the crease of my hips and drove me down. I gasped again, trying to catch my breath, impaled as I was by the ridiculously perfect cock inside me but he tapped on my ass, a signal to slid back up along his length. Nick made me keep going, sliding up just so he could shove me down—every time an assault on my pleasure senses. Just when I thought he'd let me set the rhythm on my own, his hands would come back to the nipple clamps and guide me. My whole body would contort and writhe against him.

I loved every minute of it even though my heart picked up pace as my orgasm neared. I was so lost to his touch, I couldn't tell if it was with the good or bad kind of thrumming. Honestly, not a single brain cell cared to figure it out.

He shoved harder into me and I was sure his next thrust would send me over the edge. Nick knew too. He humored me and pressed deep into me. Those amazing, wonderful, perfect waves started to wrack my body. He ripped off first one jeweled clamp then the other, thrusting twice more before coming himself. His hips kept rolling, pushing cum out onto our legs and making the sheen that had developed between us all the more sticky. I couldn't do anything but sag into his firm body, my heart still a jackhammer.

Nick emptied completely before he noticed how spent I actually was. His eyes flashed with concern just before he scrambled to untie me. My face twisted when he pulled out of me and pressed his hands up against my bruised backside to get at the ribbon.

"Jesus, Nick," I gasped.

"You're heart?"

"Is fine." I took a deep breath and he gave me one hell of a skeptical face. "It's hammering because you drive me crazy. The moment I met you it started pounding around all crazy in there. Who fucking knew it only gets better?"

I smiled and laid my hand to his heart; faint marks wound around my forearm where the ribbon had gripped my skin. His was calming down but even his heart thudded a little too hard in his chest. I flexed my fingers into his perfect skin and he understood. He even smiled and leaned his forehead to mine.

"Thank you," he breathed. "Thank you for that, for knowing what I needed and being it, without hesitation. For letting me take control. For being you. And being mine." He was so sweet and earnest that my heart did thump.

Of course he noticed but rather than get upset he lowered himself to bed and pulled me into the crook of his shoulder. Nick traced my favorite small circles up and down my arm, and I listened as his heartbeat slowed. I willed mine to match his. I could have sworn they were beating in unison when I finally fell asleep.

20.

"Shhhh Kate, calm down. Please, please, please calm down, sweet girl."
Julia slowly, almost hypnotically, rubbed my back.

I hadn't been dreaming of anything that I could remember when
I shot up from bed. Luckily, she'd been there to hold me but that didn't
change that my heart ached worse than it had since leaving the hospital. This was the kind of sharp shooting pain that made me clutch my
chest and fill with fear—the I-might-actually-die kind of fear. Eventually, I could breathe again, and I sagged into Julia's fluttery, delicate
arms.

"What just happened?" For the first time since I'd known her, Julia's voice wavered.

"It's my heart." My hands kept on rubbing at my chest.

"You looked like . . ."

"Like I was going to die." I finished the words for her. "I felt like
it." My voice shorted out too.

Now that adrenaline wasn't coursing through my veins, I was
shaken, a tear rolling down my cheek.

"Oh honey." Julia was still rubbing my back, her strokes picking
up pace. "Nicholas asked me to stay with you, to make sure you follow
Dr. Chamber's orders, but I had no idea . . ." she stuttered a little, her
eyes wide, before adding, "I'll get you some chicken soup."

She had made me pancakes the last time she tried to care for me, and I knew being busy made her feel useful, so I let her spin in ballerina-like frazzled circles on the way to the door. Honestly, I didn't know how to stop her. Or to say that, for once in my life, I desperately needed someone. Just as Nick always did, Julia must have read my thoughts because she hovered in the doorway rather than leaving. Her hand fluttered nervously against the wood the way it always did near me.

"It's that bad huh?" I leaned back into the pillows when I asked.

"Hum?" She smiled lightly, feigning confusion, but her gunmetal eyes couldn't lie.

"Not only do I feel like death, I look like it too?"

"You are gorgeous darling, even now." Julia smiled her broad, practiced smile.

In that moment the realization hit me that I'd seen Julia smile many times but it'd never lit up her entire face. Once or twice, I thought it had, but looking back her eyes never wavered. Not when we met. Not when Nick and I had gotten engaged. They changed color like Nick's but they never actually beamed or twinkled.

My compulsion to comfort overtook me as quickly and violently as it usually did with Nick. Words vomited out before I gave it a second thought. "Christopher did this. He did this because he's a psychopath and he's a fucking nut job because Francis never put a stop to him. We have to get away from him. Somehow." Her face pinched uncharacteristically. "Leave Francis. Walk away from the Winthrops. Please."

"Kate . . ." She walked back toward me, her hands still moving nervously through the air.

"Look, I'm not asking for me. Or because of this." I gestured at my chest. "Despite what Nicholas thinks, I'm strong enough to live through this. But Christopher did this to hurt your son. He will stop at nothing to take what Nicholas loves."

The thought made my heart shudder again. I masked the pain but my whole body still tensed. Julia slowly folded back down sitting on the bed, this time near my shins.

"Julia, Ari could be next. Hell, you could be next." I sighed. "Or best case scenario, he's done with us for now, but it still leaves you married to the man who beats you and supports *this*, or turns a blind eye to it, or whatever it is that Francis does."

Julia carefully wrapped her arms around her ribs as she listened. Judging by the progressive sag of her shoulders, everything I said was already a truth gnawing at her insides. My words had to mimic the ever-present jumbled dialogue in her head. I shuffled as best I could, covers in tow, to comfort her the way she'd done for me. I even rubbed her shoulder gently.

"I'm not like you, Kate. But God, I wish I was." She sagged into my arms. "For twenty-two years I have wished I had the strength to provide for my children. That I could bear the scrutiny and protect them all the same. But I'm not like you. I'm not strong enough." Her shoulders heaved. "I never was."

"Julia, once, I overheard you saying you married Francis to afford Nick and Ari opportunities they wouldn't have otherwise. Did you mean it?"

"That was my greatest hope." Julia twisted, putting us nose to nose.

Her eye color wasn't familiar to me but it pulled on my heartstrings all the same. Literally. My heart faltered. Her slight palm lifted to cradle my face, stroking my cheeks tenderly as my body trembled.

"But Julia. Look at them. Haven't you succeeded?" I implored. "Ten times over?"

"No sweetheart." She smiled a positively dejected smile.

"I don't understand. Please elaborate," I squeaked out.

"Oh darling, I'm supposed to be helping, not hurting you."

I rolled out of her grasp and rested my head on her shoulder, the way I would have if she was my mother. She sighed softly and her fingers curled fraily into mine, a ghosted mirror of Nick's. The longer we sat still, the thicker the silence became. When I almost suffocated, she cleared her throat. Just as Nick did, she waited until the last minute to start talking.

"I loved Nicholas' father. Truly, madly, deeply. I didn't care that he had money, I only cared that I saw the world when I looked at him, everything made sense when I looked into his dark brown eyes."

My heart clenched at the description I could relate to intimately.

"You see, I was born and bred to be a wife, and a mother. In my day, you only went to school to land a husband, not a career. I expected to get married, run a household, plan dinner parties but not to fall in love. That's what Connecticut family money does to you.

"When I found a man that actually made my heart pitter-patter, I almost didn't know how to handle it. I ran away for the briefest moment, but then I threw myself into him and our relationship without any concern for myself.

"I lost myself in him. In us. And I wouldn't take that back for anything. My world revolved around him and I loved it. First cooking and cleaning, then later, coordinating the household. I hosted events here and in the city. Never once did I complain, never once did I want to. But the day I found out I was pregnant all that changed."

A defensive scowl crept onto my face, but mercifully, I kept my mouth shut.

"I had the perfect life and a baby meant it was getting better. The day my doctor told me I was carrying Nicholas I knew something bad would happen. I didn't tell anyone, but I could feel it in my bones. No one deserves to be *that* happy."

The longer she spoke, the more I recognized Nick in her. She'd passed down her ability to keep a facade while feeling unworthy, and—to top it off—her fatalistic views on happiness.

"Two weeks after I found out about Nicholas, we found out about the cancer. And that stays between us. I've always told the children it was a short and sweet diagnosis. That their father didn't suffer."

Her eyes had shifted to a pale, ghostly gray. Again it wasn't a color I knew but it made my stomach churn all the same.

"We made every preparation, for the baby and for chemotherapy. It's an odd pair, life and death, right next to each other like that. But we managed. And Nicholas was a miracle."

A sad smile tugged at the corners of my lips.

"I wish you could've seen them together." Julia managed a laugh but it was through the first of giant, crocodile tears. "My husband would go tearing through the yard in Prada loafers if it meant playing catch with his son. He cooked hotdogs over the fire pit with a vintage Cartier watch on. Nothing mattered but his family. When he found out we were having a baby girl, he wept. And to this day, I don't know if it's because he was going to have a princess or because he would miss her growing up. She was a complete surprise. After the chemo we didn't even know we could conceive."

This was a whole different type of knife to the heart. It pounded in my chest, and I wasn't sure if I was okay with it. Besides my breathing, only silence filled the room, both of us choking on emotion.

"You know, he suggested Francis."

I had to bite back the *What the fuck?* that sat on the tip of my tongue.

"My husband could read my every thought. He knew I was devastated. He knew I questioned whether I could go on. And he knew I was terrified. And he, like Nicholas, stopped at nothing to solve a problem. So toward the end he suggested a wealthy, newly widowed replacement that would have me run his household, raise his child and keep me in the life I'd become accustomed to."

"Oh holy fuck." I couldn't hold it in this time. The ramifications were too overwhelming. "There's no way he meant for you to stay through . . . *this*." I wanted to throw my hands up but something in her posture said don't lose it. I'd break the spell.

"Sweet girl, you say that but you don't know what it's like. To make promises to someone you love like that."

"But I do." My words tumbled out. "Every time I look into Nick's eyes I see my world staring back. I know exactly what it feels like to love like that, to swear like that. But I also know what it is to *be* loved like that. He'd sooner die." I couldn't help that my voice got more urgent.

Or that I grabbed her hand and squeezed.

"And what would you do for the children you feel similarly about?" She looked over at me, her eyes past forlorn, far closer to hopeless. After a few deep breaths, her gaze fell away.

"I don't know much about children, but I had parents I loved dearly. I'd do anything to bring them back, of course. But what haunts me is that they died in pain. As futile as it is, I prayed I could take away their pain."

Julia's shoulders shook gently at those words. Rather than stare in wonder at the first genuine emotion I'd seen from her, I continued. It seemed far more appropriate.

"The man in Prada loafers playing catch in the yard only wanted to protect you. He wanted you happy."

"And that's all I want. Them safe and happy. That's all I've ever wanted." Her tears were small, dainty things that still managed to roll down her face and onto her shirt.

"Julia, the only sadness in Nick comes from the result of you keeping that promise."

I probably should have toned it down. I probably should have let her continue to weep on my shoulder in silence. I probably should have kept my nose out of Bryant family business. Then again, they were my family now too.

"Well then, I suppose "Oh holy fuck" is appropriate." Julia's practiced smile pulled up into place. "At least I was obedient to the end. To the end of all of us, it would seem."

My heart thudded again. This time I didn't think it was toxins but I couldn't be sure. It was far heavier and every bit as painful as it had been earlier.

I rubbed her shoulders and she sagged into me. Consoling words kept tumbling through my mind but none of them were right. None of them could be strung together to make a sentence. Or at least not one that made anything better.

"I'm so tired of playing a part, Kate, of being in this balancing act where I choose between letting down my two little hearts and my one giant universe. I'm lost every day." Her facade finally made sense; it was the only thing keeping her together.

Suddenly the right words bubbled up. "You're far stronger that you think, Julia."

Her head twisted toward me, and just like Nick, her eyes filtered to a disconcerting blue. We studied each other. Everything in the room quieted, even the ticking of the clock and vibrating of the inner workings of the building went silent.

Then it clicked, the final piece of the Julia Winthrop puzzle. Julia wasn't just a reflection of Nick, but of me too. I was staring at a version of myself. Sure, I would fight and rail on if something like that ever happened between Nick and I, but I would be obedient in the end. I hated myself a little for that. But perhaps that's why I could speak on a level no one else had. I too had seen my universe in someone's eyes.

"If your husband had anything to do with the human being Nick is, I know beyond a shadow of a doubt . . ." I paused, taking a deep breath. "Nick's dad would personally strangle Francis if he knew what Francis had done," I said as Julia leaned on my shoulder the way I had on hers. "I know down deep in my soul, he'd put nothing else above you." My hands curled inadvertently into hers. "Nothing," I added vehemently.

"Kate, that's a beautiful notion but . . ."

"No. No buts," I cut her off the same way Nick would have me.

I pulled her into a bear hug, and would have folded her into my heart if I could have.

Jaime picked that moment to deliver my soup. His arrival burst the emotional bubble, tension dissipated but neither of us could smile. My face contorted when a boulder dropped into my stomach and my heart twittered. I tried to hide it by reaching for soup. I had to ball my fist to steady my fingers before I grabbed it. Both Jamie and Julia noticed.

"Should we call Dr. Chambers? Nicholas?" Jaime asked as concern crinkled his brow, Julia's eyes went dark.

I ignored them. "So, speaking of Nicholas . . ."

"Back at the office." Jaime rolled his eyes.

"I should get back . . ."

"No, please rest." Julia smiled.

Ari chose that exact moment to make her appearance. "You actually aren't allowed to leave. We're under strict orders to keep you here and keep you safe."

"And family keeps each other safe." Julia winked just before kissing my forehead, effectively ending the exchange.

21.

When no one was looking, I snuck down to the home office for my laptop. Once I had it, I all but sprinted back to bed and built the covers up to hide behind.

My jaw fell open when I clicked on my email revealing seven unread messages. *Seven?* The last time there were so few was high school. Maybe. I zeroed in on the hundreds marked replied. I tried not to let the signature at the bottom of each infuriate me.

Nicholas Bryant, Owner, CTO
Vesper Fitness & Apparel
New York, New York

At the end of the day, he was an owner. And the Chief Technology Officer. But neither fact stopped my temper from flaring. My heart jamming against my ribs was the only thing that could. I leaned back to take deep breaths. I even started counting dots on the ceiling to calm myself enough to return to reading.

I tried—really, I did—to keep my temper in check as I returned to the threads sitting in my inbox. Nick hadn't been sleeping. Even if the time stamps didn't tell me as much, the sheer volume of work completed did. It was staggering.

I read and reread his emails, dwelling for far too long. The Fi-Tech launch was planned, marketing completed and even preliminary summer design sketches approved. I liked everything he'd done, but couldn't shake the sheer irritation over *him* doing it. I ground my teeth at the screen for hours.

"Sweets?" My head snapped up at the sound of Nick's voice by the doorway. "You behave yourself?" He arched his eyebrow and smiled that priceless crooked smile.

"What are you doing here?" I asked, piqued.

"I live here, Kate." He must have caught my mood because his face pinched. "What's going on?" He scrutinized me as he walked closer to the bed.

I looked out the windows behind him rather than at him. Night had fallen over the city, not even a rosy hue was left lingering on the skyscrapers.

"Why are you answering my personal emails?" I hadn't paused to censor my tone.

"I'm an owner concerned with Vesper's success. I'm also your fiancé and I'm concerned about your health. Take your pick."

He scowled at me as he sat on the edge of the bed.

"Don't get sarcastic, Bryant. I'm trying incredibly hard not to get pissed off right now. Do *not* make it more difficult." I couldn't help snapping at him.

"What on earth do you have to be pissed about? I've brokered a deal or two and launched a product once or twice before," he scoffed. "Everything is planned to my exacting specifications."

"That's just it. They're *your* standards, not mine," I snarled. "I worked on this for fucking ever. So much of my blood, sweat, and tears were put into this and I failed. I failed!" I threw my arms up and then reined them in across my chest. "You come in here on your damned white horse and fix it all, even coordinating the launch perfectly. I can't help it if I get a little butt hurt about the whole damn thing." I took a deep breath but stopped myself short of shouting anything stupid. "I know what an ungrateful lunatic I sound like."

"You're butt hurt about this?" Nick asked calmly, eyes bright blue; his crooked smile pulled back on his cheek.

"Yes, or haven't you heard that before?"

He leaned toward me. Before I could even flinch, one strong hand reached around my hip and squeezed. Hard. Of course I yelped.

"I'll be the only one using that phrase from now on, understood?" Everything pounded in my chest but in the best possible way, but I still faltered ever so slightly. "How's the heart?" he added seamlessly.

The life momentarily drained from his face as if his whole world hinged on my answer and his hand skated up to my chest. He pressed his hand to me and felt for a moment, his eyes laser focused on my chest. I almost rolled my eyes and scoffed but he leaned down and kissed where his hand had been. I melted.

"It's been good and bad."

Honesty was the only policy with my fiancé—particularly my sweet and tender fiancé. I sighed and let my head roll back against the headboard.

"Thank you for not lying to me."

He wormed his way onto the bed and sat against the headboard with me. The two of us stayed side by side for a little while, watching the lights of the city twinkle.

"I'll change anything you want for the launch. Tell me and I'll change it. Just promise me, you'll let me take care of it?"

I heard him roll his head against the brushed steel to look over at me. I sat there, still staring straight ahead. This was always the line. What would I give up, knowing full well what I got in return . . . Nick.

"Kate?"

"Fine. Fucking fine, Nick." I purposely rolled my head away from him and re-crossed my arms dramatically over my chest. Even now, retreat wasn't completely comfortable. We both sat silent for a little while longer.

"Victor is Christopher's puppet."

"What?" My head snapped back.

"Jaime dug into Victor's financials, he found a payment that was tied to a Winthrop bank account in the Caymans. It's massive. I can't imagine what it affords him." My heart started freaking out and I didn't know if it was the news or the bleak color of his eyes that did it.

"Kate, you've got to calm down."

"I." *Gasp.* "Am." *Wheeze.* "Calm."

"Kate." Nick turned toward me, circling his fingers on my bare thigh.

I grabbed at him and he settled his head in my lap. My fingers started running through his hair, and I closed my eyes as I leaned back. I kept trying to focus on taking deep breaths and the feel of him against my skin.

Always the feel of him against my skin.

When I opened my eyes, I sighed loud and exasperated, his hand skated up to my heart and rested there.

"Kate, I need to trap them. I don't know how to do it but I need to figure this out before it escalates further. I have to get more than a bank account to go on."

I kept combing through his hair. The slower my heart moved the more my mind raced. An idea began forming, and before I could think about the ramifications, I willingly became Nick's accomplice.

"Nick what if you made the announcement that you're going transfer major manufacturing to Dongguang due to long term growth possibilities then heavily fortify a faux-facility. Give it a complex alarm system, hi-tech surveillance, and falsities worth approaching for."

"Long term growth possibilities? Faux-facilities?" He shifted to look at up at me.

My gaze flitted down but then immediately returned to boring a hole in the window seam.

"Yes. Faux as in fake." Both of my eyebrows climbed up my forehead. "And Dongguang is the third largest exports region in China. It gets overshadowed significantly by Shanghai and Shenzhen but it is a major hub. They don't have the same financial incentives for investing but it's because they're spending heavily on infrastructure."

"What's the point of keeping the manufacturing in China if the financial incentives don't exist?"

"It's fake, Nick."

"Still, explain." He wiggled again in my lap. This time when I looked down, his eyes were more blue than expected.

"The initial cash outlay is lower than Shanghai or Shenzhen but the US tax credits are worse. But that's solely at the outlay. If you disperse them over the five-year loan amortization, they balance out around year three and half. Then surpass in year four.

"And if you want further justification, my guess is the prefecture made infrastructure a priority because they plan to start to aggressively seek foreign direct investment. They're already major players in the Taiwanese investment scene and have been slowly working on Brazilian shoe manufacturers. Brazil is a medium player in the shoe game. Which says to me, Dongguang is testing markets. They can't have an infrastructure problem when they go for major players. By the time the lesser incentives become financially unfavorable, I think they'll have implemented a revised bonus structure."

"Huh." Nick was the one focused on a window seam now.

"It's still hypothetical though." I loosened his tie. "Buy property for dirt cheap. Hire people on a contract basis to make it look like a big deal, a new manufacturing hub, but don't do anything with it. It's sure as shit a cash outlay but it meets every other requirement."

I took a deep breath again, ready to launch into the very real marketing even a fake would need when Nick let loose a husky chuckle.

"I never thought talking about manufacturing in Chinese prefectures or entrapment would get me excited but, Jesus, Sweets, I'm hard. You're brilliant." He sat up and gazed his teeth across my jaw. "And incredibly sexy." He nibbled on my earlobe and shoved the comforter away. "Quite possibly perfect."

His hands moved up my shirt and I gasped.

"I'm far from perfect," I moaned as he pulled on one nipple. "I'm stubborn and willful." *MMMmmm.* "And have a horrible temper and a weak heart."

"You are perfect for me." He peeled off my shirt and his lips moved up to my breastbone. "I even kind of like the weak heart." His raspy laugh was back.

Nick whipped off his tie and bound my wrists together before yanking me down the bed. I let my hands rest on my stomach as I watched him slowly undo each of his shirt buttons. I couldn't help but bite my lip as he slowly teased me. When he reached the bottom of his shirt, he shrugged out of it and climbed over me.

He took my hands and pushed them overhead. He hovered his perfect body above mine, just out of reach. His bright, clear eyes drank in every inch of my face and his attention shifted to my chest. I was sure he would swoop down and take my nipple in his mouth but he simply moved in close. A puff of warm breath against my sensitive skin made me moan. My nipples rose on their own and he chuckled.

Nick slid lower and my skin responded similarly the entire way. Just below my belly button, his nose grazed ever so slightly along my waistband. I groaned and arched up away from the sheets underneath me.

"Nick," I whined. "Please."

"Your heart okay, Sweets?"

"Yes." My answer was a breathy groan.

He better be asking so he can rip my shorts off and slam into me.

"Then you're going to have to hold on a little bit longer."

Oh for fucks sake.

"You bastard!"

If my wrists were free, I would have banged them into the bed beneath me.

"That's not very nice."

He nipped the sensitive skin beneath my belly button this time.

"Should I punish you for name calling?"

"Sure . . . fine . . . whatever." I just wanted him sprawled across my body and buried deep inside of me.

A spanking would get him there *and* it sounded downright delicious despite the bruises that peppered my ass.

"I was hoping you would say that."

He growled and slid to the edge of the bed. I cried out in frustration when he grabbed the landline receiver.

"You remember this game don't you?'

Oh fuck, fuck, fuck.

"Yes." My voice was pitiful.

Last time I'd lost and been denied my orgasm. I'd be damned if that happened again. He clicked on speaker and started dialing. My heart raced while the ominous tone echoed through our bedroom.

Breathe.

Nick took the opportunity to peel my shorts off with one finger.

"Wái." A voice crackled across the line.

He's fucking calling China?

"Wái Mr. Kuan." He brushed his hand up my bare inner thigh. He reached all the way up, and I steeled myself but then his hand dropped.

"Ah Mr. Bryant. So nice to speak with you."

Nick ran his hand up my other leg and rested it right against my sex. He wanted my attention.

"I was having a conversation with a brilliant colleague and she pointed out another possibility for me. I'd like to explore the opportunities available in Dongguang."

As soon as Mr. Kuan started talking, Nick plunged his finger into me. I had to bite down hard on my lip so as not to moan. As it was, my back arched, and my feet scrambled against the silky sheets. Mr. Kuan started talking but I couldn't focus on his words.

Nick grabbed my foot and planted it under his leg, keeping me still, and *wide* open. He slid his finger a few times into me then stilled; I caught bits of Chinese. He added a second finger and slowly twisted them inside of me; I lost any hope of following the conversation.

I let out a deep breath before starting to chew on my lip again. He added his thumb, brushing against my clit as he spoke. When he started to alternate between his thumb stroking me and his fingers inside putting pressure on my G-spot, the flesh of my cheek gave way.

Nick knew exactly how deep to go, when to add another finger, and when to move back to his tantalizing, but relatively innocent, circles. I had to ball my fists and dig my nails into my palms to keep from blatantly yanking on his tie. My breathing was ragged and my heart still hammered away.

I missed the sounds of him scooting toward me. The only reason I noticed was when he barked to Mr. Kuan, his words vibrated against me. He'd bent so his nose could replace his thumb at the apex of my thighs. I wanted to moan or whimper or scream or cry or *something* at the switch.

It was just so good. *He* was just so good. And he was playing extremely dirty.

Warm breath danced against my slit when Nick spoke to Mr. Kuan. And as soon as the answering voice crackled across the speaker, his tongue shot into me. How the fuck was he carrying on a conversation, I didn't know. I couldn't recall my name, let alone conduct business.

He licked and circled, both sensitive and firm. He used his fingers, nose, and tongue in between sentences to pleasure me. And it was such delightfully dirty pleasure. The tension in my body was becoming so extreme that the tie dug into my wrists. I'd rip my arms out of their damn sockets if it meant I could pull him away from my thighs and up to my lips.

Nick read my body like a book, and he saw or felt or whatever that my body was building. But this time he wasn't wrapping up the phone call. He wasn't relenting either. I dug my toes into the bed and tried to free my foot to shove at him. His fingers plunged back inside of me and he swirled.

Fuck, fuck, fuck!

I wanted to scream. No. I *needed* to scream.

He twisted on the bed, landing between my knees and shoved my legs further apart, his fingers still moving expertly inside of me. He'd moved so his other God damned hand could reach my nipple.

No, no, no.

He clamped down hard and twisted; excitement shot straight to my stomach. He chose that moment to swipe across my G-spot again.

I came. Hard and fast. Ripples danced on his fingers and through my very being. My lip flew out from between my teeth and my mouth opened in a perfect, silent, shriek. My eyes slammed shut and my back arched violently against the bed. He stayed deep inside of me while my orgasm trembled.

When I slumped down, I was close to hyperventilating. I couldn't open my eyes or slow my heart. I relished the honey feeling in my limbs but my rib cage chattered at the mercy of my heartbeats. For the slightest second I worried that it wasn't slowing. I bit my lip despite the broken skin and focused on the sound of Nick's voice. I pictured the hunger in his eyes and my heart slowly calmed.

But that's when he flicked my nipple and lightning cracked through my body.

My eyes shot open and I glared at him. Technically, I'd won, fair and square. I'd come silently, and I was pretty sure I had the permanent marks to prove it. Knowing he had my full attention, he pulled his fingers out from me and pressed them into his mouth. He sucked as he winked at me.

"Mh'gòi Mr. Kuan. Joigin."

Thank God!

I knew enough Cantonese to know he just said *thank you* and *goodbye*. And as soon as he clicked off the phone he was on me, leaning in to kiss me.

"Oh I don't think so," I panted.

He snarled at me and my toes curled at the sound. He bent down again, this time hovering barely above me. I narrowed my eyes at first but then threw my wrists, still tied, up and over his head so they could rest on his neck and pulled him down the last tiny bit. He smiled as he kissed my lips over and over. I could feel how hard he was against me.

He surprised me by grabbing my hips and pulling me up off the bed with him, his hands digging into my hips. He went to nibble on my lower lip and found the teeth marks and broken skin.

"It seems I owe you despite the fact that you've already gotten off." His voice was pure sexy, sweet honey.

"Just get inside of me and we'll call it even." I was breathy and whiny all at once.

That deep, disarming flash in his eyes had me expecting a push back down to the bed. Instead, he carried me to the bookcase wall, everything clattering when my body pressed against the dark wood.

One of Nick's hands left my hip and reappeared between my legs. He fumbled with his belt and grazed my clit in the process. I moaned into his mouth as the sound of a belt buckle unfastening then dropping to the floor echoed through the room.

His cock poked between my thighs, and my hips bucked up involuntarily to meet his. He made a point to fondle me, letting his fingers leisurely walk along the wet flesh he'd already been exploring. He smiled against my lips just before he started back in on his fevered kisses.

Finally, he shifted, kicking his pants to the side. He lifted me up along the shelving, knocking over picture frames and books as he found a ledge to take a small bit of my weight. He kissed my breastbone then my nipple, keeping me perched on the shelf just out of reach of the rock hard erection below me.

"Nick . . . please," I breathed.

My head rolled back, hitting a vase. He held me still, despite my plea, and the water that was now slowly trickling down my shoulder and onto his lips where they were perched at my breast. Without warning, he switched to my other nipple and bit down hard.

"Please!" I cried.

"Jesus Christ, Kate." His cock had barely brushed my inner thighs when he choked the words out.

He was breathing through barred teeth as he slid in the slickness there. His eyes met mine just before pulling me slowly down onto his cock. Nick peeled my hips away from the wall a tiny bit and pinned my shoulder blades firmly against one of the top shelves. He rolled his hips expertly against mine, excruciatingly slow. He wrapped one arm around the small of my back and shifted the other up to the shelf where my head rested. Something else clattered behind me.

A sweaty sheen glistened on our skin where our limbs entwined. Everything behind me jostled in time with his movements but I didn't notice things falling or digging into my back anymore. I couldn't feel my toes, or my bound fingers either.

Nick shifted again, pushing me fully back against the wood so both his hands could grip the shelf beside my head. I slipped slightly, my knotted hands catching on his neck quickly. The movement managed to settle him deeper inside me. Nick sucked in breath at the same time I cried out.

We sat nose to nose for a heartbeat but then he started thrusting slowly. Each time pushing so deep, filling me so thoroughly, I thought I might actually break. I don't know how long we were like that but my shoulders started to ache. His hands moved from planted next to me to holding my forearms. His forehead dipped against mine.

"Sweets, come for me." Nick was barely breathing. "I need to feel you roll across my dick the way you did across my fingers."

The choked whisper was so hot everything in my belly clenched. He growled his approval and started the same, slow rolls of his hips. He took my lips with his again, biting and pulling. When he let his tongue wander along the teeth marks I'd given my bottom lip, I groaned.

One of his hands moved to my hip and dug in. The sharp pain that traveled across my bruises arched my back. I curved at the same time he shoved into me and the angle changed. Everything inside me clenched then damn near exploded as I came, exactly how he'd asked. My body vibrated around him and he started coming the second those vibrations rolled up the length of his cock. Hot cum was mingling with harsh squeezes and everything got slippery.

When we started sliding down the shelves, I realized Nick had spent every last bit of energy on me. We crumpled to the floor, tangled on the carpet and the disarray of books and debris. He slipped out of me, and I winced as his semi-hard self landed back between us.

He didn't pause to ask if I was okay though, he just started kissing me again: my face, eyelids, neck, ears, and then finally my lips. I wove my legs securely around him and did what I could to hug tightly with my bound wrists.

"We're going to ruin the carpet," I managed in between his kisses; we were a mess of sweat and stick.

"If we do, we'll redo the whole damned apartment."

I laughed as he kept kissing me. My heart took one loud thud, just to ruin the moment.

"Shit," Nick swore against my lips. "What was I thinking?"

"That Chinese acquisitions are sexy." I only had a mildly difficult time getting it out.

"You're heart isn't . . ."

"Stop." I gasped rather than growled. "Stop right fucking now." I pinned his face between my elbows. "I'm going to be ok."

"What if you're not?"

"Then sex with you is one hell of a way to go."

I unhooked my arms from around his neck and did my best to push him back.

"That's not even remotely funny." He made a point of staying perfectly still.

"I hadn't meant to joke."

I sat up and slumped against the bookshelf, letting my hands fold to my chest as my heart hammered a little.

"You're taking the whole week off."

He finally bent to untie me.

"Oh for fuck's sake Bryant." I snarked as I rolled my eyes.

"Do not call me Bryant," he growled. "Not on this, Kate."

Surprisingly, I let it go.

22.

Oh Jesus Christ. Ouch. Oh fucking hell. Shit. Ouch. Ouch. Ouch.

My heart was thundering again, and worse than ever before. I clutched my chest, which usually seemed to help. But not this time. I was gasping and looked down at my hand to see it shaking. Violently. Faint marks still adorned my wrist from Nick's tie a few nights ago. I focused as hard as I could on the memory of him inside me.

He wasn't in the apartment, I wouldn't be falling apart otherwise, but I called out anyway. It was more of an impulse than anything else. And a small part of me prayed I was wrong, that he'd burst through the door any moment. I even tried to force myself to imagine what his face would look like, whether his eyes would be flat or glistening. Both of the colors were familiar, both of them were mine.

Instead, Ari burst in, the door clattering to the wall, while I writhed on the bed.

Thank God.

Her arrival helped me catch my breath.

"Kate?" Her head swiveled until she saw me clutching my heart. "Oh shit!" I whimpered as she gathered me in her arms.

"Do you need a doctor?" Her hands were rubbing furiously against my skin.

I shook my head and closed my eyes to picture the image of Nick I had conjured up. It helped me mellow enough to squeak out words.

"Something's wrong Ari."

"Well, yeah. It's been getting worse all week." She eyed me warily, worry written plain on her face.

Between her and Julia, they'd comforted fewer attacks as the week went on but each had been more intense than the last. She got up and grabbed water for me. I was still pinned to the bed by the jackhammer in my chest.

"No. This isn't my heart. This is something else. Something's actually wrong."

The harder I tried to soothe myself, the less it worked. My gut knew this was a combination of heart trouble and instinct. My intuition was using an internal blow horn to tell me shit was going sideways.

"Huh." Ari was processing. "I saw Laura this morning, she's still a little mad but she's fine. Nick and I chatted briefly when he left. And Jaime's in the living room, he'd have left if things had gone awry. Any messages on the cell?"

She arched her eyebrows as I reached for my phone. I didn't even realize I'd taken my hand from my chest until Ari snatched it mid-grab.

"Oh my God, what is on your wrists? What happened?" Her eyes went wide. "Wait is this what I think it is? Do you use handcuffs or rope or zip ties or what?" Of course Ari was revving up and speaking a million miles an hour. "I always knew you guys were ridiculously kinky. Kate, these are downright scandalous! Are they from the night mom and I were gone?"

My heart crashed into my ribs at the mention of Julia. Ari had purposely been distracting me.

"Where is your mother?" The words burned in my throat.

"She'll be back tomorrow for the launch," Ari said nonchalantly, but she wouldn't meet my gaze.

Everything in me seized.

"Ari." I meant her name to come out as a forceful warning but it was an unmistakably desperate plea.

"Kate, you need to calm down." Ari rolled her eyes but her face wasn't light or breezy.

Dread seeped thick back into my blood, and my hand crept back to my chest even though I was decidedly detached and numb.

"Where's your mother?" My heart let out one, truly explosive beat when I asked again.

Ari caved when she saw the agony I was in.

"Okay, if I tell you, you can't tell Nicholas." My heart jackhammered in my chest. I tried to keep from gulping. "I promised Mom I wouldn't say anything."

"Where?"

"She went to Connecticut. She's serving Francis divorce papers."

No, no, no. Fuckingshitpiss.

If my heart hadn't been going crazy before, it sure was now. Blood thumped through me, painfully tunneling my vision. I couldn't breathe. Guilt mingled with terror in my veins and choked me. Sure, it had been my idea, but not like this. Not without all of us there to protect her. If Francis beat her for someone else's willful actions . . .

Do not go there!

"Why isn't someone serving them for her?"

Ouch, ouch, ouch.

"She couldn't take it anymore. She saw how bad you've been, how upset Nicholas is, how hurt we all are. She finally saw that the Winthrops would be our demise."

I clamored across her body for my phone, heart be damned.

"Kate, please! Mom made me promise."

I wasn't listening anymore—I wasn't sure I physically could. But my fingers could dial.

"Sweets." Nick's voice answered roughly after half a ring.

"Your mom," I gasped.

"What about my mom?" He shifted on the leather chair behind his desk.

"Ari," I breathed.

"Wait, what about you? Kate, what the fuck is going on?" When I couldn't answer, he called out again. "Kate?" Each time his voice got a little more harsh.

I shoved the phone in Aribella's face as Nick barked. They went back and forth while I rubbed my heart. When Ari spoke, her voice was small, but "She's divorcing Francis" echoed through my soul.

Nick's answering boom was so loud Ari pulled the phone from her ear. I could hear him perfectly, his words an echo of my unspoken thoughts.

What will Francis do to her?

Ari bolted the second she was off the phone. I'd tried to keep up with her as she barreled out of the apartment but my heart forced me to stop on the stairs more than once. The elevator had sealed behind her before I even got down the first flight.

I made myself as comfortable as possible draped across the couch, unable to physically make it back upstairs. I'd resorted to counting the ceiling panels, hoping that would soothe my body, when the main elevator dinged. I held my breath wanting it to be Julia, magically back from Connecticut so quickly. Or if not her, Ari. I'd control my temper, tell her we'd face anything, even her brother's wrath, together.

But it was loud, angry, stomping footfalls that echoed through the cavernous living room. When glass scraped sharply against the wood of our bar, and was followed by the shatter of shards, I forced myself to sit up.

"Aribella!" Nick's roar shook every single window in the apartment.

"She left, Nick."

He whirled to look at me, his eyes a tumultuous tempest that even I hadn't seen before.

"What?" His howl started my heart up again.

One hand flew to my chest and the other clenched at the couch cushions.

"Kate." His whole face changed and he took two powerful steps toward me. "Sweets?"

"Is she going to be okay?"

I sagged against the couch as Nick threw his arms around me. He said nothing. He simply pulled me as close as his stance would allow. My chest unclenched at his touch but I couldn't get my shoulders to relax.

"What are we going to do?"

"*We* aren't going to do anything."

I had no desire to fight him. It had nothing to do with my heart, either.

"Okay, what are you going to do?"

"I have to try and stop her. I have to get out there, but . . . His voice trailed off and I knew exactly how he intended on finishing that sentence.

"Fuck the launch, Nick. It's just business. This is family." My hands shook as I brought them up to trace the backside of his palms. "I'll deal with the launch."

"I know your heart was bothersome today." That tone said his eyes were the agitated, unruly eyes of a mad man again.

"Yes." I couldn't hold in a sigh anymore. "But trust me when I say I can handle this. I'll even see Dr. Chambers tomorrow. You have to go. Please trust me. *Please.* I know something's wrong with your mom."

I was ready to elaborate when he cut me off.

"I know." He ran his finger across my collarbone. "This time I feel it too."

Nick had shuffled out only moments after and I hadn't heard from him in the twenty-four hours since. Ari hadn't slunk back into the apartment and Julia never returned. I'd called out for all of them each time my heart started slamming around—which it'd done repeatedly—or rather hadn't really stopped doing.

Jaime had come running each and every time instead, with his face drawn, a furrowed brow in place and dark circles under his eyes, looking more and more gaunt. I refused to let myself think about what that meant. Mostly because it would send my heart thundering.

Dr. Chambers made a house call. When I told him what had been happening he insisted I check back into the hospital. The thought of lying in a bed while my world was teetering on the brink, being poked and prodded when Vesper had business and Nick was in Connecticut and Julia was . . . I just couldn't wrap my head around it. I simply turned my back on him and asked that Jaime showed him out.

I tried to keep my mind blank as I curled in a ball on the ottoman in my closet. I reminded myself to take on one task at a time. Here, all I needed to do was stare at my expansive wardrobe and repeat *calm down*. When I had the strength, I could pick a gorgeous outfit. I'd get through the evening by staying focused on baby steps.

Sighing, I shoved myself up from the leather to leaf through the fine fabrics in front of me. My heart thumped and my stomach churned even at the slight movement. I settled on a vintage Yves Saint Laurent tuxedo and, with a Herculean effort, slipped into the black pinstriped high waisted, wide-legged trousers. I paired the perfectly tailored single-breasted jacket with a simple, sheer white v-neck. I added black patent alligator pointy-toe stilettos and a long gold pendant necklace that paired with my contoured McQueen cuff. I left my hair down and wavy just the way Nick liked it. I kept my eye makeup simple and painted my lips a dark crimson.

My exterior made it seem like there were no heart problems, like there was no Christopher, like Julia wasn't in Connecticut, or that Nick was MIA. The facade was convincing until the light fabric of my shirt or dainty chain of my necklace betrayed my stuttering heart.

I faltered when press swarmed outside of One Madison, and my heart jackknifed. Jaime noticed and all but bear hugged me to actually shove through the crowd. He was the only reason I stayed standing.

When I looked up to thank him, I noticed something was off. His eyes were red and puffy. I was focused on catching my breath or I would have questioned him.

We waded into the launch in much the same manner. I let out a massive breath when I saw Laura standing in the staging hallway, waiting. She noticed I was rubbing my chest and all but sprinted over to me. Her arms were around my shoulders, and she'd started speaking before I had a chance to apologize.

"It's fine. It's always been fine. I just don't want you to get hurt," she said, heading off the sorry on the tip of my tongue.

"Doesn't mean I don't want to apologize. I feel like an ass."

"Because I let you get drugged? Or because I screamed at your fiancé?"

She was gently rubbing my back where she held me.

"Because I didn't even listen to you, Laur."

"Honey, if I had a dollar for every time you didn't listen . . ." She waved me off. "Besides I was the one that stormed out of the hospital remember?"

"Sorry."

"Don't get all soft on me now, Elliott." She stepped back and smiled. "And speaking of the devil, where is Nicholas?"

She asked the very question running through my mind. Jaime pocketing a phone beside me pulled my attention from Laura. One look at Jaime's face and that heavy boulder of dread fractured in the pit of my stomach to form a million pinpricks of worry. A dramatic line of questioning barreled through my mind just as Gemma, Callista, Elena, and Brennan all whirled down the hallway, effectively stopping that train of thought in its track.

My heartbeat turned erratic, picking up speed and losing any kind of real rhythm. I kept it together though. Everyone except Jaime scrutinized my every move. If nothing else had happened, that would have told me something was off. Even when my knees buckled pulling Laura and Gemma to my side, Jaime kept his distance.

Oh no. Oh fucking serious no.

It took me a little while to shift my focus from the pummeling in my chest to charming the crowd, but I managed. There were lots of hands to shake and people to greet. I tried not to watch Jaime but when I looked up my anxiety skyrocketed; he was visibly upset. And he never got upset.

After cocktail hour, I was slated to give a speech and be a part of a question and answer panel. Bryant was supposed to be up there with me. I didn't know if I could do it by myself. My slightly ragged breathing said probably not.

Jaime didn't see me watching him from where I hid, crumpled behind the stage in the hopes of catching my breath. He didn't feel my gaze on him when he pulled his glasses off and wiped a tear from his cheek.

My insides skittered then froze. My chest, my breathing, my knees were all problems, but none of them even remotely compared to the fear that gripped my throat. I vaguely registered that my name boomed from the podium. On autopilot, I stood and righted my suit. For a moment, I walked toward the person introducing me, but my body had other plans. I abruptly changed directions and cornered Jaime.

"What is it? And don't even try and tell me nothing." It was probably the harshest I'd ever been with him.

"Can it wait until after?" His voice was a little shaky.

"No." I wasn't bending on this. If nothing else, I needed to start my heartbeats again, however crazy they might get. "Is Nick okay?"

"He's not physically hurt if that's what you're asking." Jaime's voice trembled.

Fuck.

Something horrible *had* happened. Whatever my heart and stomach had been trying to warn me about was real. I couldn't breathe. I couldn't feel my fingertips. I sure as hell couldn't give the speech. I needed to be with Nick regardless of where the hell he was and what the hell had happened.

My name rang expectantly over the speaker system again, sending a wild jolt of electricity through me.

"Brennan," I said sharply as I turned wildly from Jaime.

Brennan hurried over. Everyone that had been standing with him saw whatever tortured look crossed my face and quickly followed.

"I can't do it. You have to give the speech, and the specs."

"Kate you have to . . ." Callista was starting in.

I didn't let her finish, no words could stop me anyway, I just turned and blindly barreled toward a door. Any door. Anything that would get me closer to Nick.

23.

I busted through a side door and into a long, fluorescent-lit hallway. It seemed to tunnel away from me infinitely, narrowing to the size of a pinprick. I forced my legs to move faster across the linoleum. I probably looked like a wounded animal, desperate for somewhere safe to hide.

Nicholas Bryant was my somewhere.

"Kate." Jaime's voice was soft when he grabbed me. I hadn't noticed he'd caught up and my saucer-sized eyes told him as much. He only held me for a moment as he pointed toward a stairwell at the side of the hallway.

"Wait. What is going on?" Laura's voice came from somewhere behind me, whomping in and out between heart thuds.

"I don't know, I don't care. I just need to be with him."

I stumbled off in the direction Jaime had pointed, my hand bracing against the wall, my movements becoming much more labored under the strain of my heart. Despite my internal meltdown, I somehow made out Jaime's whisper to Laura low behind me.

Laura gasped and I froze.

No. No please, no.

My heart was the only noise in the corridor, and since it was going to plow right out of my chest, everyone could actually hear it. Laura and Gemma watched me, tears already pricking at the corners of their eyes.

Oh God, oh God, oh God. No!

My insides shredded, my heart was a lost cause. I couldn't force myself to face the words Jaime had spoken. All I could think of was Nick. Of needing to hold him. My temper bubbled up, but I couldn't lose it; all my anger was directed solely at me.

I should be there.

It took all the strength I had to shove open the stairwell door. My wobbly legs started careening down the concrete steps. Footfall after footfall echoed in the corridor, they sounded like landlines to me.

"Kate!" Jaime shouted after me and his footfalls picked up. "Kate! Please stop."

My knees buckled and I crashed into the wall. It barely held me up.

"Tell me that it's not true. Tell me you lied to Laura." My heart thundered and I automatically clenched at it. "Tell me it was one big fucking joke, Jaime." A sob choked my voice. Jaime's shoulders slumped and he looked down at his shoes. "Tell me it's a joke!" I screamed as I looked to Laura, shaking her head silently behind him, tears now rolling unabashedly down her face. "Please." My tears broke through. "Please, please, please, God. Tell me there was some mistake. Tell me it's not true . . ." Between my heart screeching in my chest, and the sobs wracking the rest of my body, I couldn't hold myself up anymore.

Laura reached around me just in time to keep me from plummeting to the floor.

"Julia succumbed to her injuries at 3:47 p.m. this afternoon at Norwalk Hospital." Jaime could barely speak.

Gemma wove her arms around his slouched figure and Laura squeezed me all the tighter. Tears cascaded down my face, tears I didn't know had started.

"How?" My voice didn't sound like mine.

"Francis was taken into custody at the hospital." It was explanation enough.

Violent sobs shook my body. I quaked against Laura's arms, only turning so I could burry my face in her shoulder. I'd cried many times on this shoulder but it wasn't the one that felt like home anymore.

Nick.

I had to get to him. Now. I straightened my shoulders and tried to wipe the tears from my eyes. They wouldn't stop.

"Why wasn't I told earlier?"

"The launch."

"Did Nick tell you to keep this from me?" I couldn't help the little bit of anger that flared in my voice.

"He's not exactly giving orders at present."

I swallowed my tongue and my temper. "How do I get to him? I want him now." I started moving again, bursting through another door and out onto the dark street.

"Colton is coming with the car." Jaime was doing his best to stay in control of the situation.

"I'll be damned if I'm sitting in the back of that fucking Bentley all the way to New Canaan. I'm driving."

"Kate, I have to insist. Christopher . . ." Jaime stopped short as I wheeled on him.

My insides eviscerated further at the mention of Christopher. I hadn't know there was anything left to destroy.

"Jaime, I'll wait for that damned car but you will take me to mine. I will drive. Right in front of you if need be. I will not sit idly by and play with my BlackBerry or chew on my fingernails waiting to get there."

I'd bury myself in guilt if left to my own devices.

"Please listen to her Jaime. She's not going to let this one go." Thank God Laura jumped to my defense. She probably saw the panic shimmer in my eyes. "Seriously, just let her drive." Something in Laura's voice or my face convinced him.

I clutched my heart as my vision blurred with the waterworks. The thudding hadn't really lessened nor had I opened my clawed hand as I gunned out of my parking garage. I vaguely remembered Laura depositing herself in the passenger seat, Jaime insisting on being in back. Gemma and Colton stayed in the fancy black car behind us.

City traffic came alive, a monstrous villain actively working against me. It took so damned long to get out of midtown that I actually shrieked when I came to a dead stop just before Yonkers.

"Calm down," Laura murmured from the passenger seat. "I know this is miserable but it won't do any good if you literally kill yourself trying to get there."

I shot her daggers but she was right. I tried to imagine Nick to help my heart mellow. I could only picture him battered and broken which hurt even worse. I turned on the radio and started flicking through channels so furiously that my knuckles went white. Other than the occasional groan, Laura let me flip through the stations until my fingers hurt and I shut the thing off all together.

Once I made it to the Hutchinson River Parkway, I was able to floor it. Colton behind me wouldn't be pleased with my pace but I didn't care. I'd pay whatever speeding ticket, I'd deal with whatever consequences, I just needed to get to Nick. When I pulled off Connecticut 15, I realized I had no idea where I was going. I knew Julia lived in New Canaan and that was it.

Had lived.

I choked on a giant sob as I pulled over.

"What are you doing?" Laura broke the tense silence.

"I don't know where we're going." My hands clutched the wheel, making even my forearms taut. My heart hurt worse knowing I was near. I was going to see him—soon—and my very soul was going to break the second I did.

"Jaime?" she asked but I talked right over top of her.

"What am I going to do? What am I going to say?"

"What do you mean?" Laura's voice was soft and gentle.

"Kate?" Jaime's was too.

"I don't do this well. Grief." I took a deep breath. "Matter of fact, I don't do it at all. I turn into a train wreck. A zombie. I curl into a ball and I count dots on ceilings. I don't eat and I drink asinine amounts of scotch. I have no coping mechanisms. I can't help him. What was I thinking driving up here?"

I was hyperventilating and only pried my fingers from the steering wheel to dig into my chest, I didn't even notice the Bentley pull up be-hind us. My heart was running ragged, beats sounding in my ears and thumping in my fingertips. My tears dripped in well-worn salty trails down my cheeks.

"Hey, hey, hey." Laura reached over the console and hugged me awkwardly. "There's no right way to grieve. There's no right way to comfort him either. Just go to him. Sometimes you just need the feel of someone familiar in the room."

Colton's knuckles wrapped on the window and Laura reached across me to roll it down and explain. He reached in and silently rubbed my shoulder above Laura's grip before turning back to the Bentley.

The black car idled for a moment and then pulled out, leading down the main road then onto a paved and tree lined lane. Darkness completely blanketed the world around us. I was having a hard time focusing on fuzzy taillights; the whitewashed wood slat fence peeking into my headlights on either side of the road kept drawing my atten-tion. As did the sheer terror clobbering my chest.

We turned and I realized the winding country lane was actually an estate drive that wound up a small hill to the outline of a massive, regal home. Only one light shone in the house.

Without being told, I knew we'd arrived; the very bricks of the home looked like they were mourning. And I could finally *feel* Nick.

I wasn't thinking anymore when I slammed into park and bolted up the marbled steps. I barely noticed that Laura had to shut off the engine behind me or that Terrence opened the front door in front of me until he murmured, "Most likely study. Down the hall, last door on the right."

He pointed and I took off running. My skin goose bumped when I threw open the last door.

Nick was there just as Terrence had predicted. He was sitting in the dark, his head in his hands. His jacket was flung over the seat and his tie hung untied between his knees. His vest still covered his broad back and judging by the tremble of his ribs beneath the silk backing, he was crying.

"Baby," I breathed as I shut the door behind me.

He looked up, searching for me in the dark. The way his face contorted in the pale moonlight was heartbreaking. His eyes were an inconsolable matte I'd never seen before. Tear stains streaked across his skin. A bottle of scotch lay between his feet. There was no glass in sight.

I shrugged out of my jacket, pushed the bottle to the side with my toes, and crumbled between his knees. He still hadn't said anything but he watched me like a hawk. I let my hands come to a resting spot on his thighs. When I touched him, he closed his eyes and sucked in a deep breath.

His brow crinkled making his face look both relieved and despairing. Words failed me. Everything sounded so wrong and got stuck like bubble gum in my mouth. It was all so stupid and insignificant. What had Laura said to me when my parents died? What had Nick said to me when Trevor died? I couldn't remember.

"Nick." A sob choked off my voice. "Baby, I love you so much."

The declaration just slipped out but I meant it with every fiber of my being. His face got more intense just before he melted off his seat and onto the floor with me. The leather chair he'd been sitting on tipped backwards and clattered to the floor. I would have stopped it but I was too preoccupied trying to slow his tumble.

He leaned his forehead to mine and his body trembled at my touch.

"Kate." My name was long and drunkenly slurred. "My Sweetssss. You should leave." His tears were falling faster. "You'll get hurt . . ."

Shit, we're back here.

"I'm not going anywhere, Nick. I love you."

I tried to gather his muscly frame into my arms the way he always did for me. It didn't quite work but at least I got my arms wrapped around him tightly. He shifted so his head rested on my chest. We sat like that until his tears had soaked warm and wet through my shirt. The door creaked open once and I guessed Laura was checking on us. I couldn't see from my seat and I wouldn't have taken my attention from Nick anyway.

Every so often I kissed the top of his head where I could reach. Then the skin of his forehead again while I traced circles on his arm. Finally, he responded to my lips, twisting so his could meet them. His arms wrapped around me and used my long locks to pull me down to him.

I kissed him desperately but he wanted more. He bit harder on my lips and curled his fingers further into my hair. He drunkenly sprawled on the floor before pulling my body over top of his. I straddled his chest to kiss the small bit of skin that peeked through his shirt buttons.

He hadn't said anything but he didn't have to. This was how we communicated best and now he just needed to lose himself in my flesh. I kept kissing his chest as I undid the buttons of his shirt. He let me move lower and lower, his arms resting on my shoulders. Once I reached his belt, his hands tightened and he pulled me back to his lips. I let him pull me up so his tongue could explore my mouth.

These kisses were different. Rough, harsh, but he'd linger too. His hands would claw at me and then fall away completely. Like he desperately needed me but also wanted to stop. It reminded me of the conflicted sex we'd had just before he tried to leave me. The difference was that this time I understood and wouldn't let him follow through even if it killed me.

Then he did push me away, but just for a moment. After only a few deep breaths, he grabbed me and pulled me back. Once I was against him, he scrambled to pull my shirt from my body then balled it up to throw it. The skin to skin contact made my body tingle. He grabbed my face and held it in place, taking my lips violently.

I yelped but he wasn't paying attention. There was no pause, no studying of my face or even my heart. For the first time, the roughness was a little overwhelming, but I could tell it came from Nick being overwhelmed himself. I tried to pull away but he wouldn't let me. I shifted enough that I felt his tears still flowing, now warm on both our cheeks. That was all the incentive I needed to melt back into him and roll with it.

His hands wandered across my skin. Then they'd stop and circle or claw. I softened at each light touch and winced at each scratch. My body was as confused as he was when eventually he fumbled with the zipper at my hip and then let his hands skate up my body. He was more reverential with my skin than ever before but then he painfully wrenched my breasts up out of my lace bra.

"Take your pants off," he growled at me.

Just be there for him.

I sat up and peeled the fabric off as gracefully as possible. He fidgeted with his belt and pants, barely opening his fly, then pulled me down swiftly onto his erection. I shouted and he arched his head back into the carpet, his mouth opening like he was going to groan. He didn't though, he stayed silent as he encouraged me up and down.

Nick's hands moved between my hips and my chest. Yanking and pulling first, then moving gently. The fine fabric of his pants kept rubbing against me and the longer he held me, trapped upright, the more the fine wool burned rather than tickled. The bra that had been gracelessly shoved beneath my breasts wasn't feeling pleasurable anymore either.

His frustrated grunt said he wasn't building beneath me. His hands kept curling tighter into my hips, but nothing was coming from it. Nothing like usual. I decided to take control. I pushed his hands away and laid back along his chest. I kissed his lips and neck and chest with lingering sweet kisses.

Nick was trying to push me back upright but I wrestled for his wrists. I kissed slowly along my trail again, this time with more feeling. I reached up and undid my bra, then draped myself silently on his chest. We had both stopped moving, he was simply parked inside me.

I kissed his jaw.

"I love you," I murmured.

He closed his eyes.

"I love you so much, Nicholas Bryant."

He wrapped his arms tightly around me, and we laid in silence, any kind of sex unfinished, and all our feelings unresolved. It wasn't until I shivered that he shifted, just enough to grab his suit jacket and throw it over me. His chest barely expanded underneath me, his heart beat a slow, sad rhythm, and all I could do was listen ever so closely.

24.

I woke up on the floor of Julia's study. I was wrapped in the suit jacket and Nick's arms but neither stopped me from being cold. Or heartbroken. I stirred ever so slightly and he pulled me in closer. I looked up the at scruff and sadness hanging on his face and got the feeling he hadn't slept at all.

"Baby," I whispered from my spot on his chest.

I was still lost for words; this wasn't as easy as Laura made it out to be.

"You should leave me." His voice came out gravelly and harsh. Had it been a few months ago, had I not understood him, I would have been hurt.

"Never." My answer was as simple as my feelings.

Not even on your life Nick.

"Bad things happen to the people I love." He choked on the sentence and started tearing up.

"No, Nick. Bad things happen period. End of story. They happen to you, and to me, and to a billion other people just because. It sucks and it's shitty and life gets really, really fucking hard because of it, but it isn't your fault. I'm never leaving you. Ever. Not even if this was your fault. Not even if you were some talisman for bad luck. The good far outweighs the bad. I love you."

His hands gripped into me, tightly. He was beside himself and I didn't blame him.

"I should have known. I should have seen this coming. I should have been with her. I . . . I . . ." He couldn't catch his breath.

"Oh, baby." Water pooled in the corners of my eyes again. "You know as well as I do that you had no say in it."

"I should have been more forceful. I used to be. Getting soft cost my mother her life." He started chewing on his lip.

"You're not getting soft. You're learning how to really live and love and sometimes that means letting go. I know it's hard and scary but it's worth it. Your mom thought so too."

I gulped when I recalled the last conversation I'd had with Julia. At the end of the day, it had been all about very real and bottomless love. Not to mention how hard either one was.

Nick's hands dug into me hard enough to leave marks but I knew he didn't need rough sex, he needed affection. Or sleep. I sat up and pulled him along with me. He still smelled like booze and his movements were fuzzy. I eyed him warily and decided we had to find somewhere to really curl up together. I pulled the suit jacket that'd been my blanket over my shoulders as I stood. If anyone was lingering in the halls at this ungodly hour, they'd look the other way under these circumstances.

I pulled him up and the first few steps out the door but then he took the lead. He pulled me into a room that the first fade from night was starting to illuminate. Dawn showed dark, bruise-like circles under his eyes as we passed the giant open window. I'd intended to take him to bed when the large marble tub caught my eye.

Nick willingly followed me into the bathroom and stood, lost, as I drew a bath. Still a little vacant, he let me undress him. I shrugged out of his jacket and stepped into the warm water. I held out my hand to him. He eyed it for a while, like it was a poisonous snake, but eventually he took it. I folded into the water and pulled him down with me, his back to my front, and I wrapped my arms and legs around him like he'd done so many times for me.

"Nick, relax."

His muscles stayed taut and rigid in my arms.

"Nicholas," I snarled and pulled him flush against my chest. He laid back and rested his head against my neck. I changed the pattern of my fingertips, and we sat like that until I was pruney. I had just reached for the shampoo when he decided to speak again.

"I killed her, Kate."

"How can you say something like that?" I hadn't meant to sound so appalled. "Nick, you cannot blame yourself for this."

"Of course I can," he roared and splashed in the tub. "I let her come back here numerous times. I was the one that pissed off Francis in the first place. I was the one that provoked Christopher. I brought everything down on us, on my family, and I am being punished. Punished for being successful. Or happy. Or finding you. Fuck if I know. All I know is that my mother is dead. *DEAD* because of me!" he screamed the last bit and my heart thudded.

He was so worked up that his body heaved; he didn't notice my heart misbehaving. The exaggerated beats only lasted until his anger shifted back to tears.

My poor, sweet, fiancé.

I swiveled around so I could straddle him and look into his eyes. Horrific, dark pools met me. I refused to stare into black any longer.

"You listen to me and you listen good, Nicholas Bryant. This is a horrible, awful thing. It makes my heart hurt and my stomach sick but it is *not* your fault. You did *not* send her to die. None of us begging her to get divorced did either. Christopher and Francis are fucked up, disgusting people. You can be sad, you can be angry, you can sit here like a zombie, you can drink scotch until you can't see straight. God knows I've been there. But you cannot blame yourself."

I took a deep breath before continuing.

"People around you don't get hurt because of you. That's life. Beautiful, wonderful, tragic, terrible life. And I will spend the rest of mine telling you how wonderful you are. And how perfect you are for me and that my life is better because you're in it. I vow to remind you constantly that none of this is even remotely your fault."

My voice had escalated, carried away with the depth of my emotion. I didn't notice that his eyes churned as he reached for my face before he mashed my lips to his. He took my mouth but it was different than a few hours ago. My head was trapped as he kissed every inch of my lips and face but it was back to his usual firm grip. His tongue slipped in and out, tangling up with mine in a perfectly familiar, perfectly wonderful rhythm. I grabbed his biceps and pulled myself closer.

In one swift move, his arms shifted and snaked around the small of my back. I didn't hesitate to weave my arms around his neck. To my surprise Nick stood. There were no words, just the splashing and cascading of water back into the tub. I held on tight and let him carry me, dripping wet, to the bed. He pressed me down, his lips never leaving mine. I could feel sadness in his kiss but no longer the frantic desolation from before. It was too much to hope he'd forgiven himself but it was a start.

Our skin slid across one another, beaded water everywhere. When he finally pressed into me, I gasped and my eyes shot open. Nick watched me intently as his hips started to roll against mine. His eyes were still stormy but the worst of the clouds were clearing.

"I love you Nick."

He groaned and his eyes fluttered shut. My breath caught at the familiar cadence of us together. I was a weird combination of relief, sorrow, and delight as he lost himself in sex. He lifted my hips to meet his and it was his turn for his breath to falter.

"You are perfect," I panted. "Perfect for me." His hand moved to my hip and he gripped. Hard. "I thank God, every day that I get you forever."

His lips came crashing back down to mine. His hands moved back around me too. Without ever slipping out of me, he lifted me. My wet hair fell across my shoulders and grazed his skin. His skin goose bumped where the strands brushed against him. My chest was now pressed against his, my legs straddling his.

Nick gripped the small of my back with one hand and the other wrapped around my shoulder blades. We couldn't have gotten closer together if we tried. His hips moved in synchronicity with mine and my skin tingled anew with each thrust. I was able to whisper into his ear as we moved.

"You will be my husband, but you already are my everything."

With a flex of his hips, he sunk into me further and stayed there, holding me still. It was tight and almost too much. I expected his hand to move from my low back and clutch into my hips but he didn't move.

He kissed me just below my ear and then whispered, "I need you."

Nick's voice was still wrong, a little weak, a little stifled, but I guessed his eyes would be closer to blue. He bit my earlobe and pulled as he started to thrust into me again. His legs shifted to spread my thighs wider.

My hips wouldn't roll very well against him anymore but he angled himself so I didn't really need to. He moved repeatedly into me. All I could manage was to weave my hands into his hair and moan into his ear. The friction of his skin against my clit was too much. I was building, and fast, but I didn't want to come unless he'd be there with me.

I cried out quietly in both pleasure and frustration. When the strangled sound fell from my lips, his ragged voice proved he still could read my mind.

"Sweets, I'm so close. Please come. I want to feel you." Relief washed over me. Relief he wasn't too wrapped up in punishing himself.

Nick held me tighter and pushed up into me and paused again. Every inch of my skin was tingling against his. I couldn't help but moan into his ear. He threaded his hands into my hair and pulled the tiniest bit, just enough to plant his lips to the underside of my jaw. He gracefully arced up and gently bit my lip as he pulsed into me with shallow, rapid thrusts. I couldn't hold on any longer.

I cried out as I started coming, squeezing hard on him. His fingertips digging into me told me he was in sync. Only a breath later his hot cum mixed with my rippling muscles and we slid against each other. I was breathing hard and mewling into his ear while his scraped on my skin. We sat there holding each other desperately.

"What am I going to do, Sweets?"

His voice was just as broken post-orgasm as it had been before.

He rested his forehead into the crook of my neck and kissed me once. I shifted my hands so I could rub his shoulders but keep a hold on him too.

"Mourn. Be horribly sad and terribly angry." I kissed him where I could reach. "Do whatever it is that you need to feel a little more normal and be in a little less pain each day."

"You help."

His hands wound into my hair.

"I know how hard it is. Even now I remember."

Nine years hadn't erased the pain of my parent's passing. Now it was just less sharp, less constant. I could feel it dull in the background each and every day.

"Will you tell me about it?"

His voice was so timid, so unlike himself.

"What do you want to know?"

I did my best to gather him in my arms again. He cuddled into my naked chest like a small little boy.

"I don't know. Anything. Everything. We never really talked about it."

"Sure we did. I told you I was depressed and how I put the pieces together by creating Vesper."

What else was there to say?

Then it dawned on me. He was asking about this. The time when I was raw and scared and despondent. I swallowed hard. I'd never given voice to those emotions. Not even to Laura. My voice was unexpectedly shaky when I started.

"I remember the police officers coming to my apartment. I couldn't fathom a reason why they'd be there. I think I stared at them on the stoop for a while, trying to remember what the rules and caveats were for Police search and seizure.

"It was raining. I don't remember because of the weather but because of the rain droplets on the officer's uniform. I watched them slide off his shoulders and then the toes of his boots. Laura was whispering in the kitchen on the phone and I remember thinking that it sounded more like hissing than her regular murmur as I showed the police in. Her face twisted when she saw the officers at the dining room table. Right then this boulder dropped into my stomach and I knew my whole world was collapsing."

Nick pulled me in tighter. I wasn't sure if he was trying to comfort me or if he was reliving his own memories.

"I don't remember what they said after they told me about the car. It overturned on the coastal highway. The drizzle had turned icy. They slid and were clipped by an oncoming car. It started them spinning and they went up and over the guardrail. The car tumbled something like 200 yards down an embankment toward the ocean. It took a crane and two search and rescue teams to recover their . . . their bodies."

I was choking on the words. Even now, my vision tunneled. Panic welled all over again. When my heart started thundering, Nick pulled me close and kissed my forehead. That kiss made the pain almost bearable. Almost.

"I think Laura showed them out. I don't really remember. I ended up on the couch, staring. It was the first time I started counting dots in the texture on the painted wall. I do that, you know, when my mind races or I'm falling apart . . .

"There still are no words to explain that feeling. I know Laura held me for a while, but the cold that came with that news was bone chilling. The violent sobs started when I realized I was alone, I might've cracked a rib. Who knows because my body ached all over. I couldn't make myself care about anything. Mostly because I couldn't really *feel* anything."

"I feel like that now."

His lips brushed against my skin as he spoke.

"I know." I kissed his head where I could reach. "I hope you realize you still have me. And Ari. And in a weird way, Laura and Jaime too."

"Yeah . . . It's just that there's a million things I wish I'd said. Like I'm sorry for all the times I screwed up. Or thank you for always putting Ari and I first. Or even I love you." He clutched into me. "I should've said I love you more."

"Baby, if I only know one thing about your mother, it's that she knew."

I pulled the covers up around us, lost in my own memories of Julia. Her eyes never twinkled but they were also never as blue as they were around Nick. She was proud, she adored him, she was excited for his future. Our future. My heart thudded once in my chest before settling into a slow, dull ache for her.

Neither of us moved, neither of us spoke. Eventually Nick's silence was replaced by soft, steady breathing.

He sleeps. Thank God.

In this light it was easy to study him. The sadness that hung on his features, even fast asleep, made my heart rattle. I tried to focus on the fact that he was here, *we* were here, but the scruff and sallow features wouldn't let me. I leaned my head back against the pillows and focused on deep breathing and the tight grip he kept on me.

Guilt mixed with pain over the whole situation as I stared up at the ceiling. There were so many things I would say to Julia, too, if given the chance to do everything over again. And even more I would say to Nick if he were awake now. All of it was making my head hurt every bit as badly as my heart. I closed my eyes and resolved to count book spines along the bedroom wall instead.

I faded in and out of sleep until a soft knock rasped at the door.

Shit.

The last thing I wanted to do was wake Nick. I wiggled out from under him, my body almost inconsolable without his touch. I looked over the bed, every ounce of me wanted to jump back in, whoever was at the door be damned.

The second knock and Jaime clearing his throat on the other side had me moving back through the room. I snatched Nick's shirt from the floor and wrapped it tight around me. I cracked the door just enough to peek out.

"What's up Jaime?" I whispered and he followed suit.

"The authorities are here. They have some questions for the family. Would you like to send Nicholas down or shall I try and get Laura and Gemma to bring out Ari."

I'd barely thought about Ari.

Sonofabitch.

Thank God for Laura and Gemma. And Jaime.

"I'll meet with them if you'll give me just a few moments."

He nodded and I shut the door. I realized too late that my clothes were still strewn about the downstairs study. I had to crack the door and hiss at Jaime in the hopes of getting his attention. I flushed a brilliant shade of scarlet when I asked if he could possibly retrieve my suit from downstairs.

When Jaime came back with the clothes, I slipped into them and followed him out into the expansive corridor. This was the first real look I was getting at the house that was more gloomy stone castle, complete with formal tapestries and grotesque marble statues, than a family home. I'd been wrong about the house mourning last night; sorrow was built into this place, thick as the mortar between stones and had been for years.

I saw the authorities occupied with Colton and Terrence ahead, my steps stuttered at the deja vu.

"Jaime." He turned around at the fragile sound. "How am I going to do this?"

"With help. Mine, if you'll take it." A small smile tugged on his lip.

"Are you doing okay?"

"Nope, not even a little bit. You?"

"Not one bit."

I nodded and took two steps toward him. He let me throw my arms around him, he even returned the hug and crunched my ribs a little. We only stood that way for a moment but when we broke apart, he took my hand and squeezed.

Standing face to face with the officers made my stomach churn. I'd given up on my heart ever returning to a normal patter, so I barely noticed that it was jumping in response to the officers in front of me. The moment the officers started speaking my stomach heaved, stealing all my focus anyway.

"Was there a history of abuse?"

Jesus.

"Were any police reports filed?"

Oh God.

"Did she fear for her life?"

I'm going to be sick.

"Was there a history of sexual abuse as well?"

I'd been answering steadily, but that one did it. I had to excuse myself and book it to the kitchen I could see beyond the formal living room, retching ungracefully into the big porcelain farmhouse sink. And that's how things went for the next 72 hours. Answer questions. Throw up everything. Damn near crumple to the floor.

Jaime or Laura or Gemma would help steady me then shoo me back to the bedroom. Nick was always there but barely speaking. He'd bury himself in my body, taking kisses, twisting nipples, fucking me with everything he had then holding me tightly until he fell fast asleep.

Every so often he'd whisper, "I love you" across my skin.

25.

I wasn't sleeping very well. My internal monologue was guilty, grieving, angry, and exhausted all at the same time. All those emotions were amplified as I watched the sun peek through brocade curtains and fall across Nick's face. That face made me sigh and my heart hammer. I desperately wanted to console him. I would've given anything to fix things. But I still had no idea where to start.

A cell phone disrupted my thoughts. I tried to slip out of his harsh grip, whether to answer or silence it, I hadn't decided.

"No," Nick growled and pinned me to the bed.

I bit my lip and tried to ignore the tumultuous feeling in my stomach. The phone rang again and neither of us said anything. I couldn't have freed myself from his grip if I tried. Almost as soon as the ringing stopped, the knocking started. After three knocks, Nick rolled off the bed and skulked toward the door as he adjusted the waistband of his sweats. He ripped it open and Laura was standing there, hand frozen mid knock, my ringing BlackBerry in hand. I couldn't see his eyes but the slouch and seethe of his shoulders said he was boring a hole in Laura's forehead with a steely gaze.

My feet automatically hit the floor and my knees wobbled a little. The nausea was getting worse but I didn't dare tell any of them. I grabbed my robe and slung it over my shoulders as I walked toward Laura. Nick snatched the ringing phone from her and switched it off. I gently pulled the phone from Nick's fingers and tried to elbow in front of him in the doorframe.

"Kate, we should chat." She arched an eyebrow, taking in Bryant's scruff without looking at me. "I have to go back to the city."

"Sure."

I sighed when Nick's hand dug into my shoulder, keeping me rooted in place. I pried his fingers loose one by one, only to turn it over and kiss his palm. He zeroed in on me and I held his dark gaze, shivering at my least favorite eye color. After a moment, he shook his head and slunk back to bed, pulling the covers over his head with another growl.

I followed Laura downstairs clinging to the bannister as I went.

"That thing has been ringing off the hook. Not my place to say, but you need to deal with it." Luckily, she was talking over her shoulder, and unable to see how hard each step was for me. I managed to follow her to the kitchen. "How are you holding up? Anything I can do for you?"

"I'm really fucking sad. And I hate seeing Nick like this."

"Language." She turned and smiled as she patted my shoulder. I arched my eyebrow. "Sorry. Habit. I know, it sucks to see someone you care about in pain."

I made a face and changed the subject. "Is Ari doing okay?"

"Gemma's been taking good care of her. When Nick is feeling up to it you can all go hug it out or whatever. That's not what I want to talk about . . ." Her voice got serious and she arched her eyebrow.

"Laura I do not want to hear about Nick . . ."

"No. God, no." She held up her hands in front of her chest as she interrupted. "Now I know Nicholas had good reason to act the way he did. He's had good intentions from the start."

She took a deep breath.

"But?" One was most certainly coming.

"Kate, I'm worried he's just like you. He's going to fall into that zombie-like depression you're overly fond of. You have to stop indulging him and snap him out of it. I can't. Ari can't. None of us can. You have to keep him going the way I kept you going. Don't let him falter."

I took a deep breath. This was not at all what I expected.

"He's going to say fuck it all to hell, just like you, and he's going to sit in a ball in bed and count dots on the ceiling or whatever it is you do. Don't stay wrapped up in bed with him. I know you want to."

I didn't meet her eyes, finding the grout in the tiled countertop fascinating instead. Silence hung heavy in the room while I started tracing the small tracks with my finger. My fingers ran right into a porcelain cup of coffee Laura slid in front of me. I smiled, still focused on the countertop.

"You're right. Of course you're right."

"I know. You just haven't been on this side of the issue before. I thought you might need a reality check before I left. Please don't think I'm slighting anyone's grief."

I nodded, watching my dark red nails still run along the grout.

"And don't forget to take care of yourself either. You're allowed to be sad but you better take care of that heart." She threw her arms around me.

"I love you, you know that right?" I asked where I was smooshed against her shoulder.

"Undoubtedly. I mean who couldn't?" She laughed lightly and the sound helped my shoulders release. "And I love you. You're my family and that means they are too."

She waved one hand around the kitchen and I knew that meant everyone in this giant house. Ringing interrupted our moment and I looked down to see an unknown number. That threw me, the stomach thing happened all over again.

"Answer it. You need to if he won't."

My brow creased but I answered with a clipped, "Yes?"

"Oh Kate, thank God." I recognized Julien's voice on the other end, but something was off. Way off. "I didn't know how else to get in touch with him. I am so sorry to bother you," he rattled into the receiver.

"Julien calm down. It's fine. What's going on?"

"I need to speak to him."

"He's not going to take the call."

I tried to sound firm but I came across sad.

"It's an emergency. I wouldn't be interrupting otherwise." Julien's panic overwhelmed him again.

"Julien, I said calm down. Tell me what's going on. We'll get it taken care of."

This was what Laura was talking about.

I started pacing. Laura arched an eyebrow at my shaky legs, then took my coffee away. She seamlessly poured a ton of vanilla soy and sugar in my cup while I was talking on the phone. I made a face but stayed focused on Julien.

"How much do you know about Victor Alexander?"

My heart dropped.

"A lot." I took a deep breath. "I think anyway."

"He was identified through facial recognition inside the Bryant Offices."

His voice was speeding up and getting almost squeaky.

"Fuck."

Laura mumbled, "Language" under her breath and into *my* coffee.

"The thing is we activated security sweeps to detain him but they can't find him."

Jaime and Colton came striding into the kitchen when I swore, both watching intently. I couldn't help but notice that Jaime's hand flinched toward his holster. It made me wonder what my face looked like.

"We've upped security but it's not helping."

"I need a brief emailed to me within fifteen minutes. Camera locations, actions taken following sightings, everything."

I didn't even hesitate as I ran for the stairs. Or as close to running as I could manage. "I'll be there shortly Julien. I want you and the head of security at Vesper's offices in one hour."

"You're going to get him to come and fix it?"

"I'm going to fucking fix it."

I clicked off my phone and yelled down the staircase.

"Jaime, be ready to leave in 15 minutes. We will take my car, and I don't want to hear any objections."

I busted in the door to find Nick curled just as Laura had predicted, in a ball in the corner of the bed, staring at the carpet, possibly even tracing patterns or counting stitches. My jacket and shoes laid haphazardly on the back of a chair behind him. I tiptoed toward them.

"Don't go."

I let out a deep sigh.

"I have to baby." *How did he know?* "Come with me?"

I bent down and kissed the back of his shoulder. He let his head roll on the pillow.

"I'm not going to make you, Nick," I continued. "But it's serious or I wouldn't be leaving."

"Don't go."

His tone was heartbreaking; so much so that my heart really did thunder. Painfully so. My face contorted and I doubled over. Mercifully, I was hidden behind him.

"Bryant, Victor is sneaking into your building. You said he was tied to Christopher. Something has to be done."

I was trying desperately not to claw into my skin over my heart.

"Fuck the Venture Group. I don't give a shit about the damn thing," he snarled.

"Look, Nick." I forced a deep breath. "I'll be damned if it's not standing there, the multi-billion dollar empire it's supposed to be, when you're ready."

He let those words hang in the air. He didn't flinch. Hell, he didn't even breathe.

"Please don't go. I'll beg."

That cut me deep. I had to double over again, and even reach out for a chair.

"I have to baby." I forced myself to stop shaking long enough to lean in and kiss his shoulder one more time.

"Kate, no." A sob shook his body. "Please." His voice was so small and so scared.

Every fiber of my being protested, yearning to stay fixed to him like the stars to their inky, black sky. I had to make myself repeat every word Laura had said.

"I love you, Nicholas Bryant. I love you more than words can say. I am only a phone call away but I have to."

My knees buckled again while my fingers and toes went numb. I felt the tear run down my cheek as I dragged myself away. His soft snivels behind me mimicked mine.

I'm doing this for him, I'm doing this for him, I'm doing this for him . . .

I hated myself for leaving him. My heart was even more pissed about it than my mind. I had to occupy my fingers simply so they didn't bruise the left side of my chest.

After a few miles and a few emails, I found it easier to focus. None of the messages erased my pain, or guilt—or sorrow for that matter—but they occupied enough of my mind that I couldn't drip tears over the distance rapidly growing between Nick and I.

One email in particular caught my eye. Personal condolences from District Attorney Hart. My insides lurched when I read the reminder that he was happy to help with anything.

An idea appeared, more desperate than fully formed. What I wanted more than anything was to see someone pay for what my family was going through. Victor would do just fine. If he lead us to Christopher, even better.

My fingers were flying across the keys before I gave it a second thought. DA Hart answered on the second ring. Jaime's eyes widened as I explained the situation in very broad terms. Jaime's slight twitches and infinitesimal scowls told me how compelled he was to shush me. But there was no way I was shutting up now; this was right. Even my heart mellowed moderately.

"I'm not sure about this Kate." Jaime glowered out at the road when he spoke after I hung up.

"I am." I made a point to look at him as directly as the passenger seat would allow. "We need help."

"Jaime, I'd listen. She doesn't admit to needing help very often." I'd almost forgotten Laura was in the backseat. "Or perhaps, ever."

I arched my eyebrow at her dig but she just scoffed. I think Jaime managed a tiny smile.

"These things tend to come with a price. I'm worried about what we'll have to pay."

If it hadn't been for my gut feeling, I would have been too.

"I'm not." At that, I bent back over my BlackBerry, working even more furiously with my phone than I had been before. "Besides Jaime, I'd pay any price for Nick."

26.

Vesper's conference room looked like a war council; Julien had done exactly as I'd asked. I settled into my skin as much as possible without Nick and was mid-sentence, briefing the team, when DA Hart arrived.

He was accompanied by a young man, my age, or slightly older, and built like a mack truck. I noticed his suit first—it was obviously expensive, not just because of the fabric but because of the way it was tailored to such an obscenely muscular frame. Most tongues would wag at a man like that.

But most women didn't have Bryant. I wasn't checking him out, I was scrutinizing him.

His eyes struck me next, pale green and downright luminescent. Unlike Nick's they betrayed nothing; they were ruthless but hypnotic. So much so, I almost forgot to listen when DA Hart introduced his nephew, Brooklyn.

DA Hart asked me to continue but it was Brooklyn who listened intently as I did. His face crinkled and occasionally and he'd cock his head back and forth as if he was considering my words. Most of the time he'd arch a singular eyebrow and then return to his stone faced observation.

We were reviewing the security reports when Brooklyn interrupted. "Are we sure that the facial recognition component of Bryant's software hasn't been tampered with?"

"Diagnostics were run multiple times," the Venture Group's head of security spoke up.

"Then I'd wager this is a decoy." Brooklyn's haunting eyes leveled at me.

My stomach dropped and my heart hammered, not because of what he'd said, but because I knew, in the deepest crevices of my soul, without any shadow of doubt, it was true. I'd been pushing my intuition aside for too long. It had predicted Ally, Piper, Victor, Christopher, and Julia. But I hadn't really listened. I wasn't making the same mistake again.

"Decoy for what?"

"Therein lies the real question. If you know who is behind this, because I know Victor, and it's sure as shit not him, we might be able to figure that out." Brooklyn sat up, flippantly tossing papers on the table and narrowing his gaze at me.

For the first time since leaving the Winthrop house I faltered. I rubbed my heart and looked to Jaime. A whole conversation passed between us with that look. Wordlessly we agreed to accept help.

Brooklyn arched his eyebrow as he settled back into his chair, completely aware that *something* had passed between us. And, if I wasn't mistaken, completely sure of the meaning.

Good God, he's more smug than Nick.

My heart thudded at the thought of my fiancé, crumpled in bed, and my knees wavered in time with my heart.

Jaime noticed, he always noticed, and started barking out orders. The room slowly emptied, ants scurrying to tasks, while Brooklyn and DA Hart sat still watching the melee. When the tidal wave of activity subsided, only the four of us remained in the room wrapped in a thick blanket of silence.

"If you trust them Kate, I trust them, and they need to know." Jaime nodded first at the DA then at Brooklyn.

"Philip do you trust this one?" I asked as I gestured to Brooklyn.

"With everything the Hart family is." He nodded succinctly.

I sighed and plopped into the nearest chair. Relief rushed wildly through me at the thought of having help, of having someone to lean on. My hand was still fluttering at my chest as I swiveled toward the windows.

"I don't know if it's one or both of them." I sounded tired, even to myself. "But Victor Alexander and Christopher Winthrop have been playing out this personal vendetta on a global stage for a while now."

The leather beneath both men crinkled as they shifted in their seats behind me. If I had to guess, the names alone had captured their attention. It was just so much easier to speak staring at the skyline rather than Brooklyn's piercing green eyes.

"Victor's said he's just a pawn in this and, for the most part, I believe him. But it didn't start that way." I bit my lip.

"How did it start?" Brooklyn's voice was perfectly professional.

So I started at the beginning and unloaded *everything*. Family history, personal history, business history. All the things that Nick had worked so hard to keep secret laid bare for the DA and his nephew.

When I finished I took a deep breath. I felt lighter somehow but started worrying on my lip all the same.

"Tetrahexazine?" Brooklyn finally broke the silence. The word was so disorienting that I finally turned to look at him.

"Excuse me?"

"Was that what he slipped into your drink. Tetrahexazine."

"I don't know. They were only able to say it was amphetamine based and that I needed rest or to be observed."

"That means the rumors are true." Brooklyn scowled. "The military got the bright idea that, if they could induce a controlled heart attack and make a captive *think* he was dying, the torture process could be streamlined. The physical pain, the emotional terror, death looking directly in your face, but reversible if need be, and all without any proof of torture on an autopsy. Makes torturing civilians a very real plausibility. "

I let out a heavy sigh. "So *this* . . ." I pointed to my chest then couldn't help but rub on it. " . . . may actually kill me."

"No, it *will* kill you. If left unchecked without an antidote you will have a massive heart attack. Effective torture has to have an incentive to *end* the torture."

Brooklyn rubbed his temples as his eyes darted back and forth, but I still couldn't read what was roving through his head.

"What if I just take heart medication? Something that helps prevent heart attacks?"

"As far as I know, this attacks your nervous system, sending new heartbeat patterns to your body. They get worse with stress. So something that prevents clogged arteries would be irrelevant." He sighed. "Besides, the rumor is that it wipes out every medication in your system anyway. Just to be sure it's effective."

I sat wide eyed, my fingers tracing my heart. I wanted Nick here to deflect those words more than I'd ever wanted anything in my life.

"So you're telling me I'm going to die, and stress is only going to kill me faster." My hand pushed hard enough to bruise my ribs. I didn't care. I just wanted to keep it in there. Jaime's hand came to my shoulder while DA Hart's face pinched toward Brooklyn.

Brooklyn cocked his head. "What? I'm just relaying information. I didn't poison her." Philip thwacked him on his shoulder. "Fine. I have an idea of where I can get my hands on some antidote but it's black market shit. It'll take some time." He pursed his lips. "Until then, I'd suggest you go and lie down."

"No." I managed a full-blown Bryant growl for Brooklyn. "I will fix this."

"Kate, that's what I'm here for. I fix things. You got a dead stripper in a closet? A DEA shakedown for coke smuggling? Someone who needs to leave the country? Call me."

"He's really very good when he's not being a cocky ass." Philip rolled his eyes. "I wouldn't have brought him otherwise."

"Well that's lovely for Brooklyn, but I don't give a shit if he's a dealing-with-Christopher-Winthrop specialist. I'm fixing this because it is my life, my love, and my everything. Lying in bed, playing damsel-in-distress will just stress me out more."

"That's actually the truth." Jaime's hand hadn't wavered from my shoulder.

"Stubborn?" Brooklyn arched an eyebrow.

"You have no idea," Jaime smirked. "She's always an asset though."

"She's sitting right fucking here. There's no need to talk about me like I'm a God damn puppy," I snapped.

"You, my friend, are no puppy. You're a pit bull. Which I appreciate." He smiled a positively boyish and mischievous grin. I couldn't help that my smile turned up slightly to match.

Brooklyn took over after that. We'd all taken up tasks he doled out. Security panel reviews, frame by frame photo evaluations, identification of employees. In theory, I understood what we were looking for but nothing held my attention.

I had been trying to call Nick repeatedly and when that didn't work, I phoned Terrence. He informed me Nick wasn't taking calls. Instead he was smashing scotch glasses when anyone knocked on the door. Once when Terrence was checking again for me, likely dodging glass or crystal again, I started to scribble out a list of all the offenses, large and small, that had been leveled against Nick and I. I included everything from Ally to the poisoning. I aimlessly traced the letters over and over.

Every so often I'd scan the room and catch Brooklyn studying me. The fourth time it happened I snapped. "What Brooklyn?"

"What changed?"

"Excuse me?"

"This all started up four months ago. What happened four months ago?"

I bit my lip as I thought over the past few months.

Four months ago . . . September . . .

What the fuck had changed in September? I pulled up my calendar and started looking over the notes that had been plugged in.

"Us." I mused down at my BlackBerry.

"What?" Brooklyn stood up and leaned toward me at the same time Jaime shook his head and scoffed.

"Us. We got back together in September." I met Brooklyn's eyes.

"Kate, that's not . . ." Jaime started.

"No, that's exactly it." Brooklyn's green eyes glowed. "You went public in September. The press, the partnership, the brawl, those were all in September."

"All that was very uncharacteristic of Bryant," Jaime added.

"Yeah." Brooklyn shook his head. "And those events proved pit bull over here mattered more than most."

At the exact moment Brooklyn gave voice to it, my heart shuddered. It sat so well, I didn't even pause to snark at the dog remark, *other* words were tumbling out. "He knew Nick was happy . . ." My words trailed off, at the realization that Christopher had done whatever he could to make sure Nick didn't get a happy ending.

"He pulled in Piper to push you away. Victor to pick apart the business." Brooklyn was still being succinct, efficient. "He had to know what Francis . . ." My eyes snapped up, warning him with a slightly crazed face to shut up. He had the decency to stop short and even throw in an apologetic, almost sorrowful shrug.

"They were all just pawns. In a game to ruin my fiancé. If what he had on Piper is any sign of what he has on Victor, I don't know how we make this go away." I was having a hard time not choking on the facts.

"I need a list of what's important to you as a couple."

My eyes fell to the paper I'd been doodling on.

"Outside of the people we love?" The track record of attacking them was pretty straightforward.

"People, places, anything." Brooklyn was watching me intently as if I'd had the answer all along, I only needed to unearth it.

I stared into the ghostly green of his eyes. They didn't swirl, they didn't cloud—hell, they didn't move—they just pulsed with a luminescence that cut through me. I wondered idly if he used them against people, forcing them to spill their deepest secrets, sometimes secrets they didn't even know they had.

He was dangerous. And I was grateful his powers of persuasion were on my side.

"There's no need to make a list." The answer was staring me right in the face. Well rather, it was the only thing *not* scribbled down on the yellow lined paper. I picked up the legal pad and tossed it across the desk. It spun and slid for just a moment before Brooklyn caught it with catlike reflexes, his eyes still boring into my skull. "It's Vesper."

Jaime rounded the table, reading the list over Brooklyn's shoulder. Both sets of eyes reacted, Jaime's going narrow and fierce, Brooklyn's taking on an unearthly glow.

"The decoy is to keep us busy. He knew that Nick wouldn't come. He knew that you would. He did very simple math to figure out how to take finish the job with one swift move. "

Dread settled into my bones. Thick, heavy, almost consuming. My heart started rattling again. My body was panicking because it was completely and utterly true. When the table suddenly shook beneath my fingertips, I was convinced that this was it. I was finally going to succumb to the Tetrahexa-whatever.

"That was an explosion," all eyes snapped to Brooklyn when he spoke.

"What?" I cocked my head back. Jaime's hand flew to his holster. As if on cue, the conference table shuddered again. The glass chattered too.

"Minor. Sounded like a fire extinguisher," Brooklyn continued nonchalantly as panic filled up the rest of the room.

"Yeah because types of explosions are distinguishable." I arched my eyebrow as I crossed my arms.

"They are, Kate. Quite." He shot me a look. "They explode in high heat fires," he said simply as the fire alarm started blaring through the office. The lights shut off and a strobe blared in time with the siren. Jaime flew to the phone and started barking orders as Brooklyn ran to me. The blaring fire alarm cut off Jaime's words but didn't stop Brooklyn from scooping me up like a sack of potatoes.

"Put me down." I kneed his chest to get his attention but he just kept barking instructions at any being we passed.

We were in a stairwell when the second rumble shook the structure. The lights in the stairwell flickered but Brooklyn's footsteps didn't falter in the least. Emergency lights flashed on a moment later and they gave an eerie glow to the concrete. A disembodied and utterly evil cackle floated through the air.

My heartbeats started doing things they never had before. They smashed against my ribs and flattened my lungs. I writhed on his shoulder, the unearthly howl now echoing from above was ominous but the thumps emanating from my chest, and signaling the end of my life was far worse.

The bright light blinded me.

I scrambled on Brooklyn's shoulder to shield my eyes from the daylight. We'd made it outside just in time to hear the awful crack of splintering glass. The pangs increased with ferocity, echoing off the neighboring buildings as they ratcheted to fast and furious sounds. Then the sounds stopped for a single breath, an ominous sign before a windowpane thunder clapped above. Shards of all sizes rained down on us. The boom was so loud, it wasn't a usual tinkling of falling glass, but rather a crystalline roar with accents of sharp glass screech. Smoke billowed from the now gaping hole of my twenty-second floor office.

Brooklyn swore and got me out of the spray by shoving me onto a nearby window ledge covered by a thick green awning then turned and tore away. I watched his three-piece suit disappear around the corner just before the massive shower pelted the ground. Only the window behind me caught my teetering body, The large pane clattered against my weight then came alive in time with the thumping of my heart.

My world was a mix of the crashing glass and blaring fire alarms, yet my heartbeat tried to overshadow the chaos. And when a new three-piece suit stepped in front of me, it succeeded.

"Where is your security?" Victor Alexander hissed at me.

I couldn't really hear his words over the uproar inside me. I shook my head and my eyes went wide as saucers, but that was all I managed.

"Kate, where are the bastards responsible for you?" The sirens nearing helped cut through the din and this time I could process. Processing didn't help though. If I answered truthfully, Victor would know how vulnerable I was. I'd hold the door wide open for whatever was coming next.

"We've got to get you to safety before Christopher realizes you're alone." His head whipped back and forth. "An ambulance maybe?" He was thinking out loud, more to himself than anything. His lips kept moving with options, ideas, mumbling, his eyes rolled back in his head.

"You want to help me? I still can't figure out *why*?" I couldn't help the frustration that dripped from my lips.

"Kate, I know you have no reason to trust me. But Christopher is playing with us all. He can link me to some rather *unsavory* things. I tried to warn you without implicating myself. Until I saw what he did to Piper, I thought it was worth playing along. Then he started using me to do unspeakable things. This . . ." Victor's voice trailed off as he looked up and down the street again, slower, more sorrowful this time. "This isn't revenge, it's chaos."

His hand came to my upper arm and pulled me brusquely off my stone perch. I couldn't function outside of clutching my chest; I didn't know if I would resist him anyway. My heart had jackknifed as Victor spoke and now my chest ached like the bones themselves were the splintering glass. Victor wheeled me toward the arriving emergency vehicles only to freeze one second later.

"Let her go, Victor." Jaime and Brooklyn were stalking toward us.

Both had guns raised and the most severe faces I'd ever seen. I wanted to tell them to hold on, to allow Victor an explanation but my heart was reacting all the more violently to the site of steel barrels pointed in my direction. My knees buckled and I slumped to the pavement in a heap. Victor tried to soften my fall but didn't succeed, instead falling to his knees right next to me.

Jaime and Brooklyn started barking at us, or him, I couldn't even tell anymore. My whole head swam against the current of mayhem around us. The edges of my vision were going dark as both men bore down on us. I only noticed when Victor raised his hands in surrender because my body pitched forward further, my cheek headed for the ground.

A strong pair of arms were around me in a second, stopping me from hitting the debris-cluttered pavement. Jaime pulled me up to teeter on my stilettos while Brooklyn closed in on Victor. Jaime kept hold of me while he holstered his gun, taking most of my weight and with it, a lot of my fear.

Brooklyn was giving Victor explicit instructions on surrendering with the barrel of a pistol pressed to his temple. Victor was being perfectly compliant and I guessed it had little to do with the gun. When Brooklyn was able to fasten zip ties around his wrists, he tucked his firearm away, and my breathing slowed further. I noticed that the sirens had stopped, though red and blue lights reflected off every surface along the street. There were no more alarms from inside or labored breathing from the people nearest me.

I managed deep breaths, got up, and regained my balance on sky-high heels. Jaime let out a deep breath and managed a half smile when he felt me support my own weight. Brooklyn's eyes lit up and a full-blown smug smile split his too symmetrical face as he loomed over Victor.

"Did you use me as bait, Brooklyn?" I shrieked.

"Does it matter?" His smile didn't falter.

"Yes it fucking matters." I stomped my foot.

"Kate, your heart." Brooklyn arched an eyebrow and his smile spread further. If there weren't so many witnesses I would have throttled him. "I told you, I fix things. I didn't explain my methods, nor do I intend to. Matter of fact, I believe a thank you is in order. I've taken care of Victor." He looked positively devilish when he finished and gestured at the complacent man at his feet.

"You *did* use me as bait!"

"Kate, you know that in business you have to do a cost-benefit analysis. I did one. Victor versus your heart. I was right. Stop worrying about it.

My heart rattled in my chest, a reaction to the furious temper welling up at the cocky bastard. And for finding the cocky bastard painfully charming at the moment. My hand dropped from my chest as I opened my mouth to bicker with him nonetheless, but Victor beat us all to speaking. "I promise, I'm the least of your worries."

27.

Jaime's eyes went wide when Victor spilled his guts in the alley but Brooklyn hadn't even wavered. Hell, he hadn't even responded to Victor. He'd simply turned toward me and launched into a description of the way victims of Tetrahexazine were said to hemorrhage from their ears, nose, and mouth before they died then asked if, perhaps, that deserved my attention.

An overwhelming urge to choke swiftly replaced any thoughts that he held boyish charm. The only thing that stayed my hand was Jaime collecting me—mid-sentence and without asking—to take me home. And when my heartbeat went crazy all over again, he forced me out at the entrance to One Madison alone so he could park the car. As odd as it felt, there was no one there to back us up, what with being occupied by Vesper, or still in New Canaan, and I couldn't even walk from the garage around the block.

My heart had a vicious reaction to every step I took toward the building. It jackhammered in the elevator then each step to my bedroom hurt worse. I kept checking my eyes and ears and mouth, half expecting the blood Brooklyn had described to be oozing out of me. I didn't know what had set me off between Vesper and the apartment, but I knew it was *something*.

When I fell to my knees, clutching my heart, I knew I was going to die. Every cell in my body agreed. For the briefest moment, I closed my eyes and I lay on the floor waiting for a bright white light. Instead, I saw Nick. He filled my senses the way he always did, his smell, the feel of his skin, the swirl and marble of his eyes. The will to get back to him had me opening my eyes, forcing me to my feet and the last few steps to my closet.

I shrugged out of my well-worn, days-old Yves Saint Laurent suit and it laid piled on the floor when I realized the real reason my heart had gone haywire. A man's reflection appeared in the glass next to my lingerie clad form. The twisted smile and shockingly blonde hair had snuck in behind me, blocking my only exit.

"Don't bother calling for Jaime. He's not back yet."

Christopher's laugh sent goose bumps across every inch of my skin; I wanted to itch and crawl out of it. I reached out for the dresser to steady myself.

"I see the Tetrahexazine is still in your system," he snickered. "Better not work yourself up too badly."

My heart twisted in my chest. This thud was even more painful than the one moments ago and my body sank uncontrollably back to my knees. Christopher started laughing, a loud, harsh, soulless sound.

"This is going to be easier than I thought."

His detached voice did nothing to mask the sound of him shifting off the leather of the ottoman.

"You're more beautiful up close."

If I'd been paying attention to the reflection I would have noticed him slithering up behind me. I would have known he was about to touch me.

"It's that pale, smooth skin."

Instead, I was too busy trying to breathe—no, trying not to die—and his touch shocked me. I screamed and pitched forward, away from him, knocking against the dresser as I scrambled on hands and knees. Even though my heart was thudding in my ears, his laughter spliced through like a knife. I collided with the glass before turning to face him.

"There are those deep gold eyes and perky tits."

"Get." *Gasp.* "Away." *Agh.* "From." *Gasp.* "Me."

"Oh come now, Kate. I'm not going anywhere. I had to work so hard to coordinate this." He gestured between us, feigning hurt. "I had to start a massive fire at Vesper for this. For you."

"No." I barely eked it out through barred teeth.

My head lolled back and smacked against the glass.

"Victor really is very good at creating a diversion, isn't he? Him turning himself in worked even better than the original plan. Of course they sent you home. Of course there was no one to stay with you."

My thoughts were swimming as my head rolled side to side. My fingers were clawing at the purple bruises marring the swell of my breast.

This is what it feels like to die.

I couldn't do anything when he came up and straddled my legs. Every inch of my skin crawled as he got close; my heart reacted all the more violently, too. When I could feel the heat radiating off his skin I closed my eyes. I was going to picture Nick during my last minutes if it killed me.

Well no, Christopher is going to kill you but . . .

I tried to push those thoughts from my head, filling my mind with Nick instead. Every moment danced through my mind; everything from his naked body intertwined with mine to the way he looked at me over the morning newspaper. I made myself feel his lips against mine and see the color his eyes had been when he proposed.

My mind was completely focused on Nick when Christopher ran his hand across my cheek and shoved it into my hair. My eyes flew open, and I stared up and into the soulless gaze of Satan. I tried to struggle away from him but his hand curled into my long strands and kept me thoroughly pinned. He wore a truly wicked smirk as his free hand moved to his fly.

That movement snapped me out of it. I wasn't going to sit there and let Christopher fuck me. I was going to get back to Nick or die trying. I waited until Christopher started to work his pants down before launching my whole body at him.

My chest cavity constricted and the pain was on par with what being branded by hot iron had to be. But I rocketed off the glass with a lowered shoulder and lunged straight into him. I did my best to get my shoulder into his crotch and judging by his howl something hit my mark.

I screamed for Jaime as I careened toward the door, sure he had to be up here by now. Desperately praying he was up here, I ricocheted off every surface, clattering furniture and sending clothing flying from its hangers. I didn't get a chance to cry out again because a hand clamped down on my ankle. Christopher yanked, and I crashed to the floor.

"I don't think so you little whore."

He was pulling me back into the closet.

"No!"

I clawed at the floor desperate to get to the bedroom; I'd even pull up carpeting.

If I can just get to the doorframe.

I flailed wildly hoping I would propel me forward, or him back. Any way possible.

"I like it when they struggle," he purred and it made my blood curdle.

Oh God, I forgot.

Bile rose in my throat, but I still refused to roll over and play dead. My fingers hurt where they dug at the floor.

"And I can't wait to tell my brother how you struggled. How you tried to get to him."

His unholy laugh filled the closet again and his hand moved up my leg.

"But that I fucked your ass on his carpet anyway."

Christopher's hand was on my lacy thong, pulling, when I found the strength, and mercifully the angle, to kick him in the face. He stumbled back, holding his wounded jaw. Free of his grasp, I clamored toward the bedroom door, screaming again.

Where the fuck are you Jaime?

My heart was far past painful. I was sure that Brooklyn's description of organs exploding and ears bleeding would happen at any moment, if it hadn't already. And honestly, I'd rather go that way. A ruptured, bloodied corpse wasn't pretty but my death wouldn't be on Christopher's fucked up terms.

I careened into a bookshelf as Christopher swore behind me.

"Jaime!" I finally projected my voice out into the open glass box of the apartment. The end of his name got a little mangled because Christopher caught up to me and shoved me up against the cable railing of the stairwell. One steel wire cut across my throat and closed off my airway. The other shoved against my lower ribs, hard enough to crack.

I couldn't move. I couldn't breathe.

Nick. Nick. Nick.

With every one of my last haggard heartbeats, that's what I was going to think. My knees quaked and my fingers went numb, my toes too. When my limbs went dead, I crumpled the rest of the way to the stairs where I was already limp beneath Christopher.

That crumble was my saving grace. Mostly because it turned from a collapse into a head over heels tumble down the staircase; something Christopher hadn't expected. My vision tunneled as I careened down the wooden slats and away from him.

I still couldn't hear Jaime. Matter of fact, I couldn't hear much of anything anymore. Just a constant, high-pitched ringing punctuating the *thump, thump, thump* in my chest. My legs weren't working right but I was still somehow moving forward. Well, maybe forward, directions didn't make sense anymore. Away from Christopher would have to suffice.

His hands came back to me and I shoved with all my might. The new wave of momentum sent my body tumbling, rag doll-like down the last few stairs and onto the living room floor. My cheek came to rest against the wood floor and I focused on the windows where I'd first gotten to have Nick. I couldn't move. My vision blurred then started to fade to black as I focused on the glass.

Nick, I love you.

Whether I said the words out loud or not, I don't know. All I know is I felt Christopher's hand on my ankle, pulling me toward the couch.

My body stuck slightly as it slid across the floor. Only small flashes of furniture passed in front of me.

Right before everything went black, I thought I saw shiny dress shoes shuffle in front of my face. I couldn't be sure though because at that moment my heart gave one, loud, deafening thud before stopping all together.

Nicholas Bryant . . .

28.

A familiar slow, methodical, and mechanical beeping brought me around. Just like last time, it was piercing through a deep and dreamless blackness.

"God damn it."

"Kate?" I knew that voice. I loved that voice.

"Laur, I'm in the hospital again aren't I?" I asked without opening my eyes and, this time, my voice sounded like my own.

"Yup." She emphasized the U making the word five syllables long.

"Is he here?"

"No honey, he still isn't answering the phone. Colton tried to tell him but . . ."

"But what?"

I heard the beeping pick up pace but my heart didn't thunder like before.

"But, turns out your husband has quite a temper on him." I could hear the inherent roll in her eyes. "Wouldn't even let Colton get the words out. He doesn't know. About any of it." Laura's face pinched as her small hand started to rub up and down my forearm.

"Where is Christopher," I asked, my voice cutting out on his name.

"Evading everyone like usual," Laura responded with equal difficulty.

My heart thudded, a hollow space missing the one thing that made it whole. Nick.

"I need to be with him."

"You need to rest first, Doll," she scoffed.

"She's right. You *must* give your body time to recover. You were legally dead." Dr. Chambers had joined us.

My breath naturally caught and I started gnawing on my lips. I moved to sit more upright in the bed.

"Fine."

"It's imperative for both you and the baby."

Baby? Huh?

I studied Dr. Chamber's face. Surely he'd started speaking Korean because, I couldn't process what he'd just said. When Dr. Chambers' subtle, serene smile broke across his face, I barked, "What?"

"It's quite new, so I wasn't sure whether you knew. Regardless, everything looks to be in order."

A detached part of me watched Dr. Chambers' smile grow and Laura's jaw drop. But the rest of me just sat there, staring blankly at the doctor. Nothing crossed my mind. Literally, nothing. It was just one big vacant, gaping cave-hole *thing*. The monitor picked up pace again but my chest still didn't ache.

Huh, what do you know, the heart thing is gone. Brooklyn must have found the antidote. On the black market. Does one go to the black market? Or is there a website for that stuff? On TV it's like a back door chat room. Does Brooklyn hang out in seedy places? Or just on seedy websites? Probably both. He looks like he's killed a man. . . .

I twisted and idly watched the jagged lines on the monitor.

"Kate, you're pregnant?" That still detached part of me determined Laura was somewhere between shocked and disgusted. If I was processing things, I might have felt similarly.

"She is, about a month in as far as we can tell. According to Brooklyn Hart the synthetic progesterone of her birth control was eliminated by the Tetrahexazine. You've been able to conceive since your first dose of the toxin on New Year's Eve. You'll need to see an OB-GYN. Do you have one?"

Dr. Chambers was scribbling on the clipboard and I found myself wondering if he was one of those doctors with obscenely illegible handwriting.

"Kate, do you have one?" Laura's tone shifted to worried.

"Do we know how much damage the business sustained? How far will it set back production? I need to contact Damien and see what kind of hit my portfolio takes because of this. Perhaps Callista can use her connections to locate a suitable temporary location if need be. Something available immediately. Mac will need to look over the provisions of our lease and see what we are responsible for. Does he handle insurance, too? Can you hand me my phone? "

I held my hand out to Laura. All my tubes twisted, my IV pulling at the crook in my elbow. One of the monitors started screeching but I sat there, waiting for my BlackBerry. My fingers gestured impatiently while they stayed outstretched.

"I need to get Gemma back to the city from New Canaan."

The massive to-do list auto-populated in my head.

"Ms. Elliott, you have to rest. It's critical for both of your lives." Dr. Chambers was eyeing me over the clipboard.

"Have we heard anything about the initial FiTech numbers? The marketing plan may need revisiting."

"Ms. Elliott, I'm ordering at least one week of bed rest." Dr. Chambers voice was more authoritative this time.

"She's in denial, Dr. Chambers. Either that, or she finally short circuited. Either way I'll force rest on her."

You bet your ass I'm in denial about . . . about . . . about . . . oh my God.

That was the closest I could get to acknowledging Dr. Chambers' words. More items on my to-do list started tumbling out even though I vaguely acknowledged no one was there to put them into action.

"I've been meaning to tell Elena that I think the high wasted pants are actually a phenomenal idea. The gold nautical style buttons might even be ok. I mean they're not overly functional . . ."

"When can I take her home?" Laura interrupted but I kept mumbling.

"If she's actually going to rest, I'll prepare discharge papers now."

I was still murmuring my thoughts about the fall clothing line when Dr. Chambers left, and Laura cleared her throat. My mumbles shifted to internal rants. At some point I decided to remodel the Hampton's house. Laura eyed me skeptically, particularly when I stopped answering the hospital staff and she had to become my mouth piece.

Even once we were in the car, heading back toward New Canaan, I remained consumed. I'd sent 42 emails, mostly to myself, since Dr. Chambers had told me about *the thing*. It wasn't until we were 20 minutes from the Winthrop castle and I'd run out of action items and resolutions that the problem at hand finally snapped against my skin like a giant stinging rubber band.

My breath caught in my throat as my hands smacked against the dash and the door. I couldn't help but shriek. The tires of my Porshe squealed when Laura slammed on the breaks. The rear part of the car even swerved slightly.

"Oh God! Oh my God!" I gasped. "I'm pregnant. My life is over. Ruined. He's going to leave me. Up and leave me!"

I was hyperventilating. My heart wasn't hammering anymore but that didn't stop my chest constricting in a vice.

"Took you long enough," she mumbled under her breath. "Don't you think you're overreacting slightly?" she asked more directly this time.

"First I killed his mother. Then his investment. Now, this . . . this . . . this." I just pointed my hands at my stomach, unable to even speak the words.

"Whoa, whoa, whoa. You are definitely overreacting." I saw her roll her eyes in the rearview mirror at my absurdities but I just kept on vomiting words.

"We're not baby people. He's not baby people. He didn't sign up for this. He's a business magnate, he likes to drink scotch late at night and we have sex on . . . on . . . on everything. I don't blame him for leaving me." I gasped for air and my mind raced faster than my mouth.

"Remind me never to sit on your furniture." Laura was letting me barrel on.

"Fuck! Shit! Why me? Why did I get a taste of him just to have it all ripped away." I collapsed back into the seat.

The firm rasp of knuckles against the glass didn't pull me out of my spiral. Laura held up a finger to Jaime or Colton or whoever was standing there.

"Are you ready for a reality check or shall I let you continue?" Her finger was still at the window but she'd shifted her full attention to me. I managed a weak shrug. "Kate, you have got to get your shit together and give Nicholas a little more credit than that. He loves you more than life itself. Even you two psychopaths can figure something out." She chuckled as she tried to reach for my shoulder. I jerked my arm away, hitting the passenger window instead and swearing.

"I'll never kiss him again, never hear him breathing shallow beside me. Oh God! I'll never see those bright blue eyes."

I lost it. I wrenched open the door and dry heaves shook my body. Jaime rounded the hood and growled, "What the hell is happening in here?"

"Everything's fine. She's having a delusional attack. She just needs a moment."

Jaime's hand came to my back and gently rubbed.

"I have to tell him Laura. I have to tell him . . . *this*," I sneered, disgusted.

"Tell who, what?" Jaime asked over top of my bent body and Laura murmured back but I couldn't make out the words. I was too busy getting sick again.

"Kate, he's going to be thrilled," she soothed.

"No. No fucking way!"

Oh God, he really is going to leave me.

"Language."

"Not even remotely funny."

I knew she said it to lighten the mood but it flared my temper, making me even more erratic than I already was. I wretched again.

The car sat silent for a little while, everyone letting me catch my breath. Finally, I sat back, gracelessly wiping my chin. Laura and Jaime watched intently, both unsure I should be out of the hospital.

"You know you could always get rid of it." Laura swallowed hard. "He'd never have to know."

Those words hung heavy between us. My mind started to reel and my heart picked up pace at the thought. I sat up and wrapped my arms around my stomach and let my fingers curl into my sides. If the thought of being pregnant terrified me, the thought of *not* being pregnant was like my soul bottoming out and my insides disintegrating to dust.

I couldn't get rid of a piece of Nick, no matter how small. He was the reason I kept breathing. Keeping another piece of him didn't console me, nor stop me from feeling like my world was crashing down around me. I'd reached the pinnacle of *everything* just in time to have it stolen.

Fuck. Fuckfuckfuck!

Jaime rubbed my thigh and Laura my shoulder. Nothing but the breeze interrupted the thick and heavy silence. Eventually Laura spoke up.

"Kate, you need to be in the same room as Nicholas."

I shook my head. I couldn't be in the same room with him. Face to face. I wouldn't be able to hide these things from him, and once he knew, everything we were would . . . *poof.*

"Laura's right, getting back is probably for the best." Jaime squeezed above my knee then shut the door behind him.

Laura put the car back in drive and crept onto the road. I wanted to stop her but I was too preoccupied with the turmoil rolling around in my head. Would he be pissed? Would he look at me with his icy disdain? Would I ever get a sweet moment with him again? Would I ever get a moment to myself again?

"Pull over I'm going to be sick again."

"Nope. You're not actually." Laura shrugged matter of factly.

"I think I know my body better than you. I said I'm going to puke."

"Not if you just relax. You're working yourself up over nothing."

"Nothing?" I threw my arms in the air as I screeched. "He's

probably going to leave me. Then I'll be stuck with a kid that is absolutely screwed! How is that nothing?"

"Oh my God, Kate. If your child is anything like its mother, then rebellious drama in its teens lies ahead, but you are not screwed." She sighed and let her hand wave above the steering wheel. "You have some control issues, a temper, and the mouth of a sailor but you'll rein those in as needed. You always do."

We were pulling into the long driveway of the Winthrop estate. The massive house was even more depressing this time around. In daylight, the gray stones were more befitting a dungeon than a castle; the red roof tiles completed the look. And from my seat where we idled in the circular driveway, I felt it was full of ghosts.

Laura turned the key and the slight purring beneath us stopped. She let the silence grow until it threatened to swallow me. Somewhere along the line, I started chewing on my lip and rubbing my chest out of habit.

"You're just wasting time. Time you could be spending with him." I stayed stalk still in the passenger seat and she sighed. "Kate, you've got to give him more credit. And while you're at it, give yourself a little more too."

Despite all my fears, that feeling I got around Nick started to build. He was here. Just on the other side of the stone wall in front of me. And I was sitting in the car instead of running to him. My familiar yearning tangled with dread, and reminded me of the way Nick's eyes could storm.

What color would they turn when I told him? My whole world hinged on whether they would go flat gray or shine bright blue. I could sit here and wonder, or go in and find out.

29.

I waved off Laura and Jaime, telling them I was fine.

Fucked up. Insecure. Neurotic. Emotional.

Fine.

Terrence greeted us at the door and his brow furrowed at whatever emotion was hanging on my face. I slid past him and trudged toward the study. It was just a hunch that Nick was where I'd found him last time. When Terrence stepped in front of Laura and stopped her from following me down the long corridor, I knew I was right.

I forced a deep breath into my lungs as my hand rested on the study doorknob.

It could be the last time I find Nick on the other side.

Everything in me seized. Laura could go screw herself. Two things were certain: I was going to be sick and I was going to run. I choked back bile as my hand dropped from the brass. I turned and started clipping back down the hallway. Fear hijacked my entire being making me pick up pace.

Two strong hands appeared from nowhere and caught me, wrapping around my upper arms and stopping me from breaking into a full-tilt run.

"Go back in there," Jaime spoke softly but sternly as he turned me back down the hall. "Now."

I stood still for a moment or two, even after Jaime let go. He gently nudged me, and I stutter stepped forward just to freeze all over again. The corridor seemed to stretch out further before me, like Silly Putty when it was stretched too far and went wonky. My knees wavered but then Jaime said my name, this time a fatherly warning, and somehow my feet found the ability to move.

When I reached the door, my hand limply grabbed the brass. As I held it, I turned to look back down the hall. Jaime stood, stance wide and arms crossed over his barrel chest. He cocked his head when I looked longingly to his side toward freedom. I sighed and finally managed to turn the knob and nudge the door open.

Nick was draped over a chaise lounge in the corner, highlighted by the last bit of late afternoon sun. He was wearing a t-shirt and a pair of sweats that hung low on his hips. His hair fell down into his eyes, waving in every single direction. I could trace the outline of every muscle under his shirt. He was a living, breathing wet dream.

MMMmmm.

My body reacted immediately, my muscles relaxed, and my skin goose bumped. I caught my lip between my teeth as my breathing hitched up. When I shut the door behind me, he stirred.

"Get out," he grumbled.

"Nick it's me. Are you okay?" I was trying desperately not to let my heart bottom out.

"I know isss you." He was dead drunk. "And I said ge'out."

I started chewing on my lip. Could he read my mind that well? Did he already know I was ruined? I wanted to scream, "I need you! Now more than ever!" but for the first time I didn't want to fight. I wanted to go back to those days before Hong Kong when he'd been *too* nice and things had been *too* normal.

But too much had changed.

I walked purposefully over to him and heard crunching under my shoes. As I got closer, I realized the sound came from broken glass scattered across the floor. Near his feet the pieces got larger and sharper.

"Kate, get the fuck out!" he roared and I broke.

"Nick, please." I was desperate and definitely not above begging.

"I know I shouldn't have left but it was important." My fingers dug into my palms as my knees fell to the carpet by his side, glass be damned. "Baby, I know it doesn't seem like it, but I did it all for you. You're my world. I love you. Please don't send me away." My tone was every bit as frantic as my heart had been a few days ago.

He sat up, reached down and grabbed my shoulders, his grip tighter than even I was used to.

"Ouch!" I couldn't help my yelp as he lifted me from my crouch by his knees.

He wobbled a little when he stood up close to me and it made me roll my ankle. I would have fallen to the floor if it weren't for his grasp.

Once he got his feet back under him he brusquely shoved me out of the room. He shut the door in my face, it even snapped against my nose. Tears pooled in my eyes and thick, wild sobs broke the hold I had on my lip. They echoed off the melancholy stone.

At the slamming and sobbing, Laura came running down the hallway. She gathered me into her arms as best she could and hugged me tightly.

"What happened?" Her words were sandwiched by shushes.

"He. Told me. To get. Out," I was stuttering. And hyperventilating.

"After you told him you were pregnant he kicked you out?" Her voice shot up a few octaves as she dropped her arms, turned around, and started banging on the door. "Bryant! You get out here now!" she bellowed and hammered on the door.

My arms wove around my body, trying to keep that feeling of fracturing at bay. I turned and walked away without a single word to Laura, fighting shakes as I went. What I wanted most was scotch. Scotch would warm my limbs and settle the tremors. When I remembered I couldn't have a glass, fear squeezed on the sobs making for a wholly mangled sound.

I crumpled to the staircase and dropped my head into my hands. The slightest, softest footsteps were coming toward me but I couldn't right myself.

"Hey, Kate." Ari's voice was soft and hoarse. "I didn't know you were back. He'll be happy."

Her words pushed more tears down my cheeks. I couldn't help it. She noticed, sat, and wrapped her arms around my shoulders.

"Everything will be okay." She leaned her head onto my shoulder.

Laura and Bryant's bellows ripped through the house, ping pong-ing off the stone walls and down the hall.

"Laura's here too? Is everything okay?"

"He doesn't want me anymore, Ari. He told me to get out but I . . . I . . ." The sobs choked my words and I shook again.

"Kate," Ari scolded ever so gently.

Any further conversation was interrupted by more shouting and the slamming of doors. I cringed and shrunk down into my shoulders. An instant later, Nick was in front of me, grabbing me by the shoulders again.

"Ahhh . . ." I winced as he pulled me up to standing.

He wordlessly continued yanking, this time up the stairs, more a brutish savage than his usual self.

"Nick, you're hurting me." I knew I sounded whiny and upset, but I *was* whiny and upset.

Ari, Laura, Gemma, and Jaime were all standing at the bottom of the stairs, watching us go. They all had something to say, right over top of the other, about the way Nick was handling me.

He pulled me all the way to the white room we'd claimed days ago and pushed me across the threshold. I almost stumbled but his hand found my arm again and pulled me back to my feet just before I top-pled. The door slammed shut behind us as he started roaring.

"I'll admit 'mmm drunk. I've drunk enough scotch to drown my sorrows. Twice. So I asssept that I am probably the one missing some-thin'." The words were slurry, stilted, and not what I expected. "Why was Laura yellin' at me? Wha' did I do wrong now?"

I looked up at his face, his eyes were every bit the reflection of my insides. Swirling, overwhelmed, and bewildered.

"I jusss wanted you away from the broken glasss." *What?* "I broke a couple of bottles in there." He paused and his eyes searched the ceil-ing. "Okay, like sssix bottles in there." He laughed a pitiful, heartless laugh, his lips staying in his permanent frown.

As usual, I was compelled to comfort that tormented face. I reached out and cradled his cheek with my hand. He leaned tenderly, though rather sloppily, into it.

"I jus got so angry that you were gone. Then I got angry that I couldn't pull my shit together. And then I was out of scotch." A single tear ran down his cheek and pooled against my fingertips. "This is all my fault," he whimpered. "I know it wasn't safe for you in the room with the glass but wha' did Laura ge'so mad about it?"

My poor, confused, drunk Nick.

Looking through scotch tinted glasses the whole scene made sense. I could relate and I melted.

"Oh, baby." My voice was as soft and as soothing as I could make it. "It was a miscommunication. I thought you wanted me out of this house. She thought you wanted me out of your life. I have some bad news . . ." I was going to rip the Band Aid off and tell him right here, right now but he started babbling over top of me.

"Outta this house? Why on earth would I want you outta the house? I've been counting the minutes till you were back. I tried ta leave the house to come get you but I . . . I . . . I just couldn't. I needed you. I wanted you. I want you now."

He snatched my hand from my body and pulled it to his cock. My breath caught when I touched his rock hardness through his soft sweatpants. I couldn't help it when my fingers wandered over the outline then stroked.

Drunk Nick didn't need further encouragement. He mashed his lips to mine, our teeth clanging against one another. His tongue started frantically exploring my mouth and his hands tangled up into my hair. My lips were trapped against his even as I tried to gasp for air.

This was us, this was what we did best. And us was what I was terrified of losing. I melted into him, letting him push and pull against my lips as he pleased.

Stop, you have to tell him.

The force with which my body rejected that thought was surprising. "Not now." I didn't mean to speak out loud.

Luckily, Nick didn't notice, either. As soon as my lips moved frantically like his, he wrapped an arm around me and started pulling me toward the bed. He shoved the jacket off my shoulders and it softly thumped to the floor. My undershirt wasn't tight but he struggled with the fabric as we both tumbled to the comforter.

MMMmmm.

His muscles shifted underneath my fingertips, and more importantly, his heart beat against mine. His drunken hands fidgeted at the button of my pants while my lips wandered across his face. My hips pressed against his, rubbing as we both became inpatient. I pulled away and he whimpered in response.

I was gone just long enough to peel my jeans off. A lazy smirk pulled across my face as I bent to pull his sweats off. He smiled a broad, delirious smile and made grabby hands at me. I crouched to slip them off and kissed each of his knees then stopped short.

For the first time, the thought of being on display in front of him made me nervous. What my body actually looked like made no difference; I was completely and utterly self-conscious. When I stood, I'd be naked *and* pregnant in front of him.

It took me a moment to gather the courage to slither up next to him. By the time I did, soft snoring came from his rugged frame atop the comforter. I dropped my head and it shook of its own accord.

I sighed and sat back. The knot that balled in my throat and accompanied my tears was growing. I wanted him one last time while it was simple chemistry and nothing else. But after everything he'd been through, and the undoubted sleepless nights, waking him was a level of selfish I wasn't comfortable with.

So instead, I studied his face. There were his usual firm lines, a strong jaw, and his soft long lashes. But there were more worried creases now, the dark shadow of full beard scruff filling in, and the crust of too many tears hung heavy around his eyes. The sadness that hung on his features matched my downheartedness.

With a sigh, I tucked him in, careful not to jostle the bed too much. I curled up in the comforter at his side, and even deliriously drunk, his body recognized mine, bending around my shape.

This was going to change—no—*everything* was going to change.

My mind raced. A few times I even thought my heart problems started back up. I was going to have tell him about Victor, Christopher, Vesper and the baby all at once.

I need a scotch and cell phone. Doctor's orders be damned.

I wiggled to get both, but Nick's arm kept me pinned firmly to the mattress.

A sigh slipped passed my lips, more exaggerated than strictly necessary, as I resigned myself to stay put. Panic induced to-do lists barreled through my brain as furiously as they had after Dr. Chambers had delivered the news. The compulsion to get angry or drunk grew even stronger.

I'm the last person that should be allowed to have a child.

That was a surefire way to spiral. I forced myself to memorize brocade curtain patterns, count ceiling panels, and trace book bindings where they sat on dark shelves instead. There was so much in the room that I kept occupied for hours and eventually my mind cleared.

When soft sunlight warmed my face, I realized I'd fallen asleep and shot straight up. Or tried to anyway. Nick was still woven around me.

"Thank God you're back. For a second I thought I dreamed that." Nick was mumbling into his pillow and I was going to answer when he continued, "I think I remember shouting at Laura. I definitely remember kissing you. Did you say something about bad news?"

Oh fuck. Goddamnedfuckingshitpiss.

"How are you feeling?"

"Like hell, Sweets, but that doesn't change that I need to know the bad news."

Duck, dodge, bob and weave. Then maybe, just maybe, I can stretch it out long enough to have him once more.

Mercifully, there was a knock at the door. I let out a deep breath I didn't know I was holding.

"What do *they* want?" Nick's growl sent shivers down my spine.

"Do they think they can bother me now because you're here to broker peace?"

"I doubt anyone wants to bother you at all, ever again for that matter. Particularly after last night. They're probably here to speak to me." I untangled myself from Nick and his disproving look, grabbing a sheet in lieu of a robe. Jaime was waiting patiently, face drawn, on the other side of the door.

"Kate, are you okay? You don't look like you got any sleep . . ." Jaime was whispering as he reached out to rub my arm. I tried to find a reassuring smile but nothing could change the set of my lips.

"What's up?"

Nick was tossing and turning behind me in bed. Jaime must have noticed too because he creased his brow as he snuck a glance behind me.

"Brooklyn is on the phone and he needs to speak with you. He has additional details on the fire and a few recommendations to make." Jaime sighed and I squinched my face, remembering the real world.

I nodded. "I'll be right out. Could you possibly have the staff prepare breakfast?" Nick would need something for this hangover.

"I would but apparently, he's fired everyone."

Of course he has.

It was something I would do in a fit of rage too.

"Fine. Meet me in the kitchen. I'll cook breakfast." I shut the door before he had a chance to respond and scooped my clothes off the floor. I sighed heavily as I slipped back into my T-shirt and jeans.

"This have anything to do with this bad news?" Nick eyed me suspiciously.

I simply shot him a look over my shoulder and decided I wasn't answering questions right now.

"What would you like for breakfast?"

"You're going to cook?"

"Yes, Nick. But I have business to attend to, so simpler would be better."

"What business?" He seemed equally intrigued and grouchy

about it.

"We'll discuss it later." My answer was short as I padded out the door. "Pancakes?" I didn't wait for the answer before pulling it shut behind me.

30.

Brooklyn *had* been busy. He'd been able to question Victor, draft formal charges with his uncle and had a lead on a temporary space for Vesper. He'd hired additional security for One Madison and The Venture Group properties; he simply needed the financial okay to move forward.

Christopher had vanished into thin air after he and Jaime had fought in the apartment.

I was whipping egg whites with the phone pinned beneath my ear when the room fell silent. My voice echoed off the stone and the chatter of my whisk bounced off every wall. I turned to find every single person twisted awkwardly to watch Nick as he strolled in and took a seat at the kitchen island. I paid him no attention but noticed how everyone stepped back from the hunched ball of pissy that was my fiancé.

"Thank you Brooklyn. For everything. Please make sure your uncle knows just how grateful I am as well." I focused on preparing the food in front of me rather than the way Nick's eyes narrowed when I said it.

I hung up and handed the phone back to Jaime, the whole room held a collective breath as I put bacon on to sizzle.

"Smells delicious, Kate." Nick's voice was perfectly flat and I could picture his eyes, steely and intense. "Anyone want to tell me what's going on?"

"Jaime, please move forward with everything Brooklyn recommends except the temporary space. I need to see what the final damage was to the building before making that decision."

My hand pressed into my chest out of habit.

"What's going on Kate?" Nick's temper was barely bridled.

"Jaime, I know it's not technically within your scope, either, but can you coordinate things for the Hampton's house."

"I'm happy to help." Gemma smiled as she piped up and patted Jaime's arm.

Jaime smiled down on her and nodded. Both pulled out cell phones, and stepped out of the kitchen. I could hear them both start their respective conversations.

That should be me.

"Kate, you shouldn't be cooking, let alone on those phone calls." Laura warned over top of a cup of coffee, reading my thoughts.

Did she just say that in front of Nick?

My temper balled up in my throat. Something she didn't seem to notice because she had the audacity to add, "You're under doctor's orders." That did it, the small damn holding my temper at bay, broke.

I fired, "Screw you" back at her the same moment Nick growled, "What?" in my direction.

I'll kill her.

"Bryant we will discuss it later." I slammed the giant stack of pancakes I'd finished on the island and glared at Laura. I shoved the bacon at them a moment later and it slid across the stone a few inches before I stormed out of the room.

I was angry, helpless, scared, and to top it off, pretty damn nauseous.

This is all your fault isn't it?

I found myself looking down, pissed, at my stomach.

Laura yelled, "You should eat" from the kitchen. I screamed *fuck off Laura!* in my head but didn't give her the satisfaction of an actual reaction. I turned down an unfamiliar hallway hoping no one would follow.

The warm air seeping from the end of the hall drew me in and away from the chaos. I stepped through white french doors into a solarium—into heaven. The tropical air enveloped me like a friendly hug. I wandered around for a moment, smelling different flowers and letting my fingers trail across waxen leaves. For the briefest moment I could breathe and think and relax again.

Then my stomach lurched and I lost any hint of tranquility.

I plopped ungracefully onto one of the lounge chairs tucked in the back. The sun had been warming the yellow and white striped pillow and I let it do the same to my face as I laid back and tried to curl into a comfortable position.

Closing my eyes was relaxing for a moment but then it left me trapped in my own spiraling head. I let out an exasperated growl of my own just before Ari's giggle pealed from the other side of the palms. She rounded the corner into the hidden nook with a plate of pancakes.

"Not having the best week?" Despite everything, she was smiling a small sad smile.

"Nope. How about yourself?"

"Downright shitty. Thanks for asking." Her smile grew and it was infectious.

I crossed my knees, making room for her at the foot of the lounge. She sat and handed me the pancakes.

"Everyone was adamant that you should eat something. So adamant, in fact, they started arguing with each other. I figured that, as the only sane person left in the house, I would try and help."

I took the outstretched plate even though the normally delicious smell of bacon made my stomach flip. I picked at it for a while, eventually deciding to set it aside with a deepening frown. I'd give it a try once I didn't feel like heaving all over the place. Ari watched me carefully but didn't press the issue.

She stayed put, silently rubbing on my shin the way her mother would have. Emotion built in my throat again, even my hand started shaking. My anger had evaporated and I'd landed back on hurt.

"Do you ever get over it?" she asked quietly.

"Get over what, Ari?"

Ari turned away and I guessed it was because she didn't want to see the sorrow on my face when I answered. Her big, animated personality had deflated. I moved as far to the side as I could and patted the space next to me. She turned toward the sound and managed a forlorn, almost mocking grin.

"I don't know. All of it, I guess? The realization that your parents are gone forever?" she asked as she slid into place.

I sat staring at the ceiling, realizing the pattern here was even more soothing to trace than the ones I'd found in the perfectly crisp curtains of the white bedroom.

"Get over it? No. At least, I don't think so. It does get easier though. You don't focus on the pain as much after time, you just let it hang there, like a really heavy necklace." I sighed.

"How long has it been weighing on you?"

"Nine years."

"Still miss them?"

"Every damn day." I took a deep breath. "I wish they could meet Nick. I wish they could see Vesper, or *could have* seen Vesper." I corrected myself with a loud sigh. "I wish my dad was giving me away at my wedding. I wish my mom was here for advice about . . ." I let my voice trail off. I couldn't say *the baby* out loud yet. "Sometimes I just want a hug." I leaned my head to her shoulder and started chewing on my lip again.

"I didn't know my dad well enough but I'm going to feel that way about my mom aren't I?" She shrugged and I just nodded. "Kate, I'm really glad you're part of my family." She threw her arms around me.

Don't cry, don't cry, don't cry.

A future, complete with family, was falling through my fingers like tiny little grains of sand. The more I held on, the faster it was seeping out of my fist.

"We'll see about that." I couldn't help but picture the flat steel gray Nick's eyes would turn when I finally spilled everything.

"You're mine forever." Nick's voice rang through the room with its usual sincerity.

I jumped and my heart shuddered when it realized he was standing a few feet from us. His eyes were blazing blue and his brow crinkled in confusion. My eyes fell from his face to my fingers while we all sat there in a thickening silence.

My hand instinctually rubbed my chest. The antidote had worked so well my heart couldn't hammer but the gesture was oddly comforting. Nick took two purposeful steps before crouching next to me.

"Sweets, are you okay?" His hand came to my face and he gently stroked my cheek. "What the hell is going on?" His voice stayed sweet despite swearing.

"I think that's my cue." Ari stood and wove out of the room. She paused for just a minute. "Nicholas, you be nice to her or so help me God." He turned to yell at her and then caught the severity of her look and decided better of it.

He turned back to me, fully focused on my face. "I would never . . . I love you."

My eyes dropped away from his again. "For now." I sounded pitiful even to my own ears.

"No." He crooked his finger under my chin and pulled me up to face him dead on. "For always." His voice was adamant but I still couldn't force my eyes to meet his. "Are you leaving me?"

"What? No I . . ." My voice was shaky but he interrupted.

"Did you cheat on me?" I finally met his gaze, he was smirking.

It wasn't even a real question. He was proving a point.

"Never. But Nick . . ."

"No, Kate, no buts. That's all I need to know. We will get through anything else." His eyes became that deep blue that shown only for me. "I've been a wreck, and I'll apologize forever for that, but it doesn't change how I feel about you. About us."

"I'm so sorry." My voice got quiet and my eyes fell to the floor again. More than anything, I wanted to nuzzle into his hand. I just couldn't stop picturing that hand pushing me away.

"Sweets, tell me what is happening. I will get my shit together and fix it." He didn't force my eyes up, instead he crouched lower so he could look up at my pout. "I mean it. Just tell me."

I took a deep breath, then clammed up again.

"I will spank and or fuck it out of you." He chuckled slightly at a threat he'd used before. I couldn't help but crack a small smile and look back into the deep blue eyes I adored. "There's my girl. Story time or shall I follow through?" My tears came before I could even answer. "Hey, shhhhh." His thumbs rubbed on my cheek bones. "I just wanted to see you smile."

The words suddenly became every bit as easy as the tears.

"Do you remember what I said to you when I left?"

His brow knit together as his hands moved down my neck and rested on my shoulders, his eyes searched for the memory in the mortar of the bricks on the floor. Finally, his eyes focused back on me and he shook his head. My sigh was heavy and a little choked as he shifted to perch on the lounge with me.

I started at the beginning, telling him about what Laura had said about keeping him going, keeping the business going, then about the call I got from Julien. The longer the story went on, the more I could see his edges fraying, his eyes churning back to gray as I listed each development.

"Brooklyn Hart realized it was a trap before I did." Nick's breath hitched and I didn't know if it was about New York or Brooklyn.

"Victor was a pawn after all?"

I dropped my eyes back to my fingers, slowly swirling my engagement ring as I picked the story back up. The race out of the building, the fire, the events on the street. Somewhere in the middle of the story, Nick shot up and swatted at a plant nearby, totally unconcerned that ceramic shattered and soil flew through the pristine room.

This is going to get so much worse before it gets better.

I told him about the poison, about how Brooklyn sent me home. For the slightest second I saw blue filter back into his eyes.

Fuck.

When I got to the part about Christopher, his whole demeanor changed. He didn't rage like I anticipated. The mention of Christopher in our home drained all color from Nick's face.

"I fought him off as best I could, Nick." Tears dripped off my cheeks and onto my trembling bottom lip as I relived the memory.

"Did he . . . ?" Nick couldn't even finish his sentence. For the first time all day I was grateful, so unbelievably grateful—I was able to say no. Nick let out a deep breath and wrenched my body against his chest, tangling hands into hair as he pulled on me. "Thank God."

"Nick." I was talking against his shoulder now. "The stress on my heart was too much." He pulled back and stared directly into my eyes again. "They said I was legally dead when the EMTs arrived. I'm not sure how I survived. I woke up in the hospital. Two days later. That's why it took me so long to get back here."

"What?" Panic was plain on his face. His hands scrambled against my skin where he could reach, desperate to hold me even closer.

"Yeah." I finally drew blood where I bit my lip. "And that's not even the bad news."

31.

He must have sensed my fear—because that's what it was—bone chilling fear for the future. Nick hadn't planned for this. He couldn't want it. I certainly didn't. Everything I'd ever wanted was about to tumble to my feet.

"What? Please God, tell me you're going to be okay? You have to be okay." There was a tremble in his voice that matched my shaking fingertips perfectly.

"Define okay . . ."

Fuck, fuck, fuck.

"You said you weren't leaving me." His voice cracked, his hands pulling at my hair as he crushed me further to his chest.

"Nick, I'm pregnant." My lips whispered across his shoulder.

"Sweets, what did you say?"

I tried to push back from him. I needed air. When he wouldn't let me move I started to scramble against his chest, pressing harder and harder, panicking, desperate to take a full, deep breath.

And see his eyes.

"Kate, what did you just say?"

"I'm . . . pregnant." I stuttered and continually whomped against the immoveable boulder that was his chest.

"How?" He lessened his grip on me, letting me push him back, his eyes still watching me intently.

"The Tetrahexazine. It eliminates everything in your system."

"When?"

"I don't know Nick. It's not as if we've been celibate since New Year's." I would have smirked if there was anything but terror filling my chest.

"No, no we have not." His crooked smirk played on his lips. "Is this the bad news?" My favorite deep blue eyes studied me.

One last beautiful blue.

I could only manage another meek nod.

"So not the explosion, not the hit to our company, our assets. Not that you were attacked. Or even dead. None of those things are the worst news?"

"I've had time to think about all of those things," I squeaked. "I've got people working on solutions as we speak. But this? You didn't even want a relationship when I met you and here I've shoved the whole fucking mess of a family on you."

"I'm going to be a dad." His voice was quiet, awed. He wasn't listening to me anymore. He wasn't even remotely focused on the business. "Kate, you're going to have my baby?" His smile was growing with each moment. "And you aren't happy about this?"

"No, God no. What am I supposed to do now? Give up Vesper? Be barefoot in the kitchen? Move into some ridiculously huge house in the middle of nowhere like this? Give up everything that makes me, me? Everything that makes us, us?" Tears were coming back to my cheeks. "What will be left of the person you fell for? What will be left of the person I am?"

This time Nick used his grip still tangled in my hair to force my eyes to meet his.

"Are you serious right now?" he snarled at me.

"My life is over and I'm fucking stuck! And you're not going to want to be stuck with me." I started off screaming but ended with a whimper. "I don't want to be stuck with me."

Nick's hand fell away and my head naturally fell forward. I chewed on my tearstained lip, worried I would fall apart completely without him. I was able to keep from hyperventilating simply because he used his hand to pry my knees apart then pin me down to the chair.

"Let me address your points one by one." He lowered himself partially onto me and ran his nose along mine.

"First, the answer has been and always will be, do whatever you want. I'm quite sure nothing can stop you. Second, don't even think about giving up Vesper. I know we've joked about you staying chained to my bed, but we've also discussed that no one can run it like you. If you need to share responsibility, restructure. It's not that problematic." He moved his lips so they grazed against mine.

"Third, you already are barefoot in the kitchen occasionally. It's a wondrous and beautiful thing but never an expectation. Fourth, people raise children in the city all the time. The penthouse is certainly large enough." He started kissing on my neck, my body relaxed marginally as he did.

"Finally, and perhaps most importantly, you are amazing and we are electric. And you have never amazed me more. Nor have I ever wanted you more than I do right now. The sexiest thing I have ever pictured is you, as my wife, carrying my child. It makes me extremely hard."

He kissed my eyelids and then the tip of my nose and finally my mouth. "Nothing could lessen my feelings for you." He took my lips violently this time and pressed the weight of his body fully into mine. "Nor how desperately I need you and your body." He went back to my lips and nipped gently before lifting me. "Specially not this."

Nick was careful with me as he strode to the first room outside of the solarium. He kicked the door shut behind us and stood me on my feet facing away from him. My skin goose bumped as his hands travelled over me, reaching for the hem of my shirt.

"You aren't going to walk away? You'll take me whatever happens with this, this, this . . . ?" I was still having an exceedingly hard time with the word *baby*. "My body won't be the same." The words just blurted out. I couldn't help it. Even if it ruined the mood.

"I wouldn't walk away from you, ever. May I remind you, I never have." He trailed kisses up my neck to my ear and nibbled slightly before pulling my shirt up and over my head. "I want you until you're old and gray and hunched and every single moment in between. I found you because of this . . ." He skated his hands down my body. " . . . but I'm keeping you because of this." He moved his hand over my heart; it actually pounded in response.

Without another word, his hand moved toward my zipper. He pushed my pants to the floor, sucked in a very deep breath and stepped away from me. A chair puffed then creaked behind me. "So beautiful," he whispered reverently. "Turn around."

I did as I was told and faced him, finding deep clear pools watching me. My entire universe was looking back at me. A smile played across his lips, and his muscles bunched and flexed underneath his shirt as he shifted on the seat.

If I have to be pregnant, thank God it's with some small piece of that man.

That gorgeously wonderful, perfect man loved me exactly how I was. And however I would become. My mood shifted. Nick noticed and he tried to stifle his smile and slip his sexy, steely look in place. It didn't quite stick.

"Run your hands over your body. Caress and tease your skin. Every inch." My body obeyed before I even thought about it.

I took first one finger and started to trace up my arm, I swirled ever so slightly at the inside of my elbow where the skin was so sensitive I flushed. When my skin colored pink, Nick bit his lip but otherwise stayed still. I let my fingers drift slowly across my collarbone then back. With those sultry tracks, my nipples hardened. Nick's eyes twinkled.

"Play with your breasts the way I would." His voice was already gravelly, telling me this excitement was more than just enjoying the show.

My eyes fluttered shut and I finally found a broad, genuine smile as I brought my hands to my chest to tickle and twist. My breath kept catching as I played, somehow more sensitive than just a week ago. When my thighs started to press together and shift past one another, Nick crooked one finger at me, wordlessly asking me to come closer. I did and he pinched one nipple and pulled. Hard.

Wetness spread between my thighs but my body instinctively tried to back away, making the stinging sensation more intense. He chuckled his delicious, wicked laugh and let go of my breast.

"I want to see you touch yourself. Like I would."

I arched an eyebrow then seamlessly stepped wider.

I hadn't seen this coming; that he'd know the truth and want me anyway. I hadn't given him—or rather us—enough credit, just as Laura had said. The relief was palpable and my fingers were moving before I refocused. I slipped into my slit and my senses were consumed as a moan I couldn't contain escaped my lips.

His familiar growl rumbled in his chest. I added a second finger and my mouth fell open in delight. I was lost to the game.

"Sweets." He had to clear his throat. "Look at me." It wasn't his choked request that forced my eyelids open; I wanted to drink him in anyway.

I let my palm start to rub against my clit and the friction forced my knees to knock together. Nick's eyes didn't waver from mine as he reached forward and pushed them open. I had to focus to keep them that way as I thrust and swirled inside of myself. When the arousal that coated my fingers started to drip down my leg, I begged.

"Baby, please!" My plea was rough.

Nick could take over with fingers or his cock, it didn't matter; I just needed it to be him. He arched his eyebrow, deciding whether to give in. My knees kept wobbling but I managed to keep up the rhythm and the soft brushes, whimpering while I waited for him to clear his throat.

"Stop. Go back to your nipples."

"Ahhh," I couldn't help the groan.

Or doing what I was told. The second I twisted on my hard nipple, electricity shot to my belly and more wetness dripped down my open legs. I opened my mouth to beg.

Wait, I know what to do.

My eyes fixed on his as a wicked smile stretched across my lips. I lifted my fingers to my lips. This was playing dirty and I knew it. Judging by how intently he watched the fingers that'd been inside me, he did too. He scooted forward in his chair as I let my fingers dance on my lips. I shoved them in roughly and let my tongue swirl around.

MMMmmm.

Nick swore under his breath and stood. He yanked my fingers out of my mouth and pulled them into his. He'd loved tasting me since the very first moment I met him. Literally. While his tongue swirled around my fingers I pushed my free hand down his pants.

He bit down on my fingers as I started stroking him. I kissed his jaw and yanked my fingers out. His lips chased my hand, changing direction at the last moment to crash down onto my mouth instead. I lost myself in that kiss but somehow managed to keep stroking him.

Nick yanked off his shirt and pulled me flat against his skin. We stumbled backwards to the couch. The cushions hit him just behind his knees and he fell to sitting. I clumsily fell on top of him with a laugh. My hands clutched onto the back of the couch as I righted myself and straddled him. I leaned my forehead to his and grabbed the band of his sweats to pull his cock free. His hands snaked to my hips and they gripped. Hard. In one swift movement, he had me lifted and then fully seated on his erection.

I kept my hands on the cushioned back of the couch and used it to help roll my body up and down. His hands dug deeper and deeper into my hips. It was his familiar viselike but oh-so-delicious grip. I'd probably have bruises tomorrow, and the thought made my toes curl.

That grip confirmed Nick was enjoying himself as much as I was. He wasn't hung up on any part of my story. And if he wasn't, I didn't need to be. Any trace of my anger or worry had faded. Nick groaned repeatedly as I circled on top of him, and for the moment, everything was right.

He pushed me backwards, arching me away from his body. He supported my upper back with one hand and traced his other down my breastbone. That hand moved further down my body. When he got gentle over my belly, I paused, suddenly self-conscious but then he continued further and he used his fingers to play between my thighs. That distracted me quite thoroughly.

Without warning, Nick switched to small, fast thrusts into me.

My eyes fluttered shut again and my fingers left the chair to grasp at his shoulders before he yanked me back against his chest.

His hands curled into my hips and he thrust fully into me again. Our delightful rhythm was only interrupted when he dug in further and used his grip to take me down to the floor. Once on the carpet he pulled my arms from his body and pinned them to the floor. After a few thrusts, he grabbed both of my wrists in one hand and pulled them straight up overhead. He used his free hand for support as he expertly rolled his hips against mine. It wasn't long before I was building in that far too fast way.

"Baby," I gasped. "Let me be on top." My voice was garbled and breathy.

His answering, "No" was through gritted teeth.

"Nick I don't want it to end," I gasped.

My back arched involuntarily as I moaned, our bodies still rolling together. He didn't stop or hesitate. Instead, he shifted his support hand to my hip and grabbed. Just the way I liked it. I was going to come even quicker now. My whimpers told him as much.

"We have a good six months where you'll have to be on top," he growled. "Let me stretch out over you while I can."

Those words struck me deeper. It was a promise I hadn't known I needed to hear. My whole body heated and flushed when I pictured us like that; bright blue eyes watching a round pregnant belly.

I surrendered completely. That honeyed feeling washed over my body and everything in me clenched, gripping onto him, and his cock inside me. I threw my head back onto the carpet and closed my eyes, relishing the feel of him working hard against me. The way he stretched me, the way he worked his hips, the way he possessed me, had only gotten better over time. Why had I thought that would change? Why had I ever doubted him?

"Sweets, I can't hold on much longer. Come with me." His voice was ragged. "Please."

He was begging and I loved it. All I could do was nod and give in to the sensations building inside of me. I felt his cum pour into me just as I started rippling up his hardness.

I cried out loudly before he closed his lips down on mine. He kissed me with an urgency and adoration I'd never felt before, not even from him. I couldn't do anything but whimper when he let me gulp for air. The waves of orgasm kept rolling through my body, warmth spreading through my limbs as he stayed inside me.

Nick kept my arms pinned far overhead as he started kissing down my body. He moved down to my breasts and showered each in kisses. He used his tongue, gently, to raise my nipples up to his mouth. He let out a warm breath on first one, then the other, and my entire body shivered under him.

He pressed his lips to the skin over my heart and kissed it ardently. Goose bumps rose to pepper his lips. He closed his eyes and turned to lay his head on my chest. He slipped out of me and let my wrists go, choosing instead to wrap his arms up around my neck and pull me even closer. Nick wanted to listen to my heart. It couldn't help but hammer a little at the tenderness.

My hands slowly came back to life, finding their way into his hair and gently combing through the locks. My nails grazed his skin or massaged in small circles. After a few minutes, he used my contented purr against me.

The *MMMmmm* was barely audible but my heart leapt in response. The pound reverberated against his cheek and his smile pulled up against my skin.

We lay there, tangled in each other until I shivered underneath him. Nick immediately moved to find something. When he couldn't find a blanket, he reluctantly held out my clothes. I used his wrist to pull myself off the floor. He crouched to help me step into my pants and I used his shoulder for support as I dipped one toe then other into the denim. He pulled them up wordlessly and kissed my forehead as he zipped the fly into place. After shrugging into my shirt, I noticed his eyes had clouded.

Oh no.

"Penny for your thoughts, baby?" I wove my hands around him, partially to console, partially to keep him from bolting if he'd changed his mind.

"I'm happy, very happy." He kissed my forehead again.

"But?"

"But it's hard to know my mom won't be here. She would've loved a grandchild. God knows she had to have given up hope on me ever having one."

I gripped his waist as tightly as I could.

"She never gave up on you, baby." I nuzzled into his chest. "I don't know if that makes it better or worse but you have to know that."

I kissed his chest where the warm skin ran under my lips. I felt him shudder and press his lips to my head where it rested under his chin.

"You won't give up on me, right?" he asked, staying tender.

His hands moved up to my face. He brushed them through my hair and wove them into my tangled locks. He used his cradled hands to shift my eyes up to meet his.

"Never." I smiled, "I couldn't if I tried."

"It's not going to be easy. I'm not going to be good at it." He smiled when I leaned into his palm.

"You're probably going to be great. You always are. I'm going to be a wreck. I already am a wreck." I turned to kiss his palm where it held my cheek. "We'll have each other though?"

"Always. I love you, Kate."

"I love you too," I whispered. His lips locked on mine and we stayed frozen in that kiss—that honest, wonderful, sweet kiss—for what seemed like an eternity.

32.

"Ms. Elliott." Cassie's voice rang across the intercom. My son's nonsensical babbling laced the background. "Gemma is here with Wells."

Shit.

It couldn't be 3 p.m. yet. I had far too much to do before leaving the office.

"Cassie, buy me fifteen minutes." I was abrupt, even forceful.

"Ummm, okay boss."

It wasn't what she had wanted to hear. Bryant had given explicit orders that we were leaving at 3 o'clock exactly. Gemma, Cassie, Julien, Jaime, Colton, Terrence and a few others had gotten the Bryant *or else.*

The last thing I wanted to do was anger him, but being out of the office for sixteen days was a serious request. They really couldn't leave without me anyway. Not even Nicholas Bryant could have a wedding without a bride.

Though if you don't hurry your ass up, there is a very real chance you'll say your vows pissed.

I shook my head. I had precious few moments before Nick burst through my door and I needed to focus for each and every one.

Vesper business had been easy and wrapped since 9 a.m. Everything else remaining on my plate was more beastly. I caught the glint of my engagement ring as I picked up my pen and was instantly sucked down memory lane, thinking back over the past two and a half years, every moment since I'd found out I was pregnant.

Prior to Wells' birth, I had restructured as Nick suggested, eventually folding Vesper fully into the Bryant Venture Group portfolio. We'd put a million contracts in place, making me an equal partner in the entire corporation. The negotiations had been tumultuous to say the least. It hadn't helped that the deal was the talk of the New York business scene, every single person had thought we were making an asinine move.

I'd been in agreement. Nick and I had gone far past ten rounds, and in front of legal no less. Nick ended the argument by shouting, "If I couldn't share this with you, I wouldn't share a God damn thing!" then spanking me while nine lawyers sat just outside the conference room. The result was a bruised ass and a new title—Chief Creative Officer of the largest company in Manhattan.

The only pause was simply that, a pause. My maternity leave lasted only two weeks. Wells Trevor Bryant was born on a freakishly hot September day almost two years ago. Mercifully, besides feeling like I was walking on the sun during my last trimester, my pregnancy was easy.

Nick had found me both incredibly attractive and delightfully amusing while pregnant. He iced my ankles after I insisted on wearing the highest heels I owned, even at nine months. He accommodated every single craving I had, even grabbing cronuts, personally, many mornings. He even helped me with my own odd form of nesting, in which I'd undertaken massive projects both work and remodel related.

As promised our sex life had not wavered. And thank God, because I'd never been so horny in my entire life. The wrong fabric would have me barging into Nick's office, completely unannounced, begging for an afternoon orgasm. Most of the time he was more than willing to oblige then send me back across the lobby we now shared.

Once he arrived, Wells was an amazing baby and I was floored. Nick took easier to parenthood than I did, just as predicted. He must have talked the universe into adding more hours into the day as he easily made time for both of us and the business. Effortlessly. I loved my little boy as soon as he arrived but the whole baby thing was not second nature to me. Nick's unwavering support and reassurance was the only thing that got me through the first six months.

Well, him and Gemma.

She'd happily transitioned to my personal assistant when I announced I was pregnant, helping me manage things I couldn't trust anyone outside my immediate family with. That's what she'd become after all. When Wells arrived, she naturally focused on him, becoming a nanny before any of us really realized. Now she was waiting in the lobby with Wells, ready to head to my Hamptons house for the long awaited Elliott—Bryant wedding.

My office door slowly creaked open and it snapped me back to the present.

"Your mother is being naughty isn't she Wells. She was supposed to ready to leave seven minutes ago." I looked up to find my boys nose to nose in the doorframe. Nick was tickling Well's belly but his deep blue eyes shifted to meet mine. "She's lucky she's wearing my favorite glasses. If she packs up now, all may be forgiven." I found it adorable when he used Wells to talk to me, never slipping into baby talk.

"Nick, I need a few more minutes. The marketing materials for the new development in Brooklyn are in and they're shit. They have to go to print on Monday and before you tell me we need to go, or that traffic is building, or we've hired the people to fucking take care of this, I'm going on record as saying leave it. And leave me the hell alone. I'll have it done shortly."

"You said you'd stop swearing in front of Wells. He tries to repeat things now. I'd rather he didn't learn shit or fuck."

"You're swearing in front of Wells." I returned my gaze to my work.

"I'm proving a point and you know it." They came closer to my desk and I tried not to focus on Wells babbling or the adorable way he pulled at Nick's tie. I almost succeeded but then they came closer and Wells to started repeating "mama" over and over.

I was busy writing all over the flyer mockup in bright red pen but could see Wells making grabby hands at me from the corner of my eye. He started screeching a shrill, delighted sound and wiggling wildly. He always kept this up until I took him. I barely broke my gaze from the papers in front of me as I reached up. Nick helped propped him on my knee as I returned most of my attention to the slicks in front of me.

Nick turned toward the windows and started pacing back and forth, first taking in the view then stalking elsewhere throughout my office. I simply continued my notes. Particularly since he hadn't technically ordered I stop. Wells reached for my face, his tiny fingers pulling at my hair and lips. I paused only long enough to nibble playfully at his fingers. He shrieked again, utterly thrilled, and I returned to my work. He started in at my glasses next.

"Wells, no, I need those." I pulled his hand away and kissed his knuckles.

This is why I asked Cassie to buy me time.

"Kate, send that down to Scott and let's go." Nick sighed as Wells ripped my glasses from my face.

"Nick, if Scott could take care of this I wouldn't be editing in the first place." I arched my eyebrow at the baby. "Wells, I said no."

"Send it down and let it go, Kate."

"Oh for fuck's sake Nick, you let it go. I'm assuming that you made me CCO because you like the direction I move in creatively not just because you decided to placate me. I have things to do and you will just have to wait." I hadn't meant to raise my voice but there my temper was, bubbling up in my throat.

We glowered at each other while Wells snatched my glasses again and wildly flailed his arms. I had to break my glare to swipe my glasses and keep Wells from poking me in the eye. At least the baby was still happy, chattering away in my lap. At the moment he was the only one.

I made a goofy face at him as I pushed the glasses back into place. When I looked up to stare down Nick again, he was gone.

"Hi darling." Gemma smiled as she and Jaime walked into the room. She was talking to me but reaching for Wells. "I was instructed to take the little one. Everything okay?"

"I'm still working." We'd been in this situation too many times together; I didn't need to say anything else.

"Well then." She cringed and collected Wells from my lap.

Once his feet were on the floor he started scampering around the room.

"Kate, we have about 20 minutes until traffic gets very ugly. If you want to get out there today, I'd recommend now." Jaime was simply providing an update, there was nothing forceful about it.

"Jaime, feel free to tell Bryant that it's duly noted." My eyes flew back to the paper and I desperately tried to focus on finishing.

"I'm Bryant now?" Nick had reappeared.

I only looked up to shoot him a withering look. I noticed his eyes weren't blue anymore. They looked to be stormy, swirling puddles.

Shit.

We were going to go a few rounds. That's why he'd sent Gemma in for Wells.

"What are you going to call me once you're a Bryant too? Won't have quite the same condescending effect now will it."

"It's not condescending," I snarled.

Gemma spoke under her breath. She was close enough that I caught the tail end of, "Jaime, out." She spun on her heel with Jaime poised to follow.

"Stay," Nick barked.

Great, we're all in trouble.

His eyes narrowed at me. "I have a favor to ask of you two."

Nope, just me.

"Of course sir," Jaime answered at the same time Gemma did, "anything Nicholas."

I wanted to yell *traitors* at both of them and pound my fists on my desk. I would have if Nick wasn't so obviously worked up.

"Would you two please take Wells to the house? You can drive Kate's car."

"Hey, but I . . ." I interrupted but the look Nick shot me stopped me dead in my tracks.

"We will follow later."

Gemma looked over at me and I shrugged. I wasn't thrilled but I also wasn't going to dig myself a deeper hole.

"Julien!" Bryant roared out the door.

Julien scrambled in and Nick doled out orders. He wanted a helicopter standing by at the 34th Street heliport and the Porsche delivered to the building. Between Julien, Colton, and Terrence everything was taken care of rather quickly.

I tried to ignore all the commotion and finish the work in front of me. If this is what had started the whole argument, I sure as hell was going to complete it.

When the car arrived, I stopped just long enough to thank Gemma and Jaime and kiss Wells goodbye. I returned to my desk quickly, trying to ignore the churn of my stomach at the impending face-off. I may have audibly gulped when Bryant dismissed both Cassie and Julien for the weekend, knowing full well we were alone on the floor without them. I was scrambling to get through the last little bit of promotional material when the door lock clicked.

"Put it down, Kate. Now." His voice was a raspy grumble I wasn't ready to brawl with. I set the red pen and the marketing slicks down. I watched Nick walk from his spot in the doorway to the windows behind my desk. My heart started to race. "I wasn't asking you to walk away from work for something trivial. You understand that right?" He wasn't as scary as he'd been moments ago but he was still obviously pissed.

He pulled his blue tie out from under his vest and unknotted it, slipping it from his collar. He shrugged out of his jacket as well before laying both on the bookcase along my wall. He looked devastatingly handsome in the simple shirt and the gray vest that remained. He spoke as he artfully rolled his sleeves up to his elbows.

"I've waited three and a half years to marry you."

He was pocketing his cufflinks. They were ones I'd given him, made from a dismantled F1 race car for our first anniversary.

"I would have married you at the courthouse the day I purposed. I tried desperately to get you to the altar when we found out you were pregnant. I have tried numerous times since."

He undid the buttons at his collar, making him even more sexy.

If that's possible.

"One might think you don't really want to walk down that aisle."

"Nick." I rolled my eyes. "I told you that has nothing to do with it. First, I didn't and still don't want anyone, including you, thinking that I'm marrying you because of Wells. Second, I committed to forever the day I took this ring. My heart was yours long before that. I never felt the pressure to rush into it." I'd said all this before and I thought it'd sunk in, but here we were having the same conversation. Again.

"Kate, you set a date. *You* set it. I waited as patiently as I possibly could for it to get here. And now it's here and you seem to be dragging your feet even worse."

At that I stood. I was over the conversation and having had it for what seemed like the fiftieth time, but I didn't want him to feel unimportant. He was, and always would be, my world. I shuffled between him and the windows and rested my hands on his chest.

"I just wanted to get those finished, Nick. That's all. No big, weird, secret agenda or cold feet. I knew it meant we might sit in traffic and yes, I loathe traffic, but I just thought how nice it would be to go on vacation without work hanging over my head the whole damn time." I sighed heavily, hoping that would make my point.

"You don't trust me to have everything in order?" His voice was still gravelly, his eyes still churning.

"I trust you to leave projects that are mine to me. I trust you know I will put my departments in order, on my own, before a major departure like this."

"Oh come on, Kate. Don't twist my words like that." His eyes blazed as he looked down at me. "I should punish you for that." There was a flash of lust in his eyes. "And for making us late. You should be spanked." He arched an eyebrow and my breath caught.

That was what he had wanted from the moment I challenged him. He'd been counting on my temper as a vehicle to get us there. My toes curled into my peep toe Manolo Blahniks.

He studied me. I was doing my best to stare unwaveringly back into his excited eyes. When his hand slid in between my legs, I gasped but forced my gaze to stick to his. My skirt was loose enough for him to creep all the way up, stroking me once before his hand came to rest on my inner thigh. He dug his fingertips in and used the hold to turn my chair toward him.

The heat from the June midday sun radiated through the windowpanes, but my skin goose bumped when he pulled me up and started sliding my zipper down. His hands skated up to my shoulders and pushed the fabric of my dress aside. He carefully handled it as it skated down to my ankles then helped me step out of it. Nick walked away and I watched him lay it nicely with his jacket and tie on the bookcase.

His reflection paced in the window as I stood waiting. My breathing got heavier, and as I inched toward the glass to warm my skin; it fogged slightly beneath my lips. Nick returned just long enough to peel my lace briefs down and shove them in his pocket. My nipples hardened against the matching bra he'd left on.

My thighs began their familiar rub together as I became more and more aroused; more and more uncomfortable. My ankles rolled in the Manolos Nick had left on and I pitched backward. He was there to catch me with a firm grip on my hip bones, and my hands shot back to him.

He righted me easily and shifted to the side of my body. Even through his vest, I could feel his tight muscles press against me. I could feel a thick column of hard dick through silken fabric too. I tried to sag into his firm body but he righted me again, this time weaving his hands around mine and planting my palms on the glass.

With a gentle nudge from his shoe, I spread my legs wider. Again, he stepped away. I was sure it was to look me over but I caught his back turned in the windows. He was bent over my desk just for the slightest moment. When he turned around, I heard the thwack of something heavy against his hand. I tried to remember what had been laying on my desk. Papers, millions of papers. The marketing slicks and the red pen I'd covered them in. A few portfolios and . . . I realized what it was just before the hard-backed book landed square across my ass. My breath caught but the resulting tingle sent electricity straight to my belly and racing down to my toes.

"The first time I ever saw you in those glasses you reminded me of this naughty librarian. I wanted to spank you with a book." His voice was already ragged. "And as I would like to remind you not to read me the riot act again, particularly regarding work, I think it's fitting."

Another quick snap rang across my backside. I couldn't help but moan. It spurred him to land three, hard smacks in quick succession. I could picture the vintage, woven cloth pattern from the cover and swore I could feel the small hash marks against my skin. The next time he swatted me with the book everything inside me clenched. He was going to make me come just from the spanking.

Of course, Nick read my body well enough to know.

I stood there breathing heavy, knees trying desperately to stay straight and hold me up as I waited for the next blow. Nick's gentle touch returned to my body, running his hand up my inner thighs like he had done when my dress was still on. When he hit the slick spots between my legs, he groaned with pleasure.

He stroked me once, like before, but this time much more slowly, purposely trying to tease me. I whimpered against the glass as every inch of my body reacted to his touch. My chest sagged against the window but my hips stayed out hoping he would stroke me again.

Instead, he returned to the book, knowing just how close I was, and paddled me repeatedly until I was so on edge that my body quaked. Nick moved beside me, his hard cock pushed up against me and he wrapped one arm around me. I was only distracted for a moment before the book landed harder and faster, slightly lower, at the apex of my thighs.

I came. My knees shook and the hand he'd wrapped around me caught me as I sagged backwards. He'd known I would come violently. He'd planned for it. And he was more than enjoying the waves that shook my body against his forearm.

My chest thundered in response to Nick, and he bent to listen to the familiar sound as we sank together into my desk chair.

33.

"You can sit differently, Sweets," Nick purred in my ear as I winced, my ass smarting against his thigh.

"I don't want to ruin your suit." I smirked against his skin.

Nick threaded his hands gently under my backside and shifted me on his lap. It was vastly more comfortable but I could feel the light-weight, soft fabric against every inch of my sensitive slit.

"It's just a suit." He kissed my head and continued cradling me. After what seemed like forever, he sighed and moved his lips right up against my ear. "You really don't have cold feet?" he whispered and it tickled my ear but I didn't dare giggle because of the trepidation in his voice.

Oh for fucks sake.

"Nicholas James Bryant, I love you with all that I am, all that I have. I pledge to be your faithful, loving, wife from this day forward." I stared deeply into his eyes as I said it. It was the only way I could think to reassure him.

He tried, and failed, to hold back a big, beaming, childish smile. "It's a little corny but I'll take it."

"Well the real ones are better. Did you finish writing yours?" I moved to wrap my arms around his neck and I winced as I shifted.

"Are you going to be able to sit down tomorrow?" He brushed hair behind my ear.

I laughed, drinking in his serious and sweet, deep blue eyes. I nodded and moved forward to kiss him then jump off his lap. Without looking back, I pulled my dress back on, zipped it, and adjusted my glasses. I combed my hair with my fingers and turned to look at him. I held out my hand and arched an eyebrow. He knew I was asking for my underwear but he stayed cross-armed and shrugged.

Fine.

I shrugged back and turned toward my desk. I made sure to lean far too deeply over the paperwork. He would see almost everything, even some of the color blooming across my ass.

He grumbled behind me but stood, adjusted his belt and picked up his jacket and tie. I could tell he was uncomfortably hard when he came close enough to hand me back the small scrap of lace. I took them just for the briefest second and then shoved them back into his breast pocket. I winked and shuffled the marketing slicks into an envelope with my notes.

"Got everything babe?" I said as I smiled.

He patted his pockets frantically, like something was lost, then landed on his breast pocket, letting out a deep sigh and nodding. I rolled my eyes at his gorgeous crooked smile then strode out in front of him.

I was standing in front of the elevator when Nick wove his hand into mine and pulled me to his office. He grabbed his BlackBerry, his briefcase, and picked up a landline to order a car. I waited patiently, though I couldn't force myself to stand still. The air sneaking under my skirt made sure of that. We walked hand in hand down to Scott's office to deliver the slicks then to the waiting car.

As soon as we stepped out onto the sidewalk he shifted behind me. Most likely concerned about what any sudden gusts of hot air might do. In the car he pulled me to his side and held me there. We both kept our devices tucked away. I traced the scar on the back of his palm and he aimlessly started tracing the one he knew was hidden under my dress on my shoulder. He kept his fingers on my skin all the way to the heliport and then into the darkening night sky.

Fading sunlight on the glass of the city soon gave way to the twinkling floodlights of estates along the coast. Our big gray house still stood, front and center, with the garage and racetrack to one side.

The only thing that looked different this time around was the giant tent that emanated a soft white glow from where it was positioned between the main house and the guest house. I could see the stone path we'd decided to lay for the ceremony, where it wandered from both homes to join together under an arch up against the sand line. I could picture where the chairs would go for the procession. My heart picked up pace and for the first time I was excited.

We landed in the middle of the track as usual and Nick carefully held my skirt down as he helped me from the helicopter. As we walked away from the whirring blades he undid his vest buttons and his collar. We aimlessly chatted as we walked toward the well lit main house but I got the feeling Nick was looking over his shoulder.

The night we'd watched Christopher from out here popped unbidden into my mind. My breath hitched and so did my knees. He looked over to me and he couldn't hide his darkening eyes. Unease settled in my stomach.

"Nick," I breathed.

"I know." He squeezed my hand then yanked me up against his side. The softest crunching of grass came from the right. My body tensed and Nick shoved me, planting himself between me and the sound.

"Oh good, it's you two."

"Fucking Christ Brooklyn, you scared the shit out of us," I swore over Nick's shoulder while he lunged at Brooklyn.

"I will kill you if you do that again." Nick added a few uttered profanities before and after.

"Sorry." Brooklyn chuckled his signature chuckle.

"Why are you slinking around out here?" Nick asked.

"You know why." There was no chuckle lacing Brooklyn's voice this time.

"How worried do we have to be?" My voice wavered.

"As of right now?" I saw his dimpled smile in the shadows. "The wedding should go off without a hitch."

"But?" Nick mellowed.

"There's that feeling." I finished the sentence and Brooklyn nodded right along with me.

"And that's why I'm out here." He smiled at us. "You guys should get inside."

Nick squeezed my hand and looped it up and around my neck to pin me to his body. He kept that grip as he pulled me into the cacophony of noise that was our home. Wedding planners were scurrying, Jaime was deep in conversation on the phone, Wells was screeching from a crib, and Gemma was ordering every single one of them around.

Nick and I went straight for Wells. Even over the noise we could hear a "mama" and "dada." I stepped out of my heels in the living room at the same time I bent to pick him up. Nick's hands went to shield my backside but as soon as I stood up, he slyly wrapped them around me. He bent to kiss the crown of Wells' head and then shifted up to kiss my forehead.

"See teddy?" Wells was picking aimlessly at Nick's shirt buttons when he asked.

"He got a bear from Aunty Laura when she got here." Gemma walked up behind us. "She went to a bar in town." Gemma's frown was a mirror of mine.

I felt compelled track Laura down and be her company as she drank in silence. Because that's what she was doing. Some bartender was lining up tequila sodas with muddled lime while she aimlessly swirled the highball glass on its edge.

Her last real boyfriend was Dr. Malik Waters. Something had shifted in the universe the day I met Bryant. For as long as I could remember, she'd been the relationship girl, and I'd been prone to one night stands but we'd completely flipped roles. She said she was having fun but the darkening bags under her eyes told me she was distraught and filling a gaping hole too.

"Who's she with?" Nick's fingers flexed into me and pulled me from my thoughts.

"I think Aribella, her friend, and Frank went." I let out a deep breath grateful she wasn't wallowing alone.

"You can go meet them or we can cook here. Though if you choose here, Kate, know I haven't had a chance to prepare."

"I'll cook." I bent to set Wells down and Nick moved awkwardly behind me again. "What would everyone like?"

I turned, still attached to my son. Wells was still saying, "Mama teddy" over and over and yanking on my neck even with his feet on the carpet. I looked into his pale blue eyes, realizing they were starting to churn like his father's. I couldn't help but smile widely.

"Think about dinner guys, I have a teddy to meet." I didn't pull my eyes from Wells. "Sweet pea, you have to let go so I can follow."

"Daddy teddy."

"Yes, I'll come meet your teddy too."

I stood and Wells grabbed each of our hands and started barreling down the hallway toward the bedrooms. Nick leaned in close and whispered, "Be careful about bending down like that again." He arched his eyebrow and let a mischievous smirk spread across his face.

"Do you think we need to be worried?" I asked without thinking of what it would do to his mood.

"About exposing your naked ass to the house? Yes. Apparently, very worried." He managed a crooked smirk.

"Bryant," I scolded and cocked my head at him.

"I hope not." He couldn't meet my eyes though, his gaze fixed on our son where he barreled between us.

We went about our evening like we weren't worried; like there wasn't anxiety churning collectively in our stomachs. Gemma started pulling us in opposite directions as soon as we ate, Ari making it far worse when she got back from the bar.

I was awake in bed staring at the ceiling of the buzzing house, tracing shadows across the paint when Nick shuffled back into my arms. I let out a deep breath and wove myself into him but there was still tension in our bodies. I didn't melt as we lay there, silent and awake, staring into the wee hours of the morning.

The next day was much of the same. I didn't get to see Nick much besides catching glimpses across the grounds or through the windows.

Something about it didn't sit right. Ari and Gemma helped me with bridal things, while Laura was more inclined to attend to Wells. It wasn't until I put the little man down to bed and dropped into the chair next to the crib that I had a chance to breathe.

A world weary sigh slipped from my lips. Any lesser prize than Nicholas Bryant and I wouldn't make it through a wedding.

I was singing my favorite lullaby when the telltale ripple of Nick nearby rolled across my skin. He moved silently into the room, bent and kissed Wells on the forehead, then held out a hand to me. I sighed as I reached for it and let him pull me from the room. That weight that had settled in the pit of my stomach when we arrived hadn't gone away but he made it better.

The house seemed quieter, almost empty. Gemma and Jaime were the only ones I saw in the house. They were sitting on the couch, Gemma with her legs up over Jaime's, reading. Nick nodded to Jaime, and Jaime wordlessly waved a room monitor in return.

We walked out onto the patio that overlooked the beach and the ocean. The guest house was lit up and I could hear the faint sounds of music and glasses clinking traveling on the breeze. My face fell when I thought about spending the first quiet moment we'd had in a crowded room.

That's when Nick pulled me in the opposite direction. I should have known we were heading to the garage. I smiled as Nick kept a firm grasp on me, helping me navigate the dips and swells in the grass of the side yard in my heels.

My eyes started to travel over the landscape, taking in the moon-lit grounds I tried to tell myself I was watching the beach grass dance in the warm breeze but really, I was looking for silhouettes tucked amongst the shadows.

"Don't worry." Nick's fingers skated against my skin. "Brooklyn's earning the exorbitant amount of money we pay him. And the contribution to his uncle's campaign for that matter."

He punched in the code to the garage door and it lifted to reveal the stunning fleet. We'd added only one vehicle recently, a LaFerrari and its sleek black frame fit in nicely with the other exceptional cars.

"Pick one." Nick squeezed my hip as he flipped on the museum-like flood lamps. I bit my lip and pointed to the Hennessey. We shared a knowing smile, both thinking of the illicit photos that had been taken on the hood of that car. "I had rather hoped that would be the one," he murmured.

Only then did he leave my side and walk over to the sleek black car. He opened it and pulled out a few items. Most were black boxes wrapped with delicate silver ribbons but on top was the very camera he'd taken all our risqué shots with.

"A few gifts for my wife." He arched an eyebrow, grabbed the camera, and then started to walk away. He was striding purposefully toward a stool resting against the far wall. "Open them. You'll know what to do." Blood rushed through my veins, my body already excited.

I opened the largest box first to find a gorgeous, supple white leather vest. It was matte leather but had a smooth finish. The zipper was hidden under the perfect piping and contours of the fabric.

There was no way I was naive enough to think it was just a beautiful gift. It was part of a grander scheme for the evening. The second box confirmed my hunch. The white lace briefs were delicate, beautiful, and definitely sexy. I couldn't wait to stand before Nick in leather and lace.

"Put those on before you open the third one," his voice was a delectable purr from his seat on a stool.

I turned to face him, my gaze becoming hungry as I drank in his V-neck T-shirt, fitted jeans, and sleek tennis shoes. Everything in my body was telling me to walk over and kiss him but I went to let my hair down instead. The snap of a camera told me he appreciated my restraint and it helped me settle into the game.

My fingers danced on the hem of my cream chiffon tank and pulled it slowly up and over my head. The shutter clicked a few times as I stretched out of the fabric. My hands went to the zipper of my gauzy snakeskin printed skirt and I let it flutter to the floor. Nick flat out growled when he realized I hadn't been wearing any underwear. My playful smirk stretched across my face as I stood in only cream pointy toe Tom Ford stilettos. The gold lock on their straps wiggled as my body trembled in anticipation.

Nick raised his eyebrows toward the gifts laying on the hood of the car then tucked back behind the lens of the camera, snapping photos of my naked body next to his gorgeous car. I turned and winked over my shoulder, forcing him to stop and clear his throat. I laughed lightly to myself and my hair tickled my shoulder blades.

"Sweets," he managed. "You're killing me. Please." His voice was choked as he tried to keep his composure.

Obediently I pulled on the lace briefs and adjusted the straps into place. They were thick bands of lace, one that rose above my hip bone and one that dipped below, leaving a cutout of bare skin on each hip that wrapped from below my bellybutton all the way around to above my tailbone.

I exaggerated my reach across the hood for my new vest and let my nipples brush across the polished metal. Nick had been taking photos the whole time but when my nipples got hard and my body goose bumped, he sucked in a deep breath, snapped a quick photo, then stood. I swung the vest over my shoulders just before he reached me.

Nick's lips took mine violently. He bit hard and pushed me up against the car. I could feel the heat of his skin against mine even through his clothes. My fingers scrambled against his soft shirt, desperate to get him naked.

If I was honest, I'd wanted his skin since he spanked me yesterday. The man could make me come in all sorts of different ways but it was never as good as it was with him inside me. I moved my hands to snake up his shirt but he grabbed my wrists to stop me. He shoved my hands down to my sides and kept nibbling at my mouth, alternating between lips and tongue. They burned, swollen, before he pulled away.

I let out a breathless moan when he left my skin. His chest was rising and falling harshly but he gathered his composure far quicker than me.

"Last one," he said as he picked up the final black box from the hood of the car.

I had to ball my fingers twice before they were steady enough to take the box from him. I gasped when I finally got it open. There was a large black diamond on the end of a delicate gold chain. It was simple and classic but unique at the same time. It was breathtaking and oh-so perfect for me.

Nick moved behind me and gently swept my hair to the side. His arms wrapped around me and took the necklace from its box. Deftly he clasped the necklace for me. He leaned in and his warm breath brushed against my neck just before he kissed the bare skin below my ear. I couldn't help the *MMMmmm* that escaped my lips. He answered by swearing under his breath and stepping away from me.

I turned to face him, missing his touch already. He reached out but just to zip up my vest so it stopped just below my breasts. The leather was tight but not uncomfortably so, just enough to press my breasts up and together. The gorgeous stone hung delicately in my cleavage.

"Stay." It was a clipped command as he turned for the camera. When he spun back, he took a few photos in quick succession as he inched closer. The last would be a close up of the curvature of my chest as the leather pushed it toward the gem, delicate and artsy.

When he popped out from behind the camera, he had his serious face back in place. He stepped around me to the driver's door and opened it. I slid in and adjusted the seat as needed. I wasn't particularly fond of driving in heels but I had a feeling we wouldn't be focusing on vehicle performance.

Nick leaned across me to push the key in the ignition. I pushed in the clutch and he twisted the key. I couldn't help the groan that escaped my lips when the car roared to life. His head cranked toward mine, still occupying the small space between my nose and the steering wheel. His eyes were the color that signaled lust but they were questioning. I smiled and nodded quickly before pushing him out of the doorframe and revving the engine a few times.

The rumbling of the machine along with the game made me extremely wet. Nick had disappeared for the moment and I knew it was to open the back garage door to the track. We'd added security measures that required manual opening. I adjusted the rearview mirror so I could watch his fine frame bend and haul the door up. When he had to stand on tiptoes to push it out of the way, I saw the dimples low on his back and the curve of his ass. Jeans without boxer briefs was a serious turn on. I let the engine roar again and he turned to arch an eyebrow at me.

Moments later, he slid into the passenger seat, camera still in hand.

"Take her out," he purred in time with the engine.

34.

I didn't even hesitate. I whipped the car out, even drifting a little, and then slammed into gear before peeling out. I couldn't keep the serious face anymore. Driving fast in a high performance car always made me smile. I effortlessly navigated the track, even though I could only see the small strip of pavement illuminated by the headlights.

When I urged it past 180mph on the beachside straight away, I couldn't help but giggle. Beside me there was only silence. Was he enjoying the drive too? Was he still snapping photographs? Was he happy? Or aroused? Or being ridiculously overprotective again?

I had to slow the car significantly for the sharpest curve on the course and as soon as I went to accelerate out, I got the answer. Nick shoved his hand between my legs. I faltered with the car for just a second.

As soon as I had control again he started stroking me through the fine lace of my underwear. The longer he stroked the more I wanted to surrender to him. As soon as the car decelerated and he pulled his hand away, I let out a staggered, halted groan. I was both grateful and disappointed that his hand was gone.

On the next lap, on the same corner, he pushed his hand back between my thighs. His strokes were stronger this time and he used the lace to create a friction that had me whimpering. I heard a few clicks from the camera but was trying so hard not to lose control of the vehicle that I couldn't linger on the thought. He saw when I was about to give in again and his hand fell away. This time my groan was far more guttural. I wanted him to stop, or keep going, or perhaps for my brain to explode simply so I didn't have to decide.

My skin started tingling the second I saw the curve in my headlights. This time I tried to brace myself for his strokes. Of course, he read the tension in my body and slipped his hand underneath the lace this time, up against my sensitive skin. I moaned as his fingers moved against my bare slick sex.

I was going to lose control. I couldn't help it. His touch had been devastating enough over top of fabric.

My mind raced, waiting for him to pull away at any moment, knowing that I couldn't drive with him touching me so scandalously. One long finger was tracing me, back and forth between my thighs. I did falter with my driving but Nick didn't stop.

Without any kind of a warning, he slipped a finger inside of me and I cried out. For a moment, I shut my eyes and forgot I was driving all together. The car decelerated quickly and when the transmission started to hitch I remembered myself and quickly downshifted.

He didn't stop his assault. Even though I was having severe trouble handling the vehicle, he added a second finger to swirl inside of me. Luckily, I was going slow enough I could slam on the breaks all together.

"Nick." My voice wasn't really mine, it was just a feverish moan.

He moved his fingers again, this time swiping across my G-spot. I forgot myself completely and pulled my feet from the pedals. The car stalled out beneath us, shuddering as it went quiet. Nick simply chuckled and snapped a few more photos.

Is he photographing getting me off?

Arousal dripped down my thigh and onto the seat at the thought.

"Jesus, Kate," his voice was ragged.

All I could do was bite my lip and whimper as his fingers moved in, out, and around in a hypnotic rhythm. I was building. Quickly. My body started tingling and my muscles clenched involuntarily on his fingers.

Without warning, he pulled his hand out and shoved his fingers in his mouth. He made a show of sucking them, and I could barely keep my eyes from fluttering shut. My body was a wreck. My chest heaving, my heart hammering, and my fingers clenched on the steering wheel. When he hollowed his cheeks and drug his fingers back across his lips, my body started tingling again.

"Fuck, you taste good." His voice was even more shaky now.

He busted out of his door and rounded the car. If it was possible, I got more turned on by the animal urgency he rounded the hood with. He yanked open my door and leaned across me to pull the seatbelt free.

I let him drag me from the car and pin my front against the metal frame. His muscled front was pressed hard against my backside. His erection poked against my bruised ass and the car's contours against my hip bones. It was slightly uncomfortable but my need for him was downright painful.

Involuntarily, I whimpered when the soft sound of his fly unzipping came from behind me. I could feel his warm, hard shaft resting against my flesh as his hands roughly shoved the lace down to my thighs. His fingers circled for the briefest moment against me then he pulled the wetness backward and plunged two fingers into my ass instead.

I hadn't anticipated that and I cried out when he pushed in further and further. His fingers slid easily in and out as he spun them, stretching me. My fingers tried to dig into the car frame below me. His free hand moved to the crease of my hip and he pulled my body back onto his fingers. Hard. I cried out and the sound pierced the night sky. Luckily, we were far away from everyone courtesy of the back half of the track.

My wetness was dripping down my leg and I was acutely aware of how cool it was when the breeze caressed it. Nick shifted so his cock was between my legs, his fingers still gliding in, out, and around. I had to be dripping onto his shaft now.

Both of his hands flexed, his fingers inside me moving in a new direction, his hand at my hip digging in. I swore almost as loudly as

I'd screeched earlier. That's when he replaced his fingers with his cock. I'd gotten him wet enough that I couldn't have resisted him if I tried. It was still tight but he pushed in quick and deep. My body seized and slumped over the car.

He clawed at my hips just before he started wildly rolling against my bruised backside. It was pleasure and pain and perfection. Each thrust seemed to go deeper and push me harder into the car. One of his hands snaked down and around, repositioning me then plunging into my sex.

His fingers rolled along the back of me so he could press against himself through the thin bit of sensitive skin that separated his fingers and cock. We both shuddered. Then he started alternating thrusts. He'd slam into my backside and pull out as he explored with his fingers. It was too much. Without any warning I starting coming.

Nick's name was tripping repeatedly from my lips. He kept leisurely thrusting with both fingers, tracing the outline of his shaft where it was buried inside of me. My body was clenching onto both. Repeatedly. My fingers scrambled for something to hold onto so I wouldn't crumple to the ground. My body was a big puddle of sensation, the waves of pleasure slowly rolling through every inch.

I was barely aware when he pulled me up off the hood of the car and pressed my back against his chest. In a swift move he unzipped the vest and his hands started roughly pulling on my nipples. He was pulling hard and using his grip to meet his thrusts. The hand that'd been inside me wove around my hip bones and held me flush to his body as he pumped furiously into me.

My body was responding again. I would come again if he kept playing with my breasts. He switched nipples and twisted. I didn't think it was possible but his thrusts inside me got both faster and deeper. Thankfully my thighs were still braced against the car; I needed all the help I could get staying upright.

The waves of an orgasm started building again at the same time his legs bunched underneath me. When the first shot of cum poured into me, hot and fast, it set me off or kept me going or whatever. My knees buckled but his grasp on me was so tight I hardly moved. I couldn't help but sag against him, gasping for breath.

When he'd emptied himself into me his hands pushed down to the wetness between my thighs. His fingers skated up along my leg then gently pressed inside of me. He used the opportunity to rub himself through the thin wall again. I shuddered when his cock twitched inside me.

Nick chuckled and kissed the back of my head as he pulled his fingers out of me, then his shaft. With one hand he turned me so I could face him. He saw me wobble and let me lean back against the car. Nick shoved his two fingers back into his mouth and licked. He stole my *MMMmmm* then pulled them out and unceremoniously bent to zip his pants back up. He sagged over top of me against the car. His forehead rested against mine for a moment before he kissed me deeply and passionately.

We stayed like that, making out against the car, for quite some time. When I got the feeling back in my fingers I let them wander through his hair, combing it back away from his deep blue eyes. Finally, he pulled away.

"I should let the bride get a good night sleep before her big day." He laughed lightly to himself as he found the edges of the vest and zipped it back up, though still only part way up. He pulled my lace briefs up and adjusted the straps back into place. His fingers skated across the exposed skin.

A slow, piercing clap rang from the darkness across the grass. Each one snapped across my skin and reverberated through my eardrums. I hadn't been able to catch my breath because of Nick, but now, my chest constricted and my stomach bottomed out the way it had before every terrible event over the past few years.

"Your whore still puts on quite a show."

Christopher.

My stomach churned as Nick's arms wound around me.

"I will kill you for calling my wife, the mother of my child, a whore."

We were a tangle of arms and legs as Nick tried to shove me toward the car and redirect toward Christopher at the same time. I couldn't talk my fingers out of clutching onto him.

The next few things happened so quickly it was difficult to process. Nick pushed me into the driver's seat and tried to slam the door. I couldn't get out of the way fast enough and the door caught my shins. I screeched as it bounced back and smacked into Nick as he rounded the hood of the car; it didn't slow him. A haunting shock of blonde hair came into the flood of the headlights. I wasn't thinking when I scrambled out after Nick.

"Get back in that car, Kate." Nick's icy roar was the most terrifying one yet.

"No, she should see this." Christopher's fist was flying toward Nick's kidneys before he had a chance to react.

I screamed as Nick doubled over in pain and Christopher drove an elbow down into his back.

Nick groaned and his knees wavered. I thought he was going to crumple face first onto the pavement, and I ran to try to catch him. Christopher hooked his hand around my waist and yanked me away though. I growled and smashed down on his foot with my stiletto.

His grip on me didn't even falter. Matter of fact, it got tighter, becoming downright painful. Christopher wound his other hand up around my throat. He squeezed as he laid my body back against his. I almost vomited when I felt his erection against my body.

"I said I would kill you," Nick gasped as he barreled toward us.

I knew I was going down when he careened into us but mercifully, Christopher's hands slipped away from my body. I needed to move but Nick consumed every thought and I instinctually spun to defend him.

That's when a shot rang out. The loud, metallic explosion that vibrated my bones. I hated that I recognized the sound. My body wasn't reacting to the gun just the wave of horror that overtook me. I didn't know who was shooting or from where. Or even at who.

Screams rang out piercing the breeze and my ears. Screams that weren't Nick's. I started to push up off the ground when strong hands were on me. Strong hands that weren't Nick's.

What the fuck is happening?

I was shaking as I turned to meet eerie green eyes.

"Kate, are you okay?" Brooklyn Hart was holding the still-warm steel of a gun against my skin.

I managed a nod before he dodged past me toward the howling. I turned to see blood. Everywhere. The crimson in headlights made my stomach lurch again. Jaime and Colton sprinted past not a second later.

Why are they sprinting?

Then I realized all three men had taken off in a singular direction. I also realized that there wasn't a pile of shocking blonde hair in the sticky, thick crimson. Nor was there a doubled over Nick anywhere. I was alone with the Hennessey on the track, hearing only shouts and footfalls fading into the distance. Further and further until eventually only the rhythmic splash of waves upon the sand filled the empty night sky.

My mind raced. Where were they? I guessed Christopher had been shot but I still didn't know for sure. Could Brooklyn have hit Nick? Could they have caught up to Christopher? Could this finally be over?

Will it ever be over?

My stomach flipped when gravel crunched beneath footsteps.

"Get in the car right now." That voice could call to me from the depths of hell. And with how harsh and icy it was, Nick sounded like he was Satan himself.

"What about . . ."

Jaime, Colton, and Brooklyn are still out there.

"Kate, for once, just do as you're fucking told," he growled and wrapped his fingers around my arm, yanking me toward the car again.

Part of me wanted to slap him but the other part of me was scared. No, *terrified*. He opened the passenger door then paused.

"Please." His soft, tortured word was all it took for my anger to ebb.

I guessed at the color of his eyes. It had to be the color that always compelled me to comfort him. I slid into the seat without complaint and I bit my lip as he rounded the hood and flashed in the headlights.

I thought about the blood that he'd have to weave around and my stomach lurched.

The second Nick slipped into the car beside me, his hand came to my thigh. He didn't say anything, his face pinched and his brow furrowed but he didn't let go of my thigh as he drove back to the garage. Nick stayed silent as we walked back to the house too. His hand shifted to the small of my back but I'd known him long enough to feel something was off in the way he touched me. Something I recognized from one time before.

No, not now, not tonight.

My heart hammered in a way it hadn't since Christopher had poisoned me.

I didn't speak up until I shut our bedroom door behind us. Nick's hand fell from my body and he walked away from me and toward the bathroom.

"You couldn't have prevented this. No one could. Please don't blame yourself, Nick."

"Don't, Kate," he spoke with his back still toward me.

"I mean it. After everything we've been through please don't go there. Not now, not right before our wedding."

"I should've taken the hint. There've been a million after all. I shouldn't be marrying you tomorrow." He started skulking toward the bathroom. "I shouldn't be with you at all."

"Nick, you can't mean that. I never . . ." He pulled off his shirt and it stopped me mid-sentence. "Baby!" I gasped as I ran to him, my hands fluttering around the already deep purple bruise from Christopher's elbow.

"Stop." He shoved my hands aside. "With all of it."

He pushed me far enough away to slam the bathroom door in my face. I went straight for the handle, more than ready to fight for him. The lock popped just before I jiggled it.

"Nick." I jiggled again. "Let me in." My heart picked up pace again. "Baby, please!"

I won't lose him now.

There wasn't a single sound from the other side of the door. I slid down along the wall, still in leather and lace, to set up post. I could be every bit as stubborn as Nicholas Bryant.

I started tracing shadows on the wall, counting all the spots that overlapped. Twice. When I got tired of the view in front of me, my fingers started counting individual carpet strands. There still wasn't a single sound from behind me.

The last time I remember seeing the clock it read 3:37 a.m.

14 hours until . . .

I must have fallen asleep wondering if we were going to get married after all. Panic that we might not welled in my chest and I shot straight up in bed.

Bed?

I started a frantic scramble in the covers to try and get back to the bathroom door. It took me a moment to realize that I'd been undressed, the bathroom door was wide open and steel gray eyes were watching me from a chair next to the bed.

My heartbeat slowed immediately and my lungs finally expanded to take a full, deep breath. I climbed off the bed and tiptoed over to his chair. He moved his arms to let me crawl into his lap but his face didn't change. Absolutely no blue filtered into his eyes. I curled my head into the crook of his neck anyhow.

"We can't get married tomorrow." He finally breathed into my hair.

"Fuck you," I whispered vehemently.

"I'm serious. How am I supposed to knowingly put you, and Wells for that matter, in danger?"

"Whether you like it or not we're both already pretty deep in this. Married or not won't create distance." I tilted my head and pressed my lips to his neck. "Don't think of *him*. Please. Think of me. Think of our son." I kissed his jaw. "I need you. Not to protect me, but to complete me. I can't live without you. And I've never wanted to marry you as much as I do now." I kissed the corner of his mouth.

"This is what it takes for you to want to marry me?" There was a hint of humor in his voice.

I'll take even the tiniest bit.

"Fuck you." I reached up and nibbled on his ear lobe this time.

"You're insatiable. One day you'll kill me." His arms finally wrapped around me.

"Nope. I can't live without you. You know that."

He squeezed me and my body melted like butter into his. "I feel so selfish. So irresponsible even considering . . ."

"This isn't your fault. I'll even let you blame Brooklyn or Jaime or Colton if you really want. I fully blame Christopher, maybe Francis a little, but not you. Never you. And you trust me don't you?"

"That's not fair." He smiled against my skin.

"I never said I fight fair."

He kissed my head where it rested beneath his lips.

"Kate, what are we going to do about Christopher?"

We? Thank God.

I took a deep breath and a moment to really think about it. Only one answer came to mind.

"I don't know. But we'll do it together."

35.

Arms bound me like black silk ribbon when the soft morning light fell on my face. Soft, steady breathing was comforting beside me too.

Thank God.

I turned, still encased in his arms, and burrowed further into his chest before planting a kiss on the skin below my lips.

"Sweets," he responded still half asleep.

I leaned in to kiss his chest again. I let my hand wander down to his cock and my fingers flexed against his morning wood. He rolled his hips up into my hand and purred.

"You can't check out on me like that again. One, it's not just me anymore. Two, I can't . . ." My breath caught in my throat. "Well I just can't without you." He groaned as I started leisurely stroking him. "We'll make it through anything because were together." I kissed his jaw where I could reach.

"I couldn't ever really leave you. Or Wells. I just . . ." His words trailed off, replaced by a moan.

"Get scared," I breathed against his skin. "I know. I do too. Until I remember I have you." My hand fell away from his perfect penis and I started kissing down his taut stomach. My body seamlessly slid between him and the sheets.

"Promise me you won't ever walk away," I purred just before planting a kiss on his shaft.

"I'm marrying you." His raspy words made my thighs shift against one another.

"Promise me." It was a playful warning as I bent to kiss him again.

"I swear on everything I have," he grunted and I smiled as I let my tongue trace the length of his cock. His thighs bunched in response. My lips hovered right above the tip of his dick when knuckles wrapped on the big wooden door.

"Go away!" Nick roared and it echoed in the room.

"I think you'll want an update, Bryant." Brooklyn's muffled voice came from the other side of the door.

"Shit," Nick swore as his hands wrapped around my shoulders and he pulled me back up along his body. His lips mashed wildly to mine before rolling from bed and snatching jeans from the floor. He jerked his chin toward his t-shirt and I scrambled for it before landing back beneath the sheets. Nick whipped open the door more violently than was absolutely necessary.

"Sorry to interrupt." Brooklyn arched and eyebrow and I couldn't help but giggle.

Nick shot me one hell of a look but I noticed the blue stayed in his eyes.

"What's the update?" Nick voice was still gruff but most of his usual ice had melted.

"We tracked him for a few hours but, true to form, he had a plan. Retracing his steps this morning, I realized he was purposely disorienting us. Even using the blood trail to his advantage."

"Blood trail?" My chest constricted when I remembered the crimson puddle on the track.

The air seemed to rush out of the room and a weight landed on my shoulders. I was sucked right back into the serious events of last night. Nick saw my whole posture change, and he walked toward me, letting his fingers drift across my shoulder when he walked up.

"Yes. He sustained significant blood loss when I shot him. He'll have to seek medical attention." Brooklyn sighed heavily.

"What would we do without you Brooklyn?" Nick's voice was warm and gracious, my jaw dropped. Where was the trademark temper? The utter meltdown from last night? "This might give us time to catch up to him. Should give us time to go through with this circus." His eyes twinkled when he referenced the ceremony.

Level-headed was new, and pretty damn sexy the way Nicholas Bryant did it. The urge to launch myself at him and his blue eyes was almost overwhelming.

"I have people on it. You'll be safe. Enjoy today," Brooklyn smirked and slipped out.

I sagged into Nick's shoulder as he climbed onto the bed next to me. I went to lean my head on his shoulder and caught the color of his eyes instead.

"What?" They'd shifted to steel gray after all. "What now?"

"What do you mean?" He crinkled his brow and cocked his head. His fingers hadn't stopped circling on my shoulders.

"Your eyes are gray." I shifted up to kneel on the bed, coming nose to nose with him.

"So?" He arched an eyebrow at me and the tiniest bit of blue filtered back in.

"So they always turn gray when you're angry or upset. They're brilliant blue when you're happy. I expected gray because of Christopher but just now, when Brooklyn was speaking, you managed to keep some of the blue. The full on gray came later."

"What?" He smiled and more blue filtered back.

"Your eyes change. They swirl. They tell me more than you do quite frequently." I cocked my head. "They have since the beginning."

"Really?" He rubbed his chin as his gaze fell to the bed. "And you noticed?"

"I always notice." I was trying to sound exasperated but his surprise was too cute, too genuine not to smile at. My brilliant blue was taking over as his grin went crooked. "Now stop changing the subject, why were they gray? What's was wrong that wasn't a second ago?" I bit my lip as I waited for him to answer.

Nick rolled his eyes. "Now I wish you couldn't read me like a book." I waited patiently, knowing he would continue, "I don't want to ruin your day."

"I don't care at all. The wedding doesn't mean anything as long as I get to be married to you."

He slowly looked up at me from under his long lashes. I got the sense he was searching my eyes for some similar tell.

"I don't want to be away from you. I don't want to go put on a tux in the guest house or wait for you at the end of an aisle. Today I want to be with you. I always want to be with you. "

"Done." I beamed.

No words could have made me happier and the way his eyes danced when I agreed made my stomach clench.

"It's not traditional, Kate."

"Because we've always been so traditional," I said meaning to be snarky but coming off soft.

I expected him to kiss me passionately but instead his fingers skated up along my cheeks and pushed into my hair. Nick cradled me, then ever so gently pulled my lips to his. He whispered *my wife* against them before he finally kissed me, planting a sweet kiss. Nick only paused for a moment to take a breath before he returned to my mouth and explored my lips like he'd never tasted them before. I let my tongue trace over his as if it was the first time all over again.

My fingers fiddled at his pants button for a moment then got it free. His went straight to my shirt hem. We were mid-strip when another knock interrupted us.

"Fuck," I muttered while he yelled, "Go away" again.

"You have a wedding to get ready for," Ari's whine cut straight through the wood.

"We'll be ready on time, Aribella."

Three different voices erupted on the other side of the door. Ari, Gemma, and Laura were all working themselves into a frenzy. I heard "But the stylist" and "Girls day" and "I've put up with too much" respectively. I shut them all out as Nick's hand came back to my shirt. My lips happily went back to his until Wells started crying. His howling adding to the cacophony in my hallway.

"Damnit," I whispered against Nick's lips.

"That's an understatement." He pulled back and kissed my

forehead just a second before everyone burst in.

I yanked at the covers while Nick slyly adjusted his jeans. I was still adjusting the comforter when Nick took Wells out of Gemma's hands.

"You guys, it's bad luck to see each other before the wedding." Ari shoved her hands onto her hips and glared first at Nick then me.

"Ari, we're pretty adept at dealing with shit." Nick smiled down on Wells, bouncing him as he spoke to his sister.

"This was supposed to be a girl's day," Gemma's voice was quiet and her gaze fell to her deeply bitten fingernails, which made me feel a little guilty.

"No one is kicking you out. I'm just not kicking Nick out either." Nick bit his lip when I said it but the corner of his smile went crooked all the same. "Laura, what's your grievance?"

"No grievance." She rolled her eyes. "Why on Earth would I have an opinion? Why would I want to be in here with you today?" Her voice dripped with a sarcastic venom.

I was about to shoot my mouth off when Nick spoke up. "Gemma, will you please help me get Wells fed? And Aribella, make yourself useful and grab our tuxedos from the guest house."

"But I . . ."

"Aribella," he barked.

Gemma lightly wrapped her fingers around Ari's arm and pulled her from the room. Nick swung Wells and made an airplane noise, pulling a screech from my son as they followed the girls out. Nick winked just before he shut the door.

"That was bitchy." I crossed my arms on my chest.

"Well how am I supposed to react when you replace me so completely I cease to matter at all?"

"*Excuse* me?"

"I've seen you less and less over the past two years. I miss my friend. I know you're in love. I know it's more than love but jeez . . ." She crossed her arms and leveled her gaze at me.

"What in the fuck are you talking about?" I was trying to keep my temper. "You know damn well I do my best. I know my shit gets a little out of hand, and I don't have tons of time but besides Nick and Wells, you are the only person I think of every day. You're certainly the only person I'd tolerate this shit from." I arched an eyebrow at her.

Laura crossed the room and sat with her back to me on the bed.

"If I lose you, I'm left with nothing." She slumped and it broke my heart. "My life has become a bad joke."

"Laur, you'll never lose me. But moreover, you've got plenty going for you." I leaned forward and let my hand brush down her back.

"I don't have this." She half-heartedly waved her hand around. "And I want it. I always did. I thought I was going to marry Malik. And I certainly thought I'd be getting married before *you*." My back bristled even though I knew that wasn't why she said it. She barreled on before my temper could pop up. "Instead everything keeps getting worse. Exponentially. My relationships have fallen apart that much more spectacularly. Each one faster or worse than the one before." She shrugged then let her face fall into her hands.

I shoved the sheets to the side and crawled across the bed, stepping off right next to her. I crouched between her knees and rested my hands on her thighs.

"Take it from someone who is pretty good at falling apart spectacularly, it only takes one person to show up and help you keep your shit together."

"Is that why you need him in here today? To help keep your shit together?" She only shifted enough to look up at me.

"Among other things." I started chewing on my cheek.

"Have anything to do with those bruises?" She barely jerked her head toward my shins.

I hadn't remembered until then and I shifted to inspect them. My heart constricted when I recalled the frantic events that led up to my legs being shut in the car door.

"A little, I guess." I shrugged. "A little because it's us."

"You still love him as much as you did when you first met him?" She leaned against her palm and met my eyes.

"More," I answered unequivocally.

"Sex life still everything it used to be?"

"Also more."

"I'm trying not to be upset or jealous." She sighed. "Really I am."

"I know." I stood up and turned toward the bar. "It means everything that you're trying. We both know I'd be a bitter bitch if the situation was reversed." I winked as I handed her a scotch then clinked her glass.

"Were you going to explain the bruises?"

My face fell.

"Do I have to?" I prayed she didn't hear my voice waiver.

"What happened?"

Still can't hide from her.

"The less you know the better." I slugged back scotch despite the morning hour and started worrying on my lip.

"Christopher? Really? Is everyone okay?"

Of course she knew what I meant. She shot off the bed and started pacing. She'd been through a lot with him too.

"Nick's bruises are worse than mine but otherwise, yes, everyone is fine. Shaken up though . . ." I let my voice trail off.

I found my shoulders creeping up toward my ears and my heart picking up pace.

The second there was a strong, steady knock at the door my tension melted. My body knew beyond a shadow of a doubt who was knocking on that door. And when both my boys slipped back into the bedroom my earlier calm returned. Nick's eyes met mine and for a moment, the whole world fell away. All that I could see, all that mattered, was the way he looked at me.

Laura laughed lightly and it broke the spell between the both of us. She took a small pull of scotch then looked between the two of us. "Well folks, it would seem we have a wedding to get ready for."

36.

I'd spent hours in a salon chair. The way the stylist played with my hair was so exquisite, I relaxed and let a lazy grin creep across my face. When she badgered me about doing my makeup too, my smile swiftly went from serene to phony. Laura sensed the change and ushered her out the door, her words so jumbled, I didn't think she breathed. I bit my lip so I didn't laugh at the scene. As soon as the stylist was gone I threw my arms around Laura, hair be damned.

When I was finally left alone, I stood and surveyed myself in the bathroom mirror. My dark hair was pinned up in romantic curls. A few tendrils fell into my face or trailed down my neck, framing the diamond studs my father had given me years ago. A matching pendant diamond hung down into my cleavage, a gift that Nick had given me earlier today. It would rest just above the deep sweetheart neck of my dress, the bright, clear compliment to the black one he'd given me last night.

I'd gone for dark red lips, the kind that Nick would stare unabashedly at. The bruises on my ass almost matched the color and I smirked when I realized I didn't know which he'd be more turned on by.

"I'm sorry about last night."

I jumped slightly at Nick's apology as he snuck back into the bathroom. When I settled, I turned to find him fidgeting with his tuxedo which was in various stages of unbuttoned and untucked. A completely different warm honey feeling spread through my insides.

"You already apologized." I went to him, unconcerned that my silk robe was falling off my shoulders.

"I'm sorry I was delusional enough to act like I could leave you, even for your own good." The last part got gravelly when my robe slipped even further and hunger flashed in his eyes.

I laughed loudly, and I threw my arms around his neck.

"Apology accepted." I planted a sweet kiss on his lips, then pulled back to make sure I hadn't left a crimson mark.

His fingers were circling on my back, bringing me closer to him and his growing erection. My hand slid from his neck, down his body, and straight for his cock as I leaned in to kiss him again.

"No," he said sharply. "If anything keeps us from getting married today, it'll be that." He kissed my forehead then turned to walk away.

"Nick, don't go. I'll behave. I promise." He shot me a look, with a halfcocked eyebrow that told me he didn't believe me in the least; the blue of his eyes said he didn't care.

He turned and kept walking.

"Nicholas Bryant!" I hadn't meant to stomp my foot.

"Do you want that ass a darker shade? Deep purple is a beautiful color on you." He chuckled darkly when he turned and saw me flush. "I'm not going anywhere."

He bent over the bed to mess with the garments I'd left there. When he turned around, I drank in the lethal glass of water that was my soulmate. I bit my lip as I pictured what was underneath. Nick shook his head as he walked back, crouched down and kissed the inside of my knee. He held out what he'd retrieved from the bed.

His shoulder was the perfect height for me to steady myself as he slowly rolled up one sheer silk stocking and clipped it to the white lace garter belt already hidden under my robe. He repeated the sweet gesture on my other leg, this time kissing all the way up. Instead of reaching the apex of my thighs, he rocked back and gazed at his handy work. His hands ran up and down my thighs just before he stood and turned back toward the bed.

"Bra, corset?" Nick was looking aimlessly around the corner of the bed.

"Don't need either." I arched my eyebrow.

"Of course you're trying to kill me."

He shook his head and reached for my Jimmy Choos. The platform heels were a combo of shimmery gold and silver glitter.

Nick bent and let me slide my toes into each one while his strong hands steadied my ankles. I paused long enough to take in the sight; my beautiful soon-to-be husband was bent at my feet as tender and loving as I'd ever seen. I couldn't help but bend down and hook my finger under his chin to gently pull him to standing.

He knew what I was angling for the second he looked into my eyes. Mine may not swirl like his but he knew what I wanted—he always knew—and his lips took mine. He kissed me until I went breathless then abruptly pulled away. Without a word, he turned back to the bedroom once more. This time he came back with his camera, snapping only a few innocent pictures.

"I think I like these even more than the other ones."

He smirked and I couldn't help but blush. After all these years, he still drew the strangest responses from me. My favorite full-blown crooked smile pulled across his lips at the rosy hue.

"I'll grab your dress."

"*I'll* grab her dress." Laura had reappeared and was smiling at both of us from the doorway. "I get you guys aren't being traditional, and that's fine, but you're going to get the big reveal whether you like it or not, Nicholas." She put her hands on her gray chiffon covered hips and glowered.

I tried to stifle a giggle, knowing full well how hard it was to fight with that face. By now, Nick knew too, and he held his free hand up and walked past her to the bedroom. He sat on the edge of the bed to slip into his vest while Laura grabbed the Vera Wang gown.

She shut the door behind her before she arched her eyebrow at me. "Okay with that?"

"Yeah, I think I am."

We both smiled as she crouched down, letting organza fluff out, holding the bustier for me to step into. We were both smiling as I shimmied and she pulled the fabric into place. Laura zipped me into place while I adjusted the diamond pendant to hang perfectly in the neckline. My hands wandered over a few appliqués of lace on the fitted, almost lingerie style top. Laura gently arranged all the waves of organza in the skirt and fluffed the appliqué pieces that continued cascading down. When she was happy with her work, she stood and turned me.

"You look amazing. You are amazing. And I'm so happy for you both." Her smile was so genuine, but her eyes still looked a little sad.

"You'll get it. I know it. You deserve it more than me." I put all the love I had for her in my smile.

"That's for sure." Her whole face brightened with the sarcasm but then fell all over again.

She yanked me into her chest and her shoulders shook a little against me.

"Laura, are you okay?" I hugged her back tightly.

"I love you, Kate," she managed through her small sobs.

"I love you, too." I smiled against her cheek and couldn't help the soft chuckle.

"Don't laugh at me!" Light laughter broke through her tears.

"Wouldn't dream of it." I was smiling ear to ear when she stepped back.

"I think we made Nicholas wait long enough."

"I made him wait three years, he'll survive." We both burst out in bright, loud laughter but Laura went to the bathroom door anyway and pulled it open.

Nick was messing with a cufflink when I stepped into the bedroom. He stopped in mid motion and the cufflink clattered to the floor. His jaw dropped and his eyes changed to an incredibly breathtaking shade of blue. But he didn't move. From the doorway it didn't even look like he was breathing.

"You like?"

Nick cleared his throat and his mouth opened once or twice. Laura stealing out of the room caught my attention for just a moment. When the latch clicked my gaze swept back to Nick, he still looked bewildered but he'd stood and was walking toward me. I only took one deep breath before his lips mashed down onto mine. I thought about protesting, my makeup was bound to get everywhere when he kissed me like that, but my self-control evaporated.

Nick gathered my Jell-O limbs in his arms and held me even tighter. Both of his hands dug into my hips as I snaked mine up to grip his neck. His hands found their way to my ass and he grabbed. Hard.

MMMMmmm.

I couldn't help the noise that escaped my lips as he softly bit and pulled on my lower lip.

"Damn Sweets. You'll kill me." He didn't stop kissing me. "I've never seen anything so gorgeous, then to hear that . . ." One of his hands started to travel up my body, moving into my hairline before freezing. "I should drag you out there right now so we can get this over and done with. I fucking want you."

"Why can't you just have me now?"

"Don't tease a man." His lips grazed against mine.

"I'm not," I growled. My hands rubbed down the front of him. I lingered on his erection. "Please," I breathed the words as my fingers flexed.

"Your dress?" His question lingered warm against my lips.

"Just be gentle."

He ducked down and in one swift movement lifted the hem. I was about to run my fingers through his hair when he shot back to my lips. His hands were still underneath the skirt and he used his grip to pull me closer. Slowly he started pushing me back toward the bed. The mattress was up against the back of my knees before I had the sense to stop him. That would certainly ruin my hair. Probably the organza too.

"Stop. Nick," I moaned.

His hands grasped desperately at my flesh. He redirected my body, angling for the section of bare wall between the bar and the bookcase. When my body thudded against the wall, he didn't even need me to say what would get mussed.

"Fuck, where can I take you?" His voice was garbled in between never ending kisses.

"Bathroom counter." I was breathless as we shuffled, all hands and lips, across the floor.

With very little effort, he lifted me onto the slate countertop. He gently pushed my dress out of the way to set my bare backside on the stone. Lust was every bit as palpable as electricity when he bent me backward and was rewarded with four different reflections of us tangled together. His hands went to his pants, and within seconds, he pushed my thong to the side and slid into me. Our moans of pleasure mingled together at the initial full feeling.

"My wife," he breathed as he pulled almost all the way out and pushed back in forcefully.

I cried out and my hips automatically shifted. Suddenly he was in deeper and I could only whimper. He started rolling his hips against me and it had my heart racing. My diamond necklace shuddered against my skin with the rhythm.

Nick's eyes were beautiful, and I made a point of staring deeply into them as I braced myself on the counter. His hands were digging into me harder and harder and I loved it. In that moment my bones felt how completely I belonged to him. And him to me. It made me truly, madly, deeply in love with the idea of marrying him. Finally.

I was building, the feeling becoming more electric as he continued his delectable thrusts.

"My husband." I was barely able to breathe the words.

His eyes flashed again and he pulled me up against his body. He would notice my heart hammering for him even through the fabric.

"Say it again," he growled.

I could feel the intensity in his voice, it rumbled through his chest.

"My husband," I gasped, more than happy to oblige.

His muscles bunched underneath me, his body responding equally to the words and the sentiment.

"Again." His breathing was getting ragged.

"My husband." The end of my word was a garbled cry as he used his thumb to brush against my clitoris.

My orgasm crashed through me. I still held tightly to the

countertop as his lips came back to mine. I moaned into his mouth as the familiar waves rolled through my body. I was flexing and rippling on his hard cock.

His body tensed under mine, and his fingers clawed into my hips. His talons would keep me from a bikini bottom in public on the honeymoon but I didn't care.

Who says we're leaving the room anyway?

My skin was still tingling when he came. My whole body twitched when his heat shot inside of me. Everything was jittery, already yearning for more of him. My hands clung to him while he finished, content to raise my lips to his jaw and shower it in kisses. When Nick could breathe again he uttered, "My wife." In that moment I understood why *husband* had turned him on so very much.

"My hus . . ."

He twitched inside of me. "Don't," he interrupted as he pulled out unceremoniously.

I couldn't help but wince until his lips found mine, kissing me again. From somewhere he grabbed a washcloth and was gently cleaning between my thighs but his fluttered kisses didn't stop. When he finally pulled his lips away, he leaned his forehead against mine.

"That is the most erotic thing you could say to me, and I don't think we can finish another round before the ceremony. I have no intentions of hurrying."

He pulled my thong back into place and rubbed over top of the fabric just to tease me. I smacked his chest half-heartedly before replying.

"You're going to have to hear it in front of one hundred people shortly. I certainly hope you don't cut me off to have your way with me right there."

He chuckled softly as he helped me down from the counter. I started arranging my gown, making sure everything was in place, and the organza fluffed and floated. Nick stilled my hands and took over, smoothing as needed. His hands softly skated up and down my dress and then along my ribs.

When I turned to check my makeup, only my lipstick had

suffered. I smirked as I cleaned up stray marks and filled in smudges. Nick slid right up behind me and was pushing any hairpins that needed back into place.

I turned to face him and noticed that my lipstick had left a few stray marks on his face. I chuckled as I reached for a clean rag. While I was wetting it, he checked his bow tie, vest, and coat in the mirror. He laughed at the lipstick marks and then at me as I gently worked them off. I couldn't help but let my fingers skate down his lapels just before I nuzzled into his chest.

He wrapped his arms around my shoulders and happily held me there. I would have sat and listened to his heart all evening if I could have. When I noticed the sun hanging low in the rippley June sky, I let out a heavy sigh.

"We should get going." Despite my words I didn't budge.

"Don't sound so thrilled, Sweets," Nick said brusquely.

"Oh stop that right now." I snaked my arms around him and kept him tight within my grasp. "You know damn well I want to marry you. I just love moments like this too. I'd be wrapped up with you in bed if I had my way."

There was a knock at the door and Nick's trademark "Go away" immediately followed.

"Nicholas Bryant do not make everyone wait. It's rude. Even for you," Aribella squawked through the door.

We shared one long, sickeningly sweet look before both breaking into beaming smiles. Nick kept his hand at the small of my back as we turned toward the door. He effortlessly pulled it open to find a bright red fuming Ari on the other side, complete with balled fists.

"Calm down Ari, we actually can't be late." I smiled serenely.

"Nicholas isn't even dressed." Her whole face squinched as she spoke. I turned to look at Nick and couldn't see anything out of place. I made a show of drinking in every inch of him. That's when I noticed he was missing the single cufflink that he'd dropped when Laura opened the bathroom door.

"Oh good God. It's a cufflink. I'll grab it, go get everyone ready."

"Your bouquet is on the counter." She shook her head and stomped down the hall.

Nick was right behind me when I shut the door and he kissed the back of my head carefully. I turned in his arms and, as badly as I wanted to kiss him, I simply set my hands on his chest and forced myself not to flex my fingers. I smiled and smoothed out his vest then down his sleeves to his cuffs.

Part of me hated pulling away from him, but I did it anyway, crouching to snatch the gold knot from the floor. Nick followed and held his wrist out to me. I carefully threaded the cufflink and adjusted his sleeve. As soon as I let go he used his outstretched hand to grab my waist and pull me against his body. It was a quick squeeze but it was so tender it made my heart swell.

Nick pulled me toward the door. I sagged into his side as we walked together to the kitchen. His arm moved from the small of my back to my shoulders as he kissed my forehead. I grabbed my bouquet of feathery, soft pink and white peonies. The lace ribbon binding them twisted and rolled in the breeze as we stepped out the front door.

The light of the sunset cast shadows across Nick's features, making him seem softer but searing the memory him into my mind all at the same time. His eyes turned deeper blue, that of infinite galaxies in the warm, cocooning breeze. My emotions grew sharp in contrast to the lazy evening, and a knot formed in my throat.

Nick looked at me similarly but there was a hint of a tear in his eye. My free hand came up to cradle his face, and he closed his eyes to nuzzle into my hand.

"Don't go soft on me now, Bryant."

Despite the sass, my voice betrayed how close I was to following suit. It made him laugh and take one quick swat at my ass.

I threaded my fingers through his, determined to keep a firm grasp on him the whole time. The song I had chosen to walk down the aisle to began drifting on the wind, dulcet and sweet like the gossamer hanging in the tent. Nick and I both straightened. We gave each other a once over as the guests rose from their seats.

The strings sang and my heartbeats rose and fell with the bows gliding along the violins. Each note struck me and was what finally pulled tears to the corner of my eyes.

We started walking down the long stone path just in time for a single tear to streak down my face. Just before the rows of guests, Nick stopped and cradled my face. He wiped my tear away with his thumbs. I couldn't help the smile that spread across my face even though my lip trembled.

An all too familiar camera shutter caught that moment. And the one after when a single tear trailed down Nick's face. I stood on tiptoes to kiss where it pooled on his jaw. We were frozen in that moment for a few deep, perfect breaths before we continued down the aisle.

We both stopped where Laura cradled Wells. I tickled his adorably tuxed tummy while Nick beamed down on the two of us. We both moved in to kiss his forehead. For a blissfully perfect second all three of us where framed by a breathtaking sunset. Then an even more spectacular aura of love.

Nick's hand clasped mine and he kissed my forehead as we took our place in front of the reverend. My eyes weren't really interested in leaving Nick's, not even for the briefest of moments. His hadn't stopped studying me since we'd left the house.

The reverend started and I barely registered his words. I could only think of Nick. Of the way the ocean breeze rustled the ends of his perfectly styled hair. Of the blue in his eyes and how deep it was. How those eyes were *my* eyes. My world.

I let my gaze wander down his body, taking in the custom tailored tux and how flawlessly it fit him. I could imagine the sculpted body I adored underneath. The heat rose in my cheeks and flushed across my chest when I pictured all the naughty things we did.

That always familiar tingle charged between us. So much so that I figured even the reverend could feel it. Of course Nick noticed. Only I saw the corner of his mouth turn up in a wicked little smirk. I bit the inside of my cheek to keep from losing my composure completely.

Nick cleared his throat as he reached into his breast pocket and pulled out a small piece of paper.

His vows!

The anticipation made my skin goose bump even in the warm breeze.

"Kate Elliott, light of my life." He paused and his crooked smile unfurled across his face. "I promise to protect you." He chuckled and I shook my head. "I promise to always try, both harder and smarter." His laugh was even brighter and this time I rolled my eyes. "And I promise to always come to a compromise, even if it takes some . . . um . . . effort to get there." At that, I burst out laughing, knowing exactly the kind of *effort* he was referring to.

"But most of all I promise you the world. I promise you anything and everything because even that wouldn't be enough to thank you for coming into my life." His smile had shifted to a sweet, shy one and it tugged on my heartstrings. "I didn't believe in love, I certainly didn't think that I would get it. But I needed you too much. My soul recognized it needed yours too much." His voice got lower, the words harder to choke out past emotion.

When he cleared his throat and struggled to find words, tears came unbidden to the corner of my eyes. Nick moved closer and rested his hand on my hip. Neither of us gave a damn about keeping the traditional distance.

"Kate, I will forever love you like this. Truly, madly, deeply." His hand flexed into me. "I will always put you and Wells before anything else. I will always try to be a man that makes you proud. Today I give you all that I am, all that I have. All I ask in return is that you love me, like this, for always."

Somehow I managed to choke out, "I will."

The reverend smiled reassuringly at me, asking me to share my vows. Tears just wouldn't stop streaming down my face but Nick kept trying to tenderly remove them. Wells shrieked as Ari stepped up from her chair and handed me the slip of paper on which I'd scribbled my vows. I took a deep breath then a tiny step forward almost pressing myself flush against Nick.

"I will freely admit I was a pain in the ass to get down the aisle."

The crowd chuckled but I still heard Laura mumble, "Language" from her seat. All I did was beam up at my love, unconcerned with the people watching or the tears trembling on my lips.

"But it had nothing to do with not wanting to be married. You had my forever the first day I met you. Maybe even before that. Admitting that was the hard part." That drew another low chuckle from those that knew us best as I continued, "But I couldn't deny that I *need* you. I couldn't deny it any more than I could stop the sun rising in the east or setting in the west. Because that is how simple and straightforward our truth is.

"You make me better and complete in every way a person can be. My heart races when I see you. My skin goose bumps when I touch you. I go short of breath when I kiss you. My soul is peaceful when I hear your voice. Every single fiber of my being recognizes my other half in you. You, Nicholas Bryant, are my soulmate and my utter truth."

His chest heaved and I laid my hand over his heart. His eyes twinkled with unshed tears. "You are my everything and my only vow is to love you more than anything in this universe, the best way I know how. And forever, in the truest sense of the word. All I ask in return is that you care for my heart as you always have."

It was his turn to muddle through, "I will."

A single tear rolled down his cheek as he wrapped his hands around my hips and pulled me up against his chest; I rested my head against my hand where it still covered his heart. The reverend cleared his throat but neither of us moved. I did manage to smile widely up at him. Nick must have done something similar because the reverend began again.

"Nicholas, take this ring and place it on Kate's left ring finger. We place rings on this finger because it is the only one with a direct connection to the heart. We hope this makes your commitment flow through you with every heartbeat and reminds your every fiber of this moment. Nicholas, repeat after me. With this ring, I pledge to be constant, my wife, and be the love that courses through your very soul. With this ring, I thee wed."

Nick tried to project his voice as he collected my hand and slipped my ring on. I let out one loud, completely unladylike but delighted sob in response.

"Kate, take this ring and place it on Nicholas's left ring finger. We choose rings because they are perfect, unending circles. No beginning, no middle, no end, only infinite consistency. The ring is the symbol of what your commitment should be and we hope this reminds the heart of future and perseverance. Kate, repeat after me. With this ring, I pledge to cherish our commitment, my husband, and preserve our forever. With this ring, I thee wed."

I repeated, my voice an uncharacteristic and trembling whisper. I pushed the ring onto his finger without moving a single inch away from him.

"It is with the utmost joy, and the power vested in my by the state of New York, I pronounce you, man and wife. Nicholas, you may kiss your bride."

Nick leaned down and one of his long perfect fingers tucked under my chin. He gently pulled my lips to his. His other hand moved to the small of my back, and pinned me to his frame while we shared a kiss both desperate and chaste. It was tender but his tongue traced my lips and moved ever so slightly into my mouth. My heart jackhammered against his chest, his a perfect mimic of mine.

"It is my deepest pleasure to introduce, for the first time, Mr. and Mrs. Nicholas Bryant."

With those words, Nicholas was mine, forever. To love always like this.

NOT ALL ENDINGS ARE ENDINGS AND NOT ALL ENDINGS ARE HAPPY . . .

I watched the needle against my skin. The way it dimpled deeper and deeper until it gave, the metal piercing my skin was oddly soothing. I could empty my mind as I stitched in and out, watching dark crimson seep out from my wound. The blood replaced tears. It always did.

When I tied the tiny knot in the end and pulled, I couldn't help but wince. Brooklyn Hart, combined with my dear, sweet, painfully infuriating step brother, was looking to be a lethal combination. And I didn't like who it was going to be lethal for. Nor did I understand how their endless shitshow masquerading as security was getting the better of me.

Perhaps even God himself preferred Nicholas Bryant.

I let out a deep breath as I sagged against the large tree trunk behind me. The ache in my thigh from the gunshot wound started to throb in time with my heartbeat and I had to adjust. Thankfully, my eyes were comfortable in the darkness. I could keep watch on the bloodhound Brooklyn and the gang of morons he was traipsing through the woods with. They circled relentlessly, following the bread crumbs I'd laid out perfectly.

How do these oafs get through the day?

I shifted again and sucked in a deep breath. It was loud enough to stop the crunching footsteps behind me suddenly. As best I could, I flattened myself further to the tree, hoping the small hollow spot

I'd chosen would do a good enough job of hiding me. My breathing stilled but I did what I could to hold it all the same. After what felt like an eternity, the footsteps started again.

They hadn't gone far before they broke a stick, cracking loud and sharp into the silent night. If it hadn't been so close, I would have laughed. As it was, I smirked to myself. Despite being the bleeding one, I wasn't the idiot in the clearing.

"Christopher!" Brooklyn bellowed—probably still standing on that stupid stick—and I really had to make an effort to hold in the laughter now. "For a long time this was between you and Bryant." My eyes narrowed at my step-brother's name but Brooklyn kept howling. "But it's personal now. I don't lose. I refuse to. You will pay for your sins if it's the last thing I do."

A guttural snarl built in my chest. I wanted to let it loose but the throb thick in my thigh reminded me not to. His words triggered something inside me. Something much like the time fuck-twat Nicholas told me school was easy and lacrosse was easier. It was like a switch flipped and every fiber of my being determined to prove him wrong. At any cost.

"Mark my words Christopher. I will end you." This time Brooklyn's voice was lower, deeper, chilling even. I felt my smile peel across my face in response.

I couldn't hold the laughter in this time. I'd overestimated Brooklyn. He was as moronic as Nicholas. I chuckled lightly and saw the puffs of air from my warm breath against a chilly evening. Brooklyn took off running, this time his path cut just past my hiding spot along the trail of blood I'd laid out for him. His suit sent the slightest breeze flapping against my skin.

He paused maybe a hundred yards from me but it wasn't to look around. He'd run into one of Nicholas' other suited doofuses. When the light shifted, Jaime was revealed, standing close and having an urgent, worried conversation.

"I have to get back Jaime. She's . . ." Brooklyn trailed off but he'd succeeded in piquing my curiosity with that one little word.

She who?

"I mean, they shouldn't be left alone," he backpedaled. "I need to see for myself that . . . they're okay." Brooklyn's tone made it obvious. He wasn't talking about a them. He was talking about a her. A her that meant a lot. A her that meant so much he'd leave his personal vendetta to rot in the midnight forest. A her that would be the perfect weak spot to dig into and abuse. And if Brooklyn was weak, the whole Bryant pyramid would crumble.

Maybe God isn't pulling for Nicholas after all . . .

Now to find out who *She* was and how to tear her to shreds.

ABOUT THE AUTHOR

Ace Gray is a self-proclaimed troublemaker and connoisseur of both the good life and fairy tales. After a life-long love affair with books, she undertook writing the novel she wanted to read, which culminated in her first release STRICTLY BUSINESS. When she's not writing, she owns her own business teaching Pilates and studies the art of craft beer. She loves rainy days, shellac manicures, coffee shops and bourbon—all of which are bountiful in her adopted home of Portland, OR where she runs amok with her chef husband and two huskies.

TITLES BY ACE GRAY

STRICTLY BUSINESS (Mixing Business with Pleasure Book 1)
BAD FOR BUSINESS (Mixing Business with Pleasure Book 2)
FAMILY BUSINESS (Mixing Business with Pleasure Book 3)
HOW TO KILL A LADY BONER (Because Beards Anthology Piece)

COMING SOON

TWISTED FATE (A Twisted Fairy Tale Book 1)
TWISTED DEATH (A Twisted Fairy Tale Book 2)
BROTHEL: MAGNOLIA DIARIES ANTHOLOGY

www.ingramcontent.com/pod-product-compliance
Lightning Source LLC
Chambersburg PA
CBHW051233260626
47162CB00002B/414